EVEN
WHEN
YOU LIE

EVEN WHEN YOU LIE

A NOVEL

MICHELLE CRUZ

CROOKED
LANE

NEW YORK

Published in the United States by Crooked Lane Books, an imprint of The Quick Brown Fox & Company LLC.

Crooked Lane Books and its logo are trademarks of The Quick Brown Fox & Company LLC.

Library of Congress Catalog-in-Publication data available upon request.

ISBN (trade paperback): 978-1-63910-250-1
ISBN (ebook): 978-1-63910-251-8

Cover design by Meghan Deist

Printed in the United States.

www.crookedlanebooks.com

Crooked Lane Books
34 West 27th St., 10th Floor
New York, NY 10001

First Edition: March 2023

10 9 8 7 6 5 4 3 2 1

Dedicated to the men and women who served
in the United States Armed Forces,
September 11, 2001–August 30, 2021.

CHAPTER

1

EVERY ONE OF my mental alarm bells clangs when the woman with pink hair shoves in through the glass doors separating Cade's section from the rest of the law firm.

The women who sometimes trail their husband or lover through here are normally quiet, downcast, as if they bear the burden of guilt or shame that their partner won't, shouldering it with their Louis Vuitton bags. They wear coordinating pantsuits and pumps in muted colors to avoid drawing attention to themselves, their hair inevitably blonde and slicked back, with conservative makeup—just enough to hide the evidence that they probably spent the morning crying before they armed themselves with a handful of pills to obediently trot into a defense attorney's office and stand by their man.

But not this woman.

Her cheeks are red, sweat lines her upper lip below two nose rings, and her baggy black T-shirt reveals tattoos of flowers and astrological symbols trailing up her arms. An owl's yellow eyes pierce me from one side of her neck. She wears ripped blue jeans and worn Converses, the laces frayed and untied.

She can't be a client; her dishevelment is so out of
bounds with what I've come to expect here that I think
she'll apologize and say she's lost.

But she doesn't.

For a second she stands, blinking like she's orienting
herself in the office's fluorescent light, and then she squares
her small, thin shoulders, and stalks to where Evangeline
and I stand at her desk.

When we don't immediately acknowledge her, the
woman takes a deep breath and huffs the long bangs of her
messy pixie cut out of her face.

"I want to speak to Cade McCarrick," she says. "Now."

She doesn't ask.

She doesn't say please.

She doesn't even request an appointment; no, she just
demands, like she's someone an attorney of Cade's caliber
will make time for.

Yeah, she's trouble, all right.

The kind of trouble that screams shrill voices making
demands and hurried phone calls to security guards.

That's not the kind of trouble we want around here, not
at the law offices of Holcombe & Donaldson, where even
the junior associates command retainer fees high enough
to have every local law school student dreaming of a post-
graduation employment offer.

Evangeline appears cool and elegant in her ivory pantsuit, which complements her creamy brown skin and amber
eyes. As Cade's paralegal for the last three years, she is most
likely to recognize the stranger, but she only flashes me a
sidelong glance—a warning that I don't need to step in just
yet, but I might be required at any moment.

Still, Evangeline keeps her voice low and soothing as
she says, "Mr. McCarrick's not available," and stands, her
long microbraids swinging loose down her back. "Is there
anything I can help you with?"

The woman with the pink hair glares and wraps her arms around herself. "I want *him*. Now, damn it," she hisses. "Get him here. It's important."

Evangeline gives me an almost imperceptible nod.

I shift my weight, drawing the woman's attention to me, and motion to the chair by my desk. Maybe the outline of my pistol under my pantsuit jacket will put a little more respect in her voice. "I'm Reagan, Mr. McCarrick's in-house investigator. Why don't you have a seat and tell me what this is about?"

"I knew this would happen. I knew I wouldn't be taken seriously." She shoves an envelope into my hands. "Here. He'll need this."

It's an ordinary white paper envelope with Cade's name scrawled across. "What is it?"

"He's a fixer, ain't he?" she asks, halfway to the door. "Tell him to fix this."

There is something desperate and courageous about her anger, that she knew the odds were stacked against her, and yet she walked in here anyway.

No, she's not like the other women who follow the firm's clients inside. I know I shouldn't concern myself with her, that she doesn't fit the image of who the partners want their clientele to be, but I can't help myself from saying, "Wait."

The glass door closes between us, and she never looks back.

Maybe she didn't hear.

"Reagan," Evangeline warns, but I ignore her and follow the woman.

The woman takes the elevator, but I slip past the law firm receptionist's desk to the stairwell, where there are no surveillance cameras to monitor me, because I don't like questions about my comings and goings.

I step out of my high heels and carry them down the four flights of stairs, reaching the lobby as she exits into the wave of skin-tightening heat. Her bright hair makes her easy to track through the late-lunch rush crowd in Uptown but, not wanting to spook her, I resist the urge to bolt after her.

It's summer in Dallas, sticky and sweaty, and I try to ignore the immediate perspiration rolling down the small of my back. Protest season, my granddaddy calls it, with the blithe dismissiveness of a white man who has never had to march for a goddamn thing in his life. His messages lately beg me not to go downtown, but I don't reassure him with a reminder that Cade's office and apartment are in Uptown. There's enough about Cade my family doesn't like, and they'll raise hell if they discover I sleep in his bed every night.

The woman staggers a few steps and drops to a seat on a bench.

I slow my pace to a stroll.

Her head bobs.

I stop cold, wondering how someone who was just energetic enough to weave through crowded sidewalks can now look like she's on the verge of falling asleep sitting upright.

She slumps and nearly tumbles into a man in a suit, who recoils as if she'll ruin his designer wingtips.

Instead, she hits the ground.

Someone screams.

A late luncher in khakis and a golf shirt leans over the woman and raises his head to shout, "Call 911!"

My heart pounds in my ears, but I hesitate and don't rush to her aid.

At least not right away.

I tell myself I'll just be in the way—too used to dealing with the aftermath of death to know how to help prevent it.

Then instinct overrides, and I push myself into the gathering throng.

The woman lies on the concrete, pink hair fanning out, her eyes closed.

A man says, "Get back, I'm a doctor," even though he's dressed more for the office than the clinic. He kneels beside her, his ear close to her face. "She's breathing."

She'll live, then.

My conscience eases and I slip back into the shadows, withdrawing to the opposite side of the street as the crowd tightens around her.

An ambulance howls onto the scene, and I reassure myself that there are now trained paramedics present. A police car pulls to the curb, lights flashing, and an officer steps out to speak with bystanders, his notepad at the ready.

I can't see the woman anymore, but I don't move any closer.

If I stay, someone might notice me. There might be questions as to why she visited Cade's office, and I don't have those answers . . . yet. Given that Cade is a criminal defense attorney, our office doesn't want or need additional scrutiny from law enforcement.

Nor do I particularly want to highlight myself to the firm's senior partners, potentially drawing attention to Cade's and my relationship.

I give the crowd a wide berth, forcing myself to a saunter back to the office. I only remember the envelope in my hands when someone brushes past me and I clutch it to my stomach out of instinct, as if to protect it.

This belongs to Cade, I tell myself. The woman brought it for him.

But the contents inside practically hum, rattling in my fingers like they're begging to come out and show me what's so damn important that the pink-haired woman insisted he have it.

Besides, I open his office mail all the time, after all. I should know if there's something that could be dangerous to him.

I don't go back in through the lobby doors, but circle around the building to the bench in the small oak grove, where I sit and toy with the sealed envelope flap. Carefully, oh so carefully—so later maybe I can claim it came like that—I slip a finger into a loose corner and lift until the adhesive gives way. The documents slide out almost of their own volition, slippery smooth, so cool in my hands that I almost shiver.

A Dallas County birth certificate—the paper thin and the print fading—of a thirty-four-year-old man named Cesar Morales, the son of Araceli Morales, no father listed.

A copy of a Texas Alcoholic Beverage Commission permit for Club Saturnalia in Deep Ellum.

A faded snapshot, the focus fuzzy, of a pair of teenagers leaning against a white stone wall. She's olive-skinned, black-haired, dark-eyed, and grinning, with her arms folded across her chest. He's almost pasty, standing next to her, one arm around her shoulders, his face blurred in profile as he kisses her cheek.

I breathe the still, humid air deep into my lungs until my heart rate slows. Then I shove everything into the envelope and stand. If I don't mention what I just saw, I'll have time to check into who the pink-haired woman is and what this envelope means without anyone interfering.

Evangeline glances up as I come through the glass double doors, her pen paused mid-stroke. "Well?"

"Lost her in the crowd," I say and toss the envelope in the inbox on my desk like it's no big deal. Later, after Evangeline leaves, I'll smuggle it into my purse and out of the office, where I can hunt through it again without any questions.

"You gonna tell Cade?" she asks.

"No," I say. "What would be the point in that?"

Evangeline nods. "Are you riding with him this evening to the Holcombes'?"

I play with my notepad on my desk, so I don't have to look her in the eye. "Why would I?"

She chuckles under her breath. "How long do you two plan to keep this up?"

How the hell does she know?

My jaw drops almost before I catch myself.

The precautions Cade and I take race through my brain: never arriving or leaving work together, never sharing a car, never appearing together in public where people might recognize us and we can't claim it was a coincidence, and never discussing our arrangement outside his apartment.

The firm's chief administrator strides by in the hallway on the other side of the glass doors. Her scowl is set as hard as her teased brown hair, and I automatically try to look as busy as possible, shuffling through papers on my desk.

With a half-hearted sigh, Evangeline resumes work on a deposition.

I try to force my mind back to the case I was working on before the pink-haired woman appeared.

Only now she's all I can think of, collapsing to the ground, her glassy eyes staring up at the sky, and the faint tinge of blue to her lips.

I may not have to tell Evangeline the truth, but I can't lie to Cade.

My Friday just got a helluva lot more complicated.

* * *

Cesar Morales. Dallas, TX.

I frown at the Google search results, close my eyes, and rest my fingertips on the keyboard, as if this will somehow guide me to the right page.

"What rabbit hole you running down over there?" Evangeline asks.

"Oh, nothing," I say. "Just a case for Cade."

"Aren't they all?" she asks.

I shrug and eye the envelope in my inbox. Maybe I can slip it out and scan it over without her noticing.

But no, Evangeline is smart, apparently smart enough to catch onto Cade and me. While I know she's so loyal to him that she won't breathe a word to the senior partners, three months of working side by side with her probably hasn't earned me the same discretion.

And I do need this job.

I click through the top few search results, but these Cesar Moraleses are too old, too young, and too wrong to somehow be associated with that picture in the envelope.

But the right one is out there, somewhere, and if anyone can find Cesar Morales, I can.

It was only a hobby in college, a defense for me and the girls on my dorm floor. We used to sift through their potential dates, separating the innocuous frat rats from the ones with darker reputations, and I further honed it as an Air Force intelligence officer.

But it was nothing more than that, not until three months ago, when my phone rang and the district chief of staff of the congressman I worked for demanded I find the personal cell phone number of Cade McCarrick.

I found all sorts of things that night, from Cade's high school football career in Appalachian North Carolina—where his family has farmed for eight generations—to his collegiate career playing quarterback at the University of North Carolina and law school at Southern Methodist.

Finding Cade's cell phone number, however, brought him to my door with a job offer at double the salary I made as congressional staff.

I took it and didn't look back.

Now it's June, almost July, and Cade strolls through the glass doors at three thirty with Armando Tamez, the firm's other junior partner. I quickly close all the windows on my screen relating to Cesar Morales because I don't want to explain what I'm doing just yet, and I watch Cade for as long as I can over the top of my monitor.

Six foot four, still with that athletic, muscular build at thirty-four, paired with an easy grace that must have been magic on the football field.

His black hair silky as cat's fur, those green eyes and dimples no web search could have ever prepared me for . . .

Our gazes almost meet, but we both realize it at the same time and look away.

"Evangeline." Armando smirks in my direction and raises a hand in a mock salute. "*La capitana* Reyes."

"*You don't look like a Reyes,*" he said my first day here.

That remark usually hurts, but with Armando and his grin, somehow it didn't, and so I retorted, "*Well, you don't look like a lawyer.*"

He only laughed and said to Cade, "*Let's keep this one.*"

It's possible Armando knows about Cade and me, too.

After all, Armando is Cade's regular golf and tennis companion and closest friend. Armando's shorter than Cade, his eyes as dark as his hair, and a ready smile that keeps him looking young enough for new employees to regularly mistake him for an intern rather than the firm's lead on immigration and family law. Cade might be all ambition and hustle, the engine that keeps Holcombe & Donaldson pushing, but Armando is its lifeblood, the zest and vitality that makes the days more fun.

"Ladies," Cade says, shrugging out of his suit coat.

Armando checks his watch and winks at Evangeline, then directs his attention to Cade. "You're so needy. It's not fair to keep Evangeline and Reagan here, especially with that dinner at Bridger's tonight. I sent my staff home at noon."

Bridger Holcombe is the managing partner of Holcombe & Donaldson. He's the closest to Highland Park royalty one can get in a town already bursting with wealth. The dinner tonight at his mansion is practically mandatory for all employees. That Armando let his team leave at noon now concerns me—perhaps this is a bigger deal than I anticipated, and I should have pressed Cade harder on what to expect.

"Your office is down the hall, if you've forgotten," Cade says, but he's smiling, and he motions for me and Evangeline to leave.

She stands, gathering her things. "Six?"

"Cocktail hour starts at five thirty," Cade says.

Armando and Evangeline exchange a look. He says, "I'm not getting there at five thirty."

"Six it is," Evangeline says.

From the corner of my eye, I see Cade almost glance in my direction. "You should head out too, Reagan."

"In a minute," I say, and when he moves toward the inbox on my desk, I add, "I'm not finished going through—"

"It's fine." Cade scoops up the contents, the envelope from the pink-haired woman on top. "Enjoy your afternoon."

If I argue with Cade here, in front of Evangeline and Armando, it'll only make a scene and pique Cade's infamous curiosity, so insatiable he'd turn up with a job offer in hand at the apartment of the woman who found his personal cell phone number.

I nod, grab my purse, and follow Evangeline to the elevator. Once the doors close, I ask, "You're not seeing Armando, are you?"

She examines her manicure, every fingernail polished in her signature pale pink. "One office romance is enough for Holcombe & Donaldson."

I chew the inside of my cheek for half a second and decide to play this cool in the hopes she'll either decide she has bad info or give up where she got it. "I don't know what you mean."

"You know damn well what I mean," she says. "You're not the only one around here with a nose for secrets. The truth has a funny way of coming out, and consequences can be expensive."

She's not wrong, not necessarily.

Cade may not write my checks, but he's my direct supervisor, and Holcombe & Donaldson strictly forbids romantic relationships between partners and staff. I remember very well initialing the full-page acknowledgment in the employee contract details that if one is discovered, the staff member faces automatic dismissal, and the partner is suspended from any benefits for at least a three-month period afterward—if not permanently.

But I make myself shrug, as if Cade and I have discussed this.

Like we made time for that eight weeks ago, when I caught him drinking apple pie moonshine from a silver flask in his suit coat pocket on the firm's private balcony after a rare loss, and we ended up in bed together, promising each other it was only once.

Or six weeks ago, when he slid a key to his apartment across his kitchen bar to me.

Evangeline eyes me, almost like she knows where my thoughts wander, and I say, "I'm pretty good at protecting what's mine. And we're both adults. Tell me what these dinners are like."

She smiles. "Oh, you'll see."

"That's not helpful," I say. "What do I wear?"

She's heard me complain often enough that one of the hardest parts about transitioning from the military to civilian life is determining what to wear to social events, and so it seems mean of her to say, "Something Cade will like."

"Again," I say, glaring, "not helpful."

She bites her lower lip to hide her grin. "A nice sundress with a wrap and some sandals. Definitely a wrap, though. It's Highland Park, and Mrs. Holcombe will be there."

"Bridger's wife?" I ask. "I've met Colleen."

Evangeline pats my arm. "No. Bridger's mother. *The* Mrs. Holcombe."

"Oh," I say, but I don't really understand what that means.

Not then.

No, in that moment I only know that I'll need to go shopping for a nice sundress and a wrap before Cade makes it home from the office, before we leave for Highland Park, because I don't own anything like that.

She waves at the lobby's security guard speaking with two police officers over at the reception desk. Their unsmiling faces and squared postures indicate this isn't a social call, but their glances slide across me and Evangeline, and any curiosity I have as to their presence is outweighed by my reluctance to reveal what I saw down the street.

"There's the trolley," she says as we step outside into the heat. "I'll see you tonight, okay?"

I laugh. "Six."

She races away—as fast as she can in her pantsuit and pumps—her bag slung over her shoulder and her braids swinging down her back. I watch, hand shading my eyes, until I make sure she arrives safely on board.

I need to find a dress.

And then I'll deal with Cade, so I can get that envelope back.

CHAPTER

2

I FIND A SUNDRESS that falls just below my knees and add a crocheted shrug. The outfit—which will be nice enough to wear out on a date—complements my dark auburn hair, my porcelain skin, and my eyes that can never decide if they're blue, gray, or green.

Not that Cade and I can usually risk being seen in public together outside the office.

I text a picture to Evangeline, wanting a second opinion. She sends back a smiley face, and so I pay and leave, hurrying the short distance to Cade's apartment.

For five blocks, I deliberate how I'll tell Cade about the woman and that envelope, how I'll bring the conversation around to her bursting into the office, demanding to speak to him, and collapsing on the street.

The uniformed attendant of Cade's high-rise building pulls the door open for me and says "Ma'am" as I pass, like I belong here. But each echo of my heels across the marble lobby reminds me how far I am from my blue-collar East Texas roots, that this is only home because of a relationship that can't be fully acknowledged outside these walls.

Cade sweeps me into a tight embrace almost as soon as I come through the apartment door, as if he has been waiting, coiled and ready to spring.

If it were anyone but him, it would panic me.

Instead, I grab him and breathe him deep.

Safe, as if safe has a scent, but I believe it must. I think it smells like Cade, the crisp whiff of his cologne and his Porsche's leather interior that permanently clings to him.

And now he is squeezing me as much—if not more—than I am squeezing him, pressing my head into his chest. "Where have you been? I was getting worried."

"I had to buy a dress," I say, wriggling free enough to show him the plastic bag. "For the Holcombes'. Evangeline said—"

"Right," he says and looks away, swallowing hard. "Sorry. Police showed up at the firm about a woman who died, and . . . then you weren't home when I got here."

"What?" I exhale. "A woman died?"

He shrugs. "The cops are just checking the box as a formality, I'd guess. Someone said she came out of our building, so they were bored enough to go floor by floor."

"But there are cameras in our building," I say.

"Sure, but building security won't turn over the lobby cameras without a subpoena, and our cameras have been down for a month," he says. "Don't tell anyone that, though."

I turn away to set my purse down and snip tags off my dress. "And the woman?"

"Not one of our clients, but the receptionist swears she came out of our section," Cade says. "Pink hair—"

"Yes." I'm surprised at how cool my voice sounds, even as my heart sinks and I realize that I wanted to believe the paramedics who arrived would be able to save her. "Pink hair and tattoos. She wanted to see you, but you weren't there. She wouldn't give a reason."

Behind me, water runs in the kitchen sink, splashing into a glass. "Probably didn't have a reason. The cops implied it was an overdose, and meth is a helluva drug."

His flippancy stings, but not enough to point out that I've never seen an overdose kick in so quickly, that the woman was coherent—if belligerent—in the office and seemed perfectly fine until her collapse on the bench.

I drop the scissors into the kitchen drawer and slam it shut with a little more force than necessary. "She left an envelope for you."

He scoffs. "Ah, yes, I'll get right on that. How many billable hours you think dead junkies can afford?"

"Cade." I tuck my chin and face him. "A woman is dead—"

"A woman who wasn't a client and represented a danger to you or Evangeline." He holds me by my shoulders for a brief second before gathering me back into his arms again. "You should have called security immediately. It sounds like she overdosed almost right after she left. Something could have happened to the two of you."

I huff a sigh. "I had things under control."

"Babe, I know, it just . . . worries me, the risks you take sometimes," he says. "I'll let Bridger know he can tell the cops our office doesn't have any additional information to offer, and this matter can be closed. Let's just forget about it and have a nice night, huh?"

I roll my eyes.

Of course, Bridger and Kirby—the firm's senior partners—will just want this to go away, so there's no blowback on the firm, no hint of anything unseemly that may taint its glowing reputation with Dallas's upper crust.

But if Cade doesn't care so much about the envelope, that frees my conscience so I can take it back Monday morning and look through it at my leisure. With enough

time, I can track down more on that birth certificate and
see what I can find out about that club.

Maybe even do some digging on that photo.

I wad the plastic hanging bag and the paper tags into
the trash can. "Did you look at that envelope she left?"

"Nope." He leans back against the counter, finishing
off the last of his water. "I sent you out and thought you'd
be waiting for me, so I was leaving when the cops rolled in.
When I got here and you weren't . . ."

"I didn't think you'd beat me here or I would have
texted," I say.

If the cops were industrious enough to go floor by floor in
our building, they may suspect this is more than just an overdose. I could give them the envelope, but given that almost
40 percent of homicides go unsolved in Dallas, they'll likely
put it in a box that will end up in a storage unit somewhere.
The detectives with their worn shoes and jaded expressions will
be too busy chasing high-priority cases that grab headlines.

Monday, I can take a second look, though, and decide
if it's worth passing along to the cops. By then, there may
be a preliminary cause of death, and if there's something,
I can claim that it got lost in our office shuffle of files and
paperwork—that happens in every busy law firm.

Cade slips up behind me and untwists my bun. "You're
home now, though."

I nudge him toward the master bedroom. "We need to
get ready."

"You can shower with me," he says.

"We won't leave on time if we do that," I say.

He grins and steals a last kiss. "Can't blame a guy for
trying."

I follow him into the spacious master suite. Beyond the
bedroom's picture window, downtown Dallas glints gold in
the setting sun. I reach past the overstuffed armchair in the
corner to tug the curtains closed.

The room darkens to twilight, and I cross to the other side of the king-size bed to the walk-in closet, hang my dress, and shrug out of my jacket. But almost as soon as I lock my pistol and the barely legal knife I carry as backup into the safe, Cade is there sidling up behind me to slip his hands around my waist.

"Sure you don't want to shower with me?" he asks and nuzzles my cheek.

"Cade," I say, but lean back against him.

"It's like an appetizer," he whispers into my ear. "Just a little, before the main course."

"Cade," I say, this time forcing a firmness I don't feel into my voice.

Because we both know my resolve is weakening. Cade brings the same level of skill and persistence to the bedroom that he brings to the courtroom, that he once brought to the football field as a quarterback. We could have the NFL's best defensive line separating us, but it won't do a damn thing when I'm slipping past them and into his arms.

A warning prickles between my shoulder blades and settles as a dull ache into the base of my skull.

Maybe the danger is this, that as much as my hungry gaze cannot stop itself from finding Cade and devouring him when we're in the same room together, his equally hungry hands and mouth can't keep themselves off me when we're near. At the office I can keep my head down and focus on my work, only watching him from the corner of my eye, never looking directly at him. He, on the other hand, is always careful to put something—a desk, a wall, or even another person—between us.

We may not have that at Bridger Holcombe's tonight.

If we indulge now, perhaps we can stave off the hunger until later, when we leave the dinner party and return to the safety of Cade's apartment.

Maybe Cade follows my thoughts, because almost breathing it into my hair, he says in a low voice, "Come on, Reag, it'll be fun."

And so this is how we scramble out of the shower at the time we should be leaving for Bridger's. My cheeks are flushed, and Cade carries a surreptitious sated air like a tomcat who just polished off a bowlful of stolen cream.

I roll stockings on, and he says from where he's tugging on gray chinos, "It's June, babe, too hot for that."

But I still hear my cousins chiding me—almost as soon as my grandfather is out of earshot—about my skin being too white and my inability to speak Spanish. They think maybe I'm not really a Reyes, maybe my father just felt sorry for my white mother and no one else wanted her—or me. To them, I'm a fake.

Unlike Tony, he would chortle, the actual grandson of Miguel Reyes. He will carry on the family name.

Every summer, as my cousins browned on the lake or the beaches, and I prayed that this would be the year I, too, browned, I instead burned, blistered, and peeled. Tony would laugh and say maybe it was because I was part snake.

Tony died when we were sixteen, the bystander at a shoot-out in Houston's Fifth Ward, and I'm the one who carried the Reyes name into the military.

I come back to the present and only say, "It looks better. Anyway, you normally like my stockings."

"I like to take your stockings off," Cade says.

"And you can," I say. "After dinner."

He buttons his Carolina blue polo and departs to the closet, returning to the bathroom while I dust on powder, line my eyes, and swipe on mascara. "You don't need all that."

"All the other women will be wearing it," I say.

"They're not you," he says. "You're beautiful without it."

I smile and reach over to smooth his damp hair, shining black under the bathroom lights. He catches my hand

and kisses the inside of my wrist, as if reminding me that he can't lie to me.

Beauty is subjective anyway.

"I'll zip you up," he offers, even though I don't need him to.

He runs a finger up the tattoo of a sword that runs almost the full length of my spine, the blade through a crown and the hilt nestled between my shoulders, and says, "One day you're telling me about this."

The tattoo fascinates Cade. His hands seek it out—caressing the outline like he still feels it—even when I'm fully clothed. When I'm not dressed, he often amuses himself by kissing a line up or down it until I melt in his arms.

"I've told you," I say. "I got it after my first deployment. What else is there you want to know?"

"You said once you got it to remind yourself you had everything you ever needed," he says. "But there's no heart there."

"No brain there, either, but I seem to be doing okay," I say.

His laugh is low and easy, the music of rain on a tin roof when you know you have nowhere else to be and nothing to do, and for a second, his mouth finds mine, still hungry.

"Just never had a girl with a tattoo before," he says.

I put a finger to his lips. "Don't."

It's the one other rule in our relationship, the one other unspoken promise we keep.

We don't lie to each other, and we don't talk about anything before that night he brought me here, that night that was only supposed to be a one-night stand. Because the minute we acknowledge there's a before, then we have to acknowledge there might be an after, and acknowledging something, speaking it, giving it words, gives it power.

Breathes it into life.

Makes it stronger.

Cade nods and kisses me one more time, then slips away to gel his hair before it dries.

I twist my thick unruly curls that defied my grandmothers and mother throughout my childhood into a loose, low bun resembling conventional expectations but that Cade will delight in taking down later. He offers me his arm and we arrive at his Porsche at the exact time we are supposed to be entering Bridger Holcombe's Highland Park home.

The 911 Turbo is fire engine red, bought used when Cade paid off his last law school student loan and made junior partner at the firm. It's his most valued possession, and I think if ever forced to choose between the Porsche and his apartment, he'd cheerfully live in the car.

Next to it, my sports sedan looks like a frumpy suburban housewife, but it attracts less attention when I need to go somewhere unnoticed.

Like tonight.

I fish in my purse for my car keys, but Cade huffs a sigh. "Reag. Get in."

"What if someone sees?" I ask.

"No one cares," he says, because he's a man and no one will ever question his career progression.

"But still," I say, even as I eye his Porsche and shift my weight toward it.

"People will be too busy with cocktail hour to watch from the windows, but if you're so worried about it, I know a place to park, and we can stagger arrival and departure times." He opens the passenger door and takes my hand. "Come on, you know you want to."

And he's right.

I let him help me into my seat and shut the door. He slides behind the wheel, fires the six cylinders to life, and we zip out of the parking garage.

"About tonight," Cade says, steering onto North St. Paul Street. "Bridger has these dinners at his house every year at the end of June."

Cade rockets the car into fourth gear as we merge onto the expressway, slinging us across three lanes of traffic, and I tighten my grip on the edge of my seat.

"You'll ruin the leather," he says, taking the time to uncurl the fingers of my left hand and draw it to him. "Tonight we find out who the summer interns will be—not that they'll be there—and where they'll be assigned. All the partners are there with their staff."

I crinkle my nose before I can help it. "And we have to suffer through cocktail hour and dinner for that?"

"And dessert," he says. "Make sure you speak with Mrs. Holcombe. She gets very offended otherwise, and while she may not run the firm, she pulls a helluva lot of weight in other circles. And she is Bridger's mother."

"Fine," I grumble.

He cracks a brief smile and traces an outline of a stocking top through my dress. "I'll make it up to you. You know I'm good for it."

The route leads through the heart of Highland Park, the richest zip code in Texas. Here, in the Park Cities, old money practically drips off the oak trees that line the wide avenues, sheltering multi-million-dollar homes from the summer sun and the hoi polloi.

Cade kills the engine not far from a large white house on a sprawling corner lot. It's easily the biggest home on the block, its broad semicircular drive glistening with parked cars under the portico lights. "That's Bridger's house. You want me to go first?"

I love him for asking, even if I'd never admit it.

Love, after all, is never supposed to enter the equation that is Cade and Reagan.

And I love him even more because I know he'll abide by my choice, although I suspect he's half waiting for me to say we could just leave so he can tell me we have to at least make an appearance, that he has to play the game if he wants to be a named partner one day.

"You," I say, "so I have a friendly face to look forward to when I arrive."

He squeezes my hand as if to apologize and promise he isn't ashamed of me.

And because I'm now fluent in the secret language of stolen moments that we've created since April—furtive eye contact and fingers and knees brushing under tabletops—I squeeze his hand back to reassure him I understand. I've read the employee contract, too, and I know what we're risking with our relationship.

"Stay through dessert," he says. "I'll slip out fifteen minutes after you."

He leans over and kisses me one more time, fiercely and deeply, then pulls away before I'm ready, his teeth grazing my lower lip.

"Come for me," he says the second time this evening, and slides out of his seat after caressing my cheek. The keys jingle as he puts them in his pocket, and he saunters away into the dying sunlight.

I apply lipstick to cover my lips, which are puffy from his kisses, and wait for the evening's warmth to make it believable that my glow is only from the temperature.

I huddle in the shelter of the car's flimsy fiberglass walls. It's safe in here, and rich with his scent. I'm protected from the senior partners' glances, who must surely see past these masks Cade and I wear and our game we play for their benefit.

But I can't stay away from Cade for long.

Not when I feel him waiting for me, drawing me like a magnet.

As soon as I feel it won't be too obvious, I step out of the car, lock its doors, and follow.

* * *

The air thickens with the sunset like a damp blanket pressing in close, weighting the hem of my sundress so it hangs as I make my way up the long sidewalk to the Holcombes'. Cicadas whine in trees, crescendoing to a screech, and a handful of June bugs swirl and pop around the porch lights. Gardenias bloom in waist-high flowerpots painted white to match the house, their scent heavy and sweet in the humidity.

The house looms over me, ten thousand square feet, two stories, Gilded Age excess with a portico covering part of the semicircular drive off to the side. But for all its brightness spilling out through the windows and the snow-white paint, it feels as if it's as much of an act as Cade and me, like it goes too far to pretend and so something must be wrong.

I tighten my shrug closer around my neckline, realizing that a house like this, with its age and decadence, could swallow a person whole and never think twice about it.

It's too bad my grandmothers aren't around to see their ugly duckling granddaughter sailing into a Highland Park dinner party.

That they might be watching from whatever afterlife they earned, eyebrows to their hairlines in disbelief, gives me enough backbone to approach the door.

It opens as I reach for the doorbell and a uniformed Latina maid stands before me. She is older and shorter than I am, dressed in black with a white apron and sensible work shoes.

For a long moment we look at each other, and I wonder if she wants to comment on my lateness, the curves my sundress enhances rather than hides, or my curling tendrils that Cade has pulled loose from my bun.

Instead, she holds out her hand. "I'll take your purse. Through there, ma'am, and into the backyard."

I pass the curving staircase and enter a cavernous room with intricately molded walls and a mirror over its fireplace. *The Bridger Holcombes at home*, I tell myself, and wonder how a house resembling a magazine spread can ever be comfortable enough to be home. This isn't the future I want for myself, even if Cade does, and maybe I should ask him about that before I fall any further for him.

Impostor, the mirror whispers to me when I catch my reflection, as if it recognizes me caught between worlds, none of which I fully belong in.

I turn my back to the mirror and step through double doors into the backyard, which is large enough to comfortably host the fortyish people gathered tonight inside its high stone walls without being cramped. A topaz blue pool with a fountain serves as the centerpiece, and strings of white lights zigzag overhead, strategically interrupted by paper lanterns. I linger at a topiary, shifting my weight from foot to foot, and search for Evangeline or Armando.

Not Cade.

No, not Cade, but he inevitably draws my attention, standing at the opposite end of the pool with the two named partners. When he smiles at something one of the partners says, I can't help but smile too.

"Are you stupid?" Evangeline hisses in my ear, yanking me farther behind the topiary.

"No," I say and straighten my shrug.

"Every time you look at him, it's all over your face," she says. "You couldn't make it more obvious if you carried around a sign saying you're sleeping with him. Get it together."

I huff and fold my arms across my chest, but she's right.

We stand close enough that I feel her without touching her, as Bridger Holcombe laughs and nudges Cade with his elbow. "Well, the NFL is hardly perfect, as you know," Bridger says, loudly enough it carries over to us.

Bridger, always the loudest in the room, as if he still hasn't figured out that volume doesn't equal authority or that money can't make people like him. He looks tired and paunchy next to Cade, his shirt bulging over his belt and sagging onto his chinos. Something about his salt-and-pepper hair seems too dark, making his skin pastier and the bags under his eyes redder, even under the flattering patio lights.

Cade forces a smile that doesn't reach his eyes. "SMU's not a bad place to end up."

Kirby Donaldson chuckles, and when he shakes his head, the highlights glisten in his blond hair. As Bridger Holcombe's college and law school roommate, and still his favorite golf partner, maybe he feels obliged to laugh. It's hard not to like Kirby, though; he's everyone's favorite uncle, with a well-timed corny joke always ready and is usually deployed as the more diplomatic face of Holcombe & Donaldson.

Or was, before Cade arrived.

"Over there," Evangeline says. "That's Sylvie Holcombe, Bridger's mother."

Sylvie is small, her silver hair piled high on her head, the hem of her purple dress brushing the floor. Each pearl on her necklace is larger than a marble, shimmering under the lights. She walks without a cane but smiles up at the man in a suit who escorts her closer to her daughter-in-law.

Colleen simpers at her mother-in-law, but I catch her eye roll when she looks away. Her tan is too peachy to be anything but sprayed on, and her feathered platinum hair fringes around large hoop earrings and long eyelashes.

A younger man joins the three of them. "Who are they?" I ask.

"Stu," Evangeline says. "Bridger and Colleen's son, but I don't know why he's here."

His hair is dark, but he has his mother's height, and there's something about his grin and the way he eyes Cade that I don't trust.

"And the other guy?" I ask.

"He works for the Holcombes," she says, and lowers her voice even more to add, "They call him Bear."

He's not much taller than Bridger, but he's burlier, his hands meaty and his neck thick, dwarfing the elderly woman on his arm. His eyes are narrowed almost into a permanent squint and his skin is reddened, as though he spends most of his free time outdoors. While his suit certainly matches the opulence present, it's too much for the evening, like he tries too hard. But the way he smiles at Sylvie Holcombe and pats her hand is endearing, giving the impression that he might almost be less the hired help and more a second son to her.

Armando slides between me and Evangeline. "Ladies," he says, his dark eyes merry. He wears a lime green golf shirt with navy chinos, but somehow this seems more appropriate for him than the conservative colors the older partners sport or Cade's blue.

The staff members congregate around the pool, but I stay with Evangeline and Armando, where it's safer in the darkness.

"Thank you all for joining us this evening," Bridger says, his voice thick and nasally.

He launches into a speech, detailing the firm's successes since the New Year. It feels so much like a commander's call that I'm on the verge of letting my mind drift while remaining the perfect picture of attentiveness, until Bridger mentions Cade's name.

The present snaps back into focus, and there is only Cade's easy grin as Bridger laughs and slaps him on the back. Cade and I make eye contact for a fraction of a second before I look away.

"Another year, and he won't be a junior partner," Armando says, his voice barely above a whisper. "Soon it'll be Holcombe, Donaldson, & McCarrick."

There's a warning here about Cade's and my relationship, soft as the resignation curling Armando's words, but I don't want him to realize I've noticed both.

"No Tamez?" I ask.

Armando's mouth twists. "You know better than that."

I do, of course, but I know that Armando won't leave. While there are other firms that would put his name on the mast, they lack the prestige that he has here.

I also know that Holcombe & Donaldson don't so much want an immigration attorney as much as they want to say they have an immigration attorney. This means that Armando doesn't help the people that could really use his aid, only the ones who can afford it.

Like Cade, Armando's clientele is mostly athletes, politicians, and corporate executives who want discreet assistance. While Cade's clients desire their criminal indiscretions wiped away, Armando's need to be able to cross borders to play games, import skilled workers quickly, or just keep the housekeeper and au pair their families have grown attached to.

And if Cade becomes a named partner, it promises more work and higher pay for me, so I shouldn't be concerned. But that farm boy from North Carolina wasn't born to wealth and isn't a member of the Highland Park glitterati, any more than the mechanic's daughter from the Piney Woods, and I wonder if Cade knows how quickly Bridger and Kirby would turn on him if he ever became a threat to them.

Or if Cade was ever allowed to help the people who truly needed his assistance.

"Don't you want more?" I ask.

Armando laughs under his breath. "Don't you?"

"It might be different when Cade is a named partner and can choose his clients," I say.

"Will it?" he asks, but I don't have an answer for him.

Off to the side, Colleen stands on her tiptoes and fusses with the collar of her son's shirt like he is four and not in his mid-twenties.

Bridger nods approvingly. "And our third-year intern this summer . . ."

A long silence builds.

Colleen beams.

"Stu," Bridger finally says. "Given his interest in criminal law, he'll be interning in Cade's office."

Cade plays with his watch, an indication he is less than thrilled with this arrangement. Stu Holcombe smiles and waves his thanks to the staffers who clap politely. As the boss's son, they'll pay lip service to him and there won't be any whispers about why he gets to attend this evening if no other interns are allowed.

"Great," Evangeline says in my ear. "Just what we need."

"It's just a few weeks," I say.

She raises her eyebrows and shakes her head.

"Now, I know you're all hungry, so let's eat," Bridger says. "The buffet is set up in the ballroom—you can either eat in the air conditioning or feel free to bring it out here and enjoy this lovely night."

Armando brushes past me and Evangeline as if answering an inaudible summons. He joins Cade and the other partners so Colleen can take a photo of Stu with the four men.

"Come on," Evangeline says. "Let's get dinner and find ourselves seats."

3

W E SIT AT a table off to the side, my back to the patio so I'm not tempted to watch Cade. "Don't look now," Evangeline says, "but here comes trouble."

"Cade?" I ask.

She smiles. "Different sort of trouble."

A hand brushes my shoulder and Colleen Holcombe says, "I've been looking all over for you. My mother-in-law wants to meet you."

Evangeline dabs her lips with her napkin, a sparkle starting in her eyes. "Don't keep her waiting."

"Maybe you should come too," I say.

"They've met," Colleen says, so quickly it almost stuns me.

Evangeline smirks. "Enjoy."

I flip Evangeline the bird behind my back as I follow Colleen into the ballroom.

Because of course the Holcombes must have a ballroom, and this one could easily host a gathering ten times the size of tonight's. Filmy white curtains cover the large windows, and the light from the chandeliers dances off the glistening wooden floor and Colleen's bedazzled flip-flops.

"Did you have a hard time finding the house?" Colleen's smile is tight, and she doesn't give me time to answer before adding, "Highland Park can be confusing if you're not from here."

Her words land like a backhand slap to my face with the three-carat rock she wears on her left hand, relieving any prior sympathy I might have had for her having to tolerate Bridger.

She leads me toward Sylvie Holcombe, seated in a chair at a table off to the side, as though she's queen of the evening.

Sylvie's pale blue eyes glitter. "So you found her."

"As you see," Colleen says. "Mrs. Sylvie Holcombe, this is Reagan Reyes, Cade's new investigator. Reagan, this is Mrs. Holcombe. Reagan was a captain in the Air Force, and was working for a congressman—"

"Yes, I know," Sylvie says. "Have a seat, Captain Reyes."

"Reagan's fine," I say, but I recognize an order when I hear one and sit.

Sylvie glances at her daughter-in-law. "You may leave," she says, and waits until Colleen is out of earshot to say, "New money is the worst, isn't it?"

It pays the bills just like old money, I want to say, but I don't.

Instead, I only answer, "I wouldn't know."

She watches me over the top of her bone china coffee cup and sips. "You're not what I thought you'd be, but I suppose you hear that fairly often."

Cade crosses my line of sight. I force myself to look away before our gazes meet, although I know he watches me; I can almost feel his fingers in my hair and hear his whisper in my ear that Mrs. Holcombe is important.

I fold my hands on the table and make myself still. "You could say that."

"You certainly have potential." Mrs. Holcombe's smile is almost predatory as she leans back a little in her seat, but not so far that she touches the back of her chair. "Air Force career, educated, striking looks—and you've impressed my son. Not married?"

"No, ma'am," I say.

"That's a pity," she says. "But fixable. You're practically the poster child for the new Texas with that last name and yet looking so . . . polished. Why aren't you running for office?"

I resist the urge to bolt from my chair. "I'm not political."

She laughs and reaches over to clasp my hands. "Dear, everyone is political with the right motivation. You'll come to the Ladies' Civic Club meeting next month at the country club with me."

This isn't a request, but it's not an order I'm comfortable with, nor is it one I'm sure I need to obey.

"I'll check my schedule," I say.

"You do that," she says. "Now be a dear and fetch me some pecan pie."

I resent being treated like the hired help, especially after the remarks on my last name and my looks, but I remember Cade's warning that Bridger Holcombe's mother holds a lot of influence. And so I walk to the buffet on the other side of the ballroom, swallowing my bitterness and the insult to a family name that has been in East Texas since the days when the land was still New Spain. I grab pie, only to see Kirby Donaldson trot over to Sylvie before I'm halfway back.

They stare past me, toward something I can't see beyond the ballroom doors, and as I approach, Mrs. Holcombe says low enough she might assume I won't hear, "Deal with *that* girl and get rid of her. I won't have the past repeating itself."

Kirby smiles and leans down to kiss her cheek. "I'm sure there's nothing to worry about, but I'll handle it."

He strolls past.

I paint a smile on my face like I've noticed nothing amiss and set the pie in front of Mrs. Holcombe. "Shall I get you more coffee, too?"

She twists her napkin in her lap. "No."

The man from earlier, the one Evangeline called Bear, steps closer to Mrs. Holcombe. "Ma'am, do you need something else?"

"No, I'm fine," Mrs. Holcombe says and smiles up at me. "Would you tell my grandson I want to see him?"

"Yes, ma'am," I say.

I hurry away, relieved to have an excuse to go, but can't help sneaking a glance over my shoulder, curious about the older woman's agitation. Bear bends down over her, his ear almost at her mouth, and smiles at me like I have nothing to worry about.

But Evangeline's voice draws me, her words sharp as a knife's blade when she says, "Excuse me?"

I step outside. Stu Holcombe holds a beer in one hand and uses his other to finger Evangeline's braids. Kirby stands on her other side, the angle of the two men trapping her against the house, and I don't like the way Stu leers down at her.

Suddenly, Sylvie Holcombe's smile at the table to me looks downright innocent.

I worm my way between Stu and Evangeline. "Your grandmother wants you."

Stu sighs, but winks at Evangeline over his shoulder as he slouches to where Mrs. Holcombe sits.

Kirby's gaze follows him. "He's just a kid, you know. Boys will be boys. If you have any trouble—"

"There will be no trouble, sir," I say.

He chuckles and pats my shoulder. "I expect nothing less."

Evangeline waits until Kirby walks away to say, "Let's go. Now."

We slip inside as though we're the ones who did something wrong and retrieve our purses from the maid at the door. The night envelops us as we hurry down the sidewalk toward the street.

"What happened?" I ask.

"Nothing," she says.

"Nothing?" I rest a hand on her arm. "Evangeline—"

"You think that's the first time a white college boy put his hands on me?" she asks. "You think I needed you and Kirby Donaldson to save me?"

"No," I say. "What did he say?"

She shakes her head. "It's not what he said, it's how he acted. Like he had a fucking right."

"Hey," Armando calls from behind us. "Wait up, I'll give you a ride."

Evangeline and I stand in the shadowed safety of an oak tree probably older than our grandparents until Armando arrives. Neither of us speaks, but he must know something is wrong because he slips an arm around Evangeline that she doesn't shrug away.

"Let's grab a drink," he says.

I take the back seat of his Jaguar two-door before Evangeline can offer me the front. No one talks as Armando drives us to an Irish pub, not the DART station where Evangeline needs to go, and the silence persists until Evangeline and I sit in a booth while Armando opens a tab.

I stare at the table and exhale. "You should tell Cade what happened."

"It'll only cause trouble," she says.

"Still," I say. "He should know."

"We'll see," she says. "How long do you think he'll stay, anyway?"

"He told me fifteen minutes," I say.

"You two should be more careful," she says.

"How did you figure it out?" I ask.

She laughs. "I'm not blind, nor am I stupid. Cade hasn't shown up to work hungover since you joined the staff, and that's got to be some sort of record. And half the time you smell like his cologne."

"And you and Armando?" I ask.

She shakes her head. "I'm not rushing back into anything. Not after . . ."

I nod, knowing that mentioning her ex-boyfriend's name will further dampen the evening, conjuring memories of bruises on Evangeline's arms, a confrontation in the front office that Cade stepped into with a threat to involve building security—or worse. "You're better off without that guy."

She sighs and tilts her head back to look up. "He was nice to pass the time with, though, until he wasn't," she says, before giggling. "And there's Cade. Not even fifteen minutes."

I glance over my shoulder to see Cade and Armando gather the drinks from the bartender. Armando slides into the seat next to Evangeline while Cade sits beside me and squeezes my hand under the table in greeting.

"Did I miss anything?" Armando asks, swirling his glass of mescal.

Cade drinks top-shelf whiskey, not the apple pie moonshine we drink when it's just the two of us on his apartment balcony and there are no pretenses to maintain. "Nah, they were still talking about the cops showing up at the office."

"The cops?" Evangeline asks. "At the firm?"

"A woman did die," Armando says. "You'd think they'd want to cooperate."

"I'd be amused at exactly how horrified Bridger and Kirby are if I didn't know why they're upset," Cade says and then mimics Bridger's nasally tone perfectly, "Look here, son, I don't mind attention when it's one of your damn press conferences. Those at least make us money, but this isn't the kind of attention this firm wants."

Evangeline frowns and plays with the stem of her martini glass. "A woman died at the firm?"

"No, not *at* the firm, but not far from it," Cade says. "That woman with the pink hair. Reagan said she came by the office but left after you told her I wasn't there. I handled things with Bridger and told him it was no big deal."

I hope Evangeline will leave this alone, but she tilts her head and says, "Reagan didn't mention anything happening outside."

Cade affords me a glance from the corner of his eye and releases my hand under the table. "What?"

I chug a mouthful of my mojito, its sweetness not enough to wash away the evening's increasing sour note. "I followed her."

He doesn't point out that I could have told him when we talked about the woman's death in his apartment; perhaps that's too obvious an acknowledgment of our living arrangement. He only asks, "And?"

"It's been a long week." Evangeline finishes off her drink in a quick gulp. "Armando and I'll get out of here."

Armando frowns. "Cade said he was buying the next round."

Evangeline shrugs. "There's tomorrow night. We can hit up Deep Ellum, if it's not too risky for them."

It's dangerous enough, the two of us appearing together in public like this not far from Bridger's home, but Deep Ellum—the most prominent entertainment district in Dallas—on a Saturday night will be worse.

Cade breathes out a long exhale, though, and says, "We'll come if Reag wants," like it's no big deal. When I step on his foot under the table, he mumbles into his whiskey, "I said I was buying the next round. Stay home if it's too risky for you."

"Sorry," Evangeline mouths to me as she stands, but audibly says, "Tomorrow night, then."

"I'll drive you," Armando says to her. "You shouldn't be taking the train."

They depart through the thickening crowd, and Cade says, "We should go too."

He's too quiet on the ride back to Uptown. Any other time, I might welcome his silence as an opportunity to sort through everything that happened at the Holcombes', but tonight it builds a wall between us. On the walk up from the parking garage, he shoves his hands in his pockets, like he's afraid he'll reach for me otherwise, and stares at the floor.

He unlocks the door and slings his keys on the bar, the silver glinting under the single light that shines from over the stove top. "You should've said something, Reag. Did you see what happened to her?"

I play with my purse strap. "Not exactly."

"What was in the envelope?" he asks.

I don't look him in the eye, not wanting to acknowledge how close I came to blowing past our agreement for honesty. "It's in the stack from my inbox you took this afternoon."

"But did you open it?" His tone is shorter than usual, nearly what he assumes in court when dealing with a witness for the prosecution. It's so different than what I'm used to with him that it almost physically hurts.

"Evangeline and I handle your letters and calls all the time, and I—"

"Stop," he says. "This is different, and you know it. Damn it, I told Bridger this was all nothing and that my office didn't have anything to do with her. What am I supposed to say if it comes out you were there when she died?"

I scoff and roll my eyes, disappointed that he's less concerned about the dead woman than Bridger's reaction. "Oh, because you tell him everything? What all does he know about us?"

"It's not like that," he says with a sigh. "But I thought you of all people would understand. Everything I have I owe to Bridger, and if I want to make named partner, there are certain expectations I have to meet—like not dragging the firm into complications. Now, what was in the envelope?"

"Nothing that made any sense," I say. "Just random shit. Go get it if you want it so fucking badly, so you can tell Bridger it's no big deal and your precious partnership is safe. We wouldn't want any inconvenient women fucking that up for you."

"Goddamn it, Reagan," he says and picks up his keys.

The door slams behind him as he leaves.

4

H IS FOOTSTEPS FADE.
 And for a fleeting second, I think about going
after him to finish this, to apologize for flinging his desire
for a named partnership and his relationship with the firm's
managing partner in his face.

Because if there's one forbidden subject in Cade McCarrick's life, it's the family farm's seven hundred acres of sweet
potatoes and the life he left behind of being land rich and
cash poor, of every spare dollar going to the crops and every
year being at Mother Nature's mercy. Now he keeps all that
at bay with his German car, Rolexes and cuff links, designer
clothes, and Italian leather loafers. Only once, the night
three weeks ago when we brought the last of my clothes
and things from my apartment that I wouldn't risk being
stolen, did he drink enough moonshine to acknowledge that
he still has family back in North Carolina. Even then, they
were dismissed, played off as a joke disguised as a single
warning that he'll eat almost anything, but he'll be damned
if he ever eats sweet potatoes again.

Only I'm not the type of woman who runs after a man,
and Cade knows that. We'll both respect me a little less if

I pursue this lover who I try to convince myself every day I don't need.

I remind myself I have no real claim on him, that besides a living arrangement that could be only as temporary as we want, we've given each other no titles and discussed no futures, so who the dead woman is—was—and what she wanted with him is none of my business.

But all I can think of is that key to his apartment in my purse.

The way it feels to nestle into his arms at night and fall asleep to the soft, even sounds of his breathing.

The smell of his cologne.

The flash of his grin.

I should leave, I think. Maybe that will show him if he comes back to an empty apartment. Let him come after me again. Let him show up in the middle of the night at my apartment to demand why I've left him.

But just as certain as I am that he won't respect me if I go after him, I know that he won't come after me.

Not again, not tonight, not this time, and so I stand in the center of his kitchen where he left me, trying to work up the nerve to do something.

In the end I don't do anything at all beyond pouring a glass of water. I sip it, letting its coolness slide down my throat and clean away the sweetness of the mojito at the bar and the wine I had at the Holcombes'.

Then I close my eyes and think of that envelope in my hands this afternoon, the thin softness of the birth certificate. In my mind, I run my fingers over the names, Cesar Morales, Araceli Morales, the year, Dallas County, Texas.

What I remember of the photo with the teenage couple tells me it will provide no viable leads. The paper is too old, the picture too out of focus to be of any use.

My mind tries to summon the TABC permit, but it doesn't reappear, only that the name of the club reminded me of space. I think of stars, galaxies, names of astronauts, but nothing feels familiar.

The birth certificate, though, provides a starting place. I have begun with less.

I pull out my cell phone and scroll through my Twitter list of Dallas media accounts, the beat reporters, the official police department, and the blogs that monitor the various DFW police scanners, searching for any details about the pink-haired woman's death.

Nothing.

Like she never even existed.

I grab a mason jar of Cade's beloved apple pie moonshine from a cabinet, unscrew the lid, and swallow a mouthful.

Maybe it's the combined heat of the alcohol and cinnamon, or maybe it's just the memories of Cade they summon, but my thoughts stop churning and I feel my heartbeat slow.

Tomorrow.

Tomorrow, Cade and I can talk about this. Or maybe he'll get distracted with something else by Monday, so he won't mention anything to Bridger or the cops and won't even notice if I reclaim that envelope from his desk.

And by tomorrow, or Monday at the latest, the name of the dead woman will be public record. She represents a potential lead, too, although why she came to Cade nags at me.

An overdose, Cade says the cops implied, only like no overdose I've ever seen . . .

I can't shake the vague feeling of dread that settles in the pit of my stomach, not even after I shower and brush my teeth.

The bed I've never slept in alone before taunts me from the center of the room, suddenly too large.

I pull the curtains open and sink into the overstuffed chair with a blanket.

My questions play in the lights from downtown that dance on the ceiling, weaving in and around their sparkle, but always circling back to the fact that Cade doesn't handle pro bono work and that woman didn't look like she could afford him.

I sigh and tug his pillow to me from the bed, bury my face in it, and breathe his scent.

It's two thirty when the apartment door opens. I sit up from where I've nearly fallen into a doze and push myself out of the chair.

The footsteps drag across the floor, and an unfamiliar male voice says, "Come on, Mr. McCarrick. Bedroom's this way, sir."

"Naw, naw, let her sleep," Cade slurs, his voice louder than usual. "She's pissed at me. I got the couch tonight."

I pad to the bedroom door as the lobby doorman passes by, one of Cade's arms over his shoulders. "There we go," he says, helping him onto the couch. "You get some sleep."

Cade yawns. "Thanks. You're the best."

"You just remember that at Christmas time," the doorman says, but pauses when he sees me. "You gonna be all right, ma'am?"

I nod. "Thank you for your help."

He shuts the apartment door quietly behind himself. I reach over and flip the lock, note that Cade's keys are back on the bar, and tiptoe to the couch.

"Come on," I say. "Let's put you to bed."

"You take it," he says. "I don't want you to leave."

"I'm not leaving." I help him to his feet, and we sway together until I get my footing. "We can talk in the morning, but you'll sleep better in bed."

He lets me undress him, the clothes he's usually so meticulous about rumpled and sweaty, smelling of whiskey. I tuck him under the covers and bring a large glass of water and the bottle of ibuprofen.

"Reag," he says when I sit on the edge of the mattress. "I—I'm sorry about tonight."

"It's fine," I say. "Take this."

He swallows a handful of ibuprofen and the entire glass of water. "I'll make this up to you. Tomorrow night when we go out with Armando and Evangeline?"

"Tonight," I say. "Go to sleep."

I refill the water glass, place it on the nightstand, and close the curtains, plunging the bedroom into darkness. His breathing softens and I settle in bed beside him, hoping I'll be able to do more than doze now that he's home.

Cade flings an arm across me and pulls me close. "Reagan," he mumbles, one of his hands slipping inside my nightgown. He nuzzles my neck and says, "I can't lose you, babe. I won't risk it."

I smooth his hair and kiss the top of his head. "It's all right."

"You have to leave this alone." He half yawns. "Promise me you won't dig around on that envelope. I love you."

His admission is so sudden, so unexpected, that by the time I realize that's what he really said, he's already still and heavy on top of me.

It takes a long time for me to fall into a fitful sleep.

*   *   *

I wake alone in bed to the sounds of Cade's voice, low and hoarse, and then the door closing. Water splashes in the kitchen sink, something metal plinks, and the warm scent of coffee brewing wafts into the bedroom.

Normally I sleep in on Saturdays while Cade works out and swings by a neighborhood diner to bring us breakfast, but this isn't a normal Saturday.

This is the morning a few hours after Cade mumbled drunkenly that he loves me, and I don't know if he'll even remember.

If he doesn't, I can just forget it happened, chalk it up to a night of too much liquor and me being conveniently in his bed.

If he does, it's one more thing we need to talk about, because love isn't supposed to enter into our arrangement.

This is a good time to leave, to disentangle myself from this man whom I perhaps want too much. Loving Cade and living with him is the most irrational thing I have ever done, worse than leaving the Air Force sooner than I intended, worse than moving back to Texas and taking the job with the congressman's office, and even worse than leaving that job. For someone who earned a reputation as a cold, hard bitch during military service to now risk everything with her direct supervisor makes no sense—at least on paper.

But cool logic will only carry someone so far.

At some point, there must be allowances for chemistry, for the magic that can happen in a spring twilight rich with desire, tasting of apple pie moonshine from a shared flask, and smelling of safety.

That's the one thing I never accounted for.

I close my eyes and try not to think about the way he feels in my arms or how his voice sounded when he said he loves me.

Something clinks on my nightstand. The mattress shifts, and then Cade is beside me under the covers.

"Reag," he says.

If I keep my eyes closed, maybe I'll be immune to those green eyes, so I stay in the darkness where it's safer. "Yeah?"

His fingers tangle in mine. "About last night—"

"You should rest," I say. "Get some food down and sleep. How're you feeling?"

"Like shit," he says. "Been a while since I stayed out that late drinking."

I count the few weeks back that I've lived here, remember Evangeline's remark last night that Cade stopped showing up to work hungover around the time I started working at the firm, and say, "You're out of practice."

"I don't think I'll be getting back in practice," he says.

I don't ask him what he was drinking to forget before I came into his life because I know Cade's client list by now. He won't turn down the pay and opportunities that list or his partnership provide, not when his family's sweet potato farm probably snaps at the heels of his polished oxfords, but sometimes what he has to do to earn the pay and opportunities must weigh on him.

That still leaves last night, though.

I feel him ease closer, like he's not sure how I'll react.

"I had breakfast delivered," he says. "It didn't seem fair for you not to get your french toast because I went too hard last night."

I open my eyes and look at him then, take in the ruffled hair and the tiredness that smudges his face, and put a finger to his lips. "Tell me why."

"Babe." He sighs and looks away, smooths his hair with his hand. "It'd been a long week. A long day."

"That's not what I mean, and you know it," I say. "Don't you lie to me. You walked out and left me here—"

"You could've come," he says.

"Was that what you wanted?" I ask.

He sits up and reaches for the cup of coffee on his night-stand. "No."

"Who was she?" I ask.

He doesn't ask who I mean. He doesn't need to, but he says, "I don't know yet," and he's not lying.

No, when Cade lies, the cadence of his speech changes—slower in the courtroom, faster at the firm when he's telling a social white lie—and he'll fidget.

But his hands are still, and he doesn't even play with the edge of the sheet or his coffee cup.

"If you don't know her, why'd she come to you?" I ask.

He sips his coffee. "I don't know. I thought about it until I couldn't think about it anymore."

Still the truth.

This isn't what I counted on; I thought I'd catch him in a lie and confront him, but his honesty disarms me.

I sit up and grab the cup he left on my nightstand, the coffee swirled with the perfect amount of cream. "All right. Why can't I look into what she left? You said yourself it was probably an overdose."

"You were there," he says, his voice low. "Do you think it was an overdose?"

"I'm not a doctor," I say.

He huffs, slouching against the headboard. "Based on what you witnessed, as a layperson on the scene, is that how you would describe it?"

I recall the woman's indignation in his office, but how she never slurred her words or picked at her skin, never seemed frantic or rambling out of her mind. Her movements on the street were hurried, without being erratic or clumsy.

Finally, I answer, "No."

"All right, then, she's dead, and we don't know why," he says. "But given the nature of our line of work, humor me here if I jump to conclusions and believe the worst. What if something happens to you?"

"Nothing will happen to me," I say.

"You can't know that," he says. "I can't—"

"I don't need you to protect me," I say.

"No." He uses his free hand to caress my cheek. "I'm not sure I'd respect you as much as I do if you did."

"You respect me, but you don't trust me to do what I do for your clients every day, what you hired me to do?" I ask.

He grins, flashing his dimples. "You ought to think about law school, you know?"

"Don't change the subject," I say.

"Babe." He half groans and rubs his forehead. "I just don't want anything to happen to you."

But I'm not sure I want another man telling me where my boundaries are, defining me and holding me to his expectations, and so I say, "I could leave. I could go and—"

"You could've left last night," he says. "But you didn't."

"But I could," I say.

He sets aside his coffee cup and takes mine from me so he can hold my hands in his, warm like they were that night in March on my apartment landing, like they were that first night in April he brought me here. "You could always go. You know that, right? But I wish you'd stay. That you'd want to stay."

It's my turn to look away, and the lump in my throat forces me to swallow hard because he's right.

I don't want to go.

Not really.

"Reag," he says. "I'm asking—no, begging—you to please leave this alone. This isn't a paying client. It's not worth the risk."

"So that's it, because she's not a paying client?" I sit up straighter and shake my hands free of his. "If the money was worth it, it'd be okay to risk it?"

"Damn it, Reagan." He scowls, his eyes stormy. "You know how to kick a guy when he's down, don't you?"

"We could have talked about this last night if you hadn't left," I say. "And if you hadn't left, you wouldn't be hungover, would you?"

He rubs the back of his neck and slouches against the headboard. "What do you want me to do? Tell me, what do I have to say to get you to leave this be? That I love you, that I don't want to think of the possibility of whatever happened to her happening to you, that I don't want to come home at the end of the day without you?"

The ache in his voice melts my anger and takes my breath away. This isn't a drunken mumble in the middle of the night as he drifts off to sleep. This is a confession, raw and spontaneous.

I reach for him before I stop myself, before I remind him again that even if it wasn't an overdose, there's still not necessarily a risk to me, and before I insist that a woman is dead and that's exactly why he should care.

"It was just supposed to be one night," I manage to croak into his shoulder.

"Yeah," he says. "Trust me, I know."

"Six weeks of living here," I say. "Just over two months since—"

"I have a calendar," he says.

Of course he does, on the phone and on his computer, and even on his desk at work, the dates neatly lined out, stretching from here to eternity, maybe stretching from here to a five-bedroom brick home in suburbia with a white picket fence and a homeowners association, which is probably the future Cade envisions for us.

Or worse yet, maybe a house like Bridger's in Highland Park, painted white walls confining us to their standard of perfection, a standard we may meet only temporarily, until the fickle Dallas upper crust decides we've outlived our usefulness and turns on us, sniffing that we never belonged anyway.

I squeeze my eyes shut. "Where do we go from here?"

"I don't know," he says. "Does it matter?"

Maybe, I want to say.

But I don't, because it isn't fair to ask a question he doesn't have the answer to, and I know he can't lie to me.

He kisses the top of my head. "I'm not asking for anything permanent. I just want you to think about whether this is worth it. Please."

Maybe today the newspaper will report the woman's death was an accident, an overdose despite what I saw, or something explainable, and maybe her appearance at Cade's office with that envelope is just a coincidence.

Only if it's not . . .

"I love you too," I say, and that I mean.

But my mumbled "I'll leave it alone" may just be the first lie I ever tell him.

CHAPTER

5

WE CONTINUE THE routine we've settled into over the last month and a half I've lived here, the small mundane chores that move us closer and closer to permanence—changing the sheets on the bed together, debating over which pasta sauce to select as we put in the grocery order, dropping off dry-cleaning and laundry.

A baseball game drones on in the background as we fold clothes, warm and smelling of fabric softener, on the living room couch while dusk creeps in from the east, bathing downtown in shades of purple and pink. Cade sits at his end, the T-shirt he bought stylishly faded and the pile of his clean dress socks in his lap somehow rendering the sleek modern furniture and the large canvas of abstract fractals hanging on the wall less austere and more approachable.

He turns the volume down on the television. "What'd you think of Bridger's?"

I add one of his T-shirts to the growing stack on the brushed steel coffee table and grab a new shirt to roll, concentrating on making the lines as crisp as possible just like I learned years ago in boot camp.

The worry that Cade might want a house like that, a life like that, complicates my folds, and so I shake it out and start again.

"It's not my business how others spend their money," I say. "But Bridger's house is practically in spitting distance of people struggling to decide between making rent and buying groceries."

He smirks. "Mrs. Holcombe seemed to like you, though. What'd she want?"

I roll the shirt to my satisfaction and set it aside, grabbing another. "For me to come to the Ladies' Civic Club meeting. Somehow she thinks I have potential and that I'd be good at politics."

"Oh, Reag." He grins and slides a pair of socks down the coffee table. "Please tell me you didn't tell her you weren't political."

Concern stirs, dust rising from the career I left behind as a congressional staffer. "I have zero interest in politics. Once you've seen behind the curtain, it loses its allure."

The endless cycle of fundraising churning against the buzzsaw of headlines, the pressure to placate constituents and do everything possible to win votes so the boss gets reelected—no matter the price.

"She'd be a good friend to have," Cade says.

I pluck a sock clinging to one of his T-shirts and toss it to him. "I don't pick my friends based on what they could do to help me."

"How very unpolitical of you," he says, but I hear his smile. "So how are you so qualified for politics?"

I try not to think of Mrs. Holcombe's sharp smile and the implicit danger that lurks behind the interest of rich, white, elderly women who wield money and gossip as capably as any weapon of war. "My military career, mainly, I think. Female, military officer, graduate degree, undoubtedly my last name—and what she calls my 'striking looks.'"

Cade leans forward, elbows on his knees, steepling his fingers. "She's not wrong."

I shake out another T-shirt, wishing I could let this conversation fall away with the wrinkles. "Striking looks isn't a compliment."

"Isn't it?" he asks. "I know you don't think you're pretty—"

"I'm not," I say, because pretty is for other girls, the ones with hair that is smooth and shiny, the ones with the golden tans and long legs, who don't wear being called a bitch as a compliment, as I learned to do in the military.

He laughs. "Babe, you say that because that pissant hometown of yours only has one standard of beauty. But just because you're not what some might determine to be a Certified All-American Girl Next Door doesn't mean you're not beautiful. It's like asking a Miller Lite guy to drink Guinness—some men just don't appreciate the difference."

I watch him for a long moment, trying to decide why this is suddenly so damn important to him. "You aren't planning to run for DA or judge, are you?"

"Hell no," he says. "But Bridger's eyeing the county judge seat."

I grimace. "I don't want to go."

"It can only help us," he says.

He's right, of course; we do things every day that we don't want to do but that we know will help us, like working to defend people we both know are probably guilty.

"Maybe someday we can do something that we want to do," I say.

He leans over to steal a kiss. "Mm, I know what I want to do."

"Get ready for dinner and the night out you promised me?" I ask. "Armando and Evangeline will be waiting."

He twines a loose curl around a finger. "No appetizers?"

I slip free of his grasp. "Not after you reneged on dessert last night."

It almost surprises me that he doesn't follow me into the bedroom, where I change into ripped skinny jeans and a backless tank top.

No, he waits until I start my makeup in the bathroom to lean in the doorway. We make eye contact in the mirror before I catch his gaze drifting down my outfit, and he says, "You look nice."

I admire him in the mirror, his sage green button-down that matches his eyes—the sleeves rolled to the elbows—and perfectly coordinated with his pants. "So do you."

"Might want these, though." He brings his hands from behind his back, revealing a pair of strappy open-toed high heels. "They should fit."

"Those are Louboutins," I say.

"They were supposed to be a surprise for the party last night," he says and shrugs, "but I got . . . distracted."

The smoothness of the leather and the glint of their rhinestones, much less their red soles, indicate they're more expensive than anything I own. "They're beautiful."

"So you'll wear them tonight?" he asks.

"I'll wear them." I stand on my tiptoes and kiss him, then nudge him toward the door. "No appetizers."

He flashes his dimples and runs a finger up my back, tracing the tattoo. "Maybe we'll call it an early night?"

I shiver, but say, "Maybe I'll make you wait."

"Not nice to tease, babe," he says, but retreats to the living room.

I smile at my reflection, finish my mascara, and swipe on my lipstick before following him.

* * *

Deep Ellum on a Saturday night in the summer pulses with excitement, a carnival for the senses. Cars pass in the street, blurs of white and red lights, horns honking, drivers and jaywalkers occasionally shouting at each other, while music pours out open doors—Tejano, grunge, jazz, rock, country.

Anything can happen.

The smells of the city, of motor oil and gasoline, burgers and tacos and uncollected trash, the mingling of sweat and hundreds of perfumes and colognes tinge the air.

Outside in the street, the darkness softens and blurs anything beyond the headlights, the brake lights, the neon signs, and the marquees.

But inside the bars and clubs, the darkness sharpens and enhances sensations, imbuing them with a depth that might otherwise pale in comparison to visual stimulus.

The bite of the ginger and vodka in my drink.

The scrape of my new heels on the concrete floor.

The twang of a steel guitar.

The caress of Cade's fingertips along my exposed spine.

By the time we arrive at the third club—some place Armando insists we go that's new by the looks of the blood velvet rope at its entrance and the bouncer who doesn't yet look jaded—I'm four Moscow mules in, so I don't question why Cade hesitates.

"Come on," Armando insists.

Cade glances around and then pulls me into himself, so I catch only a glimpse of the neon sign with a bright yellow sun surrounded by black and white stars before a wave of air conditioning washes over us and we're inside.

A smoky soprano sings and couples sway together on the dance floor.

"Anything?" Cade asks as the four of us arrive at a table in the back. "Water, food . . . ?"

"I'll have another drink," I say.

He grins and pulls out the high stool for me. "Better pace yourself there, tiger. It's not even midnight."

"Jell-O shots," Evangeline says. "Oh, and fries."

"Cheese fries," I say.

"Unless they have cheese tots," she adds.

Cade shakes his head. "Fine. Carbs with cheese. And the Jell-O shots, and a Moscow mule. Anything for you?" he directs at Armando.

"Beer is fine," Armando says. "Or whatever you're drinking."

"I'm drinking water," Cade says over his shoulder as he heads to the bar.

Armando chuckles and nudges Evangeline. "Jell-O shots? You're a terrible influence."

"That's what makes me fun," Evangeline says. "But last night must not have gone well if Cade's drinking water."

Armando frowns and taps his fingers on the table. "Cade hasn't touched a drop all night. You two fight?"

It's still so foreign that other people know about Cade and me, especially other people from work, that all I can mumble into my drink is, "If we fought, would we be here?"

Evangeline smirks. "What'd he say 'bout that dead woman?"

"That she's not our problem," I say.

Evangeline and Armando exchange a glance, and he says, "That's not like him," but she only raises her eyebrows and looks away.

"You're in luck," Cade says as he returns. "The kitchen is open, and they have cheese tots, cheese fries, and pretzels with cheese. They'll bring 'em with the drinks."

I snag his hand and he doesn't resist as I tug him to the dance floor. The singer launches into another song and I close my eyes and let Cade lead.

Cade, who smells safe but whose kisses taste of ambition and the promise we won't end up farming sweet potatoes or balancing the books at an auto shop, that we're more than the lies we assume for the sake of others.

Having him this near me is the most delicious torture—his hands touching my bare back, the smell of his cologne mixed with a faint hint of sweat like it so often is after we make love, the way I can almost hear his heartbeat when I lay my head on his chest.

He tangles a hand in my hair. "We could go."

"Food's coming," I say.

"I'll bet they have a bathroom here," he says.

"And I'll bet it's disgusting." I stand on my tiptoes to put a finger to his lips. "Shh, I like this song."

"Reag," he says, and there's a lure in his voice that draws me closer to him, to the door, to the street to meet an Uber, to his bedroom. Maybe he feels me sway because his hands tighten on my hips, pulling me against him, and there's almost a pleading urgency to his voice when he says, "Come on."

"Isn't the waiting the best part?" I ask.

"Really, babe?" he says. "If the waiting's the best part, I'm doing something wrong."

He looks so offended I can't help but kiss him, and he slides his hands into the back pockets of my jeans. "The hardest part," I remember. "That's what Tom Petty said. The waiting is the hardest part."

"I'll show you the hardest part," he whispers in my ear.

"Later. It's not even midnight," I say, and over his shoulder I see the waiter arriving at our table. "Let's eat."

Armando gestures at the table as we approach. "Not drinking, he says, but this asshole orders a dozen Jell-O shots."

Evangeline smirks and pushes one to Cade. "We can't toast without you."

"We're toasting with Jell-O shots?" Cade asks.

"We're classy people." She flashes her brilliant smile, her eyes dancing. "Why not? You're not driving. Or are you too good for us?"

We toast. We drink. We eat and we laugh, and the music pounds in time with my heartbeat, reminding me that we're here and alive. Shards of light from the disco ball scatter around us like thousands of diamonds, ones that we could gather and hold close in our fists, preciousness to hoard, and I realize the fifth Moscow mule combined with the three Jell-O shots have put me over the top.

Cade grins. "Ready to leave?"

"Not yet," I say.

Evangeline grabs my hand, her hair tumbling free of its barrette. "Bathroom?" she asks, in the age-old girls' code of strength in numbers at any women's restroom in a strange place.

We find it at the end of a dark hallway behind a heavy wooden door that leads to a dimly lit room, every bit as disgusting as I promised Cade it would be, and smelling of marijuana, vomit, Pine-Sol, and sweat. The trash can overflows in one corner and the door to the metal bin that sells tampons, condoms, and cheap cologne hangs half open.

"Shit," Evangeline says. I expect her to say her barrette is broken, but she doesn't; she only stares at a piece of paper taped to the wall.

"What is it?" I ask.

She rips the page away and holds it toward me, but her hand blocks most of the text. "That woman from yesterday. It's her, isn't it?"

The paper is thin, the kind bought to print flyers at home one at a time so the ink doesn't streak, even though it always does. But the woman with the pink hair and tattoos is unmistakable in the photo, and while I don't know the Latino man who has his arm around her, there's something familiar about his nose and jawline.

They look so happy—alive and in love—like Cade and I must look in those rare stolen moments together when we're away from the office that it almost takes my breath away.

"This is for a memorial service," Evangeline says. "He died earlier this week. Maybe that's why she came to Cade's office?"

I look away while I still can, before her scrutiny draws the truth from me about Cade's mumbled request last night as he fell asleep, that he loves me and doesn't want to risk me.

"I don't know," I say. "Maybe Cade knew him."

"Cesar Morales," Evangeline says. "It doesn't sound familiar."

A chill runs up the back of my neck like we're outside in December, not inside a sweltering, stinking bathroom in late June, because I know that name from the birth certificate in that envelope and I am instantly, completely sober.

But she's not Cade, so I don't have to be honest with her, not entirely.

I finish washing my hands. "You want me to ask Cade?"

She shrugs. "It's not like him to be uninterested in something like this."

Her tone is curious, a question hidden there as to why he might not be, only I don't want to discuss the events of the previous night. Instead, I snatch the flyer from her and fold it small enough to cram into a back pocket of my blue jeans, as if I can tuck away all the other problems it might bring.

On the other hand, if this is enough to persuade him to check into whatever this is all about, then I don't have to feel guilty about almost lying to him earlier when I told him I'd leave it alone.

"Let me know what he says," is all she tells me before disappearing into the bathroom stall.

When we return to the table, a petite blonde in a sheer top and a pair of Daisy Dukes chats up Armando while Cade plays on his cell phone. Evangeline slides between the blonde and Armando, resting an arm on his shoulder, and the blonde flashes a hopeful look at Cade, but scurries away when he tugs me onto his lap.

I nudge him and incline my head toward Armando and Evangeline.

"Armando told me he knew about us last week," Cade says in my ear. "But they won't tell."

"Are you sure?" I ask.

"We wouldn't be here otherwise," he says.

The band starts a new set, but the food is cold, the drinks are empty, and the people on the dance floor are too drunk to do anything more than stumble into each other. Whatever magic this place held is gone, lost like the dead woman and her lover Cesar Morales.

Cade holds me against himself like a football, and I nestle into him despite the warmth, content that nothing can harm me in the security of his embrace. The niggling concern worms its way into my mind, that the dead woman might have thought that too, when Cesar Morales held her. Perhaps she held him when he died and that's why it was so goddamn important she get that envelope to Cade's office.

"Let's go," I whisper, and even though the band plays, I know Cade hears me because I feel him shift. "Take me home."

But there is still magic in the feel of Cade's fingers that lace through mine. He nods to Armando and says to Evangeline, "We'll see you Monday, then," and she rolls her eyes at Armando.

I look back as we leave the club. The sun and stars still glow on the sign, and next to them, the name spelled out in neon tubing is "Club Saturnalia."

I shudder and hang closer to Cade.

6

WE STAND ON a corner, waiting for Ubers with everyone else abandoning the bars in the hour before last call. While the backless tank top offers little defense to Cade running the back of a finger up my spine, the flyer in my pocket reminds me I have a secret.

Cesar Morales is dead.

The woman—whoever she is—is dead, too.

Don't think about it, I tell myself. If I think about it, if I acknowledge it, he'll be curious why his usual trick isn't working. He'll ask what's wrong, and I can't lie to him.

I close my eyes and concentrate only on his touch.

I'm too late, though, because he leans down to say, "I don't like sharing."

"That's why we're leaving," I say.

"Hmm." He brushes a kiss on my cheek. "I did think you were planning to make me wait until last call."

We scramble into the back seat of a stranger's sedan, its unfamiliarity jarring enough that I can forget the flyer and lose myself in Cade when he reaches for me. He kisses me until the stranger driving us clears his throat.

"We should have left earlier," I whisper.

A stoplight illuminates Cade's face long enough for me to see his grin because he doesn't know what I found in the bar's bathroom. "Isn't the waiting the best part?"

"We'll see," I say.

"Oh, we'll see, she says, like she doesn't care." Cade laughs under his breath and ropes a hand in my hair. "You'll change your tune when we get home."

We scamper across the apartment building's lobby, past the doorman, who nods at Cade. As soon as the elevator doors close behind us, I pounce on Cade, flinging myself into his arms.

He picks me up, a hand under each thigh, and I kiss him, letting him feel my teeth. His fingers run up my spine and I tighten my grip on him with my legs. He half moans into my throat and slumps back against the wall.

I barely hear the elevator chime our floor, but he must, because he cradles me and rushes to the apartment door as if it were an end zone. By the time he fumbles the keys out of his pocket and opens the door, I'm yanking his button-down shirt over his head.

He slips his hands into the back pockets of my jeans to get a better grip before I can stop him. "What's this?"

"Nothing," I say, turning his face back to mine, hoping it's in time to distract him.

Downtown Dallas glitters beneath us on the other side of the windows, enough for Cade to read the crumpled paper he tugs free, releasing me so suddenly I almost stumble.

"Reagan," he says, wadding it up in his hand as he glances back to me. "We agreed we weren't doing this."

I don't acknowledge the disappointment and betrayal in his voice; I only shrug and say, "We aren't. I saw it and thought you might want to see it too."

"You're lying," he says, but he follows me to the bedroom.

"I'm not," I say. "Anyway, I was going to tell you—"

"But you didn't," he says.

"I'm telling you now, aren't I?"

"It's a gray area," he says tightly, almost spitting the words.

I wrench him toward me by his belt loops, pressing myself up against him. "Learned from the best, Counselor."

He turns my face up to his, swiping my lips with his thumb and letting it remain there. "Why'd you bring it home?"

It occurs to me then that we couldn't have ended up at Club Saturnalia unless he was scoping things out, that maybe he opened that envelope last night and saw something to ignite his interest.

"Why'd we end up at that club?" I ask.

"You heard Armando," he says. "It was his call."

This is a non-answer, but I've seen Cade massage enough cross-examinations that I know even on a night where I hadn't put away five Moscow mules—or was it six?—plus the Jell-O shots, I probably wouldn't be able to back him into a corner unless he let me.

But I have other tools at my disposal.

I bury a hand in his hair, digging my fingernails into the back of his neck. "Don't lie to me. Aren't you the least bit curious?"

He is, I know he is. Cade is too good a defense attorney not to be.

But he remains silent.

I suck his thumb into my mouth and swirl it with my tongue until he jerks his hand back with a hiss.

"You want to go to the memorial service, is that it?" he asks. "Go. I won't stop you."

"It was Friday, damn it," I say.

Late Friday morning.

Just a couple of hours before that woman walked into Cade's office.

Maybe it's the alcohol. Or maybe it's the stress of the last two days, the tension between wanting him and not knowing why the woman came to him, the realization that my job and even my living situation in his apartment is utterly dependent on him, and I could be left like her, leaving flyers on the wall for a memorial service and begging strangers for help. But I burst out with, "You said this morning that you were worried that whatever happened to her could happen to me. Did you ever stop to think that whatever happened to him could happen to you? And *then* what about me?"

He slides free, and for a second, I think he'll walk away.

But then he puts his hand on the wall and leans over me, kissing me until I'm breathless. "Tell me when to stop," he says, grabbing a handful of my hair to pull my head back so he can nip at my neck.

I won't, and he knows it.

He knows we'll each go as far as we want, punishing the other one because we aren't who we're supposed to be, who the world believes us to be, because we recognize ourselves in each other. And so tomorrow the remnants of his kisses on my neck or along the inside of my thighs will amuse him, just as I will smile at the fingernail marks down his chest or up his back.

I tug his T-shirt over his head as he fumbles with the straps on my tank top, until I finally push him back and take it off myself.

"No bra," he says and sighs. "You're earning church tomorrow, aren't you?"

I shove him backward onto the bed. "Says the heathen. You didn't even go to church until I came along."

"Didn't see a need to," he says. "But there's something about you . . ."

He leans up on his elbows, watching me as I roll down the skinny jeans and toss them aside, leaving only the black lace thong.

"Uh-uh, Reag," he says, pointing to the floor. "The shoes. Please?"

It's that *please* that does it. That always does it, that hint of southern charm and courtesy my parents steeped me in and Cade must have been raised in too, even as we both have done everything we could to defy our families.

I fasten the high heels on, and he is there almost immediately, his hands tugging me on top of him.

But I'm in no hurry for the night to be over, not so soon, and so I let my heels dig in a little to his thighs. "Better pace yourself there, tiger."

"Oh, no," he says, and wraps a strand of my hair around his hand, pulling my face to his so he can kiss me. "We've got all night."

And then there is nothing, nothing but us, alive and together, and I can't think of anything but this man who thrust himself into the rigidly mundane life that I had fooled myself into accepting.

His touch that sets my body on fire.

His kisses that leave my mouth and skin tingling and craving more.

His body that consumes mine even as I consume his, the joint longing we have for each other, the mutual satisfaction we both lose ourselves in together.

"I love you," he whispers when we've finally exhausted ourselves.

"I love you too," I say, and drift off to sleep to him stroking my back.

* * *

I wake first and slip free of Cade's embrace, gather the discarded clothes and Louboutins, and put them all away. In the bathroom I remove the smudged eyeliner and mascara that ring my eyes like a raccoon, brush my teeth, and step into a hot shower. By the time I emerge, cleansed of last night and wrapped in a towel, Cade appears, yawning into a cup of coffee, his hair ruffled to the point I can imagine him as a young boy.

We pass each other almost without acknowledgment.

I braid my hair, apply makeup, dress, and step into shoes. I leave the apartment before Cade gets out of the shower, the church bells pealing overhead in the still morning air.

It's a ten-minute walk to First United Methodist. The church itself is old, older than Dallas maybe, maybe older than the hymn its bells chime, the tune as familiar as my grandmother's quilt, even if the building only dates to the early twentieth century. By the time I arrive, the singing is in progress, and no one notices me steal into the darkened interior through a side door and sit on a rear pew.

My attendance here is as recent a habit as my affair with Cade. While I know well enough that the hellfire and brimstone God of my evangelical upbringing would surely consign Cade and me to the depths of Hell for the pleasures we take in his bed, and that God must know because He is all-knowing, there is something in these fleeting seconds of peace I find in my pew that draws me back every week.

Cade follows, entering halfway through the next song, as he has since a couple of weeks after I began sneaking away.

We don't speak, don't so much as glance at each other. We share a bed and the most intimate moments of our lives, but we won't look each other in the eye when sitting in a pew with God between us.

The minister preaches on justice, our duties toward the less fortunate, and our obligation to assist. Unlike the preachers of my childhood, he doesn't raise his voice, prowl the stage, or pound his hand against the pulpit.

But maybe he doesn't need to, because Cade sighs and fidgets with his watch at the opposite end from where I'm sitting.

As the closing hymn begins, I sneak out the rear doors and into the noise of traffic rumbling overhead on the Woodall Rodgers Freeway and the pungent blend of hot asphalt and last night's restaurant trash already baking. The old oak trees provide welcome shadows, and I hurry into their embrace and the slightly cooler air.

Cade joins me and brushes a quick kiss on my lips. "Thanks for waiting."

I nod.

He offers me his arm and I slide my hand through for the stroll toward the café we usually brunch at on Sundays.

Cade clears his throat and says, "What he said in there . . ."

He exhales and shakes his head, but I wait. Whatever this is that he's struggling to say needs to be said aloud rather than implied or couched in pretty platitudes. The words need time and space to breathe, the power that comes with being born into summer air ripe with dissent and dissatisfaction, the grumblings that justice has not been served.

Protest season possesses its own magic.

"Look, everything in me is warning that we don't want to mess with this, that it'll lead us somewhere we may not want to end up," Cade says. "But if we don't?"

There's a long silence and I utter the words that terrify me, "Then who are we?"

We stop walking.

We face each other and see each other, recognizing ourselves.

He exhales and looks away for a quick second before we make eye contact again. "Find out what happened to Cesar Morales," he says slowly, as if weighing the cost of every syllable.

"I can do that," I say.

"Nothing official," he says.

Even in my high heels, I have to stand on my tiptoes to kiss him. "Off the books and only if I have spare time at the office. I'll be careful."

"Please," he says.

The unspoken reminder that he loves me and doesn't like this idea fills the space between us, and I squeeze his hand.

He smiles as if he knows and steals a second kiss. "Now, may I interest you in a corner table and a chocolate croissant?"

We sit at our usual table at the café with our usual breakfasts, allowing our Sunday morning to continue in its usual manner, a luxury lost to Cesar Morales and his dead lover.

7

I ARRIVE AT THE office first on Monday morning because I prefer it before the lights are on and the rooms fill with small talk and gossip and clients. I unlock the glass door, the one that passes the law firm receptionist's desk, and then the one into Cade's section.

Everything is just as Evangeline and I left it on Friday.

I sit at my desk, power on my computer, and eye my cell phone.

It will be another twenty minutes before Evangeline enters.

An appointment at the courthouse will keep Cade there until midmorning.

I flip through my contacts and find the number I need, but it goes to voice mail. "Hey, Miller, it's Reyes. Give me a call when you get this, I have a question on a recent death in Deep Ellum."

With that done, I turn my attention to my email. By the time Evangeline drops into her seat with a sigh, I'm tracking two other people who might be able to provide Cade's reasonable doubt on another case.

Cade strolls through the glass doors at ten thirty, wearing a navy three-piece suit that he keeps in the rotation for court days because he knows the female jurors like it. "Ladies," he says, like he didn't kiss me goodbye and tell me he loved me at seven. "How's the morning?"

"Quiet," Evangeline says. "When's your new intern arriving?"

Cade shrugs. "Due an hour ago. You want me to call and get him here?"

Evangeline fixes him with a hard stare, her eyebrow upraised. "No."

"Well, lemme know when he arrives," Cade says. "I'll be in and out the rest of the day, but I have no doubt you and Reag can make him feel at home."

His unspoken reminder that we need to keep Bridger Holcombe's son placated if we all want to keep our jobs, if we want Cade's name on the masthead one day, hangs in the air. Evangeline and I exchange a glance, and I look away first.

"I'll be in my office," Cade says, then disappears inside.

My cell phone buzzes, and I answer it. "Hey, Miller."

"Reyes," he says. "What's up with this message you left me?"

Miller's a Dallas detective now, but he was a damn good Marine before. He's someone I helped when I worked with the congressman, so I know he's good for a favor.

Still, this will require a little finesse.

I put a smile into my voice and talk fast to justify my curiosity in the case. "Friend of the family. You know how it is—these people come here with some sob story or something, and the old man . . . I hear he's eyeing a run at county judge. Anyway, this dead guy in Deep Ellum, named Cesar Morales—you know anything about that? Maybe you can give me something to get everyone off my back?"

It's a gamble. If Cesar Morales died of natural causes, this is where Miller will laugh at me and say that there's nothing for him to tell and I should follow up with the family and quit wasting his time.

But on the other end of the line, Miller sighs. "Damn it, Wing-Wiper. You know how to ruin a Monday, don't you?"

"Do you want the request in crayon or something?" I ask. "Come on, you know I wouldn't ask if I wasn't taking shit for it."

Evangeline puts her pen down and stares at me with upraised eyebrows, but I turn away.

"You realize what you're asking?" he asks.

"Sure," I say and plow ahead, full speed. "You got yet another dead Latino in Deep Ellum and your resources are spread thin. I'd think you'd welcome some help, especially with the kind of resources this firm could provide."

Miller scoffs. "Really?"

"What's the harm?" I ask. "You're overworked and underpaid. If I find anything, I'll send it to you. No one has to know I took a look at it."

"I'll see what I can get you," Miller says and hangs up the phone.

I click off the call and Evangeline says, "Guess you changed his mind?"

"Not me," I say. "It's off the books."

She twirls her pen in her fingers. "Cade is worried about something."

"It'll work itself out," I say.

We make eye contact but return to our work when Cade's office door opens and he emerges, rifling through his attaché case. "How are we on Asbury?"

"I've got some leads," I say.

He nods, then turns to Evangeline. "Do we have the witness list for Yates?"

"Just arrived," she says. "I'm going through it now."

"I'll take a look at it when I get in this afternoon," he says on his way out.

The morning blends into the afternoon as we work, eat our lunch, and work some more. Evangeline watches the door, narrow-eyed, like she's ready to toss out anyone who walks in, and I know she waits for Stu Holcombe because she wants to get the re-encounter over and prove that he can't intimidate her.

Even if her shoulders are already braced and her jaw is set.

My cell phone chimes, the display lighting to reveal a text message from Miller. I'M DOWNSTAIRS.

I stand, smooth my skirt, adjust my holster, and shove my cell phone into my pocket. "I need some air," I say. "Can I get you anything?"

"No," she says.

She doesn't say hurry back, but I say, "I won't be long."

Her smile is tight and her nod is short.

The security guard waves at me from his desk when I make it to the lobby, and I wave back before I walk out the heavy doors. People hurry back and forth on the sidewalk, but I don't see Miller, not until I hear a wolf whistle from the shadows and his voice calls, "What, did you think I'd need a little more persuading so you wore that skirt just for me?"

"Just for you," I say and find him along the edge of the building, hidden from the security camera's view under the thick oak branches.

He snorts. "I'll bet. There's a rumor going around that you're fucking McCarrick. Living with him."

"Don't you have anything better to do than worry about rumors? Maybe solve a murder or two?" I ask.

"So it's true?" he asks.

I make myself look him in the eye. "Sure it's true. I fucked him and half the attorneys upstairs. Tomorrow, I'll fuck the rest of 'em."

"Shit, Reyes, I'm just giving you a hard time." He chuckles and hands me a file. "You didn't get this from me."

"Of course." I clutch it against my chest, worried he might change his mind and take it from me. "His girlfriend? Did you talk to her?"

He squints, which causes the scar in his cheek left from an IED in Iraq to crinkle. "What do you know about that?"

"Heard she died Friday," I say. "I suppose y'all have a theory?"

"Autopsy's pending," he says. "But looks like a drug overdose."

"And then?" I ask. "If it's not an overdose?"

"You know the body count this year?" He throws his hands in the air and shrugs, like this isn't his problem anymore. "We'll get to it. Maybe."

I stare down at the file in my hands. "I'll take a look at this."

"You're wasting your time," he says. "It's drug-related, plain and simple."

I frown. "Was there any evidence he was using?"

Miller shakes his head. "Mexican bartender—"

"Was he Mexican?" I ask.

He rolls his eyes. "Mexican. Latino. Chicano. Tejano. Whatever they're calling themselves now."

My grandfather might not have taught me the language of his birth or his family's customs, but he was proud of his last name, his heritage, and what his family accomplished, so I say, "There's a difference between Tejano and Chicano and Mexican, you know?"

"Gangbangers," he says. "Cartels. That's all it means these days."

I catch my breath, fury rising from the pit of my stomach like my grandmother's wail at my dead cousin's funeral. "You're wrong—"

"Not from this side of the desk," he says. "They're all just victims in a turf war, whatever their heritage."

He saunters away in the direction I followed the pink-haired woman on Friday to her death.

I wait, long enough to make sure he's gone, but also long enough for no one to suspect we were meeting. I brace the file on one side of my body and slither my cell phone out to text Cade. WE NEED TO BE MORE CAREFUL. PEOPLE ARE STARTING TO TALK.

I expect him not to answer, but he must be in a recess because his response is almost immediate. ABOUT?

YOU KNOW WHAT, I text.

Cade's reply reads, THEY NEED ME GENERATING BUSINESS. I'LL PROTECT YOU.

He can say this, of course, because he's a man. No one accuses a man of sleeping with his boss to get ahead, and I know if our positions were reversed, Cade would get lauded for it, and I'd still be the one to take the fall.

Anyway, he must know this is too simple. I drift out of the shadows, toward the building, and think of how I want to respond, finally typing, BUT THE EMPLOYEE CONTRACT? YOUR SHOT AT A NAMED PARTNERSHIP?

TRUST ME, I KNOW WHAT'S AT STAKE, he sends back.

I type as I wander across the cement clearing in front of the building. I DON'T LIKE US BEING TALKED ABOUT.

I press send and collide with a solid object that's not supposed to be there. Hands catch me as I stumble, but my phone and the file fall to the ground.

"Oh, shit," he says, and I look up at Stu Holcombe. "Shit. Way to make a first impression."

"Well, that would have been arriving on time," I say, kneeling to gather my things.

He hands me my phone and picks up the file. "Case you're working for Cade? You're his investigator, right?"

I hold my hand out for it. "Yeah."

He ignores this, though, and flips through the pages. "Interesting. No leads yet?"

I'm on the verge of demanding it back when he hands it over. My fingers curl around it almost until my knuckles are white, and I pray he doesn't ask to go through it again as I stand.

"Thanks," I say and stalk past him into the building.

He rushes in between the elevator doors to join me. "I'm Stu," he says, holding out his hand to me.

His hand is sweaty and sticky, so I release it as quickly as possible and look away, hoping he'll take the hint. "Reagan."

"You look kinda young to be an investigator," he says. "I thought they were always ex-cops. How old are you anyway?"

His gaucheness surprises me, especially as he's a Highland Park Holcombe, practically born with a silver spoon shoved so far down his throat it's a miracle he didn't choke on it, and I wonder how his grandmother hasn't lectured him into submission about asking a woman her age. "Old enough."

"I'm twenty-six," he says, like this is an accomplishment, and maybe everything in his life is. Perhaps Bridger and Colleen *ooh* and *aww* over every darling thing he does, and so he's used to the mundane providing applause.

I only raise my eyebrows and look away. At twenty-six, I was an Air Force captain with two combat deployments under my belt.

"I took a gap year and traveled some," he says, leaning back against the elevator wall and folding his arms across his chest with a smug grin. "Paris in the springtime and all that. Have you been to Paris?"

"No," I say. "Just Iraq, Afghanistan, and Korea. Do you always arrive four hours after you're supposed to show up?"

He smirks. "You wanna tell my dad on me? We can stop by his office on our way to Cade's. Maybe talk about what you might be working on that you'd need to meet someone downstairs, hiding off like that in the trees?"

That little shit.

I gulp a deep breath and focus my attention on the elevator's floor numbers.

The elevator dings and the doors slide open.

The law firm's receptionist twists a ringlet of blonde hair around her finger and smiles at Stu as we pass, but when we enter our office, Evangeline's cool stare greets us with enough defiance to make me curious all over again over what exactly was said on Friday night.

"So you finally showed up," she says to him.

He only glances at me. "Busy morning for everyone. Right, Reagan?"

"I explained in the elevator that Cade isn't here," I say. "Will he have time this afternoon for Stu?"

"Depends on how long court runs," Evangeline says. "And if it runs long, he'll be pissed enough when he gets here 'cause he didn't even want to take this one to trial."

I don't mention that Cade was just answering text messages, so they're either in a late recess or through for the day. I only gesture to the chairs against the wall intended for clients and say, "You can wait there."

Evangeline aims a pointed stare my direction, as if emphasizing there is now an invisible wall between my desk and the waiting area. "I've gone through the Yates witness list if you want a second look."

Another case Cade doesn't want to take to trial, but—as he says—Bridger doesn't want the rich client offended. Enter Bridger's pet protégé, groomed since law school to capably step in as a fixer and make everything go away with a smile and a five-figure retainer.

I nod and settle into my seat, tucking the file from Miller into a bottom drawer, and wait for Cade.

CHAPTER

8

A HAZY DUSK FALLS, wrapping Dallas in a periwinkle cloak, and I stir the pasta and flip the chicken. It's a new recipe, but Cade will eat it.

He'll eat anything, after all, except sweet potatoes.

His key turns in the lock, and he enters the apartment, suit coat folded over one arm, attaché case in hand, and his footsteps heavy like he drags a year's worth of Mondays behind him.

"Sorry," he says and kisses me. "Kid got busted with cocaine at one of the prep schools. Guess who his dad had on speed dial?"

"Bridger Holcombe," I say. "Dinner's ready."

"I see that." He grins and looks over the dishes. "You know what they say about asparagus, right?"

I arch an eyebrow. "Well?"

"It's good for you." He smirks and steals a second kiss. "Let me wash up and I'll pour the wine."

He disappears into the bedroom, returning in a pair of running shorts and a T-shirt that should be out of place with the bottle of chardonnay he grabs. But here, the juxtaposition is somehow reassuring, and we sit at the table, big enough just for the two of us, the steam floating above our plates like the fog that hovers over the Trinity River on a winter morning.

"How's the kid?" I ask after he eats a couple of bites.

"Cocky little bastard," he says. "He spent the first twenty minutes telling me how I was supposed to do my job, until I finally told him to sit down and shut up unless he could match my acquittal rate."

"Speaking of cocky little bastards," I say and sip my wine. "Stu finally showed up this afternoon."

Cade cuts a piece of chicken. "He's his father's son, in more ways than one. In all the time I've known Bridger, he's only on time if a judge is involved."

I watch him across the table from me, the broad shoulders, his long slim fingers around the glass of wine, the clean hands and perfectly cut hair. I wonder if he looks like his father, the sweet potato farmer, the one who is disappointed his son doesn't work the land like the generations before him, and I say, "There are law schools in North Carolina. Law schools in South Carolina and all up and down the East Coast. Why SMU?"

He sets his cutlery down with a clink on the plate and leans back in his chair.

Probably because this is a "before" question, a flagrant violation of our agreement we made that first morning I woke up in his bed. But if we're at the stage where we're saying we love each other, then we can't keep ignoring the details that made each of us who we are.

Finally, he shrugs. "Why the Air Force?"

"I thought I'd leave," I say. "But I didn't realize I couldn't get far enough away. Not really. Not ever. So I came back to Texas—as close as I could get without being completely sucked back into the Piney Woods."

"Just so," he says. "If I hadn't gotten out when I did, I'd never have left. Eight generations of McCarricks farming that land, buried in that ground—you think I wouldn't hear it at night, calling to me?"

I think of how sometimes I swear I hear the pine trees sway underneath the hum of the city or smell the red dirt, damp after a storm, and I nod.

"I applied to four law schools, but SMU was the best option. I thought I'd see if the stories were true about Texas," he says.

"Like what?" I ask. "The weather's shitty, we have over-inflated egos, and the Alamo?"

His easy laugh and flash of dimples are prizes I collect and clutch close to my heart. "No, that you can still be anything you want to be here, and the women are prettier."

I swirl my wine in my glass. "Well, stories only have to be 10 percent true, right? I guess there's always the Alamo."

"Anything after you will be a disappointment," he says with a wink.

We eat and clean the kitchen together. Cade trades his glass of wine for a mason jar of moonshine and settles onto the couch. When I sit beside him, I notice he's going over the Yates witness list and its corresponding documents.

"I went through that," I say. "Didn't see any issues."

He scowls. "Besides he ought to take a plea bargain?"

"Aww, but what happened to that acquittal rate?" I ask and open the file Miller gave me.

"I don't want him fucking it up," Cade grumbles. "What've you got?"

"What the police have on Cesar Morales's death," I say. "Their theory is that it's a drug deal gone bad."

"How'd you get this?" he asks.

"Don't ask questions you don't want answers to," I say.

I don't realize Cade reads over my shoulder until he says, "So no leads. This is a dead end."

"It's all I've got," I say. "You'd save me a few steps if you'd give me that envelope."

His gaze meets mine, those green eyes soft and wary. "Babe . . ."

"I'll be fine," I say. "Maybe it's all nothing. Anyway, if three deployments didn't kill me, I'm probably indestructible by now."

"Damn it, Reagan," he says. "Would you stop? There are at least two people dead because of whatever this is. You can't keep downplaying it to make it fit some narrative."

"Yeah, that's your job, isn't it, *Counselor*?" I demand. "Especially since we don't even know whatever *this* is."

"Sure, it's just a coincidence," he says. "So why don't you leave it alone?"

I glare at him, trying to determine what he knows or is guessing, and what information he could be keeping from me.

He raises his glass to me and returns to his papers.

"You're impossible," I say, and stalk from the room.

We're tired, I tell myself. It's been a long day and we shouldn't discuss this right now, but maybe this is how we end. Maybe the explosion can't go on forever. Eventually there must be a fizzle, and we deserve better than a slow decline into apathy.

But the thought of another woman coming after me into Cade's bed, that he might feel for her what he feels for me, makes me pause and wonder if it's really so terrible that he tries to protect me and wants me to be careful because he loves me.

Even if he may know more than he's telling me right at this moment.

"You're right," he says from the bedroom doorway, even though I haven't said a word since I left the room. "Let's call it a night and we'll talk tomorrow."

The small voice in my head tells me not to be a petty bitch, to make this easy for him, but I still ask, "What about the Yates witness list?"

"You checked it, didn't you?" he says. "I trust you."

Somehow this stings more than anything else he could have said, and I tiptoe to him in the thickening twilight. His arms steal around me and all the lies we cannot tell each other—that this is only an overdose, that I won't be risking anything, that everything will be fine—no longer matter.

"Cade," I whisper. "I'm sorry—"

"Don't," he says and kisses me. "Tomorrow."

"It won't change anything," I say. "I can't just let this go."

"It doesn't mean I have to like it," he says.

I almost point out to him that nothing has made sense since that early morning I ferreted out his cell phone number and he responded by tracking me down at my apartment. That if things are supposed to make sense, I would never have come home with him that night in April, or if I did, we would have ended this after a one-night stand and gone our separate ways. That he is too ambitious, that I'm a liability to his career, that I want better for him—for us—than what the firm promises.

But I don't.

Maybe life isn't supposed to make sense. Perhaps later I will wonder what could have been changed if I did argue the point, if I did insist on him turning that envelope over to me, but for now I nestle into his arms and the reassurances that he loves me enough to care.

We fall into bed, into each other, into sleep, and there are no more words because we no longer need them.

In the morning, he leaves me for an early appointment. During my yoga, between downward-facing dog and warrior poses, the rhythm of my breath stills the thoughts racing through my mind, the impulse to tear through the apartment until I find what he hides.

Something about Cesar Morales and the dead woman still troubles Cade.

I'll work with what Miller has given me and let Cade
have his space until he's ready.

*   *   *

It's Thursday afternoon before I have any more time for that
file, though. I pull it out of the locked bottom drawer of my
desk, open it up, and frown.

The pages are rearranged.

I go back through my memories, of Miller, of the file in
Stu's hands, of Cade reading over my shoulder, of the file's
condition this morning when I placed it here—

But nothing.

I click one of my purple gel pens, lean back in my chair,
and find the page I need.

Heather Hudson, age 25
Relationship to victim: girlfriend

The dead woman has a name.

Had, I correct myself, and almost wince at the memory
of her death, at my powerlessness to save her.

I note the address for Heather Hudson and stare at my
computer screen, trying to ignore the prickling on my neck
that tells me Stu watches me.

Again.

I raise my gaze to where he sits, supposedly working on
a deposition for Cade.

We make eye contact.

He smirks. "You know, the girls who carry purple pens
in law school are the ones who are usually the most fun after
a couple of drinks."

For a brief second, I almost lose myself in the memory
from college that surfaces and rushes over me, tumbling me
in its wake.

The overly sweet taste of cheap liquor in a red solo
cup.

The smell of drugstore cologne, the kind a senior wears to a frat party he's not supposed to be attending . . .

I still my hands in my lap and make my voice cool. "That so?"

"Could buy you a couple of drinks," Stu says. "If you want to conduct an experiment, just let me know."

I watch him for a long moment, this son of Bridger Holcombe, with his slicked hair and polished shoes, his wolfish leer and oversized college ring.

They're all the same, really.

Just the names and features change.

"This isn't law school," I say. "The purple pens are an old habit from the military. I like nice pens. So did the men in my squadron. But if the ink was purple, it kept them from walking off with my things."

Something in my tone catches Evangeline's attention because she flashes me a quick warning look. I make a face at her, and she shakes her head at me, as if reminding me what's at stake here, with Stu in our office.

As if I need the reminder.

I resume reading, glaring at the pages.

It's a relief when late afternoon comes and Stu heads toward the door, waving over his shoulder at us. "See you Tuesday, girls. Check your calendars for those drinks."

I wait half a minute before I mutter, "Entitled little shit."

"Told you," Evangeline says, and mimics me. "It's just a few weeks."

"Thank God we have a four-day weekend for the Fourth of July." I push away from my desk, gathering the file on the Morales investigation. "I need to poke around on something. I'll be back as soon as I can be, but if I get tied up—"

"Go." She waves a hand. "Richie Rich is gone for the day. I'll be just fine by myself."

"Well." I smile and grab my bag, tuck the file in, and pull out my car keys. "You would have been fine without me anyway."

"It is helpful to have you around," she says, pursing her mouth to hide her grin. "Happy hunting."

A security guard from downstairs sits in the law firm's main lobby as I exit through the glass double doors. The receptionist smiles at me like nothing's amiss and I make a mental note to ask Cade about it later.

I steer the car out of the parking garage, pausing at the stop sign. At the building's main entrance, Stu stands with his father and Kirby, wearing his trademark smirk. Bridger's face reddens. Kirby shakes his head, his hands shoved inside his pockets.

Another thing to ask Cade about . . . maybe.

Or perhaps Bridger and Kirby just heard about Stu's weekend plans.

I ease onto the accelerator and leave the three men behind.

CHAPTER

9

I DRIVE PAST THE gray frame duplex twice before I park at
the curb. For South Dallas, it isn't bad; the burglar bars
over the porch and windows aren't rusting, and if the grass
is higher than it ought to be at least it's green.

Still, it's South Dallas.

I tuck a couple of twenty-dollar bills inside my watchband and make sure my pistol nestles securely in its holster
before I step out of the car.

An older white woman sweeps the shared front porch.
Smoke curls from a lit cigarette clenched in the corner of
her mouth, her frayed house dress dingy at the hem above
her bare feet.

She doesn't raise her head to look at me as I walk up the
rock driveway, but only says, "Funeral was yesterday. No
one's there now."

"Guess it'd be strange if there was someone there,
wouldn't it?" I ask. "I mean, if the funeral was yesterday."

She stops sweeping and glances in my direction. "You
related?"

"Friend of her boyfriend's family," I say, the lie becoming easier each time I repeat it. "They asked me to look into
some things."

She laughs breathlessly, a wheezing haw-haw, and inhales a long drag. "If they have the money to pay for someone to look into things, maybe they can pay this month's rent, huh? How'm I supposed to make any income off this place if she's dead and no one's around to clean out their shit?"

Her eyes gleam a little, and I recognize the opportunity.

It's not exactly legal, but it's hardly the worst thing I've done, and if there's any trouble about it, Cade can fix it.

"Let me in so I can see what all's left, and I'll let the family know how many boxes to bring," I say.

"Maybe you could give me something," she says. "To make it worth my while."

I raise an eyebrow. "It's the end of the month. The rent ought to be paid through this weekend."

"I'm a poor old widow with bills to pay," she says. "And you don't look like you're doing too bad."

I slide the twenties free from my watchband and offer them to her through the burglar bars.

She purses her mouth and unfolds them, holds them overhead to the light, and sighs, as if she expected more. "Come on, then."

The porch gate creaks open, and I step through.

She jams a key into the lock on the front door and twists. "Don't suppose you know anyone that needs a place to rent, eh, Miss Fancy? I'll give a few dollars off if they can keep the grass mowed."

"I'll ask around," I say.

I follow her into a living room with cheap wood-paneled walls painted white and yellowing with age. A half-burnt stick of incense sits in its burner below a wooden sign that says, WELCOME TO OUR HOME.

The old woman sniffs and fingers the plush throw over the back of the couch. "She always liked nice things. Bitched about the carpet and linoleum like I had money for new shit."

I examine a photo of Cesar and Heather on the wall. In it, they stand on the midway of Fair Park at the State Fair, a stuffed bear held between them, and the Texas Star visible in the background, its Ferris wheel gondolas bright against a cloudless sky. Her hair is blue and they're both wearing cheesy smiles.

"You should've heard her scream when the police came about Cesar," the landlady says. "Heard her through the wall, squalling and crying. Throwing things around in the bedroom."

I try not to think of what my reaction might be if cops met me somewhere with news about Cade's death.

The old woman points a finger gnarled with age and work. "Bedroom's there. I'll go with you, just to make sure you don't take nothing."

I don't remind her that she wants their things out in order to list the property for rent. Instead, I shrug. "Did you see her much?"

"Once he got in the picture, no," the landlady says, "although he'd cut the grass for me. Then they got new jobs. That kept 'em busy, but the rent wasn't late anymore, and I liked that. Guess that was about the turn of the year."

She follows me through the sparse kitchen, the linoleum so thin it reveals subfloor underneath.

In the bedroom, clothes and shoes are strewn across the floor, the bed unmade, a picture hanging askew, the closet door yawning wide.

The old woman coughs beside me, spewing an odor of stale nicotine that swallows up any space between us. "You looking for anything in particular?"

"Who says I'm looking for anything at all?" I ask.

"You're here, ain't you?" She kicks at a pile of clothes with her foot, shoving it to a corner. "What a mess."

She's too close for me to rifle through the drawers or look under the bed without asking me what I'm searching for, so I make my voice cool and ask, "Did you go to the funerals?"

"Wasn't invited to Cesar's," she says. "And so I didn't bother none with Heather's."

"Did you need an invitation?" I ask.

She scoffs. "It's nice to be asked."

I chew the inside of my cheek and scan the room one last time, maybe just to convince myself I'm not wasting my Thursday afternoon.

A scrap of paper with a phone number scrawled in black ink sits half tucked under the lamp on the small table by the bed. I wait until the woman turns her head before palming it, folding it in half, and tucking it in my watchband.

There's nothing else useful here—no files, no papers, not even so much as a bank statement.

Just clothes and sheets and photos of two people who loved each other, who are both now dead, and who appear to have no one left to come clean out their belongings.

"If the families don't come get their things, I'll have to throw it all out," she says. "That's a lot of work for someone my age, you know."

"I'll text them right now," I say, instead of pointing out to her that if she'd gone to the funeral, she wouldn't need me as intermediary.

She huffs like she doesn't believe me and lets the gate bang shut after me. The broom resumes swishing across the cement porch, but I don't look back at her.

I drive a couple of blocks south to the large bus transit station neighboring Fair Park and fish out change from my car's console. Two buses rumble past before I walk to the pay phone in sight of the Texas Star and unfold the piece of paper.

My fingers trace the numbers, the penmanship neat and clear, but not providing a clue as to whether Cesar or Heather wrote it.

Not that it matters.

They're both dead.

I drop a coin in the slot and dial.

It rings four times, and then the recorded message begins, the voice so familiar I can almost picture his sneer, "You have reached the voice mail of Bridger Holcombe—"

I slam the phone onto its cradle with trembling hands and flee to my car. Dread knots into my stomach, but I make myself pretend to ignore it all the way back to Uptown.

* * *

Cade and I sit across the table from each other, sharing a gourmet pizza he brings home from our favorite pizzeria and a bottle of wine. Because we don't have work for the next four days, I don't protest when Cade tops off our glasses each time they drop below half full.

I swallow a bite of pizza and try to work up the nerve to tell him about this afternoon's discovery, that Heather Hudson had Bridger Holcombe's personal cell phone number in her bedroom.

But somehow, all I can manage is, "How was court?"

"Full acquittal," he says, but he won't look me in the eye. Sometimes in Cade's line of work, a win can be just as bad—if not worse—than a loss.

He doesn't ask about my day, but slouches in his chair and stares out the balcony doors with his wine in his hand like he watches something I can't see.

"I did some digging on the Morales file," I say.

"Yeah?" He chews on his lower lip and rubs the back of his neck. "Anything that can't wait until tomorrow? I'm not trying to be an asshole, babe, it's just . . ."

We have all weekend, after all.

And maybe, just maybe, it's no big deal that I found that scrap of paper.

"Sure," I make myself say. "It was a long week."

He picks at a piece of hamburger that fell off his pizza. "You ever think about those decisions you make that don't seem like such a big deal at the time, but maybe they were? And you wonder if you had done things differently, maybe—"

"You wouldn't be right here, right now?" I sip my wine and watch him over the rim of my glass.

Maybe even Heather Hudson could still be alive if only I had told her to wait, that I would call Cade, that surely no meeting was more important than someone's life . . .

Cade clasps my hand in his free one, banishing all thoughts of her. "Obviously, there are some things I wouldn't change."

I squeeze his fingers, the warmth there reassuring. "But that's it, don't you see? If you change one thing, you set in motion a whole chain reaction."

"My practical, hardheaded Reagan," he says and kisses the back of my hand. "You don't think that in an alternate universe, we're not sitting together at a table, drinking wine, but maybe I'm an accountant and you're a librarian or something?"

"An accountant and a librarian?" I smile and play with the stem of my wineglass, admiring the way the liquid sloshes up the side and leaves behind a faint trail to mark its path. "Is that what you think of us? Maybe your alternate universe persona is a cop. A detective, even, and I'm a reporter."

He grins and finishes the rest of his wine in a swallow. "I'm not drunk enough for this conversation," he says and carries his plate to the kitchen.

"Where are you going?" I ask.

"To shower after being stuck in the same room with that chickenshit bastard all day," he says. "I'll be back in a few."

Water runs in the bathroom.

I stand, clear the table, and straighten the kitchen.

The fresh scent of his soap and shampoo wafts through the apartment, and I grab the wine bottle and our glasses. I leave them on his nightstand and cross to the bathroom door.

"Room in there for two?" I ask.

He opens the shower door and leans out to kiss me. "Always. Even if you're a librarian. Or a reporter. Or something."

"Or something." I shed my clothes and step into the shower and his soapy embrace.

The world shrinks to the boundaries of the shower, its glass walls fogged and the air saturated. There is only us. There can be only us, and whoever else that other Cade and Reagan are, they aren't here, and so they don't matter.

Nothing else matters, not until the water runs cool. We race to his bed and the warmth of each other and his sheets, and my hair dries into long, frizzy ringlets while we finish off the wine.

10

MY ALARM CHIMES softly and Cade growls into my hair. "We're off today," he grumbles.

"All the more reason to get a good workout in before we slack off all weekend," I say.

He tightens his grip on me and kisses the back of my neck. "I'll give you a good workout."

"Later." I nudge him and squirm free. "You can run with me if you want."

"It's hot out there," he says. "I run inside. I'm not from here, and, anyway, with age comes privileges."

I exchange my nightgown for a sports bra and leggings. "You're five years older, not fifty."

"You just wait until you turn thirty next year," he says. "You'll be careful?"

I pull on my tank top, tuck my knife and phone into my leggings, and lean down to kiss him. "So very careful."

"Mm," he says into my pillow. "Enjoy your run. I have a surprise for you when you get back."

I reach under the covers and tickle his feet. He kicks my hand away and draws his feet up where I can't get to them, and I laugh and head out the door.

Condensation streaks the windows and the eastern sky glows pink. It will be over a hundred degrees today, and I think of the homeless man who sleeps at the trailhead and his 82nd Airborne ballcap. Another veteran, like myself, only one who perhaps has had an even more difficult transition to civilian life.

I grab a couple extra bottles of water from the refrigerator and three of Cade's protein bars. He won't miss them, and—even if he does—he can afford more.

Outside, the air crashes over me like a sultry wave. Sweat drips down my back before I finish the half-mile warm-up walk to the Katy South Trailhead, despite my thin running leggings and even thinner tank top made for the heat.

I clutch the water bottles against my stomach, looking for the Ranger, and finally see him. He's not on his park bench but huddled against a building in the shadows where the cool stone exterior provides some relief.

"Hey, Ranger," I say as I approach. "Gonna be a hot one today. Better hydrate."

The Ranger doesn't say anything but stares at the horizon, so still I don't know if he even hears me. He's younger than I initially assumed; up close I can see he's probably about my age, maybe only a few years older. His thin beard is black, and his eyes are the same honey brown as my grandfather's, set deep in his tanned olive skin. With a shave, a haircut, and a change of clothes, he'd probably be a heartbreaker.

He doesn't move to accept the water or protein bars from me, so I leave them on the corner of his blanket. "Stay safe."

I'm halfway back to the sidewalk when I hear him say, "Thank you, ma'am."

I wave in acknowledgment, turn my music on, and start my run.

The city sleeps around me, and so the sunrise is all mine, the sky glowing like a rosy iridescent pearl, shimmering in the warmth. I'm too short to be a natural distance runner, too solid in my thighs and calves, and so four miles becomes as much a mental challenge as it is a physical challenge. For those four miles, all I can think of is matching my feet with the rhythm of the music, my breathing, the sound of the birds in the trees, the anticipation of a cool shower and an afternoon nap—anything so I don't think about the tension in my muscles or the sweat dripping down my back.

My watch beeps the fourth mile and I slow to a walk, raise my arms above my head, and interlace my fingers, gulping air deep into my burning lungs.

Suddenly, someone's hands are around my throat, lifting me to my tiptoes.

My military experience kicks in and I claw at his hands, his arms, anything I can get to, before finally slamming an elbow back and connecting.

He grunts at the impact, his breath hot in my ear. "Meddling bitch. This is your only warning. Leave it alone."

Panic pounds in time with my heartbeat.

He's too strong.

I won't be able to break his grip.

Finally, I do the only thing left to do and twist to throw my weight forward enough to force him off balance.

We fall together, his weight collapsing onto me. Something—instinct, maybe—forces my hands out just in time.

Grass, slick with dew, greets my palms before he forces my face into the dirt.

My toes scrabble for traction on the sidewalk and I buck my hips against him.

But he is heavy, so heavy, and he tightens his grip on my throat while pressing a knee into my back, all his weight crushing the air from me.

I can't reach my knife or my phone in the pocket of my leggings as I thrash underneath him. I can't breathe or fight or do anything but think of Cade and how guilty he'll feel that he didn't run with me. I hope that Evangeline and Armando will tell him this isn't his fault, that I could have stayed with him, and I wish I had. I summon up feelings of lying in bed beside him, the warmth of his body against mine, the way he sighs right before he falls asleep, and waking up beside him in the middle of the night to find him wrapped around me . . .

The hand yanks sharply and releases me.

Oxygen floods my nose and throat.

I gasp and curl onto my side, color returning to my vision.

"You best run," a man's voice shouts. "You best get on outta here 'fore the cops show up. I might just go crazy on you myself. Get on! Get!"

An arm slides underneath me and helps me sit up as I flail and struggle to breathe.

"Ma'am," he says. "Ma'am, you all right? You got a phone on you? You think you can walk? Here, lemme help."

The homeless Army Ranger picks me up like I'm no more than a child and moves me against the side of the building. He twists open one of the bottles of water, snapping the seal, and offers it to me, but I shake my head.

I pant and wipe my nose with the back of my hand. It stings, blood trickling onto my fingers that I smear onto my shirt. "Did you get a look at him?"

"No," he says. "Not really. I only noticed him 'cause he wore a hoodie. Who wears a hoodie like that with it hot as hell out here? Big man, though."

"Tell me about it," I say.

The Ranger is a big man, too. Not as tall as Cade, but squared and blocky, a solid man, the kind you want playing linebacker or kicking down a door. When he notices me watching him, he asks, "You want to call the cops?"

"No," I say. "No cops."

"But, ma'am," he says.

I wrap my arms around myself to stop shivering, maybe to hold myself together so I don't put my head down on my knees and sob. "You know how this goes for me if I call them."

The cops will come. Some bored white man will stand over me and ask me questions. He'll pretend to take notes, but his face will say everything he can't.

What did you expect to happen, running at daybreak, alone, in those tight leggings and that thin tank top? You're probably lucky this didn't happen before.

He'll ask for my identification and that's when the trouble will really start because then he'll see my last name is Reyes and know I don't live anywhere near here. His questions will grow more pointed, more persistent, and I'll either have to reveal my relationship with Cade, risking the partners hearing about us, or endure his suspicions.

"No cops," I say again.

The Ranger exhales but doesn't ask any more questions. He only says, "I can't let you walk home by yourself. I know you don't live far, but what if he comes back? I got nowhere else to be if you don't mind the company."

"I don't mind," I say. "What's your name?"

"Rafi," he says.

I laugh and use the building to stumble to my feet. "Rafi? Rafael, like the angel?"

"I'm no angel," he says. "You'll be okay at your place?"

I wipe my face with the hem of my now filthy tank top. "Yeah. My um . . ."

Cade and I don't usually bother with definitions for ourselves, but then we usually don't describe our relationship to others. Boyfriend sounds like I'm in high school, lover sounds silly in daylight, and partner—well, that term is loaded enough in our world.

"He'll be there," I say.

"Good," Rafi says. "You shouldn't be alone. May have hit your head."

I shiver despite the heat and wrap my arms around myself. My leggings are torn down the front, flaps hanging open at the knees, and streaked with blood and dirt.

"What's your name?" he asks.

"Reagan," I say.

"Like the politician?" he asks.

I manage a laugh. "I'm no politician. You really a Ranger?"

He gestures at his beard. "Another life."

We go in through the side door and I press the button for the elevator. He doesn't make any move to leave me, nor do I expect him to; somehow I know if I protest, he'll insist that he's making sure I arrive at the apartment safely and that the man doesn't get a chance to attack me again.

"Nice place," he says.

"It's not mine," I say. "I'll get you some water and more food."

"You don't have to do that," he says.

"You don't have to take it, I guess," I say.

He chuckles low under his breath. "Yes, ma'am."

We enter the elevator and I relax against its wall, inventorying my injuries.

"Your man," he says. "He gonna give me any trouble?"

I shake my head. "He's probably at the gym."

Rafi follows me off the elevator, his longer strides automatically falling into step beside me. He looks around like he's worried about being seen as I unlock the door and we step into the apartment.

Cade stands in the kitchen, shirtless, gym towel around his neck, drinking a protein shake he nearly drops when he sees me. "What the fuck—"

"It's nothing," I say, at the same time Rafi says, "There was a man."

"A man?" Cade holds me by the shoulders and looks me over before pulling me against himself. "This man?"

"No, sir," Rafi says.

"He chased him off," I say.

"He chased him off," Cade repeats, like he's trying to follow the conversation. "And neither of you called the cops?"

Rafi stares at the floor. "No, sir."

I let Cade touch a damp paper towel to my cheek. "I didn't want to."

"You didn't want to?" Cade echoes and glares at Rafi. "And you just went along with her?"

"I—I got warrants," he says. "I got clean but can't be involved with no cops."

"Fuck." Cade runs a hand through his hair. "Goddamn it, Reagan. You're in shock. You have to be. We're calling the cops."

"No," I say again, and maybe the tone of my voice, the unspoken plea not to take this choice away from me does something to Cade, because he turns away and laces his fingers across the back of his neck.

For a second, he doesn't say anything, and then he exhales. "Gimme a reason, Reag. Because right now, I'd like to find the fucker myself."

"I'm fine, really," I say weakly and glance at Rafi. "There are diversionary courts for veterans."

Rafi shakes his head. "I got bad paper."

Cade frowns and looks over his shoulder. The next thing out of his mouth will be a request for an explanation, and so I say, "I'll explain later," because it seems unfair to Rafi to unpack what a dishonorable discharge is and what it can mean to someone in front of him. To Rafi, I only say, "You were in the shit over in the sandbox, weren't you?"

He nods but doesn't look up from the ground. "For sure."

"If you got bad paper for things that happened after you got back, there are ways to appeal that," I say. "I can make some calls Tuesday."

I stare up at Cade until he sighs. "I can make some calls too," he says. "See about dealing with those warrants. You got somewhere you can lay low this weekend in case that asshole decides to come back for more?"

"Maybe," Rafi says.

Cade pulls his wallet from his shorts and peels off bills. "That should get you a room and food."

Rafi draws himself up, folds his arms across his chest, and glowers. "I didn't help her for the money."

"Not saying you did." Cade scribbles something on the back of a business card and hands it to Rafi. "Call me Tuesday. I'll need the details on the warrants, and she'll need the details on . . . whatever it is y'all called that."

"Thank you." Rafi shoves the card and the cash into his pockets but pauses as he reaches for the door. "Ma'am? What branch were you?"

"Air Force," I say.

"Should've known," he says, smiling as he taps his temple. "Air Force is always thinking."

The door closes behind him and I wait for his footsteps to fade down the hall before making eye contact with Cade, but he doesn't say anything. Not at first, not for a long moment, and I almost confess everything right there, that I thought I would die and that I wanted him, that maybe I'm scared that I love him, and all I want is for him to hold me.

He looks away and says, his voice barely above a whisper, "Let's get you cleaned up," as if he's frightened too.

I sit on the bathroom counter and tuck my hands under my thighs so Cade doesn't see they're shaking. "I'm fine."

"Are you?" he asks.

I shrug.

He runs warm water in the sink and soaks a washcloth, expensive by its plushness, and I almost tell him to get an old one, a cleaning rag, something I won't worry about ruining. But I know it's a moot point. Cade is generous to a fault and won't care if the washcloth is ruined. He'll only care that I'm safe and cared for, and damn him, why couldn't we stick to our promise that we were just going to be a one-night stand?

He sponges my face. "You wanna talk about it?"

"Not yet," I say. Truthfully, I'd rather never talk about it, and some part of me wants to believe if I stall him, he'll forget.

I tell myself I can forget. That perhaps I can trick myself into believing it never happened.

"Reag," he says and tilts my head so he can examine something on my neck. "Did you see anything at all?"

"I thought we weren't talking about it," I say.

He extends one of my legs straight out and braces my foot on his thigh. "These leggings are ruined."

"I'll buy another pair," I say.

Another tank top too, I almost add, but I don't. I don't want to explain to him that I'll never be able to look at it again without remembering this morning. I don't want to voice that I couldn't even scream while a man choked me and put a knee into my back, pressing me into the dirt until I couldn't breathe.

I brush him away. "You said you had a surprise. You said when I got back—"

"Yeah." He rubs the back of his neck. "You wanna talk about that now?"

"Why not? I'm not broken," I say. "I'm not going to break down and cry about it in a corner, so if that's what you're waiting for, I'm sorry to disappoint you—"

"Reag," he almost whispers. "You could never disappoint me."

I look away and bite my lower lip before I remember it's sore. "I'm sorry."

"Stop apologizing," he says. "This isn't your fault."

But it's always the woman's fault, I want to say.

He draws me close to him and kisses the top of my head. "I'm here. For whatever you need, I'm here."

Maybe that's what scares me the most, that he is here and that I need him, and so every instinct screams for me to push him away while I still have a chance to make a clean break.

Loving someone too much is risky; it tempts fate.

But his smell is familiar and comforting and I clutch at him.

"Is it okay if I don't know what I need right now? I know I should feel something," I say. "I just . . . don't."

"Give it time," he says. "Why don't you get a shower? I thought we'd get out of town for the long weekend, just the two of us—that is, if you still want to."

I think of staying here, of that man being able to find me, and I nod. "Let's shower and pack and go."

He kisses the top of my head again and releases me. "I'll be in the kitchen if you need me," he says, but doesn't stay to shower with me.

I sit on the shower floor and let the hot water pour over me. When I close my eyes, I still feel the man's hands on my throat and his weight on my back.

But I don't call Cade.

11

I TOSS CLOTHES, A swimsuit, and nightgowns into my backpack. It's when I open my nightstand drawer to grab underwear that I find the file from Miller.

The man's whisper from earlier this morning on the trail, *This is your only warning. Leave it alone,* washes over me again.

He could have made a grab for my pricey headphones if it was a mugging, or tried to drag me into the nearest parking garage if it was a rape.

But he didn't.

He targeted me, whispered that specifically.

I go through Cade's caseload in my mind, only to come back to the one whose file I hold in my hands.

"How's the packing coming?" Cade asks from the living room.

"Fine," I say, and nestle the folder in my backpack with my pistol and knife, zipping it closed before he sees.

We load our bags into the narrow back seat of Cade's Porsche. He doesn't usually like beverages in the car, but he pulls into Starbucks anyway and orders me an iced coffee without asking if I even want it.

I take it and gulp it. The coffee is cool and numbing on my throat that hurts each time I swallow more than I will ever admit to Cade.

We merge onto I-30 and Cade opens the throttle, the buildings and cars blurring around us. Within thirty minutes, we cross the Ray Hubbard Bridge, and I turn to look back. A faint haze smudges the downtown skyline, only obvious now that we're away from the city.

"Everything all right?" Cade asks but doesn't look away from the road.

"Fine," I say and settle in my seat.

We pass through the last eastern suburbs of the Dallas-Fort Worth metroplex, the interstate narrowing to two lanes on each side and the high grass scorched white in the medians. Long stands of trees replace buildings, scrubby oaks hugging the roadway, and within another ten miles, Dallas might as well not even exist. Out here, amid the forests and wide-open pasturelands and farms, the city is only a distant dream.

Static overtakes The Ticket, Cade's preferred radio station, until he cuts the radio off altogether, leaving us with only the sounds of the engine, the race of the wind over the car, and the tires on the pavement.

The silence between us builds a barrier of unspoken words, and I know I'll have to talk to him soon.

He'll look at me like I'm weak, broken, incapable of taking care of myself, and he'll try to build a pretty prison of words and emotions. He'll tell me he loves me, that he won't let me risk my safety, that I must give all this up and settle into what life was before, what it still could be.

He exits the interstate.

The trees are taller and thicker, the northwestern fringes of my native Piney Woods, blotting out the sun. I relish their shelter, finding relief there, a welcome home and a quiet peace.

"This is beautiful," Cade says.

"Haven't you been here before?" I ask.

"No," he says.

"When I left East Texas, it was so strange to see the horizon line," I say. "The sky—it felt like a fishbowl. So open, with no shelter."

"I can see that," he says, and I wonder what the view looks like from that sweet potato farm in North Carolina, but I don't have the nerve to ask.

Not this morning, anyway.

We wind our way down a narrow road, the asphalt rutted enough that Cade slows the car to a crawl. He checks his phone and turns at a mailbox, following an even narrower gravel track. Low-hanging pine boughs whisk against the car, as if investigating our presence and why we're here.

The drive leads to an A-frame cabin and a carport centered in a small clearing. Cade parks the car and turns the engine off.

He smiles for the first time since I returned to the apartment with Rafi. "Shall we go investigate?"

I nod.

My stiff muscles complain as I clamber out of the low car seat. I lean in, grab my backpack, and follow him up the porch stairs.

Cade uses his phone to retrieve the key from a lock box. He swings open the front door and we enter, the interior cool and dark after the brightness of the interstate. The downstairs is an open great room with a stone fireplace and a large television, while a corner staircase leads up to a spacious bedroom and bathroom. A balcony off the back of the bedroom looks out over the deck beneath us. From the deck stairs, a stone path leads to a fire pit with a pair of Adirondack chairs, and beyond that to a second deck built over the water, half of it roofed, covering a porch swing and a hammock.

He steps beside me onto the balcony. "I think there'll be fireworks for the Fourth."

"Probably," I say.

"There are a few local wineries," he says. "And we'll find something to do, won't we?"

I glance over at him in time to catch him watching me. I can't read his expression, but he feels far away, like he wraps himself in some sort of impenetrable layer to protect himself from me.

That he feels he needs to do this somehow hurts more than anything else today.

"We'll have fun," I say and make myself reach over to squeeze his hand, hoping if I force a smile and add enough cheer in my voice, he'll believe I'm all right and we can go on like this morning never happened.

He nods as if he sees through me and slips from my grasp.

* * *

We unpack, we drive to town, we eat lunch, we shop for groceries.

It ought to be thrilling—or at least a little fun—that we can be seen in public together, doing normal things like a couple, only I can't let myself enjoy it. I catch myself constantly checking over my shoulder, worried that someone is there.

But being alone with Cade is somehow worse, full of uncomfortable silences and awkward averted looks, like we both know that eventually we'll need to acknowledge this morning did happen.

And I know when that happens, when we face that truth, we'll shatter.

I'll shatter.

Only I can't let Cade see it. I can't let Cade know, because I know Cade's instinct will be to piece me all back together and protect me.

Once Cade does that, he may not respect me anymore as an equal.

If I must be protected, I must be weaker.

Vulnerable.

Soft.

And so I make myself smile and speak at the appropriate cues. I suppress the urge to curl up in the shower and scrub myself again instead, as if I can wash away the handprints on my throat, the words that smeared themselves on my skin, the dirt and blood and sweat that must surely still be apparent to Cade with the way he avoids making eye contact.

The king-size bed in the center of the room upstairs is a yawning white mouth to swallow me whole, but I climb into it anyway, turn off the lamp, and lie back on my pillow.

Cade gets in on his side and kisses me, but on the cheek.

He coils himself loosely around me like I'm too fragile to squeeze close tonight and doesn't slip a hand inside my nightgown.

He whispers, "I love you, Reag," but goes right to sleep, and I'm left staring at the ceiling, wondering what will happen when we both acknowledge this morning happened.

The pine trees whisper to me, and the lake murmurs from its bank, but I can't sleep. Every time I close my eyes the panic crawls up my throat and reminds me of those hands around my neck and the man's face that I never saw.

I slide away from Cade and make my way down the stairs and out the back door.

Ankle-high solar-powered lanterns line the path, giving off enough of a glow to ensure there are no copperheads or water moccasins in the way, but not so much as to disturb the night. I step onto the deck's wooden planking, warm from soaking in the sun all day, and walk to the porch swing.

It sways as I sit, the chains creaking overhead, and I draw my knees to my chest. There is no moon tonight, only the sky's midnight velvet and the even deeper blackness of the lake ringed by the trees with a faint pinpoint of light here or there marking a dock or a porch light. The lake slaps against the support beams and the bank, and a faint breeze stirs in the pines, bringing with it a loamy scent of grass and earth, and I breathe it all deep, wishing it smelled as safe as Cade.

But Cade sleeps in the big bed upstairs, alone, and that's best for us both.

There's too much danger in loving something too well; it's an added vulnerability, and if I can't protect myself, then I can't protect Cade, either.

That man that came for me this morning could come for Cade next.

Can I live with myself if something happens to him because of me?

The swing lurches a little, and Cade's voice says, "You'll catch cold wandering around in your nightgown."

"In Texas in July?" I ask. "Hardly."

He sits beside me, near enough I can feel him without him touching me, and he rests an arm along the back of the swing. "Couldn't sleep?"

"I thought you were," I say.

"No. Not really."

The unsaid words thicken the already humid air, and a chorus of frogs sings somewhere down the shore. The stars are so bright a few manage to reflect in the water—tiny dots of light like eyes staring up from the blackness.

A high-pitched whine buzzes nearby.

Cade slaps at something. "Damn it."

I want him to stay with me, and so I say, "I saw citronella candles and some matches in the pantry."

"That so?" He stands and caresses my cheek with the edge of his fingers, and for the first time all day I don't flinch away from his touch. "Will you sit with me a while if I go get them?"

"Yes," I say.

He leaves me, and I rest my forehead against the swing's chain, the metal cool against my skin. I let myself think of reaching for him, of nestling into his arms and telling him everything, all the details of this morning that nag at me.

And then I put the idea back in its drawer in my mind.

The rational side of my brain acknowledges that Cade would never fling the events of this morning in my face, but a small voice whines, growing more persistent, that he *could*, that he *might*, that he may even remind me I promised to be careful and I'm probably fortunate this hasn't happened before.

Loud footsteps tread on the wooden planking, like he's not trying to be quiet this time.

A match flares.

"There we go," he says as the candle catches. "Take that, you little sons of bitches."

"Mosquitoes that bite humans are female," I say.

He laughs under his breath and reclaims his seat beside me. "Tough to kill and hard workers—that makes sense."

The overly sweet scent of citronella bathes the air, and he passes me a bottle dripping with condensation. I twist the cap open and force myself to take a drink, but wince as I swallow.

"I thought cold water might feel nice," he says. "You didn't eat much at dinner."

I don't want to admit why, so I only say, "Good excuse to have ice cream for breakfast tomorrow, though."

"Reag, this morning." He sighs and slides an arm around me. "I understand if you don't want to run again, but you can't let that bastard win. If you want to keep running the Katy Trail, we'll figure something out."

His face is serious in the candlelight. He's not joking.

This is the Cade I fell in love with, the one who encourages and supports me, not the one who's appeared over the last week, since Friday afternoon when I walked into his apartment to the news that Heather Hudson was dead.

I take a deep breath and another drink of water. "That's not quite the reaction I expected."

He cracks a smile. "Did you think I'd load the shotguns, forbid you to ever leave the apartment again without me, and tell you that I'd keep you safe?"

Imagining this almost brings water erupting out of my nose, but I choke my giggle into the back of a hand. "You don't even own a shotgun."

"Could probably buy one. Hell, I'll bet that place we bought groceries from sells 'em out the back door."

I tilt my head back and trace Orion overhead through the latticework roofing the swing. "This is different from last weekend," I finally say.

"I'm older and wiser." He doesn't give me time to tweak him for making light of the situation before he continues. "You were right last weekend."

Any other time, I might preen at this admission, but not tonight.

Not after this morning.

"Oh?" I ask instead.

"I trust you every day to look into things for me, and there aren't always nice people involved," he says. "And I do respect you because you *are* the type of woman who doesn't need a man to protect her and won't give up on something."

I nod and watch the candlelight play on the waves rippling across the top of the lake.

"It's not fair to either of us to expect you to change, and, honestly, I wouldn't want you to," he says. "But that doesn't mean it'll be easy."

I recognize the concession in his voice and relax into the warmth of his bare shoulder. "I don't know if I'll be up to running for a few days."

"I'll try not to text you every ten minutes," he says. "This morning . . . it scared the hell outta me. I can't imagine how it feels for you."

"I'll add you to my running app so you can track me," I say.

He kisses the top of my head. "We'll get through this," he says, and I know he's telling the truth because he can't lie to me.

I'm safe here, with him, far from the city and whatever dangers it might represent.

Nothing can hurt me now except the fragmented memories I clutch to myself. If I hold too tight, they will slice me like broken glass, but if I let them go, Cade and I can maneuver around them, examine them, maybe even sweep them up and dispose of them altogether.

And if I can trust him with this, maybe one day I can trust him with more.

"I just wish I'd seen his face," I say. "It all happened so fast."

He holds me as the words spill out but doesn't comment. Not until the end, not until I hesitate, because I'm too worried if I say anything more, I'll openly sob. He draws back enough to wipe away the tears spilling down my cheeks, and then he kisses me. He doesn't promise me that everything will be all right, because that might be a lie, but he cradles me in his lap and says, "I'm here."

For right now, that's enough for me.

We return inside and curl up together in the big white bed. The air conditioner hums, and the alarm clock on Cade's nightstand glows numbers well after midnight. Not that it matters, because the weekend is ours.

He kisses me and winds himself around me with a yawn, slipping a hand inside my nightgown. "I love you," he murmurs and nuzzles into my hair.

"I love you too," I say, and close my eyes.

Only darkness greets me, liquid soft, familiar as the night, and smelling safe like Cade.

I embrace it and sleep.

CHAPTER

12

I JOLT AWAKE WITH a gasp and flop over on my back.

An unfamiliar ceiling greets me, and then I remember I'm not in my bed nor Cade's bed, but at the cabin in the woods.

"You okay?" Cade asks.

He lies next to me, propped up on one elbow, and I roll toward him, minding my shoulders and ribs that hurt more today. "Yes. No coffee yet?"

"I didn't want you to wake up in a strange bed by yourself"—he smooths my hair—"not after . . . yesterday. And I thought maybe you were dreaming, so I stayed."

"I was," I say.

Our gazes meet.

I realize that the scrapes and bruises have had twenty-four hours to settle into my skin, and blurt out, "Does it look so bad?" before I stop myself.

"No," he says, and glances back at me, turning my face a little. "You've got that light scrape on your nose and cheek, but no real bruises. You can probably cover them with makeup."

His scrutiny of my injuries somehow feels awkward, even though I did ask, and so I try to make light of it. "The second day. It's always the worst, right?"

"Right." His jaw tightens just enough that it's detectable, before the tension vanishes so quickly I'm not even sure it was ever really there. "Sundays and Mondays were never fun during college football season."

I stretch, pretending my muscles are only their normal sore from yesterday's run. "You had pads and a helmet."

He scoffs. "Not a lot of help when the defensive end tackling you weighs over two fifty."

"Guess you should've had a better offensive line then," I say.

"Trust me," he says and kisses me. "I'd have put it on my Christmas list if I thought it would have gotten me anywhere."

But if Cade had played with a better offensive line, if he'd found more success as a college quarterback, then would he have gone to law school? Would he have come to Dallas at all?

I remember my life before him, the Midtown apartment I nominally still lease, the career path I had convinced myself could make me happy, and the life outside the military I thought I wanted.

It stings, this idea of life without him, and I whisper, "We might never have met," because I think it might hurt too much to admit it at full volume.

"I'd have found you," he says. "I'll always find you."

I nearly drown in those green eyes, finally managing to say, "Just remember who found you first."

His grin sends heat flooding through every inch of my body. "Is that how this is, Reag?"

The morning sun filters through the sheer curtains and glints off his hair, and I can't resist touching him, the scrape of two days' stubble against my palm and the warmth of his cheek reassuring.

"And if it is?" I ask.

He kisses the inside of my wrist. "I'm okay with that."

Something about the familiarity and ease of his touch soothes me. This at least is normal, and I close my eyes, content to lose myself in him and forget that yesterday happened, until his hand brushes my hip.

I flinch, and his low murmur, "Babe, maybe a couple more days, huh?" is bathed in understanding.

But I need him right now, and I need him to look past the scrapes and the bruises and last night's tears and show me he still wants me. I kiss him and say, "Just be gentle. You can do that, can't you?"

"Oh, I can do anything you want," he says.

He kisses the scrape on my right cheek, softer than a summer mist, and then the scrape on my nose. He pauses at my lips for only a second, and then moves to my neck, lightly covering my throat with his lips.

When I wiggle to hurry him along, he chuckles and peels my nightgown strap down my shoulder. "Mm, but the waiting is the best part, remember?"

"Are you still on that?" I ask. "Don't be petty."

"Me, petty?" He slides the other strap down and then lifts me enough to tug my nightgown free. "I'm hurt. I think my gentleness deserves your patience."

I bury a hand in his hair while he explores, pausing every few seconds to kiss a new place on my body. When his lips brush the scrapes on my knees, I realize he's inventorying every injury from yesterday, cataloging them and covering them with his touch, a new sensation and memory to smother—if not replace—my recollection of the prior morning's events.

He eases me onto my stomach and his fingers stroke the line up my tattoo before his lips follow, sending a wave of goose bumps across my skin.

"Cade," I murmur.

He laughs, damn him, and traces the line again, but this time blows a cool stream of air up my spine and along the back of my neck.

"You're doing this on purpose," I say and glare over my shoulder at where he sits beside me on the bed.

"And if I am?" he asks and leans down to kiss me. "You enjoy it. I enjoy you enjoying it. So what's the harm?"

He's right, of course, not that I'll admit that to him.

Not now, anyway.

He now kisses me again and lowers himself next to me, and then, almost before I realize what he does, he guides me on top of him as he rolls onto his back.

I think I hear him ask me if he's being gentle enough, but I can't be sure.

I can't really be sure of anything after that point, because every sense I have is filled up with Cade and that I want him, that he still wants me, and that yesterday frightened us both, but today we are here, together and stronger.

When I collapse against him, he slips his arms around me and squeezes me close.

We lie there and he combs out my hair with his fingers, then I feel him exhale. "Ask me to be gentle more often," he says, amusement lacing his voice.

I lift my head to see his grin and match it.

He draws my hand to his lips and kisses my fingers that curl around his. "It'll be all right, Reag."

"I know," I say.

It's afternoon before we leave the cabin.

* * *

We sit in the shade of a winery pergola, drinking something pretentious and unpronounceable, and eat tapas while a string quartet plays in the background and ceiling fans turn overhead.

"Look." Cade plays with his wineglass and gulps a mouthful. "I was thinking . . ."

"Then clearly you haven't had enough to drink," I say. "We're at a winery in the middle of nowhere, it's not respectable to think."

"Is that so?" He leans in, nudging me with his shoulder. "Respectability's overrated, don't you think?"

And that's when it hits me that he might be about to do something either very serious or very stupid. I sit back in my chair, my heart pounding, hoping he's not going to rush into a marriage proposal just because of what happened Friday morning.

"This month I enter the window where I need to either extend my lease or give notice I'm moving out," he says. "And your place—it's silly for you to keep paying rent on that apartment all the way in Midtown. I thought maybe we'd find us a place together?"

The relief that this is all he wanted to talk about is quickly replaced by the worry that this is riskier than appearing together in Deep Ellum on a Saturday night. I play with my wineglass and wonder if he has even considered the consequences of doing such a thing, or how he will take it if I point them out.

On the other hand, it could be that he has thought about those things, and he simply doesn't care. Anyway, he has promised to protect me, so maybe he has a plan.

"I thought you liked your building," I say. "Besides, you owe the doorman a Christmas bonus."

He grins. "There are bigger apartments in my building."

"With the same view of downtown?" I ask. "We like that balcony."

"I do have some very fond memories of the two of us on that balcony," he says. "If there's an apartment open in my building that's larger but with the same view, is that something you would consider?"

This is another step to the merger of our lives, and I know it, but it's not a McMansion in the suburbs or Highland Park, or even a wedding. If it doesn't work out, I can still get my own apartment and move out.

"Yes," I say. "Yes, I think that'd be nice."

He clinks his glass against mine. "We'll start looking next weekend then."

I stare into my wine. "Do you really want to listen to a string quartet?"

Cade motions for the server and asks me, "What do you have in mind?"

"Yes, sir?" The server eyes the wine flight, still half full, and the tapas platter. She smiles and her pitch goes up a little. "Did you need something else?"

"Is there a pool hall or a bar with a good country band close?" I ask.

"No, ma'am," she says. "You'd have to drive into Longview or Tyler for that."

I nod. "But there's a liquor store in town, right?"

"Oh, sure," she says. "But we've got a full bar—"

"You got moonshine?" I ask.

Cade's gaze meets mine. He passes her his credit card without looking away.

"I'll be right back," she mumbles and retreats.

At the liquor store, we buy jars of apple pie moonshine. We return to the small cabin on the lake and drink on the dock, citronella candles flickering around us while the sun sets to the sounds of David Allan Coe and Waylon Jennings.

The boat traffic dies near twilight. Cade sets his drink aside and stands. "How deep you think that water is?"

I shrug. "Deep enough to dock a boat, I guess. Why?"

His grin is pure mischief, promising that he's up to no good, and whatever it is, it will shortly involve me, whether I like it or not.

He steps out of his shorts and yanks his shirt over his head before taking a running jump off the end of the dock.

The water splashes and ripples across to where I dangle my toes, and I sip my moonshine and wait.

He bobs up and slings water from his hair. "The water's nice."

"Good," I say. "You enjoy it."

He laughs and swims toward me. "Come on, Reag."

"I'd have to go inside and get my swimsuit," I say.

"Why?" he says. "You think someone'll see?"

"They might," I say. "You don't know the game warden won't be along. They always show up at the damnedest times."

He flashes that grin again, a breaststroke's distance from me. "Guess you're coming in with your clothes, then."

"Cade." I pull my legs out of his reach and creep away from the edge of the dock. "Don't you dare."

"Live a little," he says. "Or don't you trust me?"

I stand, frowning down at him. "Of course I trust you."

"Oh," he says and splashes water at me. "You've never been skinny-dipping, have you?"

I gulp a mouthful of moonshine, white hot and tasting faintly of apples and cinnamon, and stare across the lake at the last fading rays of sunlight. My mother and grandmothers would disapprove, but then I have shed so many vestiges of being their ideal of a lady over the years, because they don't realize their way isn't the only way. Maybe I have surpassed them and no longer need to concern myself with their whispers and criticisms.

After all, being a lady isn't what brought Cade to me or what he fell in love with me for.

I unbutton my blouse and let it slip from my shoulders.

"There's my girl," he says.

I take my time undressing because I know he likes to watch. The damp air is warm on my skin, a welcoming embrace once I have left my clothes in an untidy heap, as though it recognizes me and prefers me this way. I breathe it deep, hear the frogs croak and Sammi Smith on the radio, feel the moonshine's heat in my veins, and take a flying leap off the end of the dock.

13

I WAKE SUNDAY MORNING pleasantly sore. I tell myself it's from the previous day, and I can almost convince myself the scrapes and bruises are from something innocuous.

The thoughts of returning to Dallas, going back to Cade's apartment, and somehow having to force myself to run the Katy Trail again lurk in the back of my mind, but I dismiss them. I'll think of it all later, maybe Monday afternoon when we return.

But in the back of my mind, the specter stalks of the man in the hoodie, and not even Cade can fully exorcise it.

His fingers brush my spine and I close my eyes, but even after his hand stops moving and his breathing deepens and steadies Sunday night, I stay awake.

I'm only dozing lightly when his phone rings and he grumbles, "Goddamn it," as though God has anything at all to do with his phone or whoever calls at—

I open one eye. The nightstand clock says it's just after one. "Let it go," I say.

"Can't." He yawns and sits up in bed. "It's July Fourth. Probably be a fucking miracle if I don't have to haul someone's ass out of the Dallas County drunk tank."

Ah, the perils of being a criminal defense attorney with one of the best acquittal rates in Dallas County over a holiday weekend. I sigh and snag the sheet with my toes and pull it to my chin, because without him wrapped around me the room is too cold.

"No, don't call the cops," I hear Cade say into the phone, a sudden alertness to his voice. "I can be there in a couple of hours. Just keep an eye on things."

If he leaves to go back to Dallas, that means he'll need to return for me tomorrow. I burrow under my pillow, annoyed that our long weekend together is cut short—or I realize that since I'm awake anyway, I can pack and go with him and we can have all day tomorrow together.

I roll out of bed and grab clothes from my backpack.

"What are you doing?" Cade asks as I dress.

"Going with you," I say. "It makes no sense for you to drive all the way back to get me tomorrow."

"I'd rather you didn't," he says.

I flip the bathroom switch on so the light cascades out and illuminates his face. "Why not? I'll wait in the car while you deal with that client."

He frowns and rubs the back of his head, failing to smooth the hank of hair that always stands straight up if he comes to bed straight from the shower. "It wasn't a client."

I let the shower door slam shut. "It wasn't a client, but you're going back to Dallas tonight? What's going on?"

He looks away, and I know suddenly that this is bad news, and that maybe I should let him avoid my questions and leave, but damn it, I can't.

Not when he's leaving me in the middle of the night and it's not for a client.

"Another woman?" I ask.

"What?" He crosses to me to hold me by the shoulders. "Shit, no. How the hell could you even think that, Reag, why—?"

"Tell me what's going on," I demand.

The recognition dawns in his eyes that this is no longer a request.

His hands fall away from me and he turns.

I catch his arm. "I'm sorry," I say, and I don't really know why I'm apologizing, except that I just barked an order at him and he's not one of my airmen; he's in fact never met Captain Reyes. "Whatever it is, you're not going back alone tonight. Are you safe to drive, or should I drive you?"

"I'll drive," he says and hesitates at the bathroom doorway, his hand half curled around the frame. "That was your friend Rafi, the guy from Friday. Apparently, he just watched someone break into my—our—apartment. He's keeping an eye on things."

"Oh," I say. "Oh, shit."

"I mean, everything valuable should be in the safe, right?" Cade says and sighs. "But that bastard has a two-hour head start. Who knows what he could be doing in the meantime?"

I think of a stranger walking into our bedroom, rifling through my clothes, meddling in my panties and bras, touching our pillows, seeing the extra towels in the bathroom and the makeup and hair products that obviously aren't Cade's.

My stomach turns.

Cade's apartment is our safe place, sheltered from the partners and the rest of the world, and now that may be gone forever.

"Why aren't you calling the cops?" I ask. "Do you know who this is and that's why you're going back tonight—now?"

Cade looks away and plays with the watchband on his left wrist. "Let's talk about this in the car."

And for a second, I consider screaming at him, demanding an answer, but all I can think about is his arms around me Friday night on the deck, and how he reacted just a moment ago when I barked at him.

I nod, finish packing, and follow him downstairs.

* * *

I watch in the passenger side-view mirror as the shape of the cabin merges into the trees, indistinguishable in the night because we left no lights on to indicate we weren't still sleeping upstairs.

"We'll have to get fuel," Cade says, more to himself than to me, but it's enough to make me look over at the display.

When I look back at the mirror, it's too late. He's already made the turn onto the county road, and I know even if I swiveled in my seat, some modern-day Lot's wife straining for one last glimpse of a place where we were happy, the cabin is lost to my view.

The forest lurks at the edge of the narrow roadway and gives my imagination room to grow phantoms.

Suppose we arrive at the apartment and the burglar ambushes us.

Or what if we arrive to booby traps? Maybe he tampers with the gas line so the apartment explodes when we enter, or rigs an electrical outlet to explode.

Perhaps it's simpler: he waits for us to search the apartment and convince ourselves this is only a false alarm, and when we sleep in our bed, he creeps out to kill us.

Cade first, of course, because he'll represent the greater threat. The burglar will save me for last, and I can almost feel his hands on me, his breath in my ear, another man, just like the one on the trail from Friday morning, just like the one from a decade ago. Only this time Rafi won't be there to save me—

"Reag," Cade says. "Are you cold?"

He doesn't wait for me to answer but adjusts the car's temperature settings, and I unwrap my arms from around my legs, put my feet back on the floorboard, and straighten in my seat.

"Go back to sleep if you want," he says. "I'll grab an energy drink."

"I'm fine," I say, even though I am tired.

More than tired.

I'm exhausted. I want only to retreat into his bed and nestle into his arms, breathing him deep until I can convince myself we're safe again.

But adrenaline and fear gush through my veins, and meaningful sleep will be hours from now.

If at all.

I shove my hands under my thighs and stare out the windshield at the dark road, lit only by the car's headlights, twisting and turning before us. The stop sign ahead that marks the end of the farm-to-market road is almost a relief, except it's one more waypoint on the road back to Cade's apartment.

"Cade," I say.

"We'll talk about it when we're on the interstate," he says.

"That's not what I was going to say." I reach for his hand and squeeze it. "Just . . . you know what night of the year it is and how many cops will be out."

"I know," he says.

He doesn't roll through the stop sign like he usually would but brings the car to a complete stop and then makes the right turn onto the state highway.

The Porsche's engine ticks up but stays right at the speed limit, even if the tires seem to mutter, "faster, faster," against the pavement, and the trip to the interstate from the cabin feels much shorter than the trip to the cabin from the interstate on Friday.

Cade stops to buy fuel at a truck stop at the interstate junction. He asks if I want anything before he hands me the keys and heads inside.

I lock the doors and huddle in my seat, watching him saunter across the parking lot like he doesn't have a care in the world.

Only I know he does—and not only that, but he's keeping it from me.

It's something big, too, big enough for him to drive back to Dallas without getting the cops involved.

Something . . .

Or someone.

A sense of betrayal stirs.

I prop an elbow on the windowsill and rest my head in my hand. This is a lie of omission, a gray area in our world already shaded in nuance, but it requires a reckoning of sorts.

At least an acknowledgment and a discussion.

A knock sounds on the driver's side window and I jump, only to realize it's Cade. I unlock the car and pray he didn't notice.

He slides into his seat and starts the engine, passing me a plastic bag so he has a free hand to fasten his seatbelt. "Open the coffee for me, will you?"

I pull out the can of double-shot espresso and frown. "Coffee in a can?"

"The only hot stuff they had looked like it was hours old, and I wasn't asking the lady behind the counter to make a fresh pot," he says. "Guess they don't get many visitors this time of the night."

I manage a chuckle. "Not in a red Porsche."

He floors the accelerator and lets the tires spin on our way out of the parking lot. "Well, now she'll have something to talk about. Got you those chocolate caramels you like."

"I told you I didn't want anything," I say.

I barely see his smile as he draws my hand to his lips and kisses the back of it. "I thought maybe it'd keep you from tearing up your cuticles. You could've let me go back alone, Reag."

"No," I say. "I couldn't."

The wind rushes over the hood of the car and he takes a swig of the coffee. I rip open the bag of chocolate caramels and unwrap the foil, pop a candy in my mouth, and twist the wrapper into a strip.

"You know who broke into your apartment," I say. "Who . . . attacked me Friday."

It's not a question anymore, but an accusation, and I'm grateful the car is dark, that I don't see the reproach in his eyes that I hear in his voice when he says, "Reag."

"But you do—"

"If I knew who did that Friday, I'd have already found 'em," he says. "Anyway, I tried to get you to call the cops."

"Who?" I whisper.

He takes a long drink and a deep breath. "I think the Holcombes are involved."

"What?" I almost choke on my caramel. "How . . . ?"

But then I remember again Bridger Holcombe's personal cell phone number in Heather's bedroom, that the landlady mentioned that she was constantly late on rent until about six months ago. Even if Bridger didn't know I made that phone call from Fair Park Thursday afternoon, that landlady might have given my description to someone else.

And that Stu ends up interning in Cade's office the week after Heather dies—well, that's probably no accident, either.

"In the envelope," Cade says. "That alcohol permit for Club Saturnalia. I pulled the corporate filings and tracked it through several shell corporations to SilvaCo."

"*You* tracked it?" I ask.

"I'm not you, Reag, but give me some credit. I did manage law school without you," he says, and I hear the grin in his voice without even looking at him. "And let's not forget I found your apartment."

This is our usual joke, and he probably expects me to laugh here, but I sit in stunned silence instead, digging my fingernails into my palms.

"You knew what was inside the envelope this whole time," I say.

His "Yeah" is barely audible over the Porsche's engine, almost a sigh.

The ache in my ribs and shoulders is like that man is on top of me all over again, only now it's the weight of Cade's words, that he kept something from me. "So that's why you drank until last call and came home so drunk? Because you knew . . . ?"

"I traced the shell company, and I thought if I had a drink, maybe I'd work up a way to fix this," he says. "A drink became two and then three and then—well, you know the rest."

The air conditioning blowing in my face isn't as cold as the reality I'm coming to terms with, and I make myself smaller in my seat, nestling against the passenger door. "You lied to me. You let me think you hadn't opened that envelope."

"No," he insists. "No, I didn't. You never asked."

"Would you have told me the truth if I had?" I demand.

"I don't know." His voice is soft, small even, so different than when he charms a jury or plays to the media at one of his stupid press conferences. "I like to think I would have. But I don't know."

This, at least, sounds honest, and like what I've come to believe he and I represent to each other, although it stirs my own guilt from where I've shoved it aside over the weekend.

I haven't been entirely forthcoming lately, either.

"SilvaCo?" I ask. "What's that?"

"It's a Holcombe family company, one of Bridger's dad's companies that the family still uses," Cade says. "SilvaCo—like Sylvie, see?"

The Holcombes own the bar that Cesar Morales bartended at, where he died—a drug deal gone wrong, the police believe—and then Heather, who has Bridger's cell phone number, turns up at the law firm with that envelope for Cade.

But why? Why would Heather need to die, and why would I need to be warned off checking into it?

A dull throb starts at the base of my skull, and I pop another chocolate into my mouth before stealing a quick drink of Cade's coffee.

"That's disgusting," I say.

"I've had worse," he says.

I play with the foil scraps and let the silence build, watching the speedometer. "Why didn't you tell me?"

He sighs. His hand brushes my knee, just above the scrape. For a long moment, there is only his touch, the warmth of his hand, the sounds of the engine, and the whir of the tires, and then he says, "I wanted it to go away. I hoped—foolishly, I know—if I could just stall long enough, something else would come up that needed your attention and you'd let this go."

I lace his fingers with mine. As angry as I am now with this discovery and his admission, it would have been ten times worse Thursday night.

Thursday, when I had my own news to tell him, but I didn't.

And now it's early Monday morning, nearly seventy-two hours after that man attacked me on the trail and someone is in Cade's—our—apartment, going through our things. Some small part of me wishes that Cade could have been right, that something else could have come along to distract me.

"Is there anything else?" I ask.

"That guy, whoever he is, left. Rafi texted me," he says. "You?"

"Stu Holcombe knows I have that case file," I say. "And someone may have gone through it in my desk, I think. I noticed it was rearranged before—well, I went to Heather's house Thursday afternoon. I found Bridger's personal cell phone number on a piece of paper in her bedroom."

"Goddamn it, Reagan," he mutters and breathes out a long exhale. "Shit."

"I was going to tell you," I say. "Probably when you got around to telling me about the club ownership. But you didn't seem to want to hear about it Thursday when you got home, and I thought there'd be time this weekend. But Friday morning . . . happened."

Cade doesn't say anything. He only stares straight out the windshield.

"So." My voice sounds small, almost fragile, even to myself. "That's probably why that man came for me, then?"

I try not to think of him, of his hissing whisper in my ear, the sour smell of sweat and body odor, the way his hands feel around my neck, or his weight on my back, but he's there all the same, crowding in between Cade and me.

Cade squeezes my hand. "This isn't your fault."

"Isn't it?" I ask. "Why didn't you call the cops tonight?"

"Why didn't you call the cops Friday?" he asks.

"They wouldn't have done anything," I mumble. "And there might have been . . . questions."

"Yeah," Cade says. "Our living situation complicates things."

I don't argue that I live there because he invited me, I only pick at a fingernail until he moves my hand away.

"You have that file with you?" he asks.

"In my backpack," I say. "With my pistol and knife."

"The envelope is in my bag," he says. "So there might be questions from the police about how you and I have certain items in our possession that connect back to two recent deaths currently under investigation."

"But at least we have them," I say. "So they weren't in the apartment."

He affords me a glance. "Reag, we're riding a fine line here. We're almost risking charges of tampering with evidence and obstruction if this goes much more sideways. And if Bridger or Kirby hear about any of this—"

"Yeah." I pick up the can of espresso and brace myself for another drink. "We're in too deep for the cops."

Cade says, "I did offer to get you a drink."

"I know." I twist another wrapper around my fingers, wishing I could fold away my problems in it and chuck it in the nearest trash can. "Are you gonna be okay with this?"

He clears his throat. "What do you mean?"

"Bridger," I say. "He's practically your father. Your mentor, at least."

"We'll be fine, Reag," he says, and I don't push him for a better answer.

Some part of me knows that maybe he doesn't have one.

We pass through a small town, a blur of lights along the interstate and a parked patrol car on the shoulder. The Porsche hums along right at the speed limit and perfectly between the lines, like Cade didn't drink moonshine from late afternoon until the fireworks, and the patrol car doesn't move.

"What will happen when we get there?" I ask.

"I don't know," Cade says. "I don't suppose I can talk you into waiting in the car while Rafi and I do a walk-through?"

Alone in the parking garage, so the man who broke in or maybe the one who attacked me could wait for Cade to leave me and then grab me again?

"No." I clutch at Cade's arm more fiercely than I want to, and when he side-eyes me, I loosen my grip and look away, suddenly frightened that he'll know what I'm thinking. "I mean, that's silly. You might need the help."

"Of course," Cade says, and graciously doesn't point out that I couldn't defend myself Friday.

I lean across the console so I can at least rest my head on his shoulder. "I liked that place. It was a nice surprise."

He kisses the top of my head. "We'll go back."

I close my eyes and let myself believe him.

CHAPTER

14

DALLAS SLEEPS AROUND us, the buildings dark and the streets empty. Heat lightning flickers in the distance, but its threat of a thunderstorm is empty. There will be no rain.

Cade slows the car for the turn onto North Field Street and downshifts. "You never told me what it means that Rafi has bad paper."

"Oh," I say and peer out the passenger window. Occasional lumps mark where someone sleeps in a doorway, huddling close to a building in the hopes that residual coolness will seep out the walls. "A bad conduct discharge, or a dishonorable discharge. After the surge, when you had guys who had deployed over and over again, they were handing them out like candy."

"To people with multiple combat deployments?" I hear the frown in his voice. "That's hardly fair."

The military doesn't much give a damn about fairness, only war, but Cade won't understand that. Oh, he might say he will, but he's never experienced it, and there are some things that can only be known once they've been lived.

"It's not fair," I say. "Especially when we asked so much of them."

"What will happen?" he asks.

Paperwork, I want to say, the real ammunition of the Pentagon for the endless wars waged by the generals and senior noncommissioned officers who made rank off building perfect PowerPoint slides and always knowing just whose ass to kiss.

But, given Cade's profession and his day-to-day activity with depositions and briefings, he might be able to provide some assistance.

I side-eye him. "There's an appeals process. I'll help getting the documents filed and make some calls."

"I know it's not my area of expertise," he says. "But I trust you'll let me know if you need a lawyer's name on anything to speed things along . . ."

"Of course," I say.

He drives us into the garage, just like any other time, only now my fingernails dig into his arm, and I flinch at every shadow, cringing closer to him every time I think I see movement.

We arrive at the Porsche's parking bay, and he backs the car into its spot. My car gleams under the garage lights in its spot, the glass intact and the tires whole.

A shape moves at its rear bumper.

I tighten my grip on Cade.

"Easy," he says. "It's Rafi."

He turns off the engine and sets the emergency brake, then climbs out to speak with Rafi in low, muffled tones.

Maybe they think they're protecting me, that after Friday I'll be grateful they can handle this for me, but Cade ought to know that's an impossibility.

And if he doesn't, I can remind him.

I need to take back control; control is power, and if I can at least fake it enough to convince myself, it won't be a lie, and so Cade will believe.

I pull my pistol and knife from my backpack, shove the knife into my pocket, and tuck the pistol into the back waistband of my pants. It's loose without a holster but will ride there securely enough for the time it takes to get to the apartment. I step out of the car, swing my backpack onto my left shoulder, and let the door click shut.

Rafi's gaze meets mine over the top of the car. "Reagan."

At first glance, he looks like any other Latino guy in Dallas in the summer. His hair is cut and he's clean-shaven except for his now-trimmed goatee. He's casually handsome dressed in his T-shirt, khaki shorts, and running shoes, and no passerby would guess that three days ago he slept on a bench at the trailhead.

"Rafi," I say.

"Sorry to interrupt your weekend," he says and looks back to Cade. "White man, wearing gloves this time of year? That caught my attention, so I followed him. When he went into the building, it made me nervous, especially 'cause he went through the side entrance that has no doorman. He didn't have a key to your apartment, but whatever he used to open the door, I saw him use again, like he locked everything back up so you wouldn't notice. Maybe if you got cameras in the hallways, you can get something."

Cade looks away and brushes his fingers on his watch when he says, "Maybe," and so I know this is a lie.

"I tailed him like you asked," Rafi says. "He didn't look to be carrying anything when he left, but something might have been in his pockets. His car was parked at that public parking lot down the street. It must have been there a while since it was pretty crowded down here for the fireworks. I got his plate number, if you got any friends that are cops."

"Not me," Cade says. "Her, on the other hand . . ."

Miller may not want to do me any more favors, not after giving me that file last week, so I ignore this. "He probably parked there while he was scouting. How do we know the door isn't rigged?"

"I don't think that's what he's after," Cade says. "I think he's only after the information he thinks we have."

"Kinda walked like that guy from Friday," Rafi says. "With his shoulders all hunched up by his ears. You can always pick out a man by his walk."

"That guy tried to kill me Friday," I say. "Who's to say he wouldn't try again?"

"Reagan," Rafi says, his voice low like he's trying not to startle me. "That man could've snapped your neck if he wanted to 'fore I even got there. I don't think he was trying to kill you."

My hand flutters against my neck, almost involuntarily, and I move it away just as quickly, shoving it into my pocket, hoping that the men won't notice.

But he's right.

Manual strangulation is hard, harder when you're attacking from behind, so the easier way to do it involves using a garrote.

I droop against the side of the car before I remember this is Cade's baby and I might scratch something.

For once he doesn't seem to care.

He only reaches into the back seat to grab his bag and attaché case. "Still wouldn't mind getting my hands on the bastard."

Rafi grins. "Gotta catch him first."

"You get a good look at him?" Cade asks and motions for us to follow.

"No," Rafi says. "Pure luck I saw him even."

"You just hang out here all weekend?" I ask.

Rafi shrugs. "I was worried that man from Friday would come back for a second try."

Cade presses the button for the elevator. "And he went right to our place?"

"Yeah," Rafi says.

"So whoever it was knew we were out of town," I say.

Rafi shrugs. "Maybe he scouted the garage before, and I didn't catch him."

The elevator doors open, and we enter, Cade and Rafi flanking me. I try to ignore the feeling that they both think I need protecting and instead tell myself it's because I'm the bridge bringing them together, that if it weren't for me, they would pass each other on the street and only give each other a nod, if they acknowledged each other at all.

But that only serves as another reminder that whoever is behind this, Holcombe or not, isn't going to just leave us alone.

I wrap my arms around myself and stare at the floor.

* * *

Cade turns the apartment doorknob.

The lock catches, and he and Rafi exchange a look over the top of my head.

"I know you know your business," Rafi says, barely above a whisper. "But before you look for anything missing, you'd best look for anything he left behind."

Cade nods and unlocks the door.

"Ma'am," Rafi says and holds out his hand. "Let me."

I know what he wants. As a Ranger with multiple combat deployments, Rafi is still more capable with my pistol than I'll ever be, plus he has his size and strength to back him up.

I don't bother to ask how he knew it was there, but slide it out from the small of my back and hand it over to him.

He glances at it long enough to click the safety off, then steps past me and Cade.

He opens the front hall closet, pantry doors, and powder room door.

He proceeds into the bedroom, and I follow him with my mind, checking under the bed, in the closet, under the lower racks, and back out into the master bathroom.

"It's just us," he says.

Cade says, "Good," and clicks on a light switch. He looks under the kitchen counter, behind the art on the walls, under the coffee table, behind the television, and lifts each lamp to check its base.

Rafi returns to the kitchen and hands me my gun. I check the safety and put it in my backpack, hoping we won't need it tonight.

"I'll check the bedroom and bathroom," Cade says. "And then we can look for anything missing."

I follow Cade to the bedroom as he checks the lamps on the nightstands, feels around behind the headboard and under each piece of furniture, and moves into the bathroom.

"Shit," he says. "We'd never have known that guy was here."

The surrealness blankets me. We've driven two hours and arrived here in the dead of night, only for everything to appear perfectly in place. Whoever broke in must have known we weren't here, and yet he came into the apartment anyway. Nothing appears disturbed. There are no bugs or cameras planted, so what was he doing while he was here?

"Reag," Cade says, and draws me close to kiss the top of my head. "You okay?"

I don't trust myself to answer. I only cling to him.

His grip tightens on me, and he turns my face up to his and kisses me. "Let's see if anything is missing so we can get some sleep, okay?" he murmurs in my ear.

"You think Rafi can crash here tonight?" I ask.

"Why don't you make that offer?" he says.

I step out of his embrace and open the front hall closet, grab the pillow and blanket that are there, and hand them to Rafi.

He smiles, understanding immediately, and says, "Thank you."

Cade and I search through the kitchen, but everything is in its place, the food and wine, the glasses and dishes all accounted for. Not even a bottle of Cade's pricey whiskey is touched.

I tell myself the intruder wouldn't have taken anything at all if the file and envelope were with us, that he couldn't want anything else, but some part of me knows that if he wants to scare us off, he wouldn't just be content to go through the apartment without leaving something behind to show us he was there.

My clothes all hang on my side of the closet. My work-out gear and headphones are in their spots, and every piece of underwear is neatly folded and tucked away.

Cade hunts through his ties, his cuff links, and his watches, but shrugs when we make eye contact.

I open my nightstand drawer and the box that has my Air Force medals, rank insignias, my parade gloves, and a spare flight cap.

Everything is there.

Everything except . . .

"My dog tags," I say and dump the box out on the bed. "Motherfucker."

"Your dog tags?" Cade raises an eyebrow. "You have dog tags?"

"Of course I have dog tags," I snap. "Did you think that was only for *Top Gun* or something?"

"He got your dog tags?" Rafi asks from the doorway.

I sort the medals onto their side, stack the soft rank intended for the shoulders of my dress uniform and the sub-dued rank for my everyday uniform, and shove aside the metal rank, hoping against hope that the silver tags bordered by their black silicone silencers are just hiding under something else.

"Shit," I say.

"But that's just your name and your blood type, right?" Cade asks.

"Yes and no." I rub the side of my face and exhale. "Full name, social, branch, blood type, and religious preference. Which means he has enough information to get all the background on me he needs."

"Oh," Cade says and rifles through his nightstand drawer. "My high school class ring is gone. That fucker bypassed my UNC class ring and my SMU ring to take that?"

The combination seems so random, my dog tags and his class ring, and yet intimate. An item from who each of us was before, a symbol of our other lives, buried and walked away from, and now this ugly reminder that they can come back.

I shove my things back into their box with trembling hands.

15

ONLY RAFI'S PRESENCE Monday betrays that this isn't a typical day off work for me and Cade.

Cade cooks breakfast. We do laundry and change the sheets, inventory the pantry and decide we don't need groceries, then watch a baseball game on the television. I work with Rafi on the appeal to upgrade his military discharge, and Cade gets the necessary details to make some phone calls regarding the outstanding warrants.

The veneer of normalcy endures well into the evening, even once Cade and I withdraw into the bedroom. He lies across the bed, reviewing a deposition, while I sit in the overstuffed chair, one leg hooked over its arm, and read a novel on my phone.

He yawns and rubs one side of his face, and I admire how cozy the room feels in the lamplight. Sometimes I can almost trick myself into believing Cade has always been a part of my life, that everything before him is a dream, that Friday morning is a dream, that Rafi in the next room is a dream, and moments like this lull me farther into my reverie.

Cade turns a page and says without looking up, "I've got a breakfast meeting at the country club. Any big plans tomorrow?"

It would be easy to lie to him and say no, but he deserves better.

I eye him over the top of my phone. "The veterans' service officer is first come, first serve, so I was going to drop Rafi off on my way to Deep Ellum."

"Deep Ellum?" He looks up from his reading and clicks his pen but doesn't ask why.

We stare at each other for a long moment, and I brace myself for the argument.

Cade will forbid me to go. He'll say that it's too dangerous, given everything that's happened during the extended Fourth of July weekend.

Cade shrugs. "Why don't Rafi and I go with you?"

I let my phone fall into my lap. "Go with me?"

"Sure," Cade says. "We get the lay of the land, as it were. Then I go to my meeting, you drop him off at where he needs to go, and you go to the office."

I pick up my phone and try to force the words on the screen back into some semblance of order in my mind.

But they don't make any sense, just like this offer doesn't make any sense, and so I say, "Why?"

"Because you want to go," he says. "Because you told me your plans, and I don't want to argue about it."

He's not lying.

And what's more, he's watching me with soft green eyes, and I bask in being the center of his attention—maybe even the center of his world.

"I'm trying, Reag," he says. "Meet me halfway."

I smile. "I'd love the company. Are you sure you have time before your breakfast?"

"For you?" He winks and stretches across the gap between the bed and the chair to brush my fingertips with his. "I can be a few minutes late."

I wait until he resumes reading. "Rafi can't stay here with us forever."

"I know," he says. "I'm working on it. And you'll probably need this."

I hide my smile when he reaches into his attaché case, that his hiding spaces are so obvious, but that there's enough trust in our relationship that we both know the other won't snoop—at least not on each other. He pulls out the envelope that Heather placed in my hands before she died and sets it on his nightstand.

"I'll be careful," I say.

It's my turn to reach across the space in the middle, and I revel in the way he still makes my pulse jump when our fingers brush.

"Come to bed," he says.

"I don't want to interrupt your deposition," I say.

He grins. "Is that what's stopping you?"

"I don't like sharing," I say.

He closes it and shoves it on his nightstand. "There. Happy now?"

I clamber into bed and close the space between us. "But what about Rafi?"

He dimples and steals a kiss. "If I can be gentle, you can be quiet, can't you?"

I want to tell him I can be anything he wants me to be, only I know that's a lie, that I can only ever be me, and that will have to be enough for him.

"I can be quiet," I say instead and press myself against him. "Just watch me."

He tangles a hand in my hair, roping it around his palm. "Oh, I plan on it."

*   *   *

The parking garage elevator is air conditioned, but on a Tuesday morning in July this makes little difference. Condensation drips down the walls and slickens the tile floor, tinging the air with a faint mildew smell. Cade presses the button, and the elevator chugs its way upward.

Rafi leans against the rear wall, wearing a pair of khaki shorts and a T-shirt I recognize as an old one of Cade's, his ruck slung over one shoulder. Cade stands on my other side in slacks and a dress shirt, polished oxfords, cuff links that sparkle when they catch the light, and his SMU ring. He carries his suit coat and tie over one arm that he'll put on when he can't delay it any longer, but for now it's too hot and humid to worry about such things, and maybe he'd rather be as casually dressed as Rafi.

I can't skip wearing a jacket, not even in the elevator, because my pistol shows through my almost sheer lace camisole. My only option is to roll back the sleeves and fan myself.

"August will be miserable," Cade says.

Rafi grins. "Could be Baghdad."

I smile at him over one shoulder before I catch Cade watching us both, and I worry suddenly that this may make Cade feel like an outsider, or like he's still just that hick kid from the sweet potato farm because we've been places he hasn't. I slide a hand into his to let him know we don't mean to exclude him, it's just one of the things Rafi and I have in common.

"Reag doesn't tell many military stories," Cade says without looking at me.

Rafi shrugs. "I don't blame her. I wouldn't trade it for a million bucks, but I wouldn't go back for that, either."

The elevator wheezes to a stop and the doors open, allowing the warmer air to flood the compartment.

Cade walks me to my car and kisses me. "I'll be right behind you."

"Liar." I laugh and smooth his hair. "You won't want to drive the speed limit."

He grins. "I'll try, at least."

I unlock the car and Cade opens my door, while Rafi slides in on the passenger side. "We'll meet you there," I say.

Cade kisses me again and steps into the Porsche.

"Not a Porsche," Rafi says as I program the address into my GPS.

"Too flashy," I say and move the shifter into gear. "Not my style."

The rising sun makes long shadows of the oak trees, their branches grasping hands across the cement, but I ignore them and turn south toward downtown.

In my rearview mirror, the red Porsche follows as if it's attached to my bumper.

"How'd you get mixed up in all this?" Rafi asks.

"It's a bad habit of mine," I say.

He chuckles. "Which one of you is the other one's bad habit?"

"That's the million-dollar question, isn't it?" I ask.

"Mm-hmm," he says. "You and I, though, we don't have a million dollars. And Cade don't seem the type to be okay with unanswered questions."

"I guess that's between us, then," I say, and steer us east, into the sun cresting the expressway, watching the rearview to make sure the Porsche does the same.

The parking lots are as empty as the streets. It's thirteen days after Cesar Morales was found dead in the parking lot behind Club Saturnalia, near the loading/unloading doors. I park in the row nearest the street and turn off the car.

"What do you think you'll find, anyway?" Rafi asks as we get out of the car and Cade's Porsche screeches to a halt next to us.

I survey the parking lot. "I don't know."

He motions to what appears to be a pile of clothes and newspapers on the sidewalk across the street. "I'm gonna have a word with him."

"Have fun," I say.

His footsteps fade, seeming to carry the honks and grumbles of the morning traffic with them, leaving me alone in silence to confront the faint chalk outline marking where Cesar Morales fell. This is all that's left of him, the last thing to note he was here, and it's already almost gone.

Nothing lasts forever, but this seems too far, a betrayal by the universe that if it couldn't preserve his life, at least it could keep a reminder of where he died.

I walk closer to examine it.

Cade's car door slams behind me and his footsteps follow mine, his oxfords gentler on the pavement than my pumps.

"So this is it, huh?" Cade asks.

He squints at the horizon line and looks back at the building, then at the pavement like he measures something, judging it against his expectations.

"It's pretty open," I say.

"Unless there was a vehicle parked here," Cade says. "No way of knowing that now, of course."

"So a vehicle," I say. "Did they lure him here? Or maybe wait for him to come to his car . . ."

"Anything in that file about cameras?" he asks. "Traffic cameras, security cameras . . . ?"

"No traffic camera on this block," I say. "If there are security cameras, the businesses aren't offering them up."

"So if it wasn't for you, this really could just go away then, couldn't it?" Cade asks. Amusement laces his voice and I look up into his smile.

"Maybe," I say.

He stands beside me, arms folded across his chest, crisp and clean and powerful in his work clothes, almost too much to look at directly in the daylight. It makes me miss the Cade with rumpled hair and five o'clock shadow, the Cade who laughingly bets me he can still shotgun a beer—and then does it—the Cade who will sit with me and hold me while I cry in the darkness of an East Texas night.

This Cade is all business—handsome and charming, but somehow icy cool and aloof, a politician on a fact-finding delegation who won't commit to one side or the other.

I afford him a glance from under my lashes. Maybe he does plan on running for something.

He scuffs at a rock with the toe of one oxford. "In that file, did they say anything about who owns the club?"

"No," I say. "And if it's just a drug deal gone bad, why would they check?"

"So that's still ours then," he murmurs, almost half to himself. "What do we know about Mr. Morales?"

"No father on the birth certificate." I shrug and wonder how life can be shrunk down into an envelope, into the chalk outline on the ground, and just ignored. "Read into that what you will, I guess. I didn't have time this morning to look for the mother."

He closes his eyes and rubs the bridge of his nose for a second, his disappointment and annoyance so obvious they buzz like twin yellow jackets in my ears, persistent and ready to sting. "Is this really all you've turned up?"

Work Cade is all very well and good when you need a homeless veteran's warrants dismissed, but there's a price to be paid for having such access to power. High expectations, a requirement to anticipate not only what questions he'll want answers to but what questions he may miss, and a demand to stay a step ahead of his lightning-fast mind feel far too expensive right at this second, though.

My cheeks flame. I glare at a passing car and chew the inside of my cheek.

"I'm not trying to tell you how to do your job," he says. "I'm just wondering why it feels like you're waiting on me."

I turn to stare at him, hands on my hips. "Are you fucking kidding me?"

He looks away, swallows hard enough I see his Adam's apple bob, and licks his lips. "Reag, did I miss something here? You're a better investigator than this."

A man's voice calls from behind him, "Hey, what are you two doing over there? Can I help you with something?"

Cade sighs. "I'll deal with him," he says and stalks away.

I roll my eyes and pull out my phone to snap a few pictures. The time of day is different, so the light isn't the same, but it will do for reference if I need it later.

Male voices blend behind me: Cade's and the man he speaks with closest, and then the low, lilting music of Rafi's Spanish as he speaks with the homeless man. Not for the first time am I annoyed that my grandfather refused to teach my father Spanish, so my father couldn't teach me.

There's nothing here, I decide, staring at the ground, nothing except this fading outline, which people will soon drive over and walk past and never take a second glance at, and maybe that's as much impact as any of us will have in the world.

I crouch to examine the line, being careful to balance in my heels without dropping a knee to the dusty pavement.

Footsteps approach from behind, but I know from the shadow that covers me that it's Cade.

"He says he didn't see anything and doesn't know anything," he says. "And that we should leave."

Cade doesn't sound like he believes him, but I see no point in pushing the issue here, so I stand and slip my phone back into its pocket. "Fine."

"Reag." He catches me by my shoulders and turns me to him. "The lines—they're blurred here."

My gaze falls to the smudged chalk.

"You and me," he says. "I know on paper, technically, and in the office . . . look, it wasn't my most ethically sound decision to take you back to my place that night. And maybe

I fucked everything up from the start by hiring you when I should've just asked for your number."

This isn't Cade.

Cade is always confident, always sure of himself, always knows what to say, like he's rehearsed for hours and stepping in front of a jury is nothing.

I look up at him, see the worry in his eyes, and wonder if he senses my confusion.

"But I don't think of myself as your boss," he says. "I never have. And you're so good at what you do. I'm not criticizing you. I'm just surprised you didn't—"

"Because I was busy at work, doing my actual job," I say. "And at some level, I knew you didn't want me messing with this."

"I didn't," he says. "But it seems now the choice is out of our hands."

We walk toward the cars, and Rafi approaches from across the street, as if on cue.

"I'll pick up Italian for dinner," Cade says, shoving his hands inside his pockets. "Tonight, we can . . . talk."

I sneak a sideways glance at him. "Talk?"

He grins and nudges me with his shoulder. "I love you, but you're impossible, do you know that?"

"I love you too," I say and stand on my tiptoes to kiss him, straighten his hair, and brush a speck of dust off his collar. "Don't be late for your breakfast. But don't get caught speeding."

Cade winks and steals another kiss. "The key word being 'caught,' right?"

Rafi shakes his head and slides into his seat. He waits until I program the address into the GPS to say, "Did that guy tell you or Cade anything?"

"No," I say. "Cade said the guy claims he didn't see what happened."

Rafi scoffs and slides his seat belt on. "You're looking for a black Lincoln Town Car. Newer, last couple of years. Maybe the same car I saw the other night. My guy says your dead guy was nice, always helped him out with food or water, but that manager dude didn't like it one bit. They argued a lot."

"Burglars don't drive black Lincoln Town Cars," I say.

"Not as a general rule, no," Rafi says. "You gonna tell the cops?"

"Probably not," I say. "Anyway, didn't they talk to your guy?"

He shakes his head. "You know we're invisible when we want to be."

There's a bitter note to his voice, and I can't blame him for it. I lay a hand on his arm and say, "We'll get things square."

"I hope," he says, a wariness to his posture like he doesn't want to get his hopes up.

Not just yet.

I can't blame him for that, and any reassurance I might offer seems trite at this point.

We don't speak on the brief trip downtown.

I PULL THE CAR as close to the curb as I can get. "As soon as you get that paperwork filed, you take proof of filing and that privacy release over to the congressman's office. Ask for their veterans' caseworker and have her request expedition based on your homeless status. I'll call ahead and warn her that you're coming. She owes me a favor."

Several, actually, now that I think about it.

Rafi stares at the building and clutches the manila folder against his chest, his ruck smashed at his feet.

"This guy you're seeing now," I say. "He's ex-Army. Artillery, if I remember correctly, and he's good people. He'll hook you up. Feel free to use my name, and just give me a call if you have any issues."

He plays with the ruck's strap and looks back at me, his eyes shiny. "I don't know what to say. Between this and Cade dealing with those warrants and setting me up with that place to stay—"

"I don't know why you feel like you have to say anything at all," I say and turn my head, the sudden lump in my throat thick. "It's the least we could do."

"Why, though?" he asks.

"Because you needed the help." I shrug and make my voice cool. "Why'd you help me Friday?"

"Because you saw me," he says. "You don't know what it's like to be invisible."

I squeeze his hand. "You're not invisible. You never were."

He nods and tightens his hand on mine before he slides free. "I'll let you know how things go. You be careful, you hear?"

"We'll be in touch," I say.

I stay to watch him walk into the building, and even though he fills the doorway he passes through, there's something fragile and vulnerable to the way he sets his shoulders and hugs his ruck like a schoolboy on his first day. When I can't see him anymore, I leave for the office.

It's early enough when I arrive that no one else is here, and so I have the silence to myself. I shove my backpack under my desk and power up my computer, smooth a strand of hair back, and wonder if being outside in the humid air smeared my makeup covering the fading scrapes from Friday morning.

I don't want to explain those.

Not just yet.

I open my middle desk drawer where my small hand mirror should be, only it's not in its place, and I frown. I yank the drawer all the way out, but nothing is where it's supposed to be.

The pens and Post-it notes mingle freely, sticky tabs on the opposite side from where they're supposed to be, and the box of paper clips emptied.

I tug open the other desk drawers.

Folders are no longer in alphabetical order, papers are loose beneath the files, and the labels popped off some.

I slump and think of alternative theories for how the contents of my desk could be rearranged, but nothing else in the office is out of place. Every picture is straight on the walls, the work Stu was in the middle of Thursday afternoon remains stacked in its place, and the magazines on the coffee table in the small waiting area are still in their line.

The door opens and Evangeline breezes through, flawless in a flowing pink cardigan with a brown slouch bag over one shoulder, carrying Starbucks cups in a cardboard tray.

"Morning," she says with a wink. "How were the fireworks?"

"Fine," I say. "Did you have a good weekend?"

"Probably not as good as yours." She smirks and sets a cup of coffee on my desk, sashaying to her seat with a flip of her hair.

She doesn't comment on any bruises or scrapes, so I tell myself they must not be too visible. I slide my phone out and text Cade. I THINK SOMEONE'S GONE THROUGH MY DESK.

He doesn't respond.

I open my email to access his calendar and groan inwardly. That he's at the country club is not a surprise, but that he's at the country club with the other partners—

Well, nothing I can do about that.

I scan through the emails, answer the ones that need it, and sneak a peek at Cade's current caseload.

It won't hurt anything if some of that waits.

Plus, Cade did give me permission to dig around a little.

I run a web search for Araceli Morales in Dallas, Texas, but get no results.

"How's your coffee?" Evangeline asks.

I remember the cup on my desk and take a sip. "It's great, thanks."

"Always hard to come back after a long weekend," she says.

I don't argue that it was a relief to enter a quiet office and know I had some modicum of control here—at least until I discovered someone had gone through my desk.

She glances over at me as if she expects something, so I say, "Cade and I went out to East Texas."

She props her chin in one hand and grins. "And? First road trip as a couple?"

"We didn't kill each other, and I finally got him to let me drink coffee in the car," I say.

"That's not what I'm asking you," she says, narrowing her eyes. "That man worships the ground you walk on. I've worked for him for three years, and I've never seen him act like this. Did he propose or not?"

"We aren't even officially a couple," I say.

She snorts. "You're living with him, aren't you?"

"I haven't met his family," I say. "I don't even know their names. I don't even think he's told them about me."

"He's never been close to them," she says.

"Anyway," I say. "We're not even three months into whatever this is, and I could lose my job over it. Cade's opportunity at being a named partner—"

"Bridger's not that stupid," she says. "Cade brings too much money into the firm."

"Okay, well, maybe my job then," I say. "So it's a little soon for him to propose, don't you think?"

She chuckles and shakes her head. "Any other woman would be planning the wedding, and you're over there, cool as ice water in December. You're crazy, you know that?"

I feel Cade's arms around me, his promised whisper in my ear that he's there, and the contentment that cocoons my life since he appeared on my apartment's landing.

Before I stop myself, I blurt out, "He asked me to go apartment hunting next weekend."

"See?" Evangeline raises her eyebrows. "Bet he proposes by Christmas."

And then what, I almost ask her, but don't. She won't know how to answer it anyway.

Because once Cade and I marry, either we continue our secret relationship or it comes out into the open, and there will likely be a push for me to move to another office or for me to stop working for the firm altogether. After all, none of the other partners has a wife who works alongside them.

Getting a job at another law firm in Dallas will be trouble enough, even if I want to start over outside the small found family of Evangeline and Armando that circulates around Cade and the semi-security it provides me. As Cade McCarrick's wife, I would be subject to constant suspicion and scrutiny in another criminal defense attorney's office, and working in personal injury or tax evasion—while it would pay the bills—doesn't sound fulfilling. And the idea of building yet another career, after leaving the Air Force and the congressman's office, isn't something I particularly want to think about.

"Don't worry too much about his family," Evangeline says. "He never mentions them."

I drum my fingers on my desk and wonder about Cesar Morales. Maybe he and his mother had the same relationship as Cade and his family. Maybe there's a reason searching for Araceli Morales didn't provide any results.

"There's a rumor they didn't even show at his law school graduation," Evangeline says. "I always wondered why he came so far away for law school."

I don't respond to Evangeline. Instead, I run a new web search for Cesar Morales, pairing his name with Heather Hudson's. Perhaps his social media or obituary will provide some clues.

*   *   *

Cade enters our section at nine thirty. He doesn't look at us, not even when Evangeline says, "I brought you coffee."

"Thanks, I'm good," he says and slams into his office.

Evangeline and I exchange a knowing look. "Breakfast with the partners must have been fun," I say.

She starts to say something, but Cade snaps, "Reagan, in here now," from behind the closed door.

"Lots of fun," Evangeline says.

I stand, smooth my pants, approach the door, and push it open to say, "Do you want me and Evangeline?"

"Did I ask for Evangeline?" he asks.

I glance over my shoulder at her.

She shakes her head at me and waves her hand in a shooing motion.

I flip the bird at her.

She holds up her left hand and points at her ring finger.

I roll my eyes and tiptoe into Cade's office, pausing at the threshold.

His office is easily twice the size of the space Evangeline and I—and now Stu—share as the foyer, boasting a coat closet and a private bathroom hidden behind almost invisible pocket doors. The long windows provide a view of downtown Dallas similar to his apartment and flood the room with light, contrasting the dark wood of the bookcases that hold photos of his college football days. His diplomas from UNC and SMU hang on the wall along with framed jerseys and sports memorabilia from the Cowboys, Rangers, Mavericks, and Stars. A football rests in easy reach on the hutch that I know he turns in his hands, lining his fingers up perfectly along the seams, when he works through a problem or practices an argument out of a client's view.

The large desk dominating one side of the room never has any clutter on it; every note is filed away, and his pens are organized by color. A rug in blue and gray contrasts the polished dark wood floors and the large conference table opposite the desk. Everything here looks ready to be featured in a lifestyle photo spread at any given time, in the same modern style as his apartment and yet somehow utterly lacking his warmth and charm.

I absolutely hate it.

"The door," he says.

I hesitate.

By rule, the partners don't ever speak one on one with female employees in their offices with a closed door. This is supposed to keep them safe from sexual harassment lawsuits and insulate them from any hint of wrongdoing, but Cade and I follow it to force a thick boundary between our work and home lives. Alone with the door closed, his office on any normal day may provide too many temptations to see how our bodies feel together on the plush leather sofa reserved for clients, or across the conference table.

But something thin and silver swings from Cade's desk lamp, and my heart plummets into my stomach.

Today isn't a normal day.

I close the door.

For a long moment, I can only stare, mesmerized at its glitter, not even raising my gaze to meet his where he stands behind his desk.

"Those would be dog tags?" He lifts the chain to reveal the metal tags in their black silicone silencers and folds them into his hand. "Is your middle name really Jean?"

"That's what you want to discuss right now?" I ask.

He stares at his desk and shakes his head. "So they went through your desk, too?"

"Yes." He passes my dog tags over to me. "Things are rearranged, but nothing missing."

His high school class ring sits at the base of his lamp, gold with a black stone in the center, made for the hands of an eighteen-year-old boy nearly half his lifetime ago. I pick it up and watch it glint in the sunlight, some small part of me wondering if the homecoming queen dreamed of wearing it.

"You don't usually wear gold," I say and replace it on his desk.

"School colors," he says.

I stare at the ring and the proof that someone was in his apartment, and then that someone was brazen enough to come into his office and leave these things here for him to find.

This isn't about scaring me any longer.

This is about scaring him, about letting him know that he can't protect himself, much less me or his property.

"I have a lead," I say, hoping to distract him. "I'm gonna run it down. Should be back by lunch, I think."

"Reag . . ." Our gazes meet, his eyes pleading, the concern that threatens to spike into fear almost tangible, and I think maybe I can smell it, overwhelming his usual clean scent of safety. "Whoever this is got into the office. If it weren't for Rafi, we'd never know this stuff was missing and the apartment had been gone through until we got here this morning."

"Are the cameras on our floor still not working?" I ask. "Is that the reason there's a security guard hanging around the Holcombe & Donaldson lobby lately?"

He shakes his head. "The cameras being down are causing a fault in the sprinkler and fire alarm systems, but they can't fix it until this weekend, because they need everyone out of the offices. To keep us open and in compliance with local code, we have the security guard on the floor to basically monitor for fires."

"Oh," I say. "Do you think he could have seen something?"

"I doubt it," Cade says.

"What about the cameras in the downstairs lobby?" I ask.

He settles into his seat and reaches for the football behind his desk, his fingers brushing the leather. "Yeah. The trick would be getting access to them."

"You can be very persuasive," I say. "Unless you've lost your touch, Counselor?"

"And where will you be?" he asks.

"Oak Cliff," I say.

He looks out the windows toward downtown, as if trying to peer farther south into Oak Cliff. "Maybe that's not a good idea today."

"Cade." I sigh and perch on the edge of his desk. "Do you trust me?"

"Of course I do," he says, frowning up at me. "But this—"

"Give me your phone," I say and hold out my hand.

He hands it over and I feel him watching me as I type in his six-digit code to unlock it.

"Do I want to know how you know that?" he asks.

I smile at him over the top of the phone. "You're too predictable on some things."

He raises his eyebrows, a grin tugging at the corners of his mouth. "I'll try to be more spontaneous."

"You're spontaneous enough where it counts," I say.

I search through the app store, select the one I want, and download it. While it installs, I pull out my phone and unlock it, then pair the two apps before returning his phone.

"Now you can always find me," I say. "Just an app away."

He sets the football aside to play with my fingers, then finally draws the back of my hand to his lips. "What's in Oak Cliff? That's a long way from your usual hunting grounds."

"Cesar Morales's grandmother," I say.

Cade frowns. "Not his mother?"

"No, she died when he was a teenager. I found her obituary," I say. "But his obituary listed his grandmother, and I tracked down her address in Oak Cliff."

"What if she's not there?" he asks. "What if she's at work? I mean, couldn't you just call her?"

I shrug, even though I want to say Lupita Morales won't likely be predisposed to trusting a random white-sounding woman calling her up on a Tuesday morning to chat about her deceased grandson.

"I think this one probably needs to be done face to face," I say. "You'll be in the office all day?"

"Yeah," he says. "I got some appointments this afternoon, but otherwise I'll be here catching up on paperwork."

"So I'll see you at lunch," I say.

He waits until I slide to my feet to say, "Please be careful."

It's his office, but I indulge in leaning down to kiss him anyway. "Have fun with your paperwork, and get it done so you don't have to work tonight."

He squeezes a handful of my ass. "But you like my work at night."

"I'll close the door on my way out," I say.

Evangeline smiles when she sees me walk out of his office. "So?"

"He's in a better mood," I say.

"Oh?" She smirks. "You two have gotten faster."

I ignore this and scoop up my backpack. "I'm heading out for a bit."

"What?" She slams her pen down, glaring at me. "No. No, you can't. What about Stu?"

I shrug. "What about Stu? If he's not here by now, he's probably still sleeping off his hangover from the long weekend."

"You better hope," she says.

I laugh at her before I leave and head to my car. For the first time since Friday morning, I feel that man's weight lift off my shoulders and a sense of hopefulness settle into its place.

Lupita Morales will have answers. I just know it.

CHAPTER

17

My GPS takes me to a small brick house on a wide grassy lot bordered by a white picket fence. I park three houses down, shoulder my backpack, and walk up the tree-lined avenue, appreciating the shade that cuts the July heat, leaving only the morning's humidity.

A woman sits on the porch steps, shelling peas. She is small and slim, her dark hair cut in a highlighted red, no-nonsense bob, and her lipstick matches her blouse.

I recognize her as Lupita Morales from a picture I saw on Cesar's Instagram, and wave in greeting.

She doesn't acknowledge me, just looks right through me as if I'm some ghost.

I wonder how many times others have done the same to her, and so I don't look away, remembering how important it was to Rafi that I saw him.

Instead, I raise the gate's handle, push it open, and step through. "May I help?" I ask, gesturing to the peas.

She raises an eyebrow and purses her mouth but doesn't say no.

I sit beside her and bury one hand in the soft green shells. "Used to do this with my granny."

She doesn't look at me. "Maybe you ought to help *her* then."

Her voice is softer than her words, a low murmur that stays flat in tone but is pointed all the same.

"She's dead," I say. "Both grandmothers and my grandfather. Just my granddaddy left now."

She doesn't offer condolences. She only says, "Him, then."

I shrug. "My people don't like me so much lately."

"Liking's not loving," she says. "Not as much to do with each other as people think."

"Maybe," I say.

We work in silence for several moments until she says, "Why are you here, Miss? Something tells me you didn't come all the way to Oak Cliff to shell peas."

"I need to know about Cesar," I say.

She drops the bright green pods in her lap, and we finally look at each other full in the face. Her jaw sets and she says, "You don't look like a cop."

"I'm not," I say. "Just someone who was asked to check into things."

Her black eyes glint like glowing embers in the late morning sunlight. "I didn't ask you to, so who did?"

I look away now, and my fingers work on splitting open the pod to release the peas. "Pink hair and a couple of nose rings."

"And you always do what strangers ask, just like you always sit with old women and shell peas, I guess," she says. "Aren't you helpful?"

"I'm an investigator for Cade McCarrick. He's a criminal defense attorney Uptown," I say. "Heather came in and asked for his help, but he wasn't in, so she left an envelope. She's dead now, but you probably know that, don't you?"

She breathes out a long exhale, heavy with some emotion I can't identify. "No, I didn't know that," she says.

"After our last conversation—well, no one would probably think I'd want to know she was dead."

Her shoulders droop before she sets aside the peas and stands, turning to face me, and I brace myself for her refusal to help and her order to get off her porch.

"You know my name if you're here," she says. "What's yours?"

"Reagan," I say. "Reagan Reyes."

"Reyes." Her lips twist, perhaps in disbelief, and she switches to Spanish.

I shake my head. "I'm sorry. My grandfather wouldn't teach my father and uncle the language. He wanted to make it easier for them, after he eloped with a white woman. And my father married a white woman, too, so it was just easier . . ."

"To pass?" she asks. "You don't know what all you've lost, do you?"

Maybe I do, I want to say. Maybe I know all too well what I've lost by my grandfather and my father making decisions before I was born, decisions I didn't have any agency in, that have impacted my life every day since.

But I look away, afraid of revealing too much to this stranger too soon, when today isn't about me.

It's about her dead grandson.

She cups my face with her hands and turns it up to her, looking closely for something. "To think, in a couple of generations, my family could have looked like you. No one would ever know," she whispers, almost half to herself. And then she says, "Might as well come inside. Bring those peas with you. Do you want some tea?"

I follow her across the porch to the front door. "Wouldn't turn it down."

She leads me into a small kitchen, narrow, with a window over the sink and wood cabinets to the ceiling. The linoleum is yellow to match the counter tops, and Fabuloso and bleach scent the air. She gestures at a chair at the small table across the stove, just big enough for two, then grabs a glass pitcher of tea from the refrigerator and pours two glasses, unwrapping a plate of *pan dulce* on the table.

The sweet aroma of the bread fills the room, and she pats my shoulder. "Eat, *chica*."

Instead of sitting beside me, she stands at the sink—leaving me under the watchful eye of a portrait of Our Lady of Guadalupe that hangs on the wall—and stares out the window for a long moment, as if questioning inviting me into her home.

"It's not right, you know, burying your child and grand-child. It isn't natural," she says, her voice suddenly low and thick. "When Cheli turned up pregnant, I knew that baby wouldn't come to a good end. How could it, conceived like that? I sent her to my cousin in Los Angeles after Cesar was born. The longer they stayed, the less I worried. Things would be fine."

The grief in this stranger's voice, a woman proud enough to still match her lipstick to her daily outfit, is too raw and makes me fidgety. I pick up more peas, the pods cool and smooth in the warmth of my hands.

She carries the tea to the table and sets it down, and we resume shelling together.

"Cheli got sick. I warned her not to make any deathbed confessions. Cesar was fourteen, too young to hear old sto-ries dredged up, and after the funeral, I brought him back here. I still thought everything would be . . . okay," she says.

Lupita pauses and swallows a drink of her tea, and I take the hint to sip mine. The tea's coldness bites enough to balance the sweetness, stirring memories of my granny's kitchen, the faint smell of coffee and bacon grease and the hum of the refrigerator.

"He never asked who his father was, and I thought that was for the best, that maybe he wouldn't care," Lupita says.

"When he graduated high school, I hoped he'd leave. I tried to get him to go, but he wouldn't. He was a good boy, you know, wanted to make sure I'd be taken care of. Always made sure the lawn was mowed and my car was washed. I didn't approve of him tending bar, but the money was good."

Lupita plays with her tea glass, turning it in her hands, the peas forgotten. Perhaps she thinks of all the meals she and Cesar shared at this table, and not even a car passing by on the street draws her back to the present.

I clear my throat. "Heather—"

"That girl," she says and takes another sip. "Never knew what color her hair would be. I'll give her this, though, she loved Cesar. Probably better than he deserved."

I don't tell her that Heather is likely dead because of her involvement with Cesar, that I watched her collapse on an Uptown sidewalk late on a Friday afternoon. I only say, "The envelope she brought to Mr. McCarrick's office had Cesar's birth certificate, a permit for a bar in Deep Ellum, and a picture."

Lupita presses her lips together tightly and sighs. "Let me see that picture."

I slide the envelope from my bag and lay it on the table, pull the picture out of it, and hand it over to her. Her mouth twists and she shakes her head, but sets the photo between us.

"So young," she says. "So young and so very stupid. I warned that girl."

"So that's your daughter, Cheli?" I ask, and then remember I'm not family, maybe I don't have the right to use her nickname. "That's Araceli?"

Lupita nods, and one cheek hollows as she chews on the inside of it. She then raises her gaze to me. "You don't know what you're dealing with here, do you?"

"I know the bar is owned by the Holcombe family," I say.

She shoves her chair back to stand, the legs squeaking across the linoleum, and walks out the kitchen door to the rear of the house. I hesitate, unsure if this is a dismissal or if she's returning. I stand to gather the envelope and go when she reappears in the doorway.

"You need this," she says and thrusts something glossy toward me.

Another photo, but this one is clearly focused and shows the teenage white boy's face.

A young Bridger Holcombe, looking very much like Stu, only shorter, his arm around Araceli's shoulders.

I look back to the woman standing in front of me who only comes to my shoulder, her chin quivering. A single tear rolls down her face.

"Cesar," I say. "Was he—is he—?"

"Oh, yes," she says. "Cesar was Bridger's son."

* * *

I sit back down.

Lupita sits, too. A long silence passes as she holds the photos side by side, and I watch her face.

Mothers and daughters, the universal language of regret and love and guilt and insecurity and pride, the cycle constant regardless of culture.

I think of all the teenage arguments my mother and I had, all the conversations we still have, all her little warnings and cautions and notes, all the little barriers I erect in my defense.

All the while, maybe she's just trying to ensure I don't make the same mistakes she made, not recognizing that I'm not her.

Maybe that is what parents do, try to rebuild and mold future generations into themselves, only armed with more foreknowledge and—hopefully—the ability to make better choices.

Perhaps one day I'll warn some child of mine about the dangers that men in power pose, and she'll gleefully ignore me, smiling at me with wide green eyes, pointing out that she's only following in my footsteps . . .

Green eyes like Cade's and dark hair like his, and—

"Do you have children?" Lupita Morales asks.

I hastily choke down a gulp of tea and shake my head, hoping my face didn't give away my thoughts drifting to something other than the present.

"It's hard to tell these days, of course," she says. "When I was young, if you didn't have a ring, you didn't have a child. It was as simple as that. Times change."

"Araceli's father?" I ask.

"Died in Vietnam," she says. "His commander told me because I was Mexican, I probably wouldn't get benefits. He didn't bother to find out that I was just as American as he was—probably more."

"So you never applied?" I ask.

She shakes her head. "What's the point? My husband was good enough to die for our country, but I'll only ever be good enough to be the hired help." Her lips purse, and she shreds a *pan dulce*, rearranging the pieces of bread on a napkin. "My family was from down in the Valley, outside Brownsville. I knew I didn't want to raise Cheli there, so we came to Dallas. I thought it would be . . . different. I got a job at a big house in Highland Park, cleaning and watching the kids. The lady of the house was nice enough to let me bring my girl when she wasn't in school. If I'd known how that would've ended, I might have kept *mija* at home."

"You were the housekeeper for the Holcombes?" I ask.

"Yes, ma'am," she says. "That big white house in Highland Park. You know it?"

"I've been there," I say. "Once."

"That house." Lupita rolls her eyes and folds her arms across her chest. "It belonged to Mrs. Holcombe's family.

My first day there, she pointed out the room where she was born. She was an only child, so she inherited everything. That was all ancient history—or so it seemed—when I started working there. Bridger was ten and Cheli was seven, the same age as his younger sister. They all played together and didn't know no difference. Mrs. Holcombe thought she was so progressive, but when Cheli turned fifteen, she didn't want me bringing my girl no more."

I do the math in my head. A fifteen-year-old Araceli means an eighteen-year-old Bridger, two teenagers who have grown up together.

Something stirs in a back corner of my mind, a memory of Sylvie and Kirby at Bridger Holcombe's house watching Stu and Evangeline, Sylvie telling Kirby to stop whatever was happening before history repeated itself . . .

"I needed the work, so what else was there to do? I didn't like leaving *mija* at home alone, but she was fifteen. She could take care of herself," Lupita says, and a bitter smile twists her mouth. "So could Bridger Holcombe, who had a shiny new Mustang and knew how to drive himself across town. They'd wait until I left for work and Cheli would go with him for the day. When he went to college that fall, they wrote to each other. I burned three or four shoeboxes of letters between the two of them from when he was in Austin. Childishness, all the promises he made to her, that he'd marry her when he finished law school and move her into that big white house in Highland Park—I was glad to watch them burn."

"So you found out, then?" I ask.

"Not me," she says. "Sylvie Holcombe found out, the summer of Bridger's sophomore year. I got a furious phone call on a Saturday morning and had to hightail it up to Highland Park. There we are in the Holcombe kitchen— me, Bridger, and his parents—and he admits the whole thing. And then he says he wants to marry my daughter."

I gaze down at the pictures on the table, the couple so young and naïve and obviously in love. "I take it the Holcombes said no?"

Lupita Morales scoffs and stacks the photos in her hand like they're playing cards. "We *all* said no. Do you know what kind of life *mija* would've had as Bridger Holcombe's wife in Highland Park? Oh, sure, there'd have been money and that white house, but nothing else. They'd have been shunned, their children never fitting in one side or the other, and in the end . . ." She sighs. Her fingers brush the girl's face in the photo on top. "*Pues*, I suppose you know how this goes, probably better than most," she says, and her voice softens. "Maybe nothing would have changed anyway. Maybe she and Cesar would still be dead."

"Maybe," I say, and I hear the echo of Cade's words from last week, the decisions we could have made differently and where we would be now. Maybe Araceli Morales and her son were always destined for their lives to be cut short.

"Mr. Holcombe threatened to cut off Bridger's allowance. Mrs. Holcombe said it was best I gave notice and found somewhere else to work," Lupita says. "I came home and forbade Cheli from seeing Bridger. I told her I'd send her to the Valley or Los Angeles. But it was too late."

"She was pregnant," I say.

"They were so stupid," Lupita says and shakes her head again. "If Bridger had gotten a white girl pregnant, regardless of what side of the Trinity she came from, he'd have had to marry her. But my girl—she was disposable. Not the same."

I reach over and clasp the older woman's hand. "She wasn't disposable."

"Maybe not now," she says. "It's different now. Dallas, thirty-five years ago, it just wasn't ready for that. Maybe Highland Park still isn't. But maybe if she'd looked like you, her last name wouldn't have mattered so much."

"Why didn't Bridger just marry her anyway?" I ask.

"The money," Lupita says. "Mr. Holcombe had control of Bridger's trust until he was thirty. Mrs. Holcombe told me that if Cheli took the baby and went away, she'd give her money to start over. I told my daughter that she'd ruin Bridger's life if she stayed, and she needed to think about a future for her and the child."

"And so Araceli went to Los Angeles after the baby was born," I fill in.

"God help us, she did," the older woman says and dabs at her eyes. "Mrs. Holcombe helped me get on with the nursing home to make up for my job, and I didn't say a word when I heard Bridger finished law school or married that girl."

"Did Bridger know he had a son?" I ask.

"I don't know what Bridger knows or doesn't know," she says. "Cesar didn't ask about his father, not until recently. He brought me that photo and asked me if that man was his father, and I told him to leave it alone. But they run across all sorts of people, working in bars, so who knows what he heard. Suddenly Cesar's talking about meetings and a business plan, and he starts working at that new club in January. Now he's dead."

"You said you had words with Heather?" I say.

Her mouth puckers like she tastes something sour. "She showed up here after the funeral, ranting about how they might have killed Cesar, but it wasn't the end, that she'd get what was owed him for him and their child."

A child.

Another secret baby.

I make myself still in my seat and don't play with the peas or the photo or even my tea glass. "Did Cesar have a child?"

Her eyes are hard when they meet mine. "No, he learned his lesson from his mother. I just thought she was talking off the top of her head, but you don't think she could have been pregnant, do you?"

Two thoughts occur simultaneously, and I turn them over in my mind, examining them like Cade did my dog tags earlier in the morning.

If Cesar had a child, why would it be a threat?

If Heather was pregnant, who would she tell?

"I don't know," I say. "We spoke for all of two minutes. Did she work with Cesar at the club?"

"Off and on," she says. "But the people there were practically their family, so she was there all the time."

I think of the flyer for Cesar's memorial service in the women's bathroom, the homeless man who told Rafi that Cesar was kind to him and argued with the manager.

"Why would Cesar not get along with the manager, if they were practically family?" I ask.

She smirks and looks away. "And didn't you tell me your family didn't always like you?" she asks. "They were co-managers, actually. Cesar managed the bar and the food service. Marcos managed the front of house, bouncers, and performers. Cesar would use the leftover food to feed vagrants, and Marcos didn't want the club to be known for having the homeless hanging around outside. He thought it was bad for business."

"Do you think someone could have killed Cesar?" I ask.

"It's Deep Ellum," she says. "Who knows what could have happened late at night?"

I consider the contents of the envelope that are now laid out across the table, but especially that photo of Araceli and Bridger. "Would the Holcombes have wanted him dead?"

"Even if Cesar did have a child, how could it have hurt the Holcombes?" she asks.

A Latino son and grandchild living in Oak Cliff would only have helped Bridger if he really were going to run for Dallas County judge.

It would have softened his image and made him seem more human than a high-powered law firm and a house in Highland Park would.

I take a deep breath and chew the inside of my cheek. It seems almost cruel to ask, and yet I need to know, if only to be certain. "So you didn't know the Holcombes owned the club where Cesar bartended?"

"*¿De verdad?*" She gasps, her hand covering her mouth. "Are you for sure?"

"Yes," I make myself say, even though somehow this makes me feel as complicit as the Holcombes.

Her mouth twists.

I wait for her to curse, to rage at them, at me, at the universe in general.

A single tear rolls down her cheek, but she brushes it aside. "You'll let me know if you hear anything."

It's not a question.

"Yes, ma'am." I stand and rinse my glass out in the sink. "Thank you for your time."

She places everything in the envelope, including the two photos, and puts it in my hands. "It would have been nice to see Cesar as a father."

A knot wells in my throat, and I can't trust myself to speak, so I only nod. She squeezes my hand and releases me, but I carry the weight of her hopes, the strength of her grip, and the sadness of her smile with me back to my car.

CHAPTER

18

THE CLOCK IN my car says it's just after eleven when I
start the ignition. I'll arrive at the office in time for
lunch, and I wonder if I can sneak away with Cade, because
he needs to hear this latest development, and I want to see
his face when I tell him.

A text message from Rafi pops up on my phone. I
wait until I'm at a stop light to read it. PAPERWORK FILED.
THANKS FOR YOUR HELP.

I one-hand a response. YOU'RE WELCOME.

Cesar is dead, murdered just outside a club owned by
the Holcombes. Heather is dead, moments after she left the
envelope with proof of Cesar's parentage at Cade's office. If
she knew Bridger Holcombe was Cesar's father and she sus-
pected that might be a factor in Cesar's death, why would
she walk through the front doors of Holcombe & Donaldson and come to Cade?

I tighten my grip on the steering wheel. None of this
makes any sense.

The office's parking garage is quiet, the city sounds
more muffled than usual. Or maybe it's just that my footsteps echo louder to my ears. I find myself checking over my

shoulder, one hand clutching my backpack and the other on my hip, as close to my holster as I can get without it being too obvious. I race through the back, onto our floor, and lean back against the door to catch my breath and relax.

I'm safe, I tell myself. No one would dare try anything at the firm.

A brief memory of Heather in our office surfaces, her face flushed and sweating, and I try not to think of what happened to her only a few hundred feet from the building's main door.

I smooth my jacket, make my face blank, and yank open the door to the firm's side entry right as Kirby Donaldson pushes it.

Our shoulders brush. "There you are. Been out on business?"

"Running down a lead," I say. "Was someone looking for me?"

"We were all just in Cade's office and you weren't there," he says. "I'd stay, but I'm late for a meeting. So late, I snagged a pen and a notepad off your desk."

"It's purple," I call after him.

"It'll do," he says. "Hope you don't mind!"

I do, actually, but he hurries down the hall before I have time to object.

The security guard in the lobby barely glances up as I pass, and the receptionist scribbles on a piece of paper at her desk. I dash to Cade's section before I let myself sulk over why Kirby couldn't have taken one of her pens.

Bridger, Colleen, and Sylvie Holcombe stand between Evangeline's desk and mine, chatting with Cade. While Cade no longer wears his tie, his collar is open, and his shirt sleeves are rolled back, Bridger still wears a jacket, all three buttons fastened over his vest, and Sylvie wears soft slacks and a sweater, even in the July heat. Next to the three of them, Colleen appears casual and underdressed in her strappy maxi dress with wedges, a cardigan tied over her shoulders by its sleeves, but the way she smiles up at Cade sends a chill tickling the back of my neck.

Sylvie waves at me.

I force a smile and swing the door open.

Bridger, Sylvie, and Cade turn their attention to me, but Colleen still watches Cade.

"There she is," Bridger says, his voice dripping with a false cheer. "Just the person we were here to see."

From over Bridger's head and behind his shoulder, Cade's look tells me to tread lightly, and so I say, "Oh, I doubt that. Cade's much more interesting."

Evangeline busies herself behind her monitor, almost completely disappearing.

Bridger shoves his hands in the pockets of his four-figure bespoke linen pants that perfectly match his tailored jacket. "To have only been here a few months, you've made yourself invaluable. I hardly see Cade without you right next to him."

His smile is friendly, but a water moccasin smiles before it bites, too, and they're not ones to let go quickly. They'll bite and hold on until their prey is dead.

I recognize the warning hiss even without the shaking tail. Part of me wishes I could drop the news of where I've spent my morning, that I know the Holcombe family's dirty little secret now, but the other part of me instinctively makes myself small and nonthreatening, wanting to hold the information for leverage.

"Habit, I suppose," I say. "I was the executive officer for three separate commanders in the military."

"Yes, we were just discussing that," Sylvie says. "How lucky we are to have someone with your military and congressional experience on staff, but an investigator in Cade's office is an odd fit for you."

"Is that so?" I look to Cade. "I've learned so much in my time here."

"You know, of course, that the firm's chief administrator is considering retirement in the next several months," Bridger says. "I wonder if that would be a better match for someone with your . . . skills."

Sylvie's eyes gleam. "Why don't we talk about it at lunch tomorrow? It's the monthly meeting for the women's club that I told you about. I can pick you up here at eleven thirty?"

"I'd have to check my calendar," I say.

She raises her chin a little to say, "Do you always have these issues with commitments? It's just lunch, dear, I'm not asking you to marry me."

"How hard did you have to work to bring her on board here?" Bridger asks Cade with forced joviality, then glances back at his mother. "I'm sure Reagan is available. Aren't you?"

Another warning, and I recognize the latent threat that it's the last by the glint in his eye and the firmness in his voice.

"Of course," I say. "Tomorrow at eleven thirty, then?"

She nods. "Good girl," she purrs. "I'll send my driver for you."

"Thank you," I make myself say because I know it's expected.

She clutches at Bridger. "Son, you and Cade walk us down. One simply can't be too careful in the city these days."

Colleen slides an arm through Cade's, even though he doesn't offer. As she brushes past me, our gazes meet, and she grins. "Have a good afternoon," she says. "Come on, Cade."

I make myself smile back like it doesn't matter, and hold the door for them.

"What'd I miss?" I ask as I sit at my desk.

"Girl," Evangeline says. "Don't you play that game with me. What the hell is going on?"

"I haven't the faintest idea," I say. "Did you know about that retirement?"

She shakes her head. "All I know is they came in here and wanted to talk to Cade."

I type in my password and stare at my desktop, a stock photo provided by the software company, wishing it were the lake from this past weekend. A picture of me and Cade, maybe, together at the winery or on the dock, or perhaps just him, swinging in the hammock alone until he convinced me to join him.

"About me?" I ask.

"Yes, about you, damn it," she says. "What are you in the middle of that Bridger and Kirby are suddenly concerned about what you're doing with your time? Talking all sorts of bullshit about how this isn't enough for you to do, that if we don't keep someone with your credentials challenged enough that we risk losing you. And then Bridger's mother asking questions about whether you have a boyfriend, whether Cade thinks it would be worth it to give you more responsibilities if you were going to leave when you married and had kids, because—as she says—a woman like you won't stay single."

"What did Cade say?" I ask.

Evangeline sighs and props her forehead in one hand. "What can he say?"

She's right. Cade risks giving everything away if he tells Bridger and Kirby that he doesn't think I'd be a good fit for that role, and it would be a lie, anyway. Stepping into what amounts as the chief of staff role for the firm is a natural move on my part, especially with my experience.

But Cade did say he could protect me if news of our relationship got back to the two senior partners.

"Where have you been?" Evangeline asks.

"Running down a lead on something," I say. "Did they say where Stu is?"

"Sick at home," she says. "That was their initial excuse for arriving, to explain that he came home from this weekend not feeling well."

"Well, not a lot that penicillin won't cure these days," I say.

Cade and Bridger arrive outside the glass door, but only Cade pushes through, head down and dawdling like a boy on his way to the principal's office.

Bridger steps in long enough to say, "We'll take my car, then?"

"Sure," Cade says, and doesn't make eye contact with me or Evangeline as he passes by on his way into his office. "If anyone drops by, I'll be back around one."

"Maybe one thirty," Bridger says, chuckling. "Hell, if the martinis are as good and the waitresses as pretty as Kirby says, it might be two."

A sour feeling turns my stomach.

Cade saunters past, fastening his cuff links, his coat draped over his arm but his collar still open. I feel Bridger's gaze on me, and so I keep my head down at my work and don't move.

Not until the glass door whooshes closed and the two men disappear from my sight.

*   *   *

It's nearly three when Cade returns. He closes the door to his office, and it's still closed when Evangeline and I prepare to leave at five.

Bridger's words, that the martinis might be good and the waitresses pretty, stab between my shoulder blades.

I smooth my pantsuit and wonder if I should leave a note, that I'll pick up dinner, that maybe he should walk home and not try to drive.

"He'll be fine," Evangeline says. "They used to do this all the time."

All the time she says, like I shouldn't care that the wait-resses probably adored Cade with his dark good looks and his generosity with his tips.

I shift my weight from foot to foot and tug my back-pack higher up my shoulder. "What if—"

"Go home," she says. "Take a hot bath and drink a glass of wine. Don't think about Bridger or that stupid lunch with Mrs. Holcombe tomorrow."

I give Cade's office door one last look over my shoulder and we leave.

Evangeline's suggestion of a hot bath and a glass of wine holds some appeal. Once I'm in the apartment, I grab a bot-tle of wine without considering its cost and a glass from the kitchen and retreat to the master bathroom.

The bubble bath that sits on the ledge of the oversized soaking tub is mine from my apartment. I pour globs of it under the spigot, its scent of amber and sandalwood reminding me of the last time we used it, when Cade and I spent a whole Sunday afternoon soaking.

Cade, who went to lunch with Bridger today instead of staying so he could hear my news, who may have drunk too many martinis and flirted with the waitress because Bridger was watching.

And maybe that pretty waitress won't have my com-mitment issues that Sylvie pointed out this morning, and probably wouldn't have a moment's hesitation if Cade asked her to move in with him or apartment hunt.

I fill the wineglass and take a long gulp, slip out of my clothes, and fling them halfheartedly toward the hamper. The bubbles quiver and jiggle as I slide into the water, reassuring myself that Cade won't care what Sylvie says or Bridger does.

Maybe.

Only I remember Colleen's smile up at Cade, the way she took his arm as though she'd done this before, her look at me as she passed.

I chug the remainder of my glass and refill it.

She knows.

We've given ourselves away somehow, or maybe she's just clever. Or maybe before I was in the picture, she and Cade . . .

I ignore the now empty glass and drink wine straight from the bottle, content in the knowledge that no matter how much I drink, Cade is safe for me and won't take advantage of the situation.

The water cools and the bubbles flatten. I slouch further into the tub, use my toes to unplug the drain, and turn the water faucet with my foot until heat floods the tub again, swirling around me like all the secrets and lies and histories.

I think about Lupita Morales and her daughter, her comments today that maybe one day her family would look like me, but that if Araceli had married Bridger, their children would have been caught between worlds, and I know this to be true. It's a difficult place to be, never fitting in, never meeting the standards of either side, always feeling out of place.

The thick, unruly curls my mother's mother complained about or the last name that separated me from my classmates in my predominately white school.

The fair skin and light eyes that automatically made me an outsider on the Reyes side, and my inability to speak Spanish that separated me from my few Latino classmates.

The military was supposed to look past all that, but instead I was a woman in a man's world, trying once again just to simply belong without making waves.

I take a long drink of wine and close my eyes, wishing for Cade, because he's the first home I've had, the first person to not give a damn about any of it.

Still, when the apartment door does eventually click open, I bolt upright in the bathtub, ears straining. A flicker of fear rises above the wine to remind me of the weekend's events.

"Reag," Cade calls. "I got dinner."

The panic dissipates and I giggle, and then because of the way the sound echoes off the bathroom tile, I giggle again. "In here. You should join me, Cougar Bait."

"Cougar Bait. Oh, that's nice," he says, and saunters into the bathroom.

Our gazes meet, and he grins, showing his dimples.

I blow a handful of bubbles at him. "Well?"

He unbuttons his dress shirt and hangs it on the door-knob. "Dinner will get cold."

"Bring it here," I say and hold up the empty bottle. "And more wine."

He frowns and takes the bottle from me. "Don't you think you've had enough?"

"I'm in no condition to judge that," I say. "Are you taking your clothes off, or are you coming in with them?"

"It's an intriguing offer," he says, "but I think—"

"Did you have too much fun this afternoon with a wait-ress? Colleen, perhaps?" I ask.

"Reagan." He stoops to caress my cheek and tangles a hand in my bun. "Gorgeous, jealous, *and* drunk is a helluva combination, you know?"

I snag him by the collar of his T-shirt and kiss him until we're both breathless. "Don't forget hungry."

He laughs and pulls free, rising away from me. "I'll bring food."

But he doesn't join me in the bathtub.

He sits outside it, cross-legged in his running shorts, and feeds me nibbles of focaccia and bites of lasagna.

He brings bottles of water instead of wine, and when I complain about this, he only says, "You'll thank me tomorrow."

"I don't give a damn about tomorrow," I say.

"I know," he says. "I'll run you a shower so you can rinse off."

He doesn't hop into the shower with me. When I purposely skip a nightgown, he slips a T-shirt from his drawer over my head and tucks me into bed. He sits next to where I lie and nominally reads a deposition, but I feel the distance tonight that isn't usually there, like he's holding himself back.

Evaluating something, perhaps, or waiting, only I don't know why that could be, and the amount of wine I've had makes it too difficult to concentrate for very long. I stumble through my memories, try to remember what I wanted to tell him, what I waited to tell him before I came home and drowned the day in a bottle of expensive red wine, but everything comes back to Cade.

Cade and his nearness, the usual fire that isn't mine to hold tonight, and I want to scream and beat against the walls of the box I feel him constructing to contain me.

He turns the light off and lies down in bed beside me, curling himself around me.

"Cade," I say and twist in his arms until we're facing each other.

"Reagan." He kisses my forehead. "I thought you were asleep."

I nuzzle into the hand that brushes my face and my lips find his fingers, drawing each one into my mouth just enough to taste it and allow it to feel the edge of my teeth.

He makes a sound that's part sigh, part moan, all of it barely audible, like he tried to choke it off but just couldn't, and then there's a mumbled, "Damn it."

I nudge him over in the bed with my knee and slide a leg over him so I can sit up.

"You know you'll feel this tomorrow," he says. "And it sounds like you have a very busy day."

"You let me worry about that." I walk my fingers up his chest and pause to swirl the hair there. "Do you think I have commitment issues?"

He chuckles softly and laces his fingers together behind his head. "Is that what this is about? I don't think that's what was said."

"But that's what she meant," I say.

He shifts and I tighten my thighs to keep him from dislodging me.

"What do you care what she says?" he asks.

"I don't," I say. "I care what *you* think."

"I'm not the one who brought it up," he says.

"Counselor." I reach a hand past the waistband of his boxers. "You're avoiding the question."

"I've never much worried about it," he says. "I figure as long as you're happy and I give you a reason to stay, you'll stick around, and that's enough for me."

"And were the waitresses pretty?" I ask.

Now he laughs. "Shit, what business do I have with cocktail waitresses when I can come home to you, hmm?"

He tries to sit up, but I push him back into the bed, shifting my weight forward to keep him there. "What about Colleen? The way she was looking at you—"

"Reagan Jean." He catches both my hands in one of his and kisses each of them. "She's not my type. She might flirt, but she won't risk it, not with their prenuptial."

"What do you know about that?" I ask.

"It was kind of a legend in law school," he says. "Bridger's will and prenuptial, actually. He used to brag when he was still teaching that they were so ironclad and airtight it'd take the ghost of Houdini to get out of them."

"Oh," I whisper.

He sits up and I don't fight him when he gathers me into his arms, cradling me against himself. "What's going on, babe? It's one thing for us to put away a bottle of wine together, but on your own . . ."

I squirm and attempt to wriggle free, but he's stronger. This shouldn't be a surprise, and yet that he's able to keep me firmly in place and doesn't give in adds another layer to the frustration that's built since Friday.

Friday, when another man showed me exactly how fragile I am.

Sunday night, when someone went through our things in the apartment.

This morning, when I realized that same man had been through my desk.

Bridger, today with his threats in the office.

And I'm completely powerless to fight any of them, even Cade.

But maybe I don't want to fight him.

I slump into his arms and strangle the furious sob in my throat, take a deep breath to compose myself, and wait to ensure I won't dissolve into angry, drunken tears.

"It was a long day. And . . ." I swallow hard and bury my face in his shoulder.

He rests his cheek against mine, his breath warm in my ear. "And?"

"And I got scared," I say. "I—I don't want to lose you."

"Reagan." His arms tighten around me, a reassurance that nothing can touch me here. "You have me as long as you want me."

I breathe deep his scent of safety and reach up to bring his face to mine. "I want you now," I say. "So the wine is the only thing I'll regret tomorrow."

His laugh is low and easy, full of promised delights, and he kisses me. "Just don't puke on me, okay?"

I try to think of something clever to say, something about what a romantic he is, but he pulls me down in the bed so suddenly that my head swims and I have to close my eyes so the room doesn't spin.

"You won't ever lose me," he murmurs into my ear. "And I'll always find you."

There in the darkness, we meet, fingers interlaced, his mouth against mine, limbs entwined and bodies together, and I let myself cling to that truth and his assurances.

AFTER THE THIRD trip to the bathroom, Cade makes me a bed of towels on the floor. He brings bottles of water and sits beside me in the darkness to sponge my face with a damp washcloth.

"Go to bed and let me die with dignity," I say, like he hasn't held my hair for me every time I've thrown up over the last hour.

I hear the smile in his voice. "First time with that much red wine, huh?"

The cool water feels good on my face, and the gentle way he combs my hair back with his fingers settles me.

"Fine," I say. "You can stay, but you have to be quiet, and we never speak of this again."

He arranges a bath sheet over me. "It never happened."

I swallow the ibuprofen and water he offers me and lay my head on his thigh, while he leans back against the wall.

"It's actually a little flattering," he says. "That you'd rage drink a whole bottle of wine worrying about me and Colleen or me and some waitress."

"I'd hardly consider it rage drinking," I grumble into his leg. "Anyway, it wasn't *just* about you, but go right on patting yourself on the back."

He chuckles. "I think you did enough of that for me earlier, don't you?"

I can't see him, not in the blackness that is the bathroom at night, but I can imagine his grin, the flash of his dimples, the way his eyes crinkle at the corners, and I smile, too. I find his hand with mine and squeeze it.

"Try and rest," he says. "You know you have to go tomorrow."

The thought of that damn luncheon swirls my stomach into another hellish knot, but this one I close my eyes and manage to ride out, swallowing my nausea with my dread.

"You should rest, too," I say.

"It's an office day," he says. "No court tomorrow."

I wipe my mouth with the edge of the bath sheet. "What happens if I call in sick?"

His sigh is half-hearted, as if he almost regrets having to point out, "I think you know better than that."

"But I could be contagious," I say. "Anyway, if you don't have court tomorrow, you could go."

He laughs, tickling my nose with a strand of my hair. "It's for women. Hence the name, women's luncheon."

"How very non-inclusive of them," I say.

As though there will be anything besides rich white elderly ladies at the tables tomorrow, clapping and nodding in agreement that *something* ought to be done.

Just so long as it doesn't inconvenience them or disrupt their way of life.

"You could say you were advocating for women," I say.

"I am, indeed, a fan of women. Especially when they're smart. Driven. Decisive. Passionate about what they believe." His hand strokes my eyebrows, lulling me closer to sleep. "One in particular keeps my life much more interesting."

I yawn. "You should tell Evangeline sometime how much you appreciate her."

His voice is soft, barely above a whisper. "This is a good opportunity for you. For us. Face time alone, with Sylvie Holcombe. You play our cards right with her, Reag, and who knows what could happen?"

Our cards—because it affects us both.

Only I'm the one who has to ride in the car with Sylvie Holcombe and sit at lunch with her, let her introduce me to others like her, other women who may have their own Lupita Moraleses hard at work for them at their houses, disposable and able to be fired the moment they cross the white woman they work for.

"Oh." I lurch up to a sitting position and sway, almost falling into Cade.

"Reag." Cade automatically gathers my hair, twisting it into a roll. "Are you all right?"

"Fine, fine." I shake my hair free of his hand and slump against him. "I meant to tell you today, but you left for that stupid lunch with Bridger. I found her. I found Cesar's grandmother, and you'll never believe this."

He's warm, and leaning with my head on his chest is more comfortable than using his thigh as a pillow. I nestle against him and find the familiar sounds of his heartbeat.

Cade nudges me. "I'm dying. What about her?"

"Yeah, that." I push myself upright and try to clear my drowsiness. "Bridger is his father."

"What?" He grasps me by the shoulders and holds me firmly. "Reagan. What did you say?"

"*Was* his father, I guess," I say. "Bridger was Cesar's father."

"Fuck," Cade says.

He releases me so abruptly I fall into the wall, bumping my head, and wail, "Cade."

"Shit," he says. "I'm sorry. You okay?"

I hold my hand to my head. "What's going on?"

"Listen to me," he says. "I need you to tell me exactly what she told you."

"Right now?" I ask.

"Oh, now you're ready to sleep?" he asks. "Here, drink some water."

He tugs me into his lap and cradles me there, holding a bottle of water to my lips. "I'm not a child," I say.

"I know," he says. "But you're nicer when you're snuggled. Now, try to stay awake and tell me the whole story."

"Don't you be ugly, or I won't tell you any more." I cuddle against him, playing with his fingers as I recount the story Lupita Morales told me, about the shoeboxes of letters and Mrs. Holcombe firing the housekeeper, only for Araceli to turn up pregnant anyway.

"And there's proof?" Cade asks.

"That photo in the envelope is of them," I say. "Araceli and Bridger . . . when he was young."

"Hmm." Cade kisses the top of my head. "How young?"

"Twenty-one when Cesar was born," I say. "Cesar was your age."

Rafi's age, as well.

Three different men.

Three different paths, and now they braid together, but I can't see where the road goes from here, sitting in a dark bathroom on the floor and trying desperately to keep my stomach in place.

"We need to find the lecture notes from Bridger's classes when he was teaching estate law," Cade says.

"Why?" I ask.

"Because of his will," Cade says. "I'll bet this goes back to that. Think of the Holcombe estate, if something were to happen to Bridger—"

"And if Cesar's girlfriend was pregnant," I say. "Well, Lupita thinks that now. I suppose that might have come up in the autopsy?"

"You think whatever friend you have in the police department can get you that info?" Cade asks.

Miller might be able to, but he'll want to know why, and I'll need to think of something to tell him.

"Maybe," I say.

"Will you have time for that around your lunch tomorrow?" he asks.

"Today," I say. "Lunch today."

He hugs me close. "Promise me you'll be careful."

"The absolute soul of discretion," I say.

"Maybe I should come along," he says.

"Don't be silly." I yawn. "It's a women's luncheon, and you have your own projects to work on now."

"Oh, I love you," he says.

"I love you too," I mumble. "And I'd love you more if we went to bed now."

"All right," he says. "Probably would be more comfortable, if you think you're up for that."

He carries me to bed and winds himself around me. Almost before he grows still, I slip into a hazy wine-fueled dream of a young Bridger Holcombe in a Mustang chasing me on the Katy Trail.

It's half a relief when Cade's alarm goes off.

*   *   *

Something gently shakes my shoulder, and then lips brush my cheek.

"Reag," Cade whispers. "I'm leaving for the office, but I made you breakfast and set out your clothes."

I roll over in bed and squint up at him.

Despite being awake most of the night, Cade is freshly showered, clean-shaven, his hair gelled, his khakis perfectly creased, and his button-down shirt crisp.

I rub my face with one hand. "You set out my clothes?"

"You always complain about not knowing what clothes to wear to events." He grins and smooths my tangled curls. "And I think the customary response is 'Thanks, sweetheart.'"

"Sweetheart?" I raise an eyebrow.

"Honey?" he offers.

"Mm, we'll talk about this later," I say.

He pats my leg. "Eat your breakfast and pop into the office before lunch to make an appearance, okay?"

I wait until he's almost to the door to say, "Cade?"

"Yeah?" He glances over his shoulder, flashing that All-American smile that makes me—even hungover—suddenly want him.

"Thank you," I say. "For last night."

"Any time," he says. "Well. Not any time, but once every now and then—"

"I love you," I say.

"I love you too." He winks. "Can't wait to hear about lunch."

I fling his pillow at him, which he dodges, but wait until I hear the door close to push myself up slowly, my head swimming. A cup of coffee sits on a tray beside a bottle of water, a plate with fried eggs stacked on toast, and sliced strawberries arranged in a heart atop a small bowl of yogurt.

Evangeline's words from yesterday, that any other woman would be planning the wedding, crash into Sylvie's remark that I can't handle commitments, and then I smile because neither of them understands Cade's and my relationship.

That's between us.

I make myself eat, even though all I really want is the coffee, and carry the dishes to the kitchen.

A bottle of water sits next to the sink. The note propped against it reads, *Why not drink me with some ibuprofen to help the headache?*

By the time I finish my shower, the pounding in my head softens to a dull ache. I brush my teeth, twist my curls into a braid while they're still wet and malleable, and step into the closet to dress before I apply makeup.

A new red sheath dress with the matching jacket hangs on the rack, a coordinating Coach purse shares the hanger, and a pair of red patent leather Jimmy Choo stilettos on the floor.

No backpack today, the note reads in Cade's scribble. *Can't wait to see how everything looks.*

The dress fits as if it was made for me, falling far enough past my knees that the bruises and scabs from last Friday morning won't show. I consider texting him a picture to thank him but decide the surprise might be better at the office.

Within another half hour, I finish my makeup, lock the apartment door, and leave.

"Reagan," I hear, almost the second I exit the building.

The bright morning sun hurts my eyes, even through my sunglasses, so I don't turn my head. "Rafi?"

He falls into step beside me, his presence comforting if for no other reason than he's tall enough for me to walk in his shadow. "It'd be safer to drive, you know."

"Ugh, but then I have to walk through the parking garage, deal with traffic, and walk through a second parking garage," I say. "I'll take my chances on the sidewalk."

"Cade said you'd say that," he says.

I sneak a glance at him and his untucked short-sleeve button-down shirt with pressed khaki slacks, the perfect Dallas summer business casual look. "He asked you to walk me to and from work?"

"Maybe."

This is more of a relief than I'll ever admit to either of them, but I keep my tone nonchalant. "Fine. Just slow down a little."

He scoffs and shakes his head. "Those ridiculous shoes."

"Cade picked them out," I say.

"I'll bet he did," Rafi says. "But if that man comes back—"

"He won't come back if you're here, and Cade knew that," I say. "You got big plans today?"

"I thought I might look around for a job," he says.

"In between babysitting me?" I ask.

"See, I told him you'd say that," he says.

I slide the bag higher up my shoulder. "Do y'all talk about me often?"

A trash truck lumbers past, trailing the stench of decaying food, and I choke my stomach back into its place and quicken my steps.

"I thought we were walking slow," he says.

"It's hot out here, and I don't want to ruin my makeup or smell sweaty," I say.

Rafi chuckles as if he knows but picks up his pace.

Evangeline smiles when we arrive. "Well, good morning. How's your head?"

"Fine," I say.

She plays with a section of her braids. "And who's this?"

"Oh, this?" I glance over my shoulder at Rafi and stop when I see his broad grin and the sudden sparkle in his eye. "This is Rafi, a friend of mine. Rafi, this is Evangeline."

He steps past me to shake her hand. "Pleased to meet you, ma'am."

"You, too," she says. "Reagan's never mentioned you."

"Old military buddy," I say on my way to my desk.

Three water bottles wait with a Post-it note that reads *Drink me.*

"I'll see you around then," Rafi says, although I'm not sure if he's talking to me or Evangeline.

But I say, "Yes," and watch Evangeline watch him stride out the door.

"You should bring your friends to work with you more often," she says.

"And Armando?" I ask.

"I told you, we're not a thing," she says. "That a new purse?"

"For lunch," I say. "Where's Stu?"

She huffs and rolls her eyes. "His grandmother is dropping him off at lunch, so Cade says he'll wait to take his lunch until you get back."

I open a water bottle and power up my computer to see what I can accomplish in the ninety minutes before I leave.

Maybe Bridger's will is on file with the courthouse.

S TU TRUDGES THROUGH the door, sunburned and scowling, hands shoved inside his pockets like he's hiding clenched fists. He flings himself into a chair and says, "She's waiting for you."

I lock my computer and stand. "You should let Cade know you're here."

"Good luck," Stu says. "The old lady's in a mood."

I shoulder my new purse. "I'll manage."

As I leave the building, I catch a glimpse of Rafi, sitting on a bench in the shade of the oak trees, reading a newspaper. His presence is reassuring, even if I know he can't go with me.

A black Lincoln Town Car idles at the curb.

Newish, maybe a couple of years old, and I tell myself the sudden warning that creeps up the back of my neck is silly, that there are hundreds of late-model black Lincoln Town Cars in the region.

That man, Bear, the one Evangeline told me worked for the Holcombes, steps out of the driver's seat.

His slicked-back hair gleams copper when the light hits it. A faint sheen of perspiration glistens around his sunglasses and over the collar of the starched white shirt he wears with a black tie and a matching suit.

As I approach, he smiles and leans down to say into the car, "Ms. Reyes is here."

"Good." Sylvie Holcombe snaps her compact closed as I settle beside her in the back seat. Her voice holds an unusual peevishness when she says, "I almost didn't think you'd come."

"I said I'd be here, didn't I?" I ask, making my tone bright.

Bear steps inside the driver's seat and buckles his seat belt. "The country club?"

"Yes, please," she says and tucks her compact into a large Louis Vuitton purse. "You don't fool me one bit. We both know why you're here."

The warning up the back of my neck is now an alarm blaring in my head to rival my hangover. "Oh?"

She claps her hands. "I thought once Bridger dangled that news about the office administrator retiring, you'd come running. Cade probably sent you to bring back some details, didn't he? He's always been clever about finding an inside angle, and men are the *worst* gossips. Aren't they, Bear?"

He chuckles from the driver's seat. "As you say, ma'am."

She smiles. "We don't know what we'd do without Bear around."

"It's so nice to have good help," I say and can't help but feel I'm betraying Lupita Morales by sitting here somehow.

"I imagine you must know from your military experience how important it is to have the right people in the right places," she says. "The chief administrator has been there since the firm opened. I think it would be interesting to see what you would bring to the position. I'm sure you might have a very different . . . style."

"How long, exactly, has the firm been open?" I ask.

"Thirty years," she says. "My husband staked it for the boys when Bridger married Colleen."

"Thirty years?" I echo. "Bridger must've just been out of law school."

She affords me a curt nod. "Just. Why should a Holcombe work for someone else when he could run his own firm?"

I resist the urge to roll my eyes at this idea that Bridger couldn't have learned anything by not being his own boss, and remark only, "What an interesting career he's had, between being a managing partner and guest lecturing at SMU. You must be so proud."

"He's done well," she says. "I disagreed with him picking up those classes here and there—he's busy enough already—but what else could he do, when the dean practically begged him? And I suppose the investment paid off, since that's how he found Cade."

"Right." I grasp for a topic of conversation away from Cade, away from anything that might hint I know more about him than I should if he's only my boss, and say, "Did Bridger meet Colleen at law school?"

Sylvie Holcombe scoffs and waves a hand. "Heavens, no," she says. "The only reason Colleen would have gone to law school is to find a husband. As it is, she didn't have to, not when her best friend was Bridger's younger sister."

Lying is the least of my sins these days, and yet I still pray silently for forgiveness when I say, "I didn't know you had a daughter."

Her jaw tightens and she looks away. "Vanessa. She . . . passed away. Cancer, about eighteen months ago."

"Oh, I'm so sorry," I manage to say.

"It's a terrible thing, burying your daughter. It's like losing the best piece of yourself," she says, and I almost flinch at the second reminder of Lupita Morales, at how closely Sylvie Holcombe's words mirror the woman I met with yesterday. "And Kirby—he's struggled with her loss—the family's had a lot to deal with."

"I didn't know Kirby was your son-in-law," I say. "He and Bridger have been close most of their lives, then?"

"Since preschool." She glances at me from the corner of her eye, slyness wreathing her mouth. "But that's another story."

I connect the dots in my head. There's no way Kirby can't know about Bridger's relationship with Araceli, or the possibility there was a child born—and if Kirby knows, then there's a good chance Colleen knows, too.

She sniffs and straightens in her seat. "But you're not from Dallas, are you?"

"No, ma'am," I say. "The Piney Woods."

"I suppose it's no wonder you joined the military," she says. "You seem to have turned out well enough, though, and that's a lovely dress. I can't wait to introduce you to everyone."

I make myself smile. "I can't wait, either."

*　*　*

The country club windows flood the dining room with light and a heavy odor of flowery perfume hangs in the air.

I pick at the beef Wellington and mashed potatoes, hoping the salt will ease my stomach.

The speaker drones on and I sit—back straight, not touching the chair, ankles crossed, hands folded on top of the napkin in my lap. I hope that this somehow makes up for all the times I've made my grandmothers—who would be thrilled to know I sit next to Sylvie Holcombe at the Dallas Country Club—roll in their graves lately.

Sylvie, with her seersucker pantsuit and silver hair coiled in an elaborate coif, who likely had her debutante ball about the same time my mother's mother was picking cotton or my father's mother was working as the elevator girl at the

Five & Dime, where she met the handsome Tejano soldier in his uniform, whom she would elope with over the objections of both their families.

I bite the inside of my lower lip to keep from yawning and count the seconds until I'm back at the office.

Eventually, the Lincoln Town Car returns us to the curb outside Holcombe & Donaldson and I say, "Thank you for a lovely lunch."

Sylvie says, "We'll do it again next month."

I groan inwardly but force a smile, knowing this isn't an invitation I can refuse offhand. "I can't wait."

Bear opens my car door and hands me out of the car, leaning in close to say, "You don't look like you feel well, ma'am. Why don't I walk you up?"

I look for Rafi in the place where I last saw him, but he's nowhere to be found. My head pounds and my stomach somersaults, yet I manage to say, "I'm fine. And you shouldn't leave Mrs. Holcombe."

"If you're sure," he says, a line of concern creasing his forehead.

"Thanks," I say.

I hurry through the heavy doors and relish the cold blast of air conditioning. Once safe from view in the elevator, I rest against the wall and close my eyes for the all-too-brief ride upstairs.

Stu looks up as I enter our section. "So, how was she?"

I sit and allow myself the luxury of leaning back into the chair. "As delightful as ever."

"You have to say that," he grumbles. "She doesn't try and run *your* life, does she? Was there an open bar at the country club at least?"

"It's too early for that," I say. "Anyway, you're twenty-six years old. Can't you afford your own drinks at the country club?"

"Reagan," Evangeline mutters, just loud enough for me to hear. "You don't look good. Are you all right?"

"The room was just stuffy." I fan myself with one hand and take another deep breath. "I'll drink some more water and be fine."

I unlock my computer and stare at my email without seeing it, making a mental list of the items to discuss with Cade as soon as we get a chance to talk.

The black Lincoln Town Car.

The firm's history.

The relationships between Bridger, Colleen, Kirby, and Sylvie, although surely Cade knows all this; he's spent the last decade of his life in and out of the Holcombe house.

I play with my pen, puzzling out how to approach Miller and ask him about Heather's pregnancy.

"Now that you're back, I'll head to lunch," Evangeline says.

"Sure," I say.

Evangeline grabs her purse and stands but doesn't move.

I look up from my computer as Bridger opens the door to our section, two men at his heels. One wears a police uniform with a gold star on each side of his shirt collar. The other is dressed in a suit, but not a department store off-the-rack special like Miller's is, and his shoes don't show the same level of use.

Bridger doesn't even look at his son. He only asks, "He in?"

Evangeline presses her lips together so tightly they almost disappear. "Yes, sir. If you'll wait one second—"

"No need," Bridger says, brushing past me to open Cade's office door. "Evangeline, you and Reagan join us. These gentlemen would like a word."

Evangeline and I exchange a hasty glance and follow them into Cade's office. Whoever these men are, they're important enough to haul Bridger in to question the three of us, and apparently are used to getting answers.

"Get the door, Reagan," Bridger says.

I turn and reach for the doorknob.

Stu's gaze meets mine.

He smirks.

I look away and shut the door.

Cade sits at the large conference table surrounded by old notebooks and what appears to be textbooks, sleeves rolled to his elbows.

He clears his throat. "Evangeline, Reagan, this is the district attorney and the Dallas Criminal Investigations Unit commander."

The district attorney says, "We understand someone in this office may have spoken to a woman named Heather Hudson shortly before she died."

Evangeline frowns, her head tilted to one side. "That name isn't familiar. Was she a client?"

"No," the district attorney says.

The police commander rakes me and Evangeline with a glare. "She was seen on this floor, exiting the elevator. You couldn't miss her, not with that pink hair."

"Oh, her." I try to swallow, but my mouth and throat are dry. "She asked to see Cade, but he wasn't in, and she wouldn't give her name or a reason. When I tried to get more information, she left."

The district attorney exchanges a look with the police commander. "You followed?"

Cade wouldn't ask a question he doesn't know an answer to, not in a situation like this, and so I can only assume the district attorney must already know I did.

"I lost her in the crowd," I say. "Late Friday lunch rush."

The police commander narrows his gaze, as though he's not quite sure he believes me. "And you came straight back?"

"I didn't want to leave Evangeline alone too long," I say. "I'm sure the building's security cameras are time-stamped."

"You didn't see anything interesting? Stop to talk to anyone?" he asks. "Powder your nose?"

It's all I can do not to roll my eyes. "Unfortunately, that day I left my compact in my other purse."

His lip curls into a sneer. "I don't like your tone, young lady—"

"Captain," Cade says. "Reagan's a captain in the military. And she's answered your questions."

Bridger stares hard at Cade, hands on his hips. "If you need anything else, Reagan will make herself available."

Cade stands, folding his arms across his chest. "I don't care for the implication that my staff—"

"We're not implying anything," the district attorney says. "What she says lines up with the lobby security camera footage we've reviewed, and we appreciate your cooperation."

Cade nods. "If you should have any additional questions, please let me know."

"I think we're good," the district attorney says, and glances to the police commander. "Do you need anything else?"

He shakes his head. "Oh, no, I'm sure this office will cooperate fully. A law firm of this caliber with years of good standing in the community—you wouldn't want it to appear otherwise, right?"

Bridger's posture visibly stiffens. "Of course," he says, and nods to Evangeline. "Please see our guests out. Get the door as you leave."

The door closes and the sounds of footsteps fade. I can't help but think how nice it would be to chug the bottle of water on Cade's desk and then lie on his couch and sleep the rest of the day.

But Bridger puffs himself up and looks from Cade to me and back to Cade. He pulls out a chair and sits, scowling at both of us. "Let me tell you how this office will proceed from here forward."

I FIND A POINT on Cade's wall and stare at it, hoping it will provide some equilibrium and distract me from the beef Wellington churning in my stomach.

Cade shifts his weight from foot to foot, like he's back in the pocket, football in hand, wanting to move but not having the space.

Bridger leans back in the chair, fingers tapping the armrests.

The silence blankets us, suffocating, warming the room, and I don't let myself inhale as deep as I want, because I worry that I'll gulp the air and make Bridger even more suspicious.

"I don't know what the hell you two are up to," he says.

I brace myself for the next statement, that he's discovered our relationship—Stu, maybe? Have we been too careless?—and prepare to take the fall for Cade.

I can't let him lose his partnership over us.

I'll think of something—I always have before—but this is Cade's dream.

"Whatever it is, it stops now," Bridger says. "This firm won't be complicit in obstructing justice or interfering with a police investigation. Whatever adversarial relationship you have with the district attorney's staff and the police department stays in the courtroom, understand?"

"Yes, sir," Cade says.

"Because there will be consequences if I catch you two having something to do with what was implied today," Bridger says. "Son, you know better. You wouldn't be here if you weren't ambitious and hustled like hell, but you need to channel that the right way. Getting your name highlighted like this to the DA's office isn't it."

"Of course," Cade says.

"And as for you," Bridger says, turning in my direction, "you haven't even gotten your private investigator license yet. So I expect you to make damn sure you're in your lane and everything is by the book. You understand?"

Cade's grip tightens ever so slightly on the back of the chair.

"Yes, sir," I say because there's really nothing else to say at this point.

"Good," Bridger says with a smile that is more of a warning. "We're all in agreement that the police will do their job, the DA's office will do their job, and this office will do the job it's hired to do."

"Just like always," Cade says.

"Just like always," Bridger echoes and picks up one of the books on Cade's table. He frowns and stands, flips through an open notebook, and examines a stack of papers. "This is a syllabus for one of my classes when I was guest lecturing."

"Yes, sir," Cade says.

Bridger chuckles, shuffling the pages. "Who knew you actually took notes? I was always convinced you were only in that class because of that pretty redhead, and she had something to do with your grades. Where'd she end up, anyway?"

"Umm, U.S. Attorney's office," Cade says, and catching my upraised eyebrow, he adds quickly, "East Coast somewhere."

"There a particular reason for this trip down memory lane?" Bridger rises, his head cocked to one side. "Seems an odd way to pass the time on a Wednesday afternoon, especially after our conversation yesterday."

My heart sinks. How in the world can Cade possibly explain that we're trying to find Bridger's will or any hint of what it might entail in old lecture notes?

Cade shrugs and shoves his hands into his pockets. "I'm not supposed to say anything. But the bar association is planning a roast—"

"A roast?" Bridger grins. "They only do that if there's an award involved."

"You didn't hear it from me," Cade says.

"Well, you're going a helluva ways back," Bridger says, but he's laughing now, and any threat of danger has passed.

Cade grins. "You know me. Leave no stone unturned, right?"

"I've always appreciated your thoroughness," Bridger says. He then turns to me, pats my shoulder, and says, "And I'll bet you made a wonderful impression at lunch today. Did you have a good time?"

"Lovely," I say.

His gaze drifts down my body and back up, and when we make eye contact, he winks. "Hell, sweetheart, if you're gonna wear dresses like that when the firm sends you out on business, maybe we need to start doing that more often."

Behind Bridger, Cade straightens. His jaw drops.

Bile scorches the back of my throat, but I choke it down and force myself to smile and say, "Thank you," because I know that's what's expected, even though what I really want is to tell Bridger where, exactly, he can stick that leering look on his face.

"We're so lucky to have her, aren't we, Cade?" Bridger asks but doesn't look away from me.

Cade catches my low wave-off that signals *I'll handle this*, and mutters, "Very."

"Well, I'll let you two get back to work," he says and rubs my shoulder one more time. "Come by my office later, and we can talk about career opportunities. I think you'll be quite the asset for the firm and its public image."

The door clicks behind me.

"Reag," Cade whispers and reaches for me.

I press a hand to my mouth and bolt for the bathroom, shut the pocket door, and barely make it to the toilet in time.

Cade waits a few minutes to slide the door open and sit next to where I huddle on the floor, expensive stilettos kicked to the side, and the jacket for my dress flung over the top of the shower. "There's mouthwash in the cabinet."

"I found it," I say.

He puts an arm around my shoulders and pulls me close, kissing the top of my head. "The dress does look nice."

The memory of Bridger's leer and the feel of his hand on my shoulder surfaces.

I put my forehead on my knees and try to think of anything else.

Cade says, "I'm sorry. I shouldn't have—I probably sounded like—"

"No," I say. "It's fine. You're not him."

"I can't believe he'd be that open about that," Cade says. "I was standing right there."

I almost point out what could have happened had he not been there and what has likely happened to other women at the firm, but I decide that will only nag at him more. "Guess that prenuptial doesn't apply to him?"

"Still trying to track that down," Cade says. "It's now surprisingly more difficult to locate than I thought."

I squeeze my eyes shut. "I should go. Stu will be suspicious."

"I sent him to grab coffee," Cade says. "But I do think you should go home."

"I can't," I say. "How will that look?"

"Like you took a sick day," he says. "Like maybe lunch didn't sit well?"

"I'm fine, really," I say, but my voice sounds so fragile I don't even believe it myself. "I just need some water. I can't leave Evangeline with Stu all afternoon; she hates working with him."

"Babe, come on," he says. "I'll cover for you here. I can deal with Stu."

I shake my head. "What if—"

"What if you go rest?" he interrupts. "I'll text Rafi and have him walk you home."

A chance to take a cool shower, slip into one of Cade's old T-shirts, and stretch out and nap in our bed holds some appeal, and so I nod.

"Reag," he says. "You shouldn't be this sick from a hangover. Do you think—"

"What?" I raise my head to glower at him. "I'm not pregnant."

"Who said anything about that?" he asks. "I was going to suggest maybe someone slipped something in your drink, but since you suggested that . . . ?"

"I'm not pregnant," I insist, and let him help me stand. "And I'd know if I was doped. It's just a bad hangover, and beef Wellington with mashed potatoes and brown gravy was probably too ambitious."

"Probably," he says.

I lean into his arm around me, and we walk—slowly— back into his office. "I'll take the rest of the day, but when you get home tonight, we're talking about what happened at lunch yesterday."

He tweaks my braid. "That will involve you telling me about lunch today."

"That can be arranged," I say.

He smiles and draws me into a hug, holding me close. "Get some rest. It sounds like we have a lot to talk about."

His heartbeat in my ear and the smell of his cologne relax me until he laughs, and I realize I've leaned so far into him that he's supporting all my weight.

"You're exhausted," he says and kisses the top of my head. "Go home."

I stop at my desk long enough to log off my computer and grab my purse. Rafi waits in the shade of the oak trees, his jaw set and his arms across his chest.

"This isn't my idea," I say. "This is Cade's idea."

"Don't care about that," he says. "Whose car was it that you got into for lunch?"

"It belongs to the Holcombe family," I say. "I know, it looks like that car you saw, like the car that other man said—"

"Not just that," he says. "I think that driver was the man in the hoodie. The guy who broke into the apartment. The license plate matched what I remember from Sunday, too."

I swallow hard and press the back of my hand to my mouth.

A sense of a second violation stirs, that it wasn't some stranger who attacked me and then went through our things, who swiped my dog tags and Cade's class ring and rearranged things in our work desks. It was Bear, who works for the Holcombes and probably reported everything back to Bridger.

If Bear is the man in the hoodie, the Holcombes know Cade and I live together. That means Bridger knew exactly what he was doing with that little scene in Cade's office earlier.

"You don't look so good," Rafi says.

"I don't feel so good, either," I say.

"I can call an Uber," he says.

"No." I trudge on, wishing my feet moved as fast as the thoughts racing through my head, the thoughts that Bridger knows everything so he'll probably wait for the opportune time to fire Cade and me. "It's only a few blocks. By the time the Uber picks us up, we could be there. You'll go back and keep an eye on Cade, won't you?"

"Cade asked me to stay with you," he says. "What are we gonna do about that man in the Lincoln?"

"I don't know," I say.

"That man, he works for Cade's boss," Rafi says. "You two aren't gonna be able to keep working there."

Cade's advancement to named partner slips further away with every click of my heels on the pavement, every second that the realization that Bridger knows sinks deeper, that Bridger might have sent Bear to scare me and to break into our apartment, and now today . . .

My head throbs.

"Cade and I'll figure something out," I say.

Rafi and I don't speak the rest of the way to the apartment.

CHAPTER

22

THE EARLY EVENING sun pries fingers around the closed curtains so streaks of light dance across the ceiling when I wake, but all I can think about still is Bridger's hand on my shoulder and the invitation to his office.

Bridger, who is more involved in this than we think, who knows about us.

I untangle myself from the sheets and roll over to reach for my phone, dialing Cade's number, whispering to myself, "Pick up, damn it."

But his voice mail answers, and I listen to the sound of his voice that is reassurance enough in its own way.

A text message pops up from Cade almost immediately. IN A MEETING I FORGOT I HAD. HOPE YOU GOT SOME REST. EAT WITHOUT ME.

I smile and text back, YOU AREN'T GETTING OUT OF OUR DISCUSSION.

WOULDN'T DREAM OF IT. FEEL BETTER? he replies.

YES, I text. EVERYTHING QUIET?

BELIEVE IT OR NOT, E AND I SURVIVED WITHOUT YOU, he sends. WE'LL TALK TONIGHT. LOVE YOU.

I smile and send back, LYT, and then a second text, BE
CAREFUL.

ALWAYS, he replies.

I hug his pillow to myself, breathe a deep whiff of his
cologne, and remind myself that we'll figure something
out.

We have to.

In the meantime . . .

I find Miller's number in my phone and press the call
button. It rings four times before his voice mail answers.

"Hey, gimme a call when you get a chance—I need to
ask you something," I say, but hang up before I tell him
what a dick he is for not warning me that the unit commander and district attorney were putting in an unan-
nounced appearance at the firm today.

A text message from him almost immediately lights up
my screen. I CAN'T TALK TO YOU.

CAN'T OR WON'T? I type back.

Nothing.

YOU COULD HAVE GIVEN ME A HEADS UP YOUR BOSS WAS
SHOWING UP AT THE FIRM TODAY, I send.

SORRY, he responds.

I type, WAS HEATHER HUDSON PREGNANT? and hit
send before I talk myself out of it.

He doesn't reply.

I flop back in the bed and stare at the ceiling, rub a hand
over my eyes, and smooth the tendrils around the front of
my face that worked their way free of my braid.

My phone chimes and I grab it without sitting up.

A single blue heart emoji.

A boy.

I sit up enough to lean against the headboard and mull
over the possibilities, but nothing makes any sense.

In a few months, Bridger Holcombe should have been a
grandfather, with proof that he had what my granny would

label a "youthful indiscretion" with the housekeeper's daughter.

Youthful indiscretions are hardly fatal to men, though.

Especially not one nearly thirty-five years ago, and especially not to a Highland Park Holcombe.

Can the baby of a Deep Ellum bartender really have posed such a threat?

Someone knocks on the apartment's main door, but I don't move because Rafi is here, and no one ever comes to see me and Cade anyway.

The front door opens. Muffled voices speak on the other side of the wall and the door closes again.

A soft tap sounds on the bedroom door. "Reagan," Rafi says, his voice low. "Cade sent dinner. Why don't you come try and eat?"

"I'll be right there," I say and throw on a bra under Cade's T-shirt that hangs halfway to my knees and grab a pair of my pajama pants.

In the kitchen, a large paper sack and a drink carrier with two plastic cups full of tea sit on the counter. "You look like you got some rest," Rafi says.

"I think I finally slept the last of it off," I say.

"Cade said you'd be hungry," he says. "And to remind you that you can't just drink sweet tea."

Somehow, even absent, Cade still manages to look out for me.

A week ago, this might have felt stifling.

Today, it feels like love.

"I'll finish the Gatorade too, I promise." I gulp a long swig of tea.

There's a chicken noodle soup and a grilled cheese for me and a sandwich with potato chips for Rafi. We eat on the couch, a baseball game playing on the television, but my mind roams to Cade's office, searching for him and some assurance that he's safe.

"Man." Rafi shakes his head beside me. "You remember when the Rangers were actually good?"

"But if the Astros and Rangers are both good at the same time, it upsets the balance of the universe," I say. "And there's always hockey season to look forward to, I guess."

"Not Dem Boys?" he asks.

I laugh. "Can't grow up in East Texas without them and the Texans, but I watch a lot more college football. I imagine Cade will, too."

"So you haven't been together that long?" he asks. "I thought so, since this place is all him and nothing of yours, but—"

"No," I say. "And obviously work complicates it."

He doesn't ask me to elaborate, and I'm grateful; I'm tired of thinking about the firm and Cade's and my relationship. And thanks to Rafi's military experience and the high rate of dual-military relationships within units, he likely recognizes some of the complications anyway.

He munches on a potato chip. "Speaking of work, who's that Evangeline in your office?"

"Cade's paralegal." I don't mention she's become my closest friend besides Cade, or how much I treasure the openness of her smile, the song she half hums when she loses herself in her work, or how she always seems to know just what to do. Nor do I explain that it was her steadiness in those first weeks I was in Cade's office that grounded me and let me know I had nothing to be anxious about.

"She gonna be in any trouble?" he asks.

"We're trying to keep her out of everything as much as possible," I say.

Rafi cracks a smile. "About the two of you, or about whatever mess you're involved in with his boss?"

"She found out about the first so there's a good chance she knows about the other," I say. "Why? You want to go babysit her too?"

His smile spreads to a grin and he laughs under his breath. "I wouldn't turn down an opportunity to hang around."

The crack of a bat draws our attention back to the television screen, and we finish our meals. I browse apartment listings and search Heather Hudson's social media, sifting through bread crumbs of information here and there and making a list of things that might prove useful. Pictures of her and a man named Marcos Escobedo crop up almost as frequently as the photos of her and Cesar, and the familiarity of the name tickles my memory.

A photo of the three of them outside a bar pops up, a neon yellow sun and white stars glowing, and I remember Lupita Morales saying Marcos was the co-manager with Cesar.

Marcos may know something.

I dig through his social media, run a web search to find his cell phone number, reverse search that number to a classified ad, and then track down his apartment address. He may remember me from Tuesday morning at the bar with Cade, but if he sees me somewhere he isn't expecting me, perhaps he won't make that connection.

I scroll back through the recent locations he tagged in his check-ins. The bar features heavily in the list, but there is also a coffee shop, a gym, and a park.

A public location will be best.

He checks into the coffee shop at roughly the same time every day, and I open a new memo on my cell phone and make a note of the address.

Rafi sits loosely curled in a corner of the couch, head propped in one hand, half dozing.

"Hey," I say. "Did that guy I sent you to yesterday give you any info on résumé writing or job searching?"

He opens his eyes, fully alert in that manner every military member who operates in a high-stress career field seems to innately acquire. "Nah, I remember hearing about it in the Army Transition Assistance Program a few years ago, though. Didn't really pay attention, because I knew I was getting out with bad paper. What was the point?"

I tap my fingers on the arm of the couch. "We should work on that."

"Reagan." He scoffs and shakes his head. "If I put my military experience on a résumé, someone's gonna ask about my discharge status."

"Maybe." I open a new document on my laptop and begin formatting it. "If they ask, you explain it like you explained it to Cade and me and mention it's on appeal."

"But then they might think I'm just one more crazy combat vet," he says. "You see how that could be a risk, don't you? We can't all be Air Force with our clean sheets, three hot meals a day, and perfect Wi-Fi connection."

And because I know he's only teasing, I say, "That Wi-Fi connection was shit. Too many guys downloading porn on the VPN."

He chuckles. "Guess some things about the military are universal."

"Let's just figure out what sort of job you'd like first," I say. "And we'll tailor a résumé to that."

He strokes his goatee and leans forward, something almost like hope shining on his face. "Maybe you and Cade need a driver like that guy today. You don't even like to drive, and that way he always knows what you're up to."

I laugh. "You take that up with Cade."

"Maybe I will," he says.

I open a new document on my laptop and format it for his résumé so we can work.

*　*　*

It's after eight when Cade enters the apartment, juggling his attaché case, his suit coat, his keys, and a vase brimming with white lilies.

Rafi stands. "I see this is my exit cue," and over his shoulder, he says to me, "Thanks for the résumé help."

"See you tomorrow, I guess." I laugh.

"Let me know when you're ready to go to work." He puts a forefinger to his temple as if he's tipping an imaginary hat. "Y'all have a good night."

The door closes and I take the flowers from Cade to place them in the middle of the small dining table, and admire them.

"Do you like them?" he asks, suddenly sounding shy, and kisses me. "They reminded me of last weekend at the winery, and so—"

"They're perfect," I say. "Did you eat dinner?"

He deposits his keys on the counter and his attaché case on a bar stool. "At the meeting."

I hear more of the Smoky Mountains in his voice tonight, the soft elongated twang he's normally so careful to hide that I know by now he only lets loose when he thinks it gives him an advantage or has had one too many drinks. He's sober, but I know he's exhausted by the slowness of his movements as he unbuttons his dress shirt and the heaviness with which he drops onto the couch.

A twinge of guilt stirs.

This is my fault, like the conversation we must eventually have about Bridger, and because I don't want to face my culpability—not yet—in complicating Cade's life two evenings in a row, I ask, "Do you want a drink?"

"No, I'm good." He rubs the side of his face and reaches for me, pulling me onto his lap. "You look comfy."

I watch his face by the lamp light. "I was looking at apartments."

This at least elicits a grin. "Yeah?"

I play with his watch, noting the second hand's smooth sweep around the dial. "There are some two bedrooms available in this building, but I couldn't tell if they were on this side."

"I'll send an email tomorrow," he says but doesn't quite manage to stifle a yawn.

I stand and tug him to his feet. "Let's go to bed."

He doesn't argue, just grabs his clothes from the bar stool and follows me to the bedroom. It's not even eight thirty on a Wednesday night, but we go through our usual nightly routine as if it's ten. By the time I come out of the bathroom, he's nestled under the covers with his eyes closed. Part of me is relieved that we can just sleep without discussing the Holcombes.

I turn off the lamp in the living room, double-check that the door is locked, and climb into bed beside him.

He flings an arm across me as soon as I lie down and holds me close. "I love you," he says and kisses me.

"I love you too," I say and wait for him to grow still and heavy.

But he sighs after a moment and nuzzles my neck. "We have to talk."

"And we will." I kiss the top of his head and comb a hand through his damp hair. "Tomorrow. When you're rested."

He doesn't say anything, and I hope he's asleep, that we can wait until daylight to discuss all this.

Because maybe daylight will put enough distance between the sensation of Bridger's hand on me and Rafi's revelation that he recognizes Bear as the man who tried to choke me on the Katy Trail and went through our apartment.

Cade won't like any of this and I know it.

He stirs, as if he knows my plan, and leans up on one elbow. "Tomorrow won't change anything."

"I just think we're both very tired," I say.

"Reag." He plays with my fingers like he would with his watch if he still wore one, and I realize he doesn't like what he's about to say. "I think it's time we go to your friend at the department and turn over everything we know or think we know, and let the cops sort it out."

I recoil and scramble up in the bed. "What? No. Absolutely not."

"Come on now." His voice possesses a faint wheedling tone, like I'm a child he's indulged but will soon grow exasperated with. "After that scene in the office today, and then Rafi texting me about the car—"

"He oughtn't have done that." I chew on the edge of a fingernail. "I told him I'd tell you."

He tugs my hand back to him. "Except you wouldn't have. Not tonight, and don't you tell me otherwise, because we both know that's a damn lie."

"All right," I say. "Maybe I wouldn't have, but it's only because you might have reacted just like this."

"Reagan." He sighs and sits up beside me. "This is a law enforcement issue. As Bridger pointed out today, you don't even have your private investigator's license—"

"I will in a few more months," I say.

"We're in over our heads," he says. "You do realize that, don't you? Let's give this to the cops—"

"Do you know what'll happen if we turn this over to the cops?" I interrupt.

"Sure," he says. "I think you've made a pretty good argument that this is somehow connected to the Holcombe family, so maybe they'll get off their asses and ask Bridger some questions."

I scoff. "In the unlikely occurrence that they decide this is all more than coincidental and invite Bridger to the station to answer some questions—or more plausibly, show up at the office to check the box—what do you think Bridger'll do?"

He releases my hands and doesn't answer.

"Bridger will tell them he wants his lawyer present for any questions," I say. "And he'll turn to his in-house criminal defense attorney, his own little fixer that he's groomed since law school."

"Reag—"

"You'll bury the cops and the district attorney's office in paperwork," I say. "And he'll get off, and Lupita Morales will never know what happened to her grandson, because no one gives enough of a damn to go after the truth. Not really, not if it involves a Hol—"

"Goddamn it, Reagan," Cade cuts in.

The headboard scrapes against the wall as he launches himself out of bed.

"Tell me where I'm wrong then," I say. "You owe Bridger Holcombe everything, and you won't risk becoming a named partner—"

"I'm risking it now, aren't I?" he asks. "Do you even give a damn about that?"

"A man is dead, Cade," I say. "A woman. Their child."

"And I'm sorry," he says. "But I can't bring them back. This ends now."

"Bridger will be so proud," I say.

He snatches his pillow from his side of the bed. "I'm too tired to listen to this bullshit," he says on his way out the bedroom. "We'll talk about this in the morning when you can be reasonable."

"Fuck you," I say. "I'm being plenty reasonable. I'm just not bought and paid for, and I'll be damned if I let another man get off because of who he is and who his friends are."

Cade creeps back across the bedroom door threshold, his pillow clutched to his chest. "Another man?" he asks. "What man?"

"It's nothing." I step out of bed and into the closet, shoving my work clothes aside so hard the hangers screech and a dress falls to the floor. "Go to bed. It's your bed, and it's stupid to sleep on the couch in your own apartment. I'll go back to mine—"

"No," he says. "No, that's not the point of this, Reag."

I slam a duffel bag onto the floor. "Then please tell me what the fucking point is."

"I was trying to give us space," he says. "You were right. We're tired."

My shoes go into the bag first, just like they taught us in boot camp, but I leave behind the Louboutins and the Jimmy Choos, and try not to think of what will happen to them once I'm gone.

I wipe my nose with the back of my hand, ignoring the tears pricking my eyes.

"You were right." I toss my running clothes in next, one pair of leggings and a tank top short. "Morning won't change any of this."

And I brace myself for his agreement, that I should just go, that maybe this—everything since April, maybe since March—is a mistake, and we've run our course.

But instead, I feel him behind me, his hands on my shoulders, drawing me back against himself. His voice is a low murmur in my ear. "You weren't talking about any of the firm's clients."

This isn't a question, but he's too close and my emotions too raw for this conversation right now, and so I steady my tone as much as possible to say, "Oh, you read minds now, Counselor?"

"Damn it, Reagan, enough."

He turns me to him, cradles my face in his hands, and kisses me. I know then I won't leave, that I can't just walk out that door and close this chapter of my life, because he's like a drug burning hot through every inch of my body.

I don't just want him. I've allowed myself to need him. Now I crave him and hope his presence and the sensation of his touch and his kisses can overwhelm me, drown me into nothingness, and let me lose myself in him until I wash up on the shores of reality—gasping, disoriented, and grateful to be alive.

I don't fight him when he picks me up, and I don't fight him when he carries me to bed.

"Now," he says, his cheek against mine. "The truth."

I shake my head and try to pull away, but he's stronger than me.

"Cade," I whisper.

His fingers tangle in my hair and trace a tear down my face. "Please."

I squeeze my eyes shut and ground myself here, in this moment, with him.

Cade's bedroom, Cade's bed, Cade's fingers tracing my tattoo down my spine, Cade's heartbeat in my ear, Cade's cologne I smell.

Safety.

"When I was a cadet . . ." I make myself take a deep breath and nestle closer into Cade. "I went to a party I shouldn't have been at. The cadet wing commander was there. I had too much to drink and woke up with him on top of me. He told me that he'd take care of my career if I'd . . . just go along. But then I puked on him."

Cade's arms tighten around me. "So he got what he deserved. Did you report it?"

I shake my head. "I couldn't. I was underage. It would have been my scholarship, and I'd never have been commissioned—"

"Oh," Cade says.

"When our paths crossed again, after we were both active duty, he told me we could make a better arrangement if he knew I'd learned to hold my liquor. I told him I'd pass. And he made my life hell for the rest of that deployment."

Cade's fingers brush my back. "The tattoo. Everything you needed, huh?"

I nod.

"I thought," Cade says and sighs. "I thought that there was a reporting process in place. That those things didn't happen anymore."

"If they don't get reported, then they don't happen," I say. "Isn't that how it works?"

"So he's why you left the military then?" he asks.

I swallow hard. "Ultimately. Especially once he got stationed at my base and I had to brief him at least once a week."

He draws back, almost out of my embrace. "Reag? I don't remind you of—"

"No," I say. "But today, in the office . . ."

"Oh," he says and hugs me close. "Shit."

"He knows," I whisper. "Cade, if Rafi is right, if that car he saw is the one that belongs to the Holcombes, and if Bear is the one behind the attack, Bridger already knows about us."

"Then maybe today in the office was just to see how we would react," Cade says. "I mean, why else would he do that?"

"Insurance," I say. "Just like leaving things from the apartment in the office. He wants us to know he knows, and we can't stop him."

Bridger knows how ambitious Cade is and must know Cade wants to be a named partner. Our relationship will be a piece of information he holds over Cade, just like that little tidbit about me drinking underage at that party kept my mouth shut. Bridger will use that information any time he needs Cade's agreement—whether it's in a meeting of all the partners or if Bridger needs a defense attorney for a murder charge.

"I promised you I'd take care of you, didn't I?" Cade asks. "Let me handle this."

"By going to the cops?" I ask.

"No," he says. "No, I don't think we can. I think you're right. We'll have to find some other way."

"Today Sylvie mentioned Kirby is—was—married to Bridger's sister," I say. "That they have been friends since preschool."

Cade yawns and lays me in bed before stretching out next to me. "Yeah, they go way back. It's caused some issues the last couple of years."

"Why?" I ask.

"Did their relationship come up at lunch today?" he asks.

"Sort of," I say. "Sylvie briefly mentioned Kirby was married to her daughter, and how long he and Bridger had been friends. So I don't see how Kirby doesn't know about Bridger and Araceli, or that there was a child."

"Bridger's sister, Vanessa," Cade says. "When she died, she reverted her share of the Holcombe money she inherited back to the family trust, with Bridger in charge of it. Kirby can't touch it. It's made things . . . uncomfortable at times. I think he had different expectations."

I almost feel sorry for Kirby, to lose his wife and then to discover that maybe she didn't trust him with her family's money or that he didn't belong, that he wasn't one of them, so he couldn't touch it.

But then who knows what their marriage was like?

Maybe even Bridger and Colleen's marriage . . .

"Did you find Bridger's prenuptial?" I ask. "Or his will?"

"I got tied up today. Tomorrow," he says, and rolls over in the bed to lay his head on my shoulder.

I rub his hair and kiss the top of his head. "You should sleep."

"Are you going to be okay with this?" he asks. "I know all this has to hit close to home, even beyond the military."

"What do you mean?" I ask.

"It hasn't escaped my notice that his last name is Morales," Cade says.

"It's complicated," I say.

"I like complicated things." He nuzzles into my neck and brushes a kiss there. "But that doesn't answer my question."

"He could be me," I say. "And he was all his grand-mother had left. The Holcombes ruined her family because they could, and no one will be held accountable. I guess I should be grateful that most people assume I'm white because it does make things easier and I don't put up with a lot of the same shit, but . . . I don't know. The things peo-ple say to you when they think you're white can sometimes sting just as bad, and then you either keep your mouth shut and feel like you're betraying your family, or you say some-thing and separate yourself."

"Like the military," Cade says.

"I just want to belong somewhere," I say.

He squeezes me close. "You belong here. With me."

His words wrap themselves around me, an embrace all of their own, and I squeeze my eyes shut so the sudden tears don't spill out.

"I like that," I manage to say.

He laces his fingers with mine. "I know we agreed not to talk about . . ."

"Before," I say. "I guess we're gonna need to rethink that, huh?"

"Yeah." He yawns again and kisses my fingers that curl around his. "Do you have any questions for me? About before?"

"Tomorrow," I say and try to think of how to ask him about the redhead in his law school class or whoever was in his bed prior to me.

Or if I even want to know the answer to either of those questions.

"Tomorrow," he says. "I love you."

"I love you too," I say. "Go to sleep."

I hold him close and stare at the ceiling while he grows still and heavy in my arms. I listen for the change in his breathing and then I let myself doze.

CADE BRUSHES A kiss on my cheek and whispers, "I'm heading to the gym," and I growl into my pillow.

He laughs and tickles my feet as he leaves.

I'm halfway through yoga when Cade returns. Cabinet doors open and shut, the refrigerator door jingles, and then he drops onto the couch.

"Now that I know what you're up to, I might start hanging out in the mornings," he says.

I scowl at him over my shoulder, and he lifts his protein shake to me in a mock toast.

I stretch into an up-dog position and ignore him, too relieved that a good night's sleep seems to have restored Cade to his usual self to be annoyed. He types on his phone, but I catch him watching me through the remainder of my workout.

He waits until I finish to ask, "Big plans today?"

"I thought I'd go talk to that guy Marcos, who co-managed the club with Cesar," I say.

He stands, brushes the lilies with his fingertips, and glances over at me. "Let me know what you hear. I'm planning to be in the office this morning, so I'll keep an eye on Stu."

"Do you think he knows anything?" I ask.

Cade rolls his eyes. "Ah, yes, if I'm going to mastermind a criminal operation, I'll definitely involve dumb frat boys who get so drunk over a four-day weekend they almost end up hospitalized."

I almost laugh. "You'll have to tell me sometime about college and law school. Especially that redhead."

"You know I'm a sucker for a redhead with a Texan accent," he says and steals a kiss.

"Cade." I turn to pour a cup of coffee into my protein shake and take a sip. "About the office."

"Yes, that." He slides his hands around my waist, tentative at first, like he's not sure how I'll react, and then draws me back against him to rest his chin on the top of my head. "Give me a chance to gauge the mood. I'll let you know something around lunch."

I almost point out to him that I can't stay away forever, that there will be tomorrow and next week and the week after that.

But I don't.

I'm too relieved that he understands, that maybe he shares my reluctance for me to return. I only say, "That's fine," and nestle there in his arms to finish my coffee.

"Are you okay with all this?" he asks and leans down to kiss my cheek. "Really?"

His concern doesn't feel as stifling as it might have two months ago; it's comforting that he cares, and maybe it makes me love him more, because I know he'll use my response to determine how we pursue this.

"I'm fine," I say.

"You'll tell me if you aren't?" he asks. "Promise?"

"I promise," I say.

"We'll get this right, Reag," he says and kisses me again.

Cade can fix anything, I remind myself. *He'll fix this.*

I slip free and run hot water in our cups. "Why don't you start the water in the shower? We'll have to hurry, so you can get to work . . ."

But he's already halfway to the bathroom, shedding his clothes.

I laugh and gather them all before following him.

*   *   *

The coffee shop is on a corner in Deep Ellum, not far from Club Saturnalia, so it makes perfect sense why Marcos would check in almost every morning. I compare our location and the club's location to where his apartment is and note the proximity. He's a creature of habit *and* convenience.

"So we just sit here and wait?" Rafi asks.

"He'll be here," I say and sip my latte, but its richness only reminds me that next week I need to start running again.

Maybe Cade will agree to run with me for a couple of weeks.

Just until everything is settled.

Rafi plays with his paper cup of coffee, black because that's how Rangers drink it, he says, and I wonder if he had breakfast.

"I'm getting a kolache," I say. "Do you want one? Or a breakfast burrito maybe? We can't just sit here, or it'll start looking suspicious."

"If they have a kolache with the jalapeño sausage and cheese," he says.

I order two of what would be Texas-sized pigs in a blanket anywhere else in the world and return to the table with them and a newspaper.

"I thought you were getting you something," he says.

I shrug. "I really wanted a chocolate croissant, but I already had a protein shake. And the latte. And . . ."

"And you're not running this week, but it doesn't kill you to allow your body a chance to heal," he says.

I ignore this and open the newspaper to the classifieds.

"Cade doesn't seem the type to give a damn here or there about a couple of pounds," Rafi says and pushes the kolaches to my side of the table. "If you don't get a chocolate croissant, I'm not eating these."

I frown and go back to the counter for a chocolate croissant, but I carry it to the table like a dragon with its gold.

Rafi smiles and unwraps the first kolache. "Cade played college football, didn't he?"

The croissant's flaky crust practically melts in my mouth, and I take a quick drink of my latte. "Mm-hmm."

Rafi eats a second bite and chews. "Why'd he quit?"

"Didn't get drafted by the pros," I say. "So law school."

"You don't just end up at SMU's law school. It's too expensive, and they don't let everyone in," he says. "You need a plan for that."

I lean back in my chair and pretend I've already thought this through, that Cade hasn't fooled me with how easy he makes everything look.

Because Rafi is right. Cade must have gone into the NFL combines knowing law school had to be a possibility; no one wings LSAT scores and grades and letters of recommendation on a spur-of-the-moment decision that qualifies for entrance to one of the Southern Ivies.

"You say I'm always thinking," I say. "Did you think I'd be with someone who isn't always thinking too?"

"That where he met his boss?" Rafi asks.

"Yeah," I say. "Back when he was guest lecturing a law school class or two every semester."

"And he just picked Cade out of the crowd?" Rafi asks.

"He offered Cade an internship," I say. "But Cade was already leaning toward criminal law, so Bridger introduced him to some people. Cade got some experience, and then came back to the firm as their in-house criminal defense guy and made partner last year."

Rafi nods and eats another bite. "Not easy being a king-slayer. Especially when the king you're taking out is who made you what you are."

"I know that," I say.

"Of course you do." Rafi sips his coffee, and our gazes meet over the top of his cup. "You're always thinking."

I crumple the croissant wrapper into a ball and resume looking through the classifieds. "Here's a job for a bouncer. You speak Spanish, right?"

"Better than you," Rafi says. "Which isn't saying much."

I ignore this. "You could do that at night and go to school during the day."

"Go to school for what?" he asks.

"I don't know, something besides being a bouncer," I say. "Once we get your discharge status changed, you'll be eligible for veterans' benefits and the GI Bill to pay for college, so you'll have options."

He doesn't say anything, and I drink my latte, frown at the classifieds, and listen to Luna Luna playing softly over the coffee shop's speakers.

"Maybe I work for Cade and go to paralegal school," he says. "Maybe there are other veterans that need legal help."

"There are plenty of those," I say. "But they don't pay much."

"Cade's firm has enough money," Rafi says. "They ought to be giving back to the community."

I raise my eyebrows and turn a newspaper page. "One would think."

"So it bothers you too, then," he says. "What he does."

I sigh. "Some of them are innocent."

"Some," he says. "But a lot of them, you know if they couldn't afford Cade, if they looked like me or their last name was Reyes, maybe they'd be punching a ticket to prison."

"Yeah." I play with the cup. "I've broached the subject with Cade a few times, that he could do wonders for some pro bono clients, but Bridger is adamantly against the idea."

Rafi scoffs. "I'll bet he is."

This, of course, could change if Bridger really is going to run for county judge, and I wonder if it might be a good time to revisit the idea with Cade. If nothing else, it would be great public relations for the firm.

The entrance bell jingles, jarring me from my thoughts. A man swaggers past our table, a pencil-thin mustache and goatee razored around his mouth, his black hair slicked back and the sides shaved. He's not much taller than I am, but his muscles bulge through his thin white T-shirt. He grins at the cashier and greets her by name, and she answers back with a cheerful, "Hey, Marcos. Your usual?"

"That's him," Rafi whispers. "How you want to play this?"

"Solo," I say. "You're along for the ride, remember? Look through the classifieds and see if there's anything you like."

"Reagan," he growls, but I walk away from the table and out of the café, dropping my cup and the paper wrapper in the trash.

Outside the air is still and muggy. I stroll as close to the buildings as I can, staying in shade as much as possible, both for coolness and concealment. The pistol in its holster is a welcome weight.

Deep Ellum at night may be a carnival for the senses, but during the early morning heat it's like the Vegas Strip without the crowds: forlorn and empty. Anything can still happen here, even in broad daylight, which means I need a location private enough for Marcos to talk to me, but public enough to keep him from doing anything stupid.

I find an alley along his likely route to the club and step far enough inside for him not to notice me as he approaches, but not so far that the smell of rotting garbage overwhelms me.

Footsteps pound the sidewalk, too loud for someone trying to conceal themselves.

I peer around the corner.

Marcos lopes toward me, holding a cup of coffee in one hand and a paper sack in the other.

I step out of the alley.

He smiles at me.

I smile back. "Hi, Marcos. I need to talk to you about Cesar Morales and Heather Hudson."

He freezes for half a second. He doesn't see Rafi rounding the corner behind him, and I pretend not to notice.

"I don't know you," Marcos says. "And I don't know what games you're playing, but I don't have to talk to you."

He turns to walk away and runs smack into Rafi, who only says, "I think the lady wants a word."

Marcos looks from Rafi to me and back to Rafi. "What is this, good cop, bad cop?"

"Sure," Rafi says. "But we're not the cops."

"Look," Marcos says. "I don't know anything. I didn't see anything. I'm just a coworker."

"Don't sell yourself short," I say. "You were friends with Heather. Good friends, by the looks of it, and good friends with Cesar, too. Now, we're not the cops, but we'd like to see whoever is responsible for their murders brought to justice. Wouldn't you?"

"Justice," Marcos scoffs and glances at Rafi. "You believe this bullshit?"

"Man, she's trying at least," Rafi says.

Marcos shoves past me anyway, muttering something under his breath in Spanish that causes Rafi to square up, but I snag Rafi's arm.

"You knew she was pregnant," I say to Marcos. "Did you know it was a boy?"

He stops.

For a second he just stands there, and I wait, keeping my hand on Rafi's arm to tell him to let this play out. I need Marcos to process what this might mean and for his conscience to get the better of him.

"How'd you know that?" Marcos asks and turns back toward me.

"I have friends too," I say.

Marcos jerks his head toward the alley, and the three of us step into the shelter of its ivy-lined red brick walls.

"So tell me how a bartender and a restaurant general manager scrape together enough cash to open up Club Saturnalia," I say.

"He had backing," Marcos says. "Deep pockets. I didn't ask where it came from. Heather—she'd waited tables for me, and she introduced us."

"But Cesar's backing knows your name now, don't they?" I ask. "Did they make promises that they'd keep funding the club if you kept your mouth shut?"

Marcos exhales slowly and looks away. "Maybe."

"Why would Cesar and Heather need to die?" I ask.

"Aw, shit." Marcos shakes his head and rubs the back of his neck, finally meeting my gaze. "If you don't know that, then you don't know nothing."

"I know that you found Cesar's body that morning," I say. "I know that witnesses say you two argued. Not to mention the dozens of pictures I could use to make the argument you and Heather had a relationship that's not so platonic. So if anyone's gonna get pinned for this, it'll be you, and soon you may want to tell someone about that black Lincoln Town Car—"

"You have no idea who you're dealing with," he says and walks away.

"I can help you," I call after him.

"I'll take my chances," Marcos says.

Rafi folds his arms across his chest. "So . . . that went well."

"Fuck you," I say and glare at the shrinking figure of the club manager. "He knows something. I just need to figure out what that is."

"He knows you don't know, and if you don't know, the cops won't know," he says.

"Well, someone knows something," I say. "Maybe we're just not asking the right questions."

"Or you're talking to the wrong people," Rafi says.

He's not wrong.

"All right," I say. "Let's go to the office."

"I thought you weren't supposed to be there," he says. "I thought Cade wanted you to lay low until he texted—"

"Well, he doesn't always get what he wants," I say. "You coming with me or not? Or maybe you don't want a chance to see Evangeline?"

"Right behind you," he says.

*   *   *

The law firm receptionist waggles the fingers of one hand as we pass by her desk but keeps talking into the phone. I give her a quick smile and heave open the glass door to Cade's section.

Stu slouches at his work but doesn't say anything.

Evangeline raises her gaze and straightens in her seat, a warning frown on her face.

"Hey," Rafi says to her.

"Hey, yourself," she says to him, and then lowers her voice almost to a whisper. "Cade said you weren't coming in just yet."

"I got bored," I say. "Is he in?"

She shakes her head. "Apparently some bigwig from Preston Hollow grabbed the wrong golf clubs this morning, and when he went back to his house, his business partner's car was in the driveway, and his business partner was—"

"Parking in the wife's driveway?" Rafi says.

"I think we all got there," I say. "So murder or manslaughter or—"

"Cade's sorting that out," she says.

"Reporters involved?" I ask.

She smiles. "Work your magic and see what bread crumbs you pick up."

"What I don't understand," Stu says, "is why the hell wouldn't he just go straight to a divorce attorney? Why risk your business and prison for two people who obviously don't give a damn?"

"You're cute, kid," Rafi says. "How old are you?"

Stu glowers at Rafi. "Old enough."

"Rafi, this is Stu Holcombe," I say, knowing the Ranger will catch the implication. "Stu, this is Rafi Velasquez. He's helping me and Cade on something."

"Hmm," Stu says.

And because I feel Stu's questions coming as to what, exactly, Rafi might be helping with, I say, "You're right, there's probably a prenuptial clause for cheating—"

"Of course there's a prenuptial with a clause for cheating," Stu says and leans back in his seat with his fingers laced behind his head. "Even my parents' prenuptial has that. Since my father's will has this proviso about everything going to the firstborn son, there's also a clause in there about what might happen if my mother had children born out of wedlock."

I stare at my computer screen and make myself keep typing. "Your mother, but not your father? That's some sexist bullshit."

"It *is* Holcombe money, after all," Stu says. "Do you think my mother does anything besides spray tan, Botox, and get sloshed by the pool?"

"I guess it's a good thing you're your father's only son, then, isn't it?" I ask.

"I guess." His smirk slouches into something that's almost a pout. "Only I have to be thirty to even access the trust or inherit. Some stupid family tradition my great-grandfather started. If anything happened to dear ol' Dad before then, I'd have to run everything through the executor he appointed in his will."

"Poor baby," I make myself say, even as my mind races.

Stu is only twenty-six, he told me that the first day in the elevator. Four years away from accessing his trust or being able to inherit everything, but Cesar, at thirty-four . . .

"I wonder if that prenuptial had any clauses about him cheating," Rafi says as if he knows what I'm doing, and maybe by now he does. "That woman could have felt like she had no other recourse, because if she divorced him, she would've lost everything."

"There's usually a clause both ways," I say. "Of course, Stu's the one who's about to be a third-year. And it sounds like his parents have a pretty airtight prenup."

"Legendary," Stu says, grinning. "Somehow, the old man worked it around so if she initiates a divorce, regardless of the reason, she only gets half of his net worth at the time of their marriage."

"That's thirty years ago," I say. "Your grandmother told me yesterday that your grandfather staked the firm for Bridger right *after* they married—"

"Insurance," he says.

Evangeline crinkles her nose. "Why would she sign something like that?"

"True love?" Stu shrugs and raises his hands, palms up. "And thirty years ago, Dallas was a different place."

He's right, as much as I don't want to admit it. A prenuptial then would have been almost scandalous, an insurance policy for something good families didn't do and never needed. How Bridger managed to convince his fiancée to sign one at all must have taken some persuading.

There isn't even so much as a tweet about the early morning murders, not even on the various outlets covering the local police scanners, and I wonder how quickly this guy called Cade and what strings Cade is pulling with his friends in the press pool.

Maybe Cade dangles information on another murder, one that might be even juicier, and I take a deep breath.

Because if Cesar Morales could prove his parentage, he was old enough to lay claim to the Holcombe fortune.

If anything were to happen to Bridger . . .

I glance at Stu around my computer monitor.

Stu may be in this deeper than we thought.

Movement on the other side of the glass doors draws my attention, and from the corner of my eye I see Evangeline raise her head, too.

Cade stands, one hand on the door handle, facing away from us, carrying his attaché case with his suit coat folded over his arm. His jaw is set, and his eyes are narrowed.

Bridger's smile is tight. Kirby has his hands shoved inside his pockets but wears a slight smirk.

Bridger points toward the back of the firm and reaches past Cade to yank the door open. "Reagan," he says. "Join us in my office. Now."

"Girl," Evangeline says under her breath. "You better be careful."

I nod and stand, brush the wrinkles from my pants, and straighten my jacket. "I'll be right back."

Bridger's office is in the rear of the law firm, the largest office in the building. I walk down the long hallway from Cade's section, trying not to notice the sounds of my heels on the floor next to the soft whisk of Cade's shoes, past the bay of cubicles housing the secretarial pool. No individual secretary guards its door; no, every secretary pauses at their work to watch as we pass, a full army of gatekeepers, ready to turn away anyone who isn't supposed to wander this far back unattended to bother the firm's managing partner.

The door is open, the office's bright light spilling across the dark wood floors like milk.

I follow Cade across the threshold, my high heels sinking into plush carpet.

"Get that," Bridger says, motioning to the door.

Cade ushers me past, then closes the door.

The windows that run down two sides of the large office overlook downtown behind their sunscreens, rendering the skyline a flat, dim gray. Bridger sits at his large desk in the high-backed leather chair, a king in his throne room, and Kirby stands at his right, leaning back against the hutch.

I make my way to the large leather chairs across from the desk, separated by a small glass table. Bridger doesn't say anything about sitting, and so I don't, letting my fingertips brush the cool, smooth back of the chair in front of me.

Cade doesn't wait for Bridger to invite him to sit; he flings himself into the nearest chair. "Do you want to tell us what the hell's going on? I'm in the middle of something—"

"I'm sure you are," Bridger says, his voice slick and oily. "I'm so glad I could catch you both. Certain questions have been raised regarding Reagan's and your relationship, and we're now invoking the romantic relationship clause in her employment contract."

24

THE ROOM IS silent, so silent I hear the ticking of the clock on the wall, the rattle of the air-conditioning duct, the chatter of the secretaries, the sound of Cade's hopes of a named partnership draining away . . .

"What?" Cade demands, straightening in his seat. "This is some bullshit. I'm the partner that supervises her—you can't just waltz into *my* office and make decisions about *my* staff—"

"Oh, I think we can," Bridger says, folding his hands on the desk.

Cade gives me a glance from the corner of his eye, as if to say, *Let me handle this.* "On what grounds?"

"Reagan," Bridger says. "Where have you been this morning?"

"Don't answer that," Cade says to me, and then to the two men, "Again, what's it to you where she's been? She works for me."

"That's exactly the problem," Kirby says.

"How I run my office isn't your problem," Cade says. "Nor is it any of your business."

"It is when her conduct is raising questions about the integrity of this firm," Bridger says, and his gaze swivels to me. "Did you or did you not confront someone this morning about the criminal case I specifically told you and Cade to leave alone yesterday?"

I think of all the arguments I can make, that I was on personal time, that Bridger could only know this if Marcos called him, and, thus, Bridger is also somehow connected with the case, or maybe that the meeting was by chance.

But I say nothing.

"So you did," Bridger says, a faint triumphant note to his voice. "I believe I explained the consequences to this behavior yesterday. Was I unclear?"

"No, sir," I say.

He scoffs and points at Cade. "This is where you should say you'll fire her. But we both know you won't. And why you won't."

Cade doesn't even so much as raise an eyebrow; he's as cool as I've ever seen him. "I resent your implications—"

"I resent the fact that you're thinking with your dick," Bridger says. "Son, you're better than this, and you're not meeting the expectations of this firm."

"I'm not your son," Cade says, his voice low.

Cade and Bridger lock gazes and Bridger's eyes narrow almost into a squint. "I warned you to get your bitch back on her leash."

The words hit, they hurt, and I slough them off yet again because this isn't the first time I've been called a bitch and it won't be the last.

But it's the first time Cade hears it, and he reacts almost immediately, launching himself out of his seat. "We're done here."

"Cade," Bridger says. "You think this through. What happened to that hungry, young attorney who wanted a named partnership before he was forty? Are you really gonna jeopardize that—your career—for . . . *her*? Use your head, son."

"Damn it, I'm not your son," Cade retorts. "And maybe you two should think through a few things before you threaten my partnership status, huh? When's the last time either of you brought in a five-figure retainer or even held a press conference? If I walk out of here, the future of your firm goes with me."

"Oh, you're still a partner," Bridger says. "But suspended from any voting or profit-sharing until you're willing to fulfill your duties. All of them."

Kirby shakes his head, his frown that of a disappointed father. "She signed a statement acknowledging what would happen if she engaged in a romantic relationship within the firm. As did you, for that matter. There are consequences for your actions. For both of you."

I swallow hard.

If I leave now, Cade won't be required to fire me. He'll have a chance to salvage something—anything—of his partnership, and maybe I can figure out why Marcos would go straight to Bridger and tattle about our conversation.

"My resignation letter will be on Cade's desk by tomorrow morning," I say.

Bridger sneers. "That's very gentlemanly of you to take the fall for him."

Bridger and I make eye contact for the first time.

I allow myself the liberty of a small, thin smile, and can't resist saying, "I think there's at least one woman you've let take the fall for you."

His face loses color for half a second and then reddens like a tomato. "You have fifteen minutes to be off the property."

I nod and leave the room, head high. Cade arrives at his section half a step behind me, close enough that he reaches around me to keep me from opening the door. "Wait," he says. "I'll fix this."

"Yes," I say. "But not today."

He bites his lower lip and looks away. "No, not today."

"Cade"—I grab his hand—"even if this—even if you can't fix this—I wouldn't change anything."

He drops his attaché case and suit coat, tugs me into his arms, and kisses me in the middle of the corridor. "I *will* fix this," he murmurs as he pulls away. "I promise."

"I know," I say and look away because I'm worried if I spend one more second drowning in those green eyes I'll lose all composure and sob into his shoulder like a frightened child.

"I'll be home as soon as I can," he says, his voice suddenly thick with unspoken words, as if he knows exactly how I feel, and he shares it.

"Be careful," I say. "If you want to be a named partner—"

"They'll give me what I want," Cade says and grins. "I know where all the bodies are buried, remember?"

He does, of course, know where the bodies are buried—literally and figuratively—for most of the DFW metroplex's upper crust at this point, but I'm not sure that will stop Bridger.

He brushes my hair and kisses me again, like he sees my concerns play out across my face. "I'm a big boy, Reag. I can take care of myself."

"Who do you think he's protecting?" I ask.

Cade shrugs. "Stu, maybe. You'd be amazed at how far parents will go for their sons."

But not Cesar, I almost say, and Cesar was his son, too.

"Go home," Cade says. "We'll sort this out tonight."

He opens the glass door and holds it for me. I go to my desk, log off the computer, and gather my things.

"Get the car, please," Cade says to Rafi. "Take Reag home and keep an eye on things, will you?"

"Yes, sir," Rafi says, and to me, "I'll meet you downstairs."

Evangeline pushes back from her desk. "What's going on?"

"Reagan's going home for the rest of the day," Cade says. "I'll be in my office, but if anyone short of the governor walks in, I'm unavailable."

"Is everything all right?" Evangeline asks.

"It will be," he says and glares at Stu. "Get out of my office."

Stu scrambles to his feet. "What the hell, Cade? I can help you—"

"Yeah, help from anyone named Holcombe has too many goddamn strings attached," Cade says. "Get the fuck out."

Evangeline and I exchange a glance and she mouths, "Text me."

"I'll see you tonight," Cade says to me.

I shoulder my bag and walk out. Once the elevator doors open downstairs, I step out and wave at the security guard one last time like everything is perfectly all right.

I don't know it then, but it will be the last time I walk out of the Holcombe & Donaldson doors without a gun to my head.

* * *

"So that's it?" Rafi asks. "They just fired you?"

The words fall, one by one, shattering in my heart so painfully that I almost wince. It's as if they're mocking me, reminding me that I'm a failure, that I've sacrificed my career for a man, that I've done something so incredibly stupid.

Still, I have my pride.

"I resigned, actually," I say. "Effective immediately."

I stroke the passenger side armrest and think how strange it is to be leaving the office before lunchtime with no intention of going back, and to not know what to do with myself for the rest of the day.

The rest of my life.

"Huh." Rafi steers the car toward the parking garage's exit. "You want lunch or something?"

I shrug. "I'm not very hungry. Maybe that chocolate croissant."

"Maybe," Rafi says, but it doesn't sound like he believes me.

"Anyway." I fumble my sunglasses on and chew the inside of my cheek until I know I can hold my voice steady. "Cade said straight to the apartment."

"You don't always do what he wants."

I make myself take a deep breath. "Let's give him this today."

Because even if Cade manages to bring me back, even if Cade does keep his partnership, his name will never be on the letterhead. Too many people saw him kiss me in the hallway. Rumors will spread through the secretaries and the paralegals, whispered over cubicle walls and picked apart via instant messaging. Whatever Bridger and Kirby's indiscretions, they keep them behind closed doors, out of sight of the staff.

Or in Oak Cliff.

No, Cade can fix a lot, but he can't fix this, not completely. Bridger and Kirby will never trust him again.

I sniff and squeeze my hand into a fist so tightly, just to give myself something else to think about, that my fingernails cut into my palm.

Rafi glances over at me. "But if Cade's boss knows about your relationship and that's what this is all about, how come you're the only one resigning?"

"Because Cade is a partner," I say. "I'm not the one bringing in the money."

"But it's not like you're the only one who participated," Rafi says.

I shrug and stare out the window. "It's not so different from the military."

Rafi sighs but doesn't argue anymore.

At the apartment, I leave Rafi in the living room and shut the bedroom door to change clothes, trying to shake the restlessness nipping at my heels.

Cade will work the bail hearing and arraignment all day for that new client, so this evening will be the first chance I have to tell him about Marcos's refusal to talk and what Stu mentioned about his parents' prenuptial and his father's will.

Or how I now know the two are connected.

I retreat to the closet and swap my pantsuit and high heels for a tank top and leggings. The dry cleaning and laundry are in their hampers, and I sigh and sort through them. If I handle some of the weekend errands today, we have more time for apartment hunting on Saturday.

How I'll come up with a job to pay for my share of that apartment will be a problem for another day.

Rafi paces at the balcony doors, looking out over the city, and doesn't even notice me open the doors in the hallway to access the washer and dryer.

"Do you think we could drop off the dry cleaning?" I ask. "We could grab you some lunch."

"As long as that's it," he says.

"It is," I say. "As much as I'd rather . . ."

"You're giving him this today," Rafi says.

"Right," I say.

We drop off the dry cleaning, pick up lunch, and take it back to the apartment to watch reruns of *The Golden Girls* and wait for Cade.

The traffic sounds increase.

The afternoon sun moves farther to the right, sinking toward the western horizon, but Cade doesn't call or text.

I switch the television channel over to the local news and start scanning my social media feeds, searching for any

word about the arraignment or that Cade has a press conference scheduled.

A phone call from Evangeline lights up my screen.

I answer it. "Hey."

"Lemme talk to Rafi," she says, a tremor to her voice.

I roll my eyes. "Evangeline—"

"Now, Reagan," she says, and something like a sob
chokes her.

I offer Rafi the phone. "It's Evangeline."

He smirks and holds it up to his ear. "Mm, *chulita*, I
knew I should've gotten your number."

His gaze darts to me.

"What is it?" I hiss.

"Yeah," he says to Evangeline. "All right. We'll be on
our way."

He clicks off the call and tosses me the phone without
looking at me.

"On our way where?" I ask.

He sighs and rubs his knees. "Something . . . happened."

I straighten in my seat. "What?"

"Cade," he says. "They're taking him to the hospital."

My mouth goes dry, and the room is suddenly very hot.

The earth stops spinning underneath me, a giant carou-
sel lurching to a halt, the calliope screeching off-tune, and I
sway as if to compensate.

"Reagan," I barely hear Rafi say, like he's somewhere
down a long tunnel, far away from me.

Of all the thoughts that race through my mind, the
only one I can comprehend is that something has happened
to Cade.

Something has happened to Cade, and I can't imagine
my life without him.

Cade, grinning at me as I fastened his cuff links this
morning, his dress shirt unbuttoned and his hair damp and
glistening from our shower.

Cade, his kiss still hot on my mouth, his whispered promise that he'll fix this.

Cade, and the future I've allowed myself to begin dreaming of with him . . .

Possibly gone.

Because of me.

"Reagan," Rafi says again, only now his hands are on my upper arms, hauling me to my feet.

I blink and look up into his dark eyes.

"Yes," I make myself say. "Yes, we should go."

"Listen to me," he says. "You know you won't want to leave him. Pack a change of clothes, a hairbrush, and a toothbrush, you hear me?"

I nod, because I know he's saying that we don't know how bad Cade is, we don't know if I'll need to stay or run, and I'd better be prepared for both.

Because if they can get to Cade, if they can kill Cesar Morales and Heather Hudson, then I'm not far behind.

"Maybe pack some of his things, too," Rafi says and lets me go with a gentle nudge toward the bedroom. "Five minutes."

I shove the knife and pistol into my backpack with my laptop, the file from Miller, and the envelope from Heather Hudson.

"It may not be anything," Rafi says from the bedroom door, coiling a cell phone charging cord around his hand.

I don't point out that if it weren't anything, Cade would have called himself, not Evangeline sobbing and demanding to speak with Rafi.

"Sure," I say instead, and put the charging cord in my bag.

On autopilot, I grab the military essentials for both of us: underwear and socks, toothbrushes, soap, his razor, a hair tie for me.

When there is still room in my bag, I add pajamas for each of us and a spare outfit for me. One of his old UNC sweatshirts, faded and worn thin, sits on the closet shelf with his clean gym clothes, and I grab it.

"Let's go," I say.

Rafi follows and stands at my elbow while I lock the apartment door, and then we hurry to the parking garage and the car.

CHAPTER

25

THE HOSPITAL DISTRICT is just over two miles north of Cade's apartment. Most of the time, it's a quick trip up I-35, five minutes from parking spot to parking spot.

But it's rush hour on a Thursday evening, and red brake lights glow along the interstate.

I bury my face in my hands in the passenger seat.

"I got it," Rafi says and floors the gas. "I'm from here, remember? I know these streets."

He swerves onto a side road, the sports sedan powering us down tree-lined streets and around cars stopping and starting.

My heart races with the engine until he stops, parking as close as he can get us to the emergency room doors. I'm out of the car almost before he presses the ignition button, slinging my backpack over one shoulder and scrambling for the entrance, but Rafi is somehow right on my heels, matching me step for step.

A woman in scrubs glances up from behind a counter as I rush through the doors. "Cade McCarrick?" I blurt out.

"Are you immediate family?" she asks.

"I'm his . . . ," I begin and realize I still don't know how to classify our relationship.

"Wife," Evangeline says from behind me. "This is his wife."

I turn my head enough for us to make eye contact, and I catch her warning look. "Yes."

"They have his insurance card from his wallet," Evangeline says. "But no one to sign the consent papers. Of course, now that you're here—"

"I'll let the doctors know you've arrived," the woman in scrubs says and plunks a clipboard down in front of me. "You'll need to sign these. Full name, please. Do you have your driver's license with you?"

"I do," I say and pass it over. "But I haven't updated it yet."

She clicks her tongue against her teeth and shakes her head. "It'll do, I guess."

Armando saunters over and hugs me. "Any issues?"

"No, just that Reagan's ID doesn't have her married name on it," Evangeline says.

"Oh, well, that," Armando says and smiles at the woman in scrubs. "It was a lovely wedding. I think I have some pictures on my phone if you want to see—"

"That won't be necessary," she says.

The four of us sit in a corner of the waiting room and Rafi watches the hospital's exterior doors like he waits for something.

Or someone.

I sit with a view of the exam room doors, hoping that any minute now, Cade will walk out, saying this is an elaborate joke.

"What happened?" Rafi asks.

"Good question," Armando says.

"We don't know," Evangeline chimes in. "The paramedics called me at the office because it was on his business card."

"So he wasn't at the office?" I say.

She shakes her head. "Obviously. I thought he was just going out to get some air."

"Someone will need to go for his car, wherever it is," Armando says. "If something happens to *that*—"

I shove my hands under my thighs and try to think of where Cade could have gone on a Thursday evening when he should have been working a bail hearing or an arraignment for his Preston Hollow client.

"Did Bridger . . . did he and Cade have more words after I left?" I ask Evangeline.

Armando straightens in his seat. "They had words?"

"The senior partners asked for my resignation this morning," I say. "Didn't you know?"

"No one told me," Armando says, but his bitter smile and the way he shrugs tell me the senior partners leave him out of most meetings.

"They invoked the romantic relationships clause in my employment contract," I say, flipping through the pages on the clipboard. "So . . ."

"So you're out of the office, and Cade's wings are clipped for a bit," Armando says. "Don't worry, Reagan, he's Bridger's golden boy. He'll bounce back with no serious damage done, and in a few days he'll probably convince them to rehire you, just in a different office."

"Maybe," I say, because Armando doesn't know that Bridger Holcombe probably killed two people.

I fill out the paperwork and sign the consent forms, forcing my hand to go through the motions of scrawling Reagan J. McCarrick in the signature blocks. When I'm done with the stack, I trace a finger over the dried ink on the top page, feeling the indentation in the paper.

"I'm sorry," Evangeline whispers. "But otherwise his nearest next-of-kin is in North Carolina, and I didn't think he'd want his family involved."

I nod. As curious as I am about his family, this isn't the way Cade needs to reunite with them, nor how I want to meet them, but part of me still wants to admit that Reagan McCarrick is an impostor, a no one.

A fraud.

Maybe just as much a pretender as Reagan Reyes, who couldn't even save herself last week or Cade, much less Heather Hudson almost two weeks ago . . .

"He'll think it's funny," Evangeline says.

I make myself smile.

"It's not for real," she says, and maybe that's the problem.

Maybe I can imagine it being real, each swirl of my signature making it more tangible, but some part of me knows that if something happens to Cade, this is only as real as it will get.

"Has anyone told the senior partners?" Armando asks.

"I didn't," Evangeline says. "Not after this morning."

"Someone will have to," Armando says.

"Tomorrow," Rafi says.

Armando frowns at Rafi as if just now seeing him, but I leave Evangeline to introduce them and carry the clipboard to the counter. The woman takes it from me without comment, but I linger until she looks up at me.

"Do you know . . ." I bite my lower lip and force my voice steady. "Is he all right? Can I see him? Please?"

"His doctor will update you when he has a chance," she says and turns back to her computer monitor. "They'll let you know when they get him in a room."

"So they're admitting him?" I ask.

She exhales heavily.

We make eye contact and her expression softens.

"Look," she says. "I'll take this paperwork back so they can proceed with the tests they need to run. As soon as his doctor can speak with you, he will. In the meantime, send one of your friends to get dinner because it may be a long night."

"Thank you," I say.

Rafi glares in the woman's direction. "What'd she say?"

"That it may be a long night, so we should get dinner," I say.

"Like you'll eat it?" Rafi asks, and I shake my head.

The two men exchange a glance and Armando nods and stands. "I'll be back. I know just the trick."

He disappears out the hospital doors and Rafi says, "I think I'll go to the gift shop and see if they have any crossword puzzles. Air Force needs to do some thinking, or they get destructive and start blowing shit up."

"I thought that was your job," I say.

Rafi grins. "Exactly."

"Where did you find him?" Evangeline asks as Rafi saunters away.

"You wouldn't believe me," I say.

"That man is fine," she says. "And smart. Was he really in the Army?"

"Yes," I say. "A Ranger, with the Purple Heart to prove it."

"I bet he looks nice in that uniform," she says.

I consider telling her that, yes, Rafi probably does look nice in that uniform, but there's a price to pay for all those ribbons and medals, dark nights of memories that may flood in unexpectedly, a military discharge status that's under appeal, and the potential for all that to affect any relationship. But that's for her and Rafi to discuss, and so I only say, "What about Armando? I know what you said last week, but you're always together, and I thought—"

"Reagan." She cocks her head to one side and frowns. "Do you really not know?"

I lean back in my seat and pull Cade's sweatshirt over my head, nestling down in it and relishing the smell of him in the collar. "Know what?"

She chuckles. "I'm not Armando's type. And you're not Armando's type. Cade, however . . ."

"Oh," I say.

"Not Cade specifically, necessarily," Evangeline says. "But Armando and I are strictly friends and wingmen. Wingwomen. Wing . . . whatever."

"Why hasn't anyone said anything?" I ask.

"Girl," she scoffs and flips her braids over one shoulder. "Do you know what Bridger and Kirby would do if Armando was out?"

"That's illegal," I say.

"That wouldn't be what they'd fire him for, but they'd find something, and you know it," she says. "Cade has always been good at protecting people and their secrets."

"Part of his job description, isn't it?" I ask.

"Maybe," she says. "Armando and I were happy to return the favor when it came to you two, especially when we saw how happy he was."

I play with the sweatshirt's cuffs. "Today . . . it was almost a relief, in a way. To have everything out in the open. Only now . . ."

I can't voice my concerns about the case Cade and I aren't supposed to be working, because I don't want to drag Evangeline into this.

I can't admit my fears about what will happen if Cade doesn't wake up, because it seems disloyal to doubt Cade.

But Evangeline doesn't need me to.

She reaches over and squeezes my hand. "Cade will fix this. He can fix anything."

I have nothing else to hold on to but her beliefs, and so I accept them and make them mine.

Cade will wake up.

Cade will fix this.

He has to.

*   *   *

Armando returns, laden with bags, and he is right—at the first whiff of guacamole and chicken fajita meat, I rediscover my appetite. The four of us settle down to a feast of chips, salsa, guacamole and queso, chicken fajita tacos, and *tres leches* cake.

When I sigh at my last forkful of cake, Armando grins. "Your Spanish may be shit, but I figured you had enough in you that you couldn't turn down tacos and *tres leches*."

Rafi glares at him and looks like he might say something, but Evangeline says, "No one turns down tacos and *tres leches*. But you could have brought us back margaritas."

Armando grins sheepishly. "I did think about it, but I knew the nursing staff probably wouldn't like it."

We clean up the remains of our dinner. Rafi and Evangeline whisper together in their corner over a crossword. Armando settles beside me and scrolls through his emails on his cell phone. I pick up an old magazine from an end table, some relic from a decade ago, and thumb through it.

"Any word from the partners?" I ask.

"No," he says.

I swap the magazine for my cell phone and open a book, but I can't read. All I can think about is that Cade is nearby and I can't be with him and it's my fault.

"Mrs. McCarrick?" a man's voice calls. "Mrs. McCarrick?"

Armando elbows me in the ribs. "She's right here."

I stand and slide my phone into my pocket. "That's me."

"Do you know where your husband was this evening?" a man in scrubs, probably a doctor, asks.

I shake my head. "Doesn't he know?"

"He's not awake yet," he says. "When he passed out, he may have hit his head . . ."

"Oh," I say.

"The MRI will tell us if the head injury is more serious than we think. I'll let you know when I have something more."

I take a deep breath and work up the nerve to ask, "Why'd you want to know where he was?"

He looks away for half a second, long enough to tell me that there's something wrong. "Your husband had very high levels of GHB in his system—"

"GHB?" I ask. "Like the date-rape drug?"

"Yes," he says. "Normally this would metabolize out of his system fairly quickly, and it wouldn't trigger a collapse like this."

"And if someone was going to dope him, his wallet, watch, and car keys would have been taken," I say. "But they weren't?"

The doctor raises his eyebrows. "I'm not the police. Does he have a history of recreational—"

"No," I say. "I won't say I've never seen him less than sober, but his habits run more to liquor or wine."

"I thought as much," he says. "But I have to ask. And it just seems very strange."

"Indeed," I say.

Evangeline waits until the doctor leaves to look at me, her head cocked to the side and one eyebrow arched. She puts her hands on her hips and taps a foot.

"What?" I ask.

"Don't you 'what' me," she says. "What the hell are you and Cade mixed up in?"

I sigh. "Let's sit down. It's probably best I tell you and Armando at the same time."

The four of us sit in our corner, the crossword puzzle and cell phones forgotten, and I confess everything—from the contents of the envelope to the news that Cesar Morales would have soon had a little boy, that Stu unintentionally revealed the proviso of his father's will that everything goes to his firstborn son, and that if that son is over thirty, he can administer his inheritance however he sees fit.

"Holy shit," Armando breathes. "So you think—Cade thinks—the Holcombes . . . ?"

I nod. "And we got too close."

"If Cade had been in the office when that woman with the pink hair came in," Evangeline says and shakes her head. "This would've started some shit on a Friday afternoon."

"I'll bet she thought she'd use Cade to get money out of Bridger," Armando says and slides an arm around me. "But GHB isn't usually fatal. Why would they dope Cade?"

"To scare him, maybe?" Evangeline asks.

No, I want to say, because I know how Cade has reacted every step of the way, wanting to protect me and for me to just leave all this alone.

Cade is already scared; he admitted he was when I was attacked Friday. Firing me today might have pissed him off enough to start making threats to Bridger, but Bridger has to know that if he placates Cade, then Cade will fall back in line.

This is aimed at me.

Bridger must realize that in firing me, he cut me loose from his supervision and oversight. Now he can't do anything to me anymore except scare me and hope I don't leverage whatever contacts I have in local law enforcement to find someone to listen to me.

"Cade will be fine," Armando says. "I'll bet he's home by tomorrow night."

I force a smile, but when I glance at Rafi, he looks away. He knows too.

I scroll through my text messages and look at the last message from Miller yesterday afternoon, the blue heart emoji, and I wonder if he'll believe a word I say, or if he'll be willing to act on it.

Probably not.

Not if he's been told not to talk to me anymore, and he's not even willing to buck that to answer a question.

Once Cade wakes up, he'll be able to tell us where he was this afternoon.

Maybe then we'll know what to do.

CHAPTER

26

Twilight falls and floodlights bathe the sidewalk outside the hospital in amber, but the man in scrubs doesn't return.

I try not to think about his remarks that GHB usually doesn't last this long.

Something is wrong and no one wants to tell me.

I wrap my arms around myself and pace, knowing that Rafi, Evangeline, and Armando watch, and that each of them must be wondering if they need to step in or if they should wait for one of the others to do it.

But no one does anything, maybe because they're scared too.

Cade is their friend, my lover, the keeper of all our secrets, the shield that protects us at the office—and now he may be gone.

The doors to the patient area of the emergency department whisk open and I turn in time to see the doctor from earlier approaching.

He smiles.

This is a good sign, I tell myself. *He wouldn't smile if there was bad news.*

"No brain injury," he says. "We're moving him to a room now."

Every muscle in my shoulders and back and hips and legs rushes to relax, and it's only then I realize how tense I have been. I put a hand on the back of a chair to steady myself, but Armando stands and slips an arm around me, pulling me close, as if he knows.

"That's great news," Rafi says.

"Is he awake?" Evangeline asks.

"No, but we expect him to sleep everything off by morning," the doctor says. "Mrs. McCarrick, you can stay with him tonight. But it's after visiting hours—"

"Of course." Armando squeezes my shoulder. "We'll check in first thing tomorrow."

I nod and take my backpack from Rafi. "You'll drop Evangeline off?"

"I'll take good care of her," Rafi says. "And your car."

Evangeline hugs me. "You tell him that if he ever scares us like this again, we *will* call his parents."

I follow the doctor through the doors to an elevator, and he waits until it creaks upward to say, "He should be awake at some point tonight, but probably won't remember what happened. A lot depends on the combination of the GHB and the fall. He could lose a few minutes, or it could be a few hours, even a couple of days."

"Right," I say.

But if Cade is in a room, his phone and wallet should be there too, and maybe they'll hold clues as to where he went and what he did this afternoon.

"He's pretty lucky," the doctor says. "In anyone else, the GHB wouldn't have hit that hard, but that old kidney injury saved his life."

An old kidney injury, something that happened in the "before" time that Cade and I don't talk about.

But I make my face blank, because Cade's wife would know about this, and murmur, "Who would've thought?"

The doctor shakes his head. "He could've been driving on the freeway when it hit, and good luck explaining that to the cops if he'd caused an accident or got pulled over for driving under the influence."

The possibilities of what could have happened to Cade send new shivers of fear darting into my heart, icy fingers that threaten he's still not safe, and somehow I manage to make myself say, "We're so lucky."

The elevator doors open, and I follow the doctor down a maze of corridors to a door at the end. He opens it and ushers me into the room.

A dim half-light glows a circle around the bed where Cade sleeps, pale and still, guarded by a wall of monitors that beep and click, the wires and connectors all leading back to him.

"The nurses make their rounds every two hours," the doctor says. "But they'll do their best to be quiet. Blankets and pillows are in that closet."

"Thank you," I say.

He nods and makes his way out.

I set my backpack on the small sleeper sofa under the window and draw the chair up to the bed.

Cade doesn't move.

I sit and eye the monitors, watch his blood pressure, his heart rate as steady as a metronome, and reach over to smooth his hair.

All the things I want to say, all the apologies for not leaving things alone, that if only I had walked away from this when he had asked, that if I had just not been so persistent at unraveling the puzzle, choke unspoken in the back of my throat.

"I love you," I whisper instead. "Please wake up."

I huddle my knees to my chest and wrap my arms around them, rest my forehead on them, and pray silently he'll be all right.

* * *

Something like ocean waves softly breaking whoosh-whooshes nearby, but it's cold and I snuggle down further in Cade's sweatshirt without opening my eyes.

A hand strokes my hair.

"Reag," Cade mumbles.

I sit up, blinking. A faint impression marks the edge of the bed where I fell asleep, resting my head on my forearms, but other than that, the room is perfectly as it was when I entered. I rub my face, look at the monitors, and try to decide if I imagined it all.

"Will you get that light?" Cade asks without opening his eyes. "It's too bright."

"Cade," I breathe and squeeze his hand, stand to kiss his forehead, and press the button to turn the light off completely. "Do you know where you are?"

He yawns and shifts in the bed. "Mm, no, and I don't care. Should I?"

I brush his hair with my fingers, avoiding the place where he hit his head. "There was an accident. You're in the hospital."

"My car," he mumbles.

"You weren't driving," I say.

"How could there be an accident if I wasn't driving?" he asks.

"We'll talk about it tomorrow, when you've gotten some rest."

"You'll stay, won't you?" he asks.

"Yes," I say.

I find a blanket and pillow in the closet. The couch feels too far away from him, so I settle back into the chair and let myself doze until a hand on my shoulder makes me jump.

"Shh, it's me," Evangeline whispers.

I open my eyes. "Is it visiting hours already?"

"No," she says. "We snuck in to bring you breakfast."

"Chocolate croissant and a latte," Rafi says with a wink as he places a wrapped paper bag and two coffee cups on the tray table. "Got him a couple of kolaches and a black coffee. You mind if I go with Evangeline to the office?"

The office, because it's Friday morning and Evangeline needs to carry on like everything is normal.

"The office," I say. "Cade—"

"Armando is handling it with the senior partners," she says. "I'm clearing Cade's schedule."

I rub the side of my face and eye the paper bag, smelling the richness of the chocolate croissant even through its wrapping. "Okay."

"You'll check in?" Rafi asks.

"Yeah," I say. "Will you two?"

Evangeline smiles and nods, kisses the top of my head, and slips a hand in Rafi's as they leave.

I open the blinds and sunshine drifts into the room, the soft golden rays bathing Cade in their light. For a moment, I watch him sleep, the rise and fall of his chest somehow reassuring and deceptive in its normalcy. It's only when I look closely that I see the remnant of blood or antiseptic that wasn't cleaned off his face and neck the night before, and so I tiptoe into the bathroom.

Without checking the mirror, I know that I'll be pale, that dark circles will ring my eyes, and my hair is a tangled mess. I splash warm water onto my face, smooth my curls, and hope Cade will be too tired to notice.

The door opens as I soak a washcloth in warm water. I step out of the bathroom warily, but only a nurse stands at the end of the bed.

"Good morning, Mrs. McCarrick," she says and makes notes on the whiteboard hanging on the wall. "Do you need anything?"

"Can he eat when he wakes up?" I ask.

She eyes the bag and coffee on the table. "Maybe ask the doctor just to be sure."

"Thanks," I say.

She leaves and I lean over Cade to dab at his face. A hand grabs my ass and I yelp, startled, only to realize it's Cade.

I swat him away. "Holy shit," I say, but suddenly I don't know whether I want to laugh or cry.

He grins without opening his eyes. "Mrs. McCarrick, I believe? Please tell me I didn't fuck up the proposal, Reag. I can't wait to hear."

"Well, it was either we told them I was your wife, or we called North Carolina," I say. "As a lawyer, it's pretty fucking irresponsible for you not to have a power of attorney to make medical decisions when you're going to collapse and be unconscious for hours."

"Y'all managed," he says, drawing the back of my hand to his lips. "That coffee?"

"Not yet," I say. "You heard her."

He opens his eyes and manages to dimple up at me. "Are you finishing the sponge bath, or do I have to wait on the doctor to clear that, too?"

"Yes," I say.

"To which one?" he asks. "The lights, Reag, and can you close those blinds? What the hell was I drinking last night to end up in the hospital unconscious and still have a hangover this bad?"

"You weren't drinking," I say, closing the blinds and dimming the lights once more. "Do you remember yesterday?"

"I remember you leaving," he says. "And working through lunch. And I went to the arraignment. But after that . . ."

"Someone slipped you GHB," I say. "Enough to knock you out since yesterday afternoon, but they think part of that is the head injury from when you fell. And that happened because—"

A knock on the door interrupts me.

"Come in," Cade says.

"You sneaky bastard," a man in scrubs says as he enters. He's younger than the doctor from last night, only a decade or so older than Cade, and grins at me. "How many years have you been my patient and you don't tell me you got married?"

Cade opens one eye long enough to squint at the man. "Oh, they called you? Hell, it must've been serious."

The doctor laughs and looks at the tablet he carries. "No idea how the GHB got in your system still, I take it?"

"We were just discussing that," I say.

"Shit, if it weren't for that wonky kidney of yours, the effects probably wouldn't have been as immediate or as severe," the doctor says. "Just imagine how badly you could have fucked up evening rush hour. Still have the Porsche?"

"Mm-hmm," Cade says and nestles further into the bed, his eyes closed again.

The doctor glances over Cade, raises his eyebrows, and returns to his tablet. "I spoke with your nephrologist, and he wants to see you within the next couple of weeks instead of waiting for your next checkup."

"Fine," Cade says.

"You do also have a minor concussion," the doctor says. "A couple of days of rest, though, and you should be as good as new."

"Can he have breakfast?" I ask.

"Small bites," the doctor says. "Given the concussion combined with the GHB, you'll be sticking around until tomorrow morning. I'll send a nurse in a few minutes to unhook you so you can get up and walk, though. Lemme know when you're up for a round of golf so I can beat you again."

"Like hell you will," Cade grumbles. "You only win 'cause you cheat."

"Oh, I cheat? Damn lawyers," the doctor says but smiles at me. "Nice to meet you. Hopefully he won't be too terrible."

He exits the room and I drop into the chair by the bed, my head practically spinning with the events of the last twelve hours.

Cade blows out a long exhale and his hand finds mine. "So now you know."

"No," I say. "Not really."

"It was one of those 'before' things, you know?" He shrugs and closes his eyes. "My next to last game. I, umm, was in the pocket. I didn't see the guy until the last minute and I tried to scramble. I slipped the first tackle, but he ended up coming down hard on my back. And then it seemed everyone piled on. I was sore the next day. The next week. But there was a bowl game coming up, so I didn't say anything. I just thought I pulled a muscle, maybe, or there was a deep bruise."

"And so you played the bowl game," I say.

"Played the bowl game. Got sacked a few times. Pissed blood after, but I was almost twenty-three years old, so I figured—I mean, shit, Reag, you know I wasn't exactly a saint—"

"Right," I say, because I see the gazes that follow him now, and I can only imagine Cade at twenty-two, a college quarterback, handsome with that grin, those green eyes, his dimples, and his charm, with the world at his feet.

And while he's always been very conscientious about offering a level of protection that we're both comfortable with, a twenty-two-year-old college quarterback can sometimes be a long way from a thirty-four-year-old attorney.

"But all the tests were negative," he says. "The doctors and trainers insisted on more tests because of the back pain and everything else, especially with the NFL combines coming up. And so that's how we found out I'd damaged my right kidney to the point it barely functions. They told me no NFL team would touch me and I'd better get a backup plan ready.

"I went through with the combines anyway, just hoping that maybe my performance would buy me a seat on a bench, but . . . they were right. A damaged kidney means no contact sports, and my playing career was done."

"So law school," I say.

"So law school," he repeats.

I trace a line on the hospital blanket with my fingertip. "And your parents?"

"My father thought the only advantage to me playing football was quick money for that damn farm," he says. "And if I couldn't deliver on that, I was supposed to come home and work. It didn't matter what I wanted. We had words."

"It's been eleven years," I say. "Must have been some words."

He rubs his forehead. "I think his side culminated in that I was disloyal and thought I was better than them and too good for the farm. I told him where he could stick his farm, that I didn't need it and never needed it, nor them. He told me that they wouldn't put a dime toward law school, and I reminded him that they hadn't put a dime toward my college anyway. And so he said I should just . . . not come home."

"And your mother?" I ask.

He turns his face away and shrugs, his voice dropping almost to a whisper. "She said it was best if I just went. If I wanted a life without the farm, they could want a life without me."

I almost stop myself.

But in the end I can't, and so I ignore how small the bed is and crawl in beside him, pulling him to me so I can hold him, because after yesterday I know I'll never want a life without him.

"They were in a bad spot," he says. "I know that now. And life on a farm—it's not easy. You have to make hard choices."

"Everyone makes hard choices," I say. "But eleven years and no one's said anything? Not even your sisters?"

"They were a lot older than me and always thought Mom and Dad spoiled me too much anyway, so of course they sided with them. Look, I sent invites for my law school graduation and they were returned unopened, so that pretty much told me where I stood, and it just got easier to let it be," he says. "They clearly wanted to pretend I was dead, so why shouldn't I let them?"

The things families do to push each other away and tear each other apart, to shred the flesh and pick the bones, when all they should really want is to nest together. Maybe in the end we're all the heroes and villains in the same story, each family member trying to live up to some standard of our parents and grandparents as we blaze our own trail and establish our own identities while ensuring we have a place to come home to and put down roots.

So in twenty or thirty years our children can defy us in the same manner, and the cycle will begin again.

He nuzzles into my shoulder. "We need to figure out what happened. Did you go through my cell phone or my things yet?"

"No," I say. "I thought about it, but by the time they put you in a room last night, all I wanted to do was make sure you were okay."

He squeezes me close enough I feel him breathe, and then he says, "Yesterday was a long day for you."

"For you too," I say.

"The office," he says. "Have they—"

"Armando and Evangeline are covering for you," I say. "Rafi and Evangeline came by and brought breakfast and coffee."

"Food does sound nice," he says. "After the nurse leaves, let's have that, and then we can worry about yesterday."

CHAPTER

27

CADE SIPS THE coffee and nibbles a kolache while I find the sealed bag with his clothes, attaché case, and belongings, pouring them across the bed.

The Italian leather loafers he wore yesterday.

A dress shirt and T-shirt, each sliced up the front, and I move those to the trash.

Tan suit coat, his favorite blue pen still in its breast pocket, and the matching dress pants.

Cuff links, watch, wallet, car keys, and cell phone all in their own small bag.

He fastens his watch back on his wrist and examines it, then smiles at the cuff links. "Good, I'd have missed those if something happened to them."

I roll my eyes and press a button on his cell phone, but the screen doesn't light up. "Battery's dead. I brought a charger, though."

"So wherever I was, I needed the suit coat." He rifles through the attaché case and pulls out his tie. "But not this."

I plug the phone in and hunt through the pockets of his pants, but they're empty.

He turns out the suit coat pockets and produces two receipts from his wallet, examines them, replaces one, and gives me the second. "I must have stopped for a drink."

"Did you have a bar association or a criminal defense association meeting?" I ask.

"Wouldn't have a tab for those," he says.

"This address is in Highland Park," I say. "Did you meet someone?"

He sighs and shakes his head. "I don't remember."

"It's fine," I say and squeeze his hand. "We'll sort it out."

The single drink at a bar on a Thursday evening nags at me, right at the start of happy hour, when he should have been coming home to me.

I hand it back to him. "What's the other receipt?"

He grins at me over the top of his coffee cup, green eyes glinting in the low light. "A surprise."

"Hmm," I say. "Will I like this surprise?"

"Maybe," he says. "I'm a little fuzzy on the details myself, but yes. I think so."

"You don't remember what you bought," I say.

His smirk tells me he knows exactly what he purchased.

"You're impossible." I open my backpack to tug out his pajama pants and a clean T-shirt for him. "Also, if you're feeling well enough to be difficult, you can shower, and I brought your toothbrush and razor."

He huffs and folds his arms across his chest. "I hardly think I'm being difficult if I can't remember, Reag. I *do* have a head injury. Maybe you could help a guy out, you know?"

"I'm not giving you a sponge bath," I say. "You're perfectly capable of taking a shower."

"But by myself?" he asks. "I could fall if you leave me unsupervised—"

"Then you should shower while I brush my teeth," I say. "And at some point today, Rafi or Evangeline will come sit with you so I can shower at our place."

He preens. "You said 'our place.'"

I ignore him and retreat to the bathroom with my clothes and toothbrush, closing the door behind me in case a nurse or one of our friends should drop in. I brush my teeth, pull my hair up into a ponytail, and step out of yesterday's clothes, pulling on fresh underwear and a clean pair of blue jeans.

Cade calls, "Reag, I meant to ask. About yesterday . . ."

"What about?" I ask.

"Bridger," he says. "What he said, about you talking to someone about the case yesterday morning. What'd you find out?"

"Oh," I say, tugging on a T-shirt. "I went back and talked to the club manager, but he wouldn't talk to me. He said if I didn't know why Cesar and Heather had to die, I didn't know anything at all. Only then at the office, Stu said something about the prenuptial that got me wondering."

"That just happened to come up?" Cade asks.

"We were discussing your new case in Preston Hollow," I say.

"Ah, yes," Cade says, and I can hear the eye roll in his voice. "Catching your wife banging your business partner is not an automatic not guilty by reason of insanity plea, by the way."

I slide back into Cade's old sweatshirt and step out of the bathroom. "Stu said it was stupid not to invoke the prenuptial and divorce her. He mentioned his father's will and prenuptial. Did you know that if Colleen is caught cheating, he has grounds for divorce, but if she divorces him, she only gets half of his assets as valued at the time of their marriage?"

"Well, no one said she was smart," Cade says.

"And apparently the will states that if something happens to Bridger, everything goes to his firstborn son and their heirs," I say. "If Heather was pregnant with Cesar's child and made that known . . ."

"Shit," Cade breathes. "That's a helluva motive. So even if Cesar was dead, that she was pregnant with his child meant that she and the baby had to die, then?"

"It points back to Stu or Colleen, if you think about it," I say. "Because why would Bridger have cared? Honestly, the way the will is written makes it sound like he's giving the finger to his family."

"Colleen and Stu aren't this bright," Cade says. "Stu only wants to be a lawyer so he can make some quick money until he can access his trust at thirty. And Colleen—this takes a helluva lot more planning than a cocktail party."

"It doesn't seem fair that everyone's always putting her down," I say. "Look, I get the dumb blonde stereotype, but did anyone stop to consider it might be an act?"

Cade smiles. "It'd have to be a pretty long-running act. I'd believe it of Stu before Colleen, and certainly of Bridger if he now regrets his earlier actions and needs to cover everything up to launch his golden boy out into the world."

And I almost echo Armando's words from last night in the emergency department's waiting room, that Cade is Bridger's golden boy, but that only reminds me of another unacknowledged similarity between Cade and Stu.

"That assumes Stu wants the firm and the money," I say. "Do you want your family's farm?"

Cade eases himself out of bed and pads to the bathroom. "The farm doesn't come with seven figures in assets, a house in Highland Park, and a law firm. How could Stu not want all that?"

I sit cross-legged on the end of the bed and pick up the receipt from the bar again to examine it. After he brushes his teeth and I hear water run in the shower, I open his wallet and withdraw the other receipt.

A Highland Park jewelry store.

One thousand dollars.

I catch my breath, remind myself that's not enough for an engagement ring, not with Cade's spending habits. And, anyway, he knows enough by now not to spring a surprise like that on me, surely he wouldn't . . .

He leans around the doorframe. "I knew you wouldn't be able to resist."

"It's not like there's anything here," I mutter, glaring at him.

He laughs. "I love you, Reag."

"I love you too," I grumble.

"This shower is too small," he says. "You think you could talk them into letting me leave earlier?"

"No." I flop back on the bed and stare at the ceiling. "You should stay until the doctor says you can go."

"Oh, he's just trying to prevent a malpractice suit," Cade says. "I don't need all this babying. I'm fine."

"You were just complaining that you needed me to help you in the shower," I say. "You can't have it both ways."

He laughs. "Who says?"

I smile because it's Cade and he can say that; he's a man and he doesn't understand there's often a price that won't just go neatly on a debit card.

The familiar smell of his soap washes over me and I breathe it deep. "So you went to a jewelry store?"

He chuckles and the water stops in the bathroom. "Apparently."

I examine the time and date stamps on the receipts and compare the addresses. The bar and jewelry store are in the same Highland Park shopping center.

"You were at the bar first," I say. "Do you remember what you were drinking? The receipt doesn't say."

"I don't know," he says. "I wish I did, but . . ."

"It may take a few days," I say. "We'll sort it out."

He steps out of the bathroom, towel around his waist, and leans down to kiss me, his damp hair tickling my cheek. "I think after I lie down."

I laugh and rub the scruff on his cheek. "Like for a nap? You hate naps."

"No, I just got a head rush when I bent over," he says. "I need to lie down."

"Oh." I race to support him, barely getting an arm around him in time. "Come on, let's get you dressed and back to bed."

He leans on me and eases into the mattress. "I knew you wouldn't be able to resist getting in bed with me."

I wriggle free of his attempts to yank me down with him. "We're putting your clothes *on*. Not taking them off."

"No fun," he says.

I toss him his clothes. "Fun will happen when the doctor says you're well enough to go home. And maybe when you can tell me about that jewelry store receipt."

"I told you." He pulls on pants, grinning at me. "I can't remember."

"This head injury is very convenient," I say.

He grasps my hand and kisses the back of it. "If I get out of the hospital in time tomorrow, do you think we can still look at apartments?"

That I don't have a job to help contribute to this larger apartment doesn't seem to have crossed his mind.

But something might come up, after all.

And it's nice to know that, regardless of yesterday's blowback at the firm, he still wants a more permanent arrangement than what we have now.

"Anything you want," I say.

"Except you in the shower," he quips.

I kiss the top of his head. "Don't be petty."

He tugs me into bed with him and snuggles close, his head on my chest. "You'll stay?"

I almost point out to him that I have nowhere else I can go, nowhere else I want to go, but maybe he needs the verbal reassurance, and so I turn his face up to mine and kiss him. "I'll stay."

As long as you want, I don't say, forever even. I have a feeling he already knows that.

He yawns and says, "I love you."

"I love you too," I say, and hold him and think about how lucky we are, about how much worse yesterday could have been, until I feel him fall asleep in my arms.

* * *

It's late afternoon by the time Cade wakes again, but he must feel better because he requests his favorite lunch from the deli near the office and opens the window blinds. He sits in bed, pulls the blue pen from his suit coat pocket, and marks up a deposition from his attaché case while a baseball game plays on the television.

I stand at the window and watch the early rush hour traffic building. A sudden longing for the stillness of the lake among the pine trees, the soft creaking of the hammock, and the blackness of the sky without the city lights washes over me.

Cade tosses his wadded-up sandwich wrapper into the trash can and says, "I'm sorry this isn't the weekend we thought we'd have."

"Did we think we'd have any sort of weekend?" I ask. "Anyway, it's not your fault. Who goes around expecting their drink to get spiked?"

He smiles at me and sips his lemonade. "I have a feeling you're very careful with your drinks when you're out."

I shrug. "Do you think it was a stranger? It'd have to be someone you'd grab a drink with on a Thursday evening."

"Well, whoever it was, know I'd rather have been at our place drinking with you," he says. "And doubly so now."

I drag my backpack out and open it to smash in the bag of our dirty laundry. "Rafi will probably be here soon with my car. I can go get more clothes for us and pick up anything you want from home. Do you need anything in particular?"

"I'm leaving here by lunch tomorrow," he says. "But I suppose shoes would be helpful."

"You don't think you'd like to walk out of here in pajama pants and loafers?" I ask.

"No." He laughs. "Shorts, a T-shirt, and a pair of running shoes, please."

I hand over my laptop, the file from Miller, and the envelope Heather brought us. "Is there room for those in your case? I'll be able to fit more in here without them."

He nods and tucks everything away. "I'll take good care of them."

"Speaking of taking good care of things," I say. "Your car has probably been parked by that bar all day today. Rafi and I can go get it, or I can grab an Uber, but I'd like to move it for us to have it tomorrow when you're discharged."

Cade leans back against the pillows, frowning. "I don't usually let anyone else drive my car."

"Bullshit," I say. "You let them drive it to service it, don't you? To wash it and wax it and check the tires?"

"That's different," he says. "It's a closed lot then. Not on the streets."

"And have you considered that your doctor may say that you can't drive through the weekend?" I ask. "Wouldn't you rather the car is here and then comes home with us, instead of sitting over in a lot in Highland Park?"

Cade sighs and chews the edge of his lower lip. "There's that."

"I'll be very careful," I say.

"This is just . . ." He pulls his car keys from his bag and twirls them on one finger. "It's a big step for our relationship."

I raise an eyebrow. "Bigger than moving in together?"

"You make a good point." He smiles sheepishly and hands me the keys. "Take good care of her."

"Her?" I ask.

"What can I say?" he asks. "I'm a sucker for a Texas redhead."

"It's a German car," I say.

"Bought in Texas," he retorts.

His phone rings and I stash the car keys inside my backpack before he changes his mind. If I slip away now while he's distracted, he's less likely to complain any further, so I request an Uber from my phone. Rafi is probably occupied with Evangeline, and there's no sense in interrupting him.

"Hey, man," Cade says into the phone, and to me, whispers, "It's Armando."

"Of course," I say.

"Reag says hi. So no one's said a word?" Cade covers his phone, and says, "Can you bring me my pillow, too?"

I can't make out what Armando says on his side of the phone conversation, but Cade narrows his eyes.

"Are you kidding?" he asks.

"I'm sure everyone misses you," I say.

Cade flips me the bird, but says to Armando, "Hell, I didn't expect balloons and flowers, but I thought someone would've asked or something."

I kiss him goodbye. "Back soon."

He grins and winks. "I love you. Be careful."

"Oh, I won't hurt your car," I say. "I love you too."

It's half a relief to step out of the hospital, even if the air is warm and heavy, smelling faintly of smog and concrete, but it's preferable to the sterile fluorescent hallways and industrial tile floors. Daylight fades, draining the city's color with it, jeweled fingers glittering on the downtown skyline and casting long shadows, and I wish Cade's doctor had cleared him to go home tonight. I decide I'll smuggle in some moonshine and a burger from that place Cade likes, the one right around the corner from his apartment building, where he took me the first night that we ate dinner together.

I close my eyes, breathe in the city, and summon memories of moonshine in a shared flask, salt from the french fries, and the bacon in his burger, all the flavors I tasted when he kissed me.

A car engine startles me from my thoughts, and I check my phone, match the car to my app, and wave to the driver.

I slide into the passenger seat of the sensible sedan, beige upholstery smelling of air freshener and carpet cleaner.

The driver meets my gaze with an apologetic smile. "It's rush hour. Hope you're not trying to get anywhere in a hurry."

My evening will probably consist of Cade falling asleep halfway through a baseball game while I read a book on the small sofa next to his bed.

I buckle my seatbelt and say, "It's fine."

Cade can manage on his own for a bit. He'll probably doze back off and not even notice how long I'm gone.

Taillights seethe red along I-35, bumper to bumper traffic like last night, when Rafi brought me here, and I almost text him to ask that he go sit with Cade.

But maybe he's having the Friday night with Evangeline that Cade and I should be having together. And he'll fuss that I'm leaving at all, that I'm by myself, and I roll my eyes and shove my phone into my bag. I'm not the one who's recovering from a GHB overdose.

Knowing what I know now about Cade's kidney, it only makes sense if whoever slipped him the GHB didn't have the same information. If the plan had Cade wrecking the Porsche on the expressway home from the bar, this might not just be about scaring me. It would be about having Cade out of the way—

But from what?

I lean back in my seat and comb through Cade's current caseload in my mind.

Certainly none of his clients benefit if Cade is out of the picture.

Nor the firm either; Cade may be suspended temporarily from profit-sharing, but they do need him bringing in retainers and billable hours.

What did Bridger say about the NFL that night at his house two weeks ago, with that smirk of his so like Stu's, like he knew something no one else did?

Bridger, Cade's mentor from the time he started law school.

If he knows why Cade isn't playing pro football, why Cade is an attorney instead, then he can't have been the person to dope Cade.

I'm missing something, I tell myself, *something big and important.*

My head aches suddenly, and I rub the side of my face.

"Too warm?" the driver asks and reaches for the temperature control. "We've been lucky so far, that the summer's been so mild. But this heat today—the weatherman said it's the hottest day of the year so far. Some rain sure would be nice, wouldn't it?"

"Mm-hmm," I say automatically. "But be careful what you wish for, or we'll have a tropical storm on top of us. This is Texas."

He laughs. "The weather here."

I pick up my line of thought where I dropped it when the driver interrupted and retrace my steps.

It makes sense that it would be Bridger that Cade met at the bar. There would have been a promise that they could work something out over a round of drinks, a restoration of their long-standing mentor/mentee relationship, and Cade could be Bridger's golden boy once again.

"Son," Bridger calls him, when he barely acknowledges Stu.

Maybe the GHB really is just a warning to me, maybe just to scare me off, that I'm too close to something that can embarrass Bridger or the Holcombe family, a reminder that they know about Cade and me and they can hurt him in more ways than just costing his partnership.

But if it isn't Bridger . . .

A shiver runs up my spine and I close my eyes, allowing my intuition to steer me the same way it pushes me when I'm running down a rabbit hole online, following the bread crumbs.

Stu can't access his trust until he's thirty, even if Bridger is dead, even if Cesar is out of the way.

So someone who needs Bridger *and* Cade out of the way, and Bridger's oldest, illegitimate son.

Colleen wouldn't benefit if Cesar inherits, but if something happened to Bridger before Stu is thirty, she'd have control of the trust—

Except that isn't a given, I remind myself. Not after how Bridger's sister left Kirby without access to her trust, leaving it all in Bridger's control.

I sit up so suddenly in my seat that the driver glances over at me. "Are you all right?" he asks.

"Yes," I say, but tuck my hands under my thighs so he doesn't see they're trembling.

Kirby.

Bridger's best friend from pre-kindergarten, his college and law school roommate, his brother-in-law, his original law firm partner—

Only for it to all come crashing down around him eighteen months ago when his wife died. But why act now, why kill Cesar and Heather, and why try clearing Cade off the board like he must have yesterday?

The car slows.

I open my eyes as the driver steers us into a shopping center parking lot in Highland Park. Cade's Porsche gleams in the setting sun, and I say, "This is fine. You can drop me here."

"Nice car," the driver says. "Park Cities don't mess around."

He's harmless enough that I grin. "It's not mine. I just have the keys tonight."

"Better enjoy it then," he says.

He waits without me asking until I unlock the car and give him a thumbs up. I watch his small sedan chug away, off to his next stop, and tip him and give him a five-star rating on my phone before I open the door.

The familiar smell of leather and Cade's cologne washes over me.

I duck into the car, the seat warm from the day's sunlight. Papers are strewn across the passenger seat, as if someone carelessly tossed them there, and I lock the door, shove my backpack into the floorboard, and start the car before gathering the documents.

Cade's partnership agreement.

Notes and underlines in purple ink, only I know I didn't make these.

I remember the blue pen in Cade's coat pocket, the blue pen he always carries, and then a second memory surfaces, of Kirby passing me in the hallway, laughing over his shoulder that he borrowed a pen from my desk.

That bastard.

I skim through the scribblings, clearly not in my handwriting or anything resembling it, so maybe Kirby's plan isn't to frame me. It's almost as if he left these to point out potential leverage for Cade in the agreement, with a running list of Cade's cases and the dollar amounts compared to Cade's shares in the firm, and how much of Cade's raw income goes to Bridger as the managing partner.

Like Kirby needs to convince Cade that he isn't getting his fair share and what he could earn if someone besides Bridger was in charge.

But why would Kirby need to divide Cade and Bridger?

And what could this accomplish that the scene yester-day in Bridger's office didn't?

I frown and tap my fingers on the Porsche's shifter.

Despite the income Cade generates for Holcombe & Donaldson, his partnership agreement has no loopholes for him to leave without significant financial penalties, none of the wiggle room here Cade can find in the criminal code to delight juries with during arguments in the courtroom. I recognize the syntax and pacing from the last couple of months reviewing law firm documents; this is obviously written by Bridger, and it makes me wonder what Kirby's and his partnership agreement must look like, if the junior partners' agreements have this elegance.

The Porsche's engine idles at a low growl and the air conditioning kicks in, cooling the interior to a pleasant chill. Outside the car, other vehicles arrive, couples in busi-ness casual attire laughing and chatting on their way to the bar, a few window-shopping at the jewelry store.

It's Friday night.

Cade and I ought to be together right now, maybe hav-ing a drink on his balcony, debating over what to order for dinner, planning our weekend while his green eyes flirt with me over his glass, his fingers playing with my hair and promising more to come.

Only right now he's laid up in a hospital bed.

I lean back in my seat, let the warmth of the leather soak into me, and consider my options.

If I go to the apartment and return to Cade, tell him my theory that Kirby is behind Cesar and Heather's deaths, he'll listen. But his first phone call will be to Bridger, and their inclination will be to handle this in-house. Mitigate risk to the firm.

Bridger, after all, doesn't seem very inclined to cooperate with a police investigation into the deaths of Cesar Morales or Heather Hudson; even the knowledge that Kirby might have been behind them likely won't be enough to sway him. He'll only want to cover up any scandal.

Kirby being arrested for murders—or accessory or conspiracy to commit—in conjunction with the attempted coup will be the talk of the Dallas legal community.

However, the law firm is on the way to the apartment, and it will be empty.

I have Cade's keys, and there are no cameras right now. Besides, I can always say I'm just cleaning out my desk if there are questions.

But maybe I can slip into Cade's office, use his computer, his password, and poke around on the network. There, I might be able to find Bridger and Kirby's partnership agreement, and maybe even the proof that Kirby may have committed or been party to the murders.

Or at least that he had motive.

I can take that to Miller, who won't give a damn about any Uptown scandals. He'll arrest Kirby if it means closing a case.

I can tell Cade about it if I find anything. There's no point in worrying him needlessly if I don't.

It's a gray area, not quite a lie of omission, but not exactly the truth.

I pray silently for Cade's forgiveness, that I'm adjusting his mirror and his seat, that I'm borrowing his car and maybe skirting a boundary. I push the clutch in, move the shifter into gear, and drive south toward Uptown.

CADE'S PORSCHE CRUISES into the parking garage, easily navigating the hairpin turns and growling up the ramps, making me half envious that this will probably be the only time Cade lets me drive it. *Maybe I'll slip out later*, I promise myself, once Cade is asleep, and I can take it for a run up the North Tollway or around the Bush Turnpike, where no one will care how fast I'm driving.

And if I do get a ticket, Cade can manage that.

The garage is deserted, because of course it is. It's Friday night, and even the reserved slots for the partners and senior associates are empty. I park in Cade's spot and eye the employee entrance to the law firm.

No one should be there except the security guard stationed on the floor until the cameras and sprinklers are fixed next week, but he won't know I quit yesterday. I consider taking my bag but decide to leave it; the more I carry in, the more suspicious it looks. With no holster and no way of discreetly holding my pistol, I leave it in the backpack. But my knife might be useful, so I clip it into the center gore of my bra and tuck the bag behind the driver's seat where it won't be obvious.

I slide out of the car, slip my phone into the back pocket of my jeans, and click the alarm, flinching at the chirp that seems to echo more loudly than usual. For a second, I hesitate, listening to it reverberate off the cement walls, wondering if anyone else hears it.

But so what if they do? If anyone stops me, I'm just picking up my things, I have a perfectly valid reason for being here.

Stop looking so damn guilty, I tell myself. *Get in there or don't; no one is making you do this.*

Cade's keys are warm in my hand, reassuring somehow. I find the key to the law firm's entrance, turn it, and pull the door handle, only to realize the door is now locked.

I twist the key again and pull.

The door opens, having been unlocked all along.

Only it shouldn't be, not at this time, not with all the cars gone from the employee spaces. No one should be at the firm.

I clutch the keys against myself at a low ready, wishing I can make them the pistol I probably should have brought with me, and pad down the hall.

The front desk is empty, the lights lowered. The security guard isn't in his chair.

Everything appears exactly as it's supposed to be.

But I try the glass door back to the offices before I use a key, and it's unlocked too.

A faint shiver of fear tickles my spine and runs the length of my tattoo, but I shake it off. Of course the door would need to be unlocked if the security guard is in here, making his rounds.

Still, I keep my footsteps soft and watch every shadow as I make my way to Cade's section.

Its door is locked.

I breathe a sigh of relief, but then I hear men's raised voices.

Bridger and Kirby's voices.

In Bridger's office.

I press Cade's keys into my pocket so they won't rattle and tiptoe toward the back of the firm.

If Bridger and Kirby are in Bridger's office, maybe Kirby's is unlocked.

Kirby's office, the firm's other corner office, tucked behind the secretarial pool next door to Bridger's that I've never been into, that I've never needed to enter.

Only now it may have everything I need to bring him down.

I duck through the secretarial cubicles, sneak to Kirby's door, and turn the handle.

It opens.

I push it wider and slink inside.

Like Bridger's office, it boasts thick carpet; I can feel its richness beneath the thin soles of my sandals. Its windows don't overlook downtown like Cade's and Bridger's, though, but the neighboring buildings, so only their lights and what filters up from the street beneath us soften the darkness of the deepening dusk.

I creep toward the desk and file cabinets.

"Goddamn it," Bridger shouts from his office, and I freeze, my ears straining to hear more.

But there are only low, harsh tones, a masculine chuckle—Kirby, maybe—and I resist the urge to press my ear to the wall between us.

The desk's surface is clear, and the computer is powered off. I squat between the chair and the desk, ease a file drawer open and run my fingers over tabs, squinting in the low light rather than using my cell phone.

In the back, I find a folder labeled "Important Documents" and grab it, opening it to skim through.

Death certificate for Vanessa Holcombe-Donaldson.

Kirby's medical power of attorney, naming Vanessa Holcombe-Donaldson as agent.

His financial power of attorney, naming Vanessa Holcombe-Donaldson as agent.

His will, naming Vanessa Holcombe-Donaldson as sole beneficiary.

Their marriage license.

Bridger's and his partnership agreement.

A cramp starts in my thigh, and I sit, knees over opposite ankles, and read.

This partnership agreement isn't as refined as Cade's; it's clear it was written earlier in Bridger's career, but its exit penalties are a silk garrote wielded by Bridger's capable pen.

If Kirby leaves, he leaves with nothing. He can only take his client list with him if he pays, and he can't cash out his shares in any form.

If Kirby retires, he only gets a retirement funded by the other partners if he leaves his clients behind. He forfeits his retirement the day he takes a case as an independent attorney or as anything beyond a consulting attorney for Holcombe & Donaldson.

Kirby doesn't carry that heavy of a caseload; his days lately consist of three-martini lunches and golf games. Retirement would be no great hardship for him, except that it isn't quite as lucrative as being a senior partner.

Whatever Kirby is up to, he must need money—badly.

The kind of money access to a hungry young partner like Cade provides, with his five-figure retainer fees and splashy publicity, because why else would Kirby be trying to lure Cade away?

But it must be money that Kirby can't or won't ask Bridger for, money Kirby thought he would get when his wife died, only for it to all go to Bridger.

Even while Kirby named her beneficiary in the case of his death, she didn't extend him the same courtesy.

I shake my head, replace the partnership agreement in its file, and the folder back in the drawer.

A loud slam echoes in Bridger's office, like a hand hit-
ting a table.

I straighten, listening, but hear nothing else, so I close
the file drawer and move to the drawer above it. Two squatty
liquor bottles cover a stack of *Playboys*, and I roll my eyes.
Underneath them, though, is a photograph, old by how thin
it is and the way its edges crinkle, and I hold it up to what
little light there is.

Four teenagers.

I pick out Bridger and Araceli right away; I recognize
them from the photos I have in the envelope I left with
Cade. This must have been taken the same summer, as they
appear the same age, but in this picture, a teenage girl about
Araceli's age is with them, her dark hair and smile a softer
version of Bridger's. She stands between him and a teenage
boy, his blond hair shaggier but his grin just the same, his
arm thrown around her.

Kirby.

This is the proof he knew all along about Bridger and
Araceli's relationship, that maybe he at least served as an
accomplice and a co-conspirator in the murders of Cesar
and Heather, and I tuck the photo into my back pocket.

I stand, roll my ankles to shake the tingling feeling
there, and get the blood flowing again. It's almost nightfall
outside, and my stomach growls, as if to say, *Yes, it's time to
get out of here, get what Cade needs from the apartment, and
grab dinner.*

The photo will be enough, maybe, to show leverage. And
now that I know the gist of Kirby's partnership agreement, I
should be able to convince Miller to get moving. Cade won't
be nearly as hasty in wanting to protect Kirby as he would be
if Bridger is involved, and maybe between Cade and Bridger
and Miller, they can work something out quietly.

Something where Kirby still gets punished for what he
did, but where it doesn't drag the firm through any mud.

I turn the door handle, gently pull it to me, and step out into the secretarial pool.

Bridger's office door is still open, the lights shining, but if he and Kirby are still there, they aren't talking.

Not that it matters; I have what I need.

I steal in the opposite direction, back through the secretarial cubicles to slip past Bridger's open door, arriving at the safety the darkness represents with an almost audible exhale.

Home free.

The rest is easy, a few quick steps down the hallway, past Cade's section, through the glass doors into the lobby, out the side exit to the garage, and into Cade's car.

To Cade's apartment, to pick up dinner, to the hospital and the safety of his embrace.

I take one step, then a second.

An arm, thick and heavy, snags me, wrapping itself around my waist.

A hand clamps over my mouth.

"You sneaking bitch, today you gonna learn your lesson about not being where you ain't supposed to be," a male voice says in my ear, and then raises his voice to call, "We got a visitor."

*   *   *

The smell of perspiration, the sensation of being lifted off my feet, his breath hot against my neck combine and drag me back to the Katy South Trailhead. I recoil, knowing that whoever this is, it's who attacked me, and Rafi isn't here to save me this time.

I kick against him, but his grip tightens as I thrash and squirm, half carrying me, half pushing me toward Bridger's open office door, finally flinging me across the threshold.

A flip-flop band breaks as I stumble, getting my feet under me, my bare toes sinking into the carpet.

For a second, Bridger stares across his desk at me, perspiration beading at the open collar of his dress shirt. "What the hell . . . ?"

Kirby angles in his seat in one of the leather chairs to smile at me over his shoulder. "Reagan."

"Caught her snooping," the man behind me says. "Again."

Meaty hands give me another push, but I glimpse his face this time.

Bear, wearing a T-shirt with black jeans, a black leather motorcycle vest, and boots despite the heat. He appears even more ridiculously out of place here in the law firm's luxury than I do, especially when compared with Kirby in his linen trousers and pale blue dress shirt, monogrammed cuff links winking at me from the French cuffs.

"It's fine." Kirby picks a fleck of lint off his trousers. "Did she come alone?"

"McCarrick's Porsche," Bear says, "but only her."

Bear pats me, as if searching for something, and I slap his hands away. "Put your hands on me again and—"

"Let her be," Kirby says. "Have a seat, Reagan. You're late to the party, but there's always room for one more."

"I'll stand, thanks," I say, shifting so I can keep the three men in my line of sight and the chair between us.

"Suit yourself." Kirby rolls a glass half full of an amber liquid between his fingers. "How is Cade?"

I bite the inside of my cheek and think about how to answer this, the advantages and disadvantages either way. Finally, I say, "His doctor thinks he'll make a full recovery."

"I'm sure that will be a great relief to you and Bridger," Kirby says.

"His doctor?" Bridger frowns. "I thought this whole being too sick to work today was a ruse, that he was just blowing off some steam about yesterday—"

"No," I say.

Bridger's face reddens and he glares at Kirby. "What the fuck did you do?"

"Cade and Reagan should have left all this alone," Kirby says.

My phone vibrates in my back pocket, buzzing.

"What's that?" Bear asks.

"Nothing," I say.

Kirby says, "Give him the phone, or I'll have him take it from you."

I pull my phone out of my pocket. Cade's name and the picture of us at the winery last weekend flash on the screen as I hand it over.

"It's McCarrick," Bear says.

"Answer it on speaker phone," Kirby says to me. "You're a smart girl, Reagan. Do the right thing here for Cade."

I swallow hard and swipe the answer button, then set it on speaker. "Hey."

"Reag," Cade says. "Where the hell are you?"

Kirby's gaze meets mine, an icy warning of what can still happen to Cade if I don't cooperate.

If I don't warn Cade the only way I can.

"At the apartment," I say. "Just like we agreed."

"Oh, really?" Cade asks. "Then why is Rafi telling me that you aren't there?"

"There must be a mistake," I say. "Maybe I was in the shower when he knocked. I'm here, at your apartment, and then I'm stopping to get dinner on my way back to the hospital. Those sweet potato fries from the diner you asked for?"

"Fucking sweet potato fries . . . ," Cade scoffs and then catches his breath on the other end of the line, almost a gasp. He must know now, but he keeps his tone nonchalant. "Hurry back then, okay?"

I eye Kirby across from me, see Bridger watching us both. "Traffic's a bitch."

"I'll wait up," he says. "I love you. Be careful."

"I love you too," I say, but I don't promise him I'll see him soon.

Because that may be a lie, a real lie this time, and I can't lie to Cade.

Not about this.

One lie is enough, the only lie I'll ever tell him, and I already hate myself for it, even if I know it's for his own good.

Bear holds out his hand when I hang up the phone. "Give it to me."

"Fuck you," I say, forcing bravado I don't feel into my voice. "Clearly you heard it ring and I cooperated."

"Leave it," Kirby says. "It's fine."

He's letting me keep my phone as a way of placating me temporarily; Bear is big enough to take it whenever he or Kirby decide they want it.

I sit in the leather chair, encase myself in its thickness, cross my ankles, fold my hands in my lap, and say, "Now, why are you two here on a Friday night?"

"You shouldn't be here," Bridger says. "You're not supposed to even be on the premises—"

"But she is." Kirby's smirk is somehow menacingly triumphant, only I can't figure out what he accomplishes by me being here or what it means.

Whatever it is, it makes Bridger wilt a little more in his seat. He drums his fingers on his desk, as if considering his options, and finally asks, "Cade's in the hospital?"

"Someone slipped GHB in his drink last night," I say. "Cade doesn't remember who he was with, but I found Cade's partnership agreement in his car, with Kirby's handwriting all over it. I'm no lawyer, of course, but from the looks of it, Kirby's trying to rope him into a hostile takeover. Not that he's doing so hot, if he has to drug Cade."

Kirby chuckles beside me. "I should have known why Cade was so adamant about hiring you. How long did it take you to get him into your bed—or were the two of you already together, and that's how you convinced him to give you a job?"

"She's good enough to track you, isn't she?" Bridger rubs his face with one hand, but that doesn't hide his down-turned mouth. "Look, whatever plan you have isn't going to work."

Kirby sneers. "If she had anything at all, the police would be here. Did you call the police, Reagan?"

If I talk fast enough, if I can make myself not a threat and convince Kirby I'm on his side, then maybe we all walk out of here alive tonight.

I raise one shoulder in a half-shrug, force a smile, and keep my tone casual. "Should I have?"

"See?" Kirby smirks at Bridger. "I talked to the police when they were here on Wednesday. They have nothing. I made sure of it, and unless you want to raise some hell about that dead bastard of yours, they're not gonna give a damn."

"That's a gamble, of course," I say to Bridger. "Eventually, someone might get motivated in the department and wonder about that connection from a Deep Ellum night club to your family. And that Heather was pregnant—well, who knows what might be said about that?"

"She was pregnant?" Bridger hisses.

Kirby glares in Bear's direction. "I thought you said you had things under control."

"I couldn't go with her everywhere," Bear says. "'Specially not once she had that Mexican guy tagging along after her."

"He's not Mexican; he's as American as we are, and if you want to get technical about it, his family is from Guatemala," I say. "But still, I don't see why things can't just go on like they were before."

"Oh?" Kirby asks. "You don't?"

"I go back to the hospital," I say. "I'll tell Cade you two want to make a deal. Cade becomes a named partner, I come back on staff, and this gets . . . handled."

Kirby smiles as he looks over at Bridger. "Hear that? She wants things handled."

"If you don't keep Cade, you're letting a lot of money walk out the door," I say. "And if you don't make him a named partner, then you risk some other firm in Dallas doing that."

"That puts us in a difficult spot, though, don't you see?" Kirby glances at me now. "If we keep Cade, we keep you, and that puts us back at square one."

"But if I'm here, then you can keep an eye on me," I say.

Kirby snorts and slams back a mouthful of his drink, emptying the glass. "If I thought that would actually be effective."

"If I'm good enough to uncover this about Bridger's family—*your* family—imagine what other dirt I might be able to find for you two," I say. "And when this blows up in your face, you'll need a damn good defense attorney. It's pretty handy that you already have one. Right here in the office. Whose name is on the masthead."

Bridger actually cracks a smile as he leans back in his seat a little. "Have you thought about law school, Reagan? Maybe your talent *is* being wasted in Cade's office."

"Your mother seems to think as much," I say.

"Let's leave my mother out of it," Bridger says.

"She's already involved, though," I say. "Because we wouldn't be here if she hadn't told you no all those years ago. If she'd just let you and Araceli have the future that you wanted together. If she hadn't paid Lupita off to send Araceli away, out of your reach."

Bridger's mouth twists and he looks away, glowering. "So you know that too."

"And your prenuptial. And your will," I say. "What I couldn't figure out, though, was how Cesar found out who his father was and just turned up with the club."

"Oh," Stu says from behind me. "That's all my fault."

CHAPTER

29

"KNEW I'D SEEN whiskey in Cade's liquor cabinet," Stu says, ambling past with a bottle of Macallan 18. He looks fresh from the tennis court in his whites and sweatband holding back a mop of still-damp hair curling around his ears.

"Cade's been holding out on us, in more ways than one," Kirby says. "But then his taste has improved drastically over the last several years. We're a long way now from the hooch his family probably bootlegged a couple of generations ago, huh?"

"Distilled properly and aged right, even hooch might surprise you," I say.

"I guess you'd know." Kirby sneers and says to Stu, "Get a glass for Reagan. She's joining us."

"I think I learned my lesson yesterday about having a drink with you," I say.

"Clever girl," Bridger mutters and frowns in Kirby's direction. "You've probably had enough, anyway."

"Not yet, especially not if it's coming out of Cade's stash." Kirby leers at me, the whiskey on his breath overpowering even at this range. "You should have a drink."

Stu grins. "Good luck. I tried to get her to come out with me for a drink and she turned me down cold."

"Well, now we know why, don't we? Let's be fair, Stuey, you're not and never will be Cade the Great." Kirby shoves the small end table between us backward and yanks my chair closer to him. "I'd like to see you when you get that edge off you. I'll bet that's when you and Cade really get down to fun, when he's convinced you to relax a little."

"Enough," Bridger says. "She says she's not having any."

"It's really not up to you or her tonight, is it?" Kirby asks. "Pour her a glass."

Stu glowers at his uncle, sullen suddenly—maybe the reference to Cade?—and sets out three additional glasses from a cabinet in Bridger's hutch behind his desk.

"Don't forget Bear," I say.

"He's not staying," Kirby says, and flicks his fingers toward the open door. "Back to guard duty."

Stu opens the bottle and fills Kirby's glass, but the other three tumblers only halfway. He slides one across to me, our gazes meeting for half a second.

For once, he looks away first.

"Drink," Kirby says.

"But what are we drinking to?" I ask.

"To beautiful women," Kirby says. "May they be worth every bit of the trouble they cause and the heartbreak they bring."

Bridger scowls. "Fuck you. You never deserved her."

I sip the whiskey and let it slide down my throat, wishing it was moonshine.

Moonshine from a shared silver flask with a hint of apples and cinnamon, the scent of Cade's cologne promising I'm safe, his arm around me . . .

Just like Bridger's around Araceli, like Kirby's around that girl who must have been Bridger's younger sister.

"Araceli or Vanessa?" I ask. "Which one did he not deserve?"

"I was never after the little Mexican bitch," Kirby says. "At least not like *him*."

"She had a name," Bridger says through what sounds like clenched teeth. "Say it. Or can't you?"

"Take some advice here, Stuey," Kirby says. "Mexican girls come in all shapes and sizes and range of colors, but they're only good for cooking, cleaning, weeding, and fucking—not for marrying."

Bridger's face reddens.

Stu snorts. "Shit, it's like some relic from a time machine. Do you honestly believe that?"

"Oh, he does," Bridger says, turning his whiskey glass in his hand.

"She knows it's true," Kirby says and brushes my cheek with the backs of his fingers. "Don't you? Aren't you a little worried that's what Cade thinks, that maybe secretly you're just a placeholder until he finds that girl who can really take his career where it needs to go?"

"Cade's career must be doing just fine, or you wouldn't have been trying to lure him away last night," I say.

Kirby chuckles but moves his hand away. "Hell, Stuey, you ought to be more grateful. Without me, you wouldn't know the first damn thing about your daddy's little bastard, would you? The Great Bridger Holcombe, brought down because he couldn't keep his fucking pants zipped in college."

Stu slouches against the hutch, arms folded across his chest, and when we make eye contact, he says, "I didn't know it'd come to . . . all this."

"That's the problem with you Holcombes," Kirby says. "Always so convinced you're thinking two steps ahead of everyone else, when you're actually half a step behind."

"I just wanted to be treated like an adult for once in my life," Stu says. "At least to have my father treat me the way he treats Cade. For once. Is that too much to ask?"

"So you went to him?" I ask. "To Kirby?"

"I found letters in the attic from some girl named Araceli," Stu mutters, half into his whiskey glass. "All it took was caddying on Sunday for Uncle Kirby and keeping the flask full of his favorite scotch. I went hunting for Cesar and found him, and I swear to God I just wanted to have dirt on Dad for the next time he told me no. I just didn't count on Bear ratting me out to Dad."

"Bullshit," Bridger says. "Bear works for *me*."

"Does he?" I ask and incline my head toward Kirby. "Because he seems to be working for *him*."

Kirby snickers. "She does have a point."

I sneak a glance toward the dark cubicles. If I make a break for it, how far will I get before Bear or Kirby attempt to intercept me?

"The only vested interest Bear has in you, you two-faced shit, is that you're up to your ears in gambling debt to his buddies," Bridger says. "And I refuse to cover you."

I squirm to the edge of my seat, hoping against hope that maybe Bridger and Kirby will get so involved in their argument that I can slip away.

Stu smirks, as if he knows what I'm thinking and dares me to go through with it, and I want to hurl my glass at his head.

That all of this could come about because that entitled shit just wanted dirt to hold over his father's head . . .

Bridger sighs. "Maybe if I'd done things differently, none of this would have happened." He hunches in his chair, his eyes red and watery, clutching his glass like it's a lifeline, suddenly rendered small.

Weak.

Ineffectual.

He shakes his head. "Maybe if we'd recognized how badly Vanessa's loss impacted us all. Maybe if I'd kept a closer eye on Kirby, maybe if I'd told Bear that he couldn't drive Kirby, that he wasn't there to keep him from the consequences of his actions."

"I didn't need a goddamn babysitter," Kirby says. "I needed my wife to be loyal to me. Not to you. Not to her family. I needed to know I was important to her, but you couldn't even let me have that, could you? Always interfering, always meddling, and even when she died, I couldn't plan her funeral, because your mother took that from me, and then you took everything else. And tonight, I'll take everything from you, Bridger."

"You can't," Bridger says. "Because you'll go down with me. Did you think I was so stupid I wouldn't have safeguards in place?"

Footsteps approach from the dark hallway, their owner apparently unconcerned about being quiet or seeing a need to sneak anywhere.

"Bear?" Kirby calls. "Is everything all right?"

But it's Cade's voice that snarls from the darkness, "My car is here, so where the hell is Reagan?"

* * *

From the secretarial cubicles comes the sound of a scuffle, the sharp intake of breath, a low male grunt, the thwack of a punch.

I half rise from my seat, only for Kirby to grab my wrist and say, "Sit down."

And I don't question him.

Not then.

Bridger stands, long enough for Kirby to say, "Do you want to see what can happen if you don't sit down and shut up?"

I'm surprised that Bridger sits, that he doesn't even make an argument.

But he does.

Outside the office, a chair rolls and slams into a wall.

Glass shatters.

Cade stalks into the room.

Our gazes meet for half a second.

I almost blurt out an apology for my lie, an explanation that it's not Bridger behind all this, it's never been Bridger, but I'm too busy deciding if I'm relieved that Cade is here or concerned that we could both be in danger.

But now really doesn't seem to be the time to explain things, and maybe I don't need to. Not with the tableau spread out before Cade, not with Bridger slouched in his chair, Stu scowling and half perched on the hutch, Kirby still holding my wrist.

Cade looks away from me, green eyes practically sparking, jaw narrowed, and bristling like an angry tomcat.

He knows.

Blood spots the knuckles of his right hand, and his tousled hair, two-day beard, T-shirt, and yesterday's rumpled tan dress pants are as sloppy as I've ever seen him appear in public.

But then he wouldn't have many options coming straight from the hospital.

I cock my head to one side. How *is* he out of the hospital?

Apparently, the question occurs to Kirby as well because he says, "Ah, if it isn't Bridger's little insurance policy. Should you even be out of bed?"

Cade's grin is sharp as a knife's blade. "Ask Bridger's driver. Your fucking hitman. Whatever you want to call him."

Oh, yes. Cade knows.

"Goddamn it, McCarrick," Bear half moans, stumbling into the room with a tissue pressed to his nose. "You fucking lawyers always cheat. It's not fair to cold-cock someone like that."

"Was it fair to jump Reagan on the Katy Trail, you chickenshit son of a bitch?" Cade asks. "Next time you want to hit someone, pick on someone your own damn size."

Kirby laughs, a hearty guffaw, and slaps a knee. "He's got a point, Bear. Cade, you want a drink? It's your bottle of whiskey."

"Shove it up your ass," Cade says. "I only came for Reagan."

Kirby releases my wrist with a shrug. "We were just discussing some things."

"Odd how discussions with you seem to wind up with people dead," I say. "Were you discussing some things with Cesar Morales in the bar parking lot a couple of weeks back? Or when Heather came by the office?"

"Collateral damage," Kirby says. "You know a thing or two about that, don't you?"

"I have nothing to discuss with you." Cade jerks a thumb toward the door. "Reag, let's go. Now."

I stand and take one last look at the group Cade and I'll leave behind.

At Stu, who stares into his glass and apparently started all this in a misguided attempt to blackmail his father into cash and freedom, because he felt Bridger never valued him the way he valued Cade.

At Bridger, who has gone ghost-white pale, his mouth hanging open, so he soundlessly gulps air.

And at Kirby, sipping his whiskey like this is just a normal Friday night.

I cross to Cade and slip a hand in his.

Cade nods, as if to say we'll discuss this later or maybe not at all; maybe we can just leave here and call Miller, have him meet us at the hospital or at the apartment, tell him everything there and see what can be done.

A gun cocks behind us.

"I didn't say you two could leave," Kirby says. "Sit down."

Cade and I turn, his arm closest to me sweeping me back, behind him. The look on his face tells me he wants to handle this himself, and I can almost feel him making the calculations as to what will be the best approach.

Kirby holds a snub-nosed revolver, finger on the trigger, hammer cocked.

Bear shoves me, pushing me into Cade. "He said sit down."

"Watch it," Cade says over his shoulder, stepping sideways to place himself between not only me and Kirby, but also me and Bear too. "You're dispensable, and I'd remember that. You might want to consider whose side you're on here."

Bear grunts something unintelligible in response.

I glance back toward the door, evaluate the distance, and attempt to gauge how far that gun will be accurate, how fast we can make a dash for the cubicles—not that they'll be much protection—or if it would be best to make a break for Bridger's coat closet or the bathroom.

"This has gone a little far," Cade says, his tone easy and light, a marked contrast from his previous sharpness. "But we can handle this in-house, right? Nothing's been done here tonight that can't be explained away. We can work this out, Kirby."

Kirby laughs. "Hell, you are good. You almost had me there for a second."

"Bridger, you should've brought this to me in the beginning," Cade says. "I could've fixed it. Why didn't you come to me?"

Bridger shakes his head and swallows a long drink of whiskey, setting the empty glass on the table with a sigh. "Would you have been honest with me if I'd been honest with you?"

I don't see Cade flinch, but I feel it in the way his hand tightens on mine, the way he shifts his weight to his back foot.

Stu raises his head from his glass. "Go ahead. Answer him. I can't wait to hear how Cade the Great took his eye off the ball, fucked around with a staffer, and finally managed to disappoint Daddy Dearest."

"He's not my father," Cade says, but gentler than he might have said it yesterday.

Kirby chuckles. "Isn't he, though? Maybe not biologically, but how many years has it been since you went home to the farm?"

"That's hardly germane to this discussion," Cade says.

"You have a whole helluva lot more in common now with Bridger than your daddy," Kirby says. "German sports car, expensive suits, SMU ring, a taste for top-shelf whiskey and pretty women that'll get you in trouble—you're probably already checking on properties in Highland Park, aren't you?"

Cade takes his hand from me to fold his arms across his chest, and I hear him mumble, "Maybe."

"So much not Bridger's son that he named you executor of his will," Kirby says. "Now, how 'bout that?"

Stu's jaw tightens.

Bridger slumps in his chair.

Cade only demands, "What?"

"Oh, yes," Kirby says. "If something happens to our dear Bridger before Stuey turns thirty, you have complete and utter control of the Holcombe Trust and the law firm. Not Sylvie, not Colleen. Not even me."

"There must be some mistake," Cade says.

"Imagine my surprise too, when I found that out," Kirby says. "His oldest friend. His brother-in-law. His partner. And when I need money, when I need the smallest shred of assistance and compassion from him, not only will he not give it to me, but he puts it entirely out of my reach and hands it over to a fucking upstart hillbilly whose foundational skill is how to throw a goddamn football."

"For just this reason. I knew I could trust him to do the right thing and not gamble away what my family built or run it into the ground," Bridger snarls, but then gentles his tone to say to Cade, "I should have told you everything. If I'd been here the day Heather came to the office, maybe I could have stopped this. She must have known who was behind Cesar's death and was trying to warn me. What did she say to get you two involved?"

"She left an envelope for Cade," I say. "With his birth certificate, the alcohol permit for the club, and the picture of you and Ara—Cesar's mother."

"All this from that." Bridger shakes his head again. "Your talent *is* being wasted."

"She's very good at her job," Cade says, his arm stealing around my waist.

Kirby sneers. "I'm sure that's why you keep her around."

"I wouldn't have looked into it without her," Cade says.

Bridger's mouth tightens, his lips pressing together into a thin line. "I know. No one would've ever known or cared without Reagan."

And maybe that's the real tragedy of this whole damn thing, that if not for a little curiosity and persistence, their deaths would have been for nothing, and no one would have thought to look any further. There must be other Cesar Moraleses and Heather Hudsons out there, who die too young and leave behind grieving families, but no one cares enough to pursue the bread crumbs back to the murderers.

"So you killed them," I say to Kirby. "Or did you have Bear do it?"

"I didn't kill Mr. Holcombe's boy," Bear says. "And all I did was follow the girl. Rough you up when Mr. Donaldson said you were meddling about his gambling debts. Go through McCarrick's apartment and office to scare him off."

"Shut up," Kirby hisses.

"Fuck you," Bear says. "You're not pinning this on me."

"I'll pin whatever the fuck I want on you," Kirby says. "Cade was right. You are dispensable."

And almost before it registers that Kirby pulls the trigger, that the sound I hear is a gunshot, Bear drops to his knees and topples backward.

He doesn't move.

"Holy shit!" Stu screeches and rushes to the body.

"Okay," Cade says, breathing it out, "let's just talk through this, Kirby. We can still fix this."

"Oh, Bridger, listen to your boy." Kirby chuckles, stands to reach across the desk to grab the whiskey bottle, splashes a tumbler full, and drops back into his chair. "Do you think I give a flying fuck about fixing this now, Cade?"

"Do something," Stu hisses, maybe to me, maybe to Cade.

Maybe to Bridger, who still slumps in his seat, propping his forehead in one hand.

Kirby laughs. "What do you expect them to do? I have the gun, you entitled little shit. Do you know how many bullets it holds?"

It's an old-school .38 special, the kind of gun a guy like Miller probably carries in an ankle holster as a backup piece, one I might slip into a garter, but nothing that Cade will have ever seen outside a courtroom.

Certainly nothing that Stu will know anything about.

"Five," I whisper for him.

Five bullets, but now there are four, and there are four of us remaining.

Kirby can clean up everything here tonight and walk away. With Cade out of the picture, Kirby can take over the law firm and no one will be any wiser. Colleen and Sylvie won't challenge him, and Kirby can use the firm as his own personal piggy bank to clear out his gambling debts.

Kirby's gaze meets mine and his sneer sends a chill crawling up my back. "Oh, you are too clever, Reagan. Figured it all out, haven't you? Saved me some steps too. I wasn't quite sure how I'd deal with you and Cade, but now that's a moot point."

Cade moves back between me and Kirby. "Look, even if you don't want to fix this, no one else has to die tonight. We can all still walk away from this."

"Cut it out," Kirby says. "This isn't a press conference or a closing argument. You're not charming your way out of this one."

Behind Cade, safe from Kirby's view, I slide the switch-blade from my bra. I don't open it, not yet, but its warmth reassures me.

Four shots, four of us remaining.

But now one of us has a knife.

Stu says, "This isn't what I wanted," and almost trails off in a sob.

"Poor little rich boy," Kirby says. "You've spent the last eleven years bitching about your daddy and Cade McCarrick. I give them up to you on a silver platter and you lose your nerve."

"He had nothing to do with this," Cade says. "You did this."

"Yes," Kirby hisses. "I did. I beat Bridger Holcombe. Game, set, match. I'm hanging the bastard in his own loop-hole. Everyone will know that family isn't who they claim to be, that they're all impostors and fakes and hypocrites after I get through spinning the scene tonight, explaining about Stu killing everyone in a jealous temper. Even you and Reagan, as unfortunate as that is, all because the two of you were trying to pretend you belong here. You fit in better than you think, lying, even to each other that you can fake your way through this—"

"Reagan never lies to me," Cade says. "How else do you think I knew something was wrong earlier and came here?"

"That'll be your last mistake," Kirby says and raises the gun.

I flick the switchblade open and lean around Cade to throw it.

The knife catches Kirby just inside his right arm and he fires wide, hissing as the knife clatters to the desk and the gun falls to the floor.

Bridger moves now, lightning fast as a snake striking, grabbing the knife and plunging it through Kirby's right hand into the desk.

Kirby howls.

Cade pushes me. "Get out of here."

I reach for him, but he slips free of my grasp and rushes for the gun.

Kirby kicks at it, sending it clattering away, toward the far wall. He manages to tug the knife out of his right hand and swings it at Cade.

Cade should have the advantage—he's sober, with age and height and a gym habit on his side. But even though I know he just felt well enough to punch Bear a few minutes ago, I also remember that the doctor wanted him to rest through the weekend, that the head injury had him dizzy and sleepy earlier in the day, and that he's not even supposed to be out of the hospital.

He's only here because of me.

"Get up and help us!" Bridger bellows at Stu as he charges toward Cade and Kirby. "For once in your goddamn life, be a man."

But Stu freezes, cringing behind me.

Kirby lunges at Cade with the bloody knife.

Cade feints left and darts right, reaching low.

Kirby follows.

Bridger sails in with a tackle, rolling him and Kirby against the wall.

Both reach for the gun.

The gun fires.

Kirby flings Bridger off him.

I launch myself into the fray to help Cade.

The gun fires again.

A hand tangles in my ponytail and yanks.

"I'll shoot her," Kirby says, panting. "So help me, I'll do it. Is that what you want?"

Cade steps back and Kirby pulls me up harder against himself, pressing the gun to the left side of my head.

I eye the blood soaking the right sleeve of Kirby's dress shirt, dripping onto his pants and ruining Bridger's carpet. "He's only got one shot. He can't kill us all."

Kirby holds me close enough I can feel his ribs expand as he breathes. "Maybe you haven't noticed, sweetheart, but you and Cade are the last two standing."

Bile creeps up the back of my throat, burning the roof of my mouth, but I swallow it.

Bridger pushes himself up to a seated position, blood darkening his right side. "Stu," he croaks.

Stu's face is ashen, pressing his hands to the left thigh of his tennis whites. "I—I'm okay."

"Let her go," Cade says.

"This isn't a negotiation." Kirby slams his right arm across my throat, the coppery smell of his blood sending a second wave of nausea crashing over me. "Get Bridger and Stu on their feet."

Cade leans down so Bridger can hold onto him with his left arm and ease to his feet. Stu uses his father's desk to pull himself up, hopping to balance on his right leg.

"To my office," Kirby says.

"Fuck you," Stu says.

"Get him under control, Cade, or you'll be holding her while she dies in your arms," Kirby says. "Is that what you want?"

I sink my fingernails into Kirby's arm. "Don't listen to him."

"No," Cade says, although I'm not sure he's talking to me or Kirby.

"And you," Kirby whispers. "You be a good girl, or I'll shoot Cade. I won't shoot to kill. I may have forgotten that bad kidney of his yesterday, but I remember it now. Do you want to find out if they can perform an emergency transplant of his other one tonight, or if he'll bleed out before an ambulance gets here?"

I release my grip and let my hands fall to my side. "Okay."

Kirby waits for the men to pass, a trail of blood dotting the floor, and pushes me after them.

Kirby removes the gun from my head long enough to backhand a single light switch. "The bathroom."

Cade glances over his shoulder. "The bathroom?"

"Funny thing," Kirby says. "While Bridger was off feeling up cocktail waitresses over his long lunches and you were slipping off—to fuck a staffer, as it turns out—I was preparing for the day I might have to hide out from Bear's friends coming to collect their money. So I put a biometric deadbolt on my bathroom door."

"A biometric deadbolt." Stu pants and leans against the wall. "What the hell even . . . ?"

"I didn't want Bear's friends hiding in the bathroom to ambush me. But I also needed a place to hide if they came," Kirby says. "So it requires a thumbprint—my thumbprint—to unlock it from either side if it isn't already open. As it is now, so get in there."

Stu hobbles into the bathroom, leaning against the sink and peering around Cade to say, "We'll get out."

"Oh, now you're a big man, Stuey," Kirby says. "We'll see if that's before or after you or Bridger bleed out or if the smoke gets you first."

"You don't have to do this," Cade says.

"No," Kirby says. "No, but I want to."

"Look, let Reagan go," Cade says. "You don't need her."

"I need your partnership agreement paperwork from the Porsche," Kirby says. "Wouldn't want anything to point back to me, would we? And since I'm already there, at your car, I might as well take it to get home. But I can't drive it, not with this hole in my hand."

"Take me," Cade says.

"No." Kirby's chuckle is almost a wheeze in my ear, his breath brushing against my hair. "As amusing as the idea is of Bridger's golden boy begging me for a favor, I want you to die knowing you couldn't save her. That in the end, Cade the Great failed. If you have any parting words, you'd better say them now."

Cade's and my gazes meet for a long moment, and I drink him in.

The last time I'll ever see him.

He doesn't say I love you.

He doesn't say this is my fault.

He only says, "I'll find you," and that's all he'll ever have to say, because I know what it means.

It means "I love you," and "I forgive you," and "I need you to stay alive," and "I'm doing this for you, for us, so please stay strong," all neatly wrapped into three words that no one else will ever know how much mean to us.

I nod, fear and dread lumping so much in my throat that I can barely say, "Not if I find you first."

"Shut the door," Kirby says.

The door swings shut, and Kirby presses me to the wall, left hand holding the pistol at my head while he grunts and raises his right hand long enough for the biometric lock to click the deadbolt into place.

"That door's shit," I say. "Why would you waste the time putting a biometric lock on a standard door?"

"Oh, Reagan," Kirby scoffs, leaning into me. "The lock was only ever to delay Bear's goons for me to get security up here or for the secretaries to call the cops."

"Cade and Stu will break out," I say.

"Will they?" He laughs softly. "Maybe they could have, before Cade got the wind taken out of him in that fight and Stu got shot. But now . . . well, now we go to my desk. The center drawer, please."

He shoves the gun into my back as if to emphasize what will happen if I don't cooperate, and we walk to his desk. I pull open the center drawer, tears blurring my eyes and spilling onto his arm.

"The lighter, Reagan," he says.

"You can shoot me," I say. "I won't help you."

The gun moves away for a fleeting half second and he breathes in, quickly, almost an audible wince, but just before I bolt, the gun shoves into my back and he yanks the lighter from the drawer.

He pins me to the desk with his hip on my back, opens another drawer, and crashes a glass bottle next to me.

The crisp, alcohol smell of vodka wafts through the room.

Kirby clicks the lighter and tosses a wad of burning paper onto the desk. He yanks me upright, pausing to click the lighter at the fabric wall of the secretarial cubicles.

"Should we set fire to Cade's office?" he asks. "Maybe your desk?"

"Go to hell," I say.

"You're right," he says. "Wouldn't want to waste much time."

The hallway's reflection is orange in the glass doors by the time we arrive. I open it enough for us to pass through, praying to God that if He still hears me, that security guard will have returned and be at his post.

But as we pass the receptionist's desk, I see his shoes and follow the line of his pants to where he must be crumpled underneath.

I choke a sob.

No one is coming.

We make our way down the hall, out the exit into the parking garage, and Kirby makes me open the passenger door and climb over the center into the driver's seat. He settles inside and doesn't fasten his seat belt, only turning so he can push the gun into my ribs.

"Drive," he says.

I swallow hard and lick my lips. "Where?"

"Cut over to 75 north," he says. "My place is in Addison, but I don't want us tracked on the Tollway."

I press the key into the ignition and turn, hoping against hope that the car won't start.

But it does.

As we leave the parking garage, I glance up, one last time, hoping to see nothing, only darkness, maybe Cade waving to me that he broke out of the bathroom and he's safe.

But the windows glow orange, smoke beginning to curl.

"People will notice," I say.

"Maybe," Kirby says.

Bridger won't last long. He'll be the first to go. And Stu will likely bleed out; gunshot wounds to the leg are always tricky. But once that fire starts going, Cade will have only a matter of minutes.

I drive, blinking away tears.

"Don't worry," Kirby says. "I'll make it quick. Quicker than Cade's, anyway."

"Do you think Colleen and Sylvie will just step aside so you can manage everything?" I ask.

"They're sheltered women," he says. "They just want to be taken care of. And who knows? Maybe I'll comfort Bridger's grieving widow in more ways than one."

"I can't believe you'd do this to him," I say. "To Cade."

"Cade should have stayed out of it," he says. "And if it weren't for you, he would have. That's on you, sweetheart. And since I can't blame Stuey anymore for all this, it'll have to be you that takes the fall. I'll tell everyone this was a lover's quarrel between you and Cade, and Stu and Bridger interfered. And now they're all dead. Because of you."

Kirby sounds smug, sure he'll get away with it.

And why wouldn't he?

He's white and male and educated. After he gains control of the Holcombe Trust and the law firm, he'll have all the money he could want.

And not only will Kirby get away with it, Cade will be dead and won't be able to stop him.

Cade will be dead and won't make good on his promise to find me.

Cade will be dead, and I'll be damned if a single ounce of blame comes back on me.

The rage hits then, white hot like moonshine and tasting like apples and cinnamon. It soaks through me, replacing my panic and grief, and I let it steady my hands and clear my mind.

The Porsche's engine hums along as we merge onto the expressway north, and I consider my options.

My cell phone is in my back pocket.

My gun is in my bag, but it's in the seat behind me.

An open stretch of road looms before us, a rare gift from heaven on a Friday night, like God makes amends for not rescuing me and Cade earlier when we both might have lived.

Maybe I don't need a gun to kill Kirby and stop him.

I floor the accelerator.

The V-6 responds immediately.

Kirby thrusts the gun more firmly into my side. "What the hell do you think you're doing?"

"Having a little fun," I say. "Might as well. You're gonna kill me anyway."

"Stop this, right now," he says.

The speedometer ticks up.

Eighty-five miles per hour.

Ninety.

Ninety-five.

"Or what?" I ask. "You'll shoot me? I dare you."

One hundred five miles per hour.

He grabs for the wheel, but I hold it steady and jab at his bloody right hand.

"Bitch!" he screams and yanks at my hair.

I push the accelerator harder.

He tries to knock the shifter out of gear, but the car is engineered too well, and he's too weak now, cradling his wounded hand and the gun to his chest.

I swerve into the far right lane.

"Reagan!" Kirby shouts.

I yank the wheel hard to the left, right foot hard on the brake, left foot engaging the clutch to kill power to the engine completely while I pop the emergency brake.

The Porsche squeals into a spin, only its low center of gravity keeping us from rolling. It impacts the highway barrier hard on the passenger side with a sickening jolt, all screeching metal and shattering glass, a grunt from Kirby, and the explosion of airbags.

And then everything is still.

CHAPTER

31

THE PARAMEDICS WILL later swear that I never lost consciousness, that when they found me still buckled into the driver's seat covered in blood, my eyes were so wide open they thought I might be dead.

But I don't remember that.

I don't remember them pulling me out of the car.

I don't remember them placing me onto the stretcher.

I only remember staring up, the amber lights from the highway mixing with the red and blue emergency lights to make the night sky an angry seething bruise.

It's cold, so cold, and I can't feel anything because I'm a block of ice, floating in an ocean far away from here, where no one will ever hurt me again.

A man nearby, his voice frazzled to the edge of his patience, says, "Sir, you can't be here, you can't—"

"Damn it, I'm her family, let me through!" Cade shouts, and then he bends over me, his face streaked with soot and ash.

His hand strokes my face and I gasp at his touch, hot tears burning my eyes, because I know this is only a dream, a beautiful dream.

Cade is dead.

Or maybe I'm dead.

Or maybe we're both dead, and this isn't the worst outcome, because at least we're together.

But his hand feels warm and solid, and underneath the smoke and sweat, I smell him.

I smell safety.

"You're dead," I blabber. "We're both dead, and I—"

"No, babe, no," he murmurs, his voice too low, too husky, too twangy, too much like he's trying to keep the emotion from it. "I'm not dead. And you're gonna be all right, you hear me?"

He kisses me and breaks away before I'm ready for it to end, and I remember.

His Porsche is smashed to pieces, and it's my fault.

"I'm sorry about the car," I croak.

"Goddamn it, Reagan." His voice breaks and he presses his cheek to mine, like he's hiding his face from me. "I don't give a shit about the fucking car. I can replace it. I can't replace you."

The sky blurs over me and I blink away the tears.

Someone grabs his shoulder. "Sir—"

"Please let him stay," I say. "Please."

"I love you," Cade says. "I won't leave you. I'll be right beside you the whole way."

A needle stings my arm.

"I love you too," I say.

Cade grins. "And I didn't buy another watch at the jeweler's."

I manage a smile and say, "I know," through thickening lips.

The night sky descends to wrap me in its blackness, and there is nothing, not even dreams.

A tile ceiling replaces the blackness, a dark room lit only by a dim light over me.

I move my hand and it finds another hand, but I know it's Cade's because of the way my skin tingles when we touch.

He stirs where he sleeps in the chair beside my bed, his head propped on his opposite hand.

"Cade," I say, my voice so low and gravelly it's almost a growl.

He opens his eyes and eases upright in the chair. "Hey, babe."

"You found me," I say.

"I told you I would." He squeezes my hand and laughs. "That app on my phone sure helped, though."

My body aches and my mouth is dry, but I'm alive, and it seems ungrateful to expect anything more than that.

"What happened?" I ask. "Am I . . . ?"

His smile is weary but relieved. "You'll be fine," he says. "A mild concussion, a black eye, and a busted lip from the airbag. No internal bleeding, though, and no broken bones. Because you were wearing a seat belt, you just have some bruises and maybe a couple of sprains. The cops were impressed how you managed to do that."

"I suppose there are some perks to being a mechanic's daughter and growing up on a steady diet of car races and dirt roads to experiment on," I say.

He looks away for half a second. "Speaking of your family, I didn't call them. The hospital staff thought you were my wife anyway, and so it . . . just seemed easier to go along."

"Fair enough." I wiggle my toes and fingers just to reassure myself, and then I take a deep breath. "And . . . ?"

"Bridger is upstairs in the ICU. Stu is in recovery from surgery." Cade clears his throat and takes a deep breath. "And Kirby is dead."

"Oh," I breathe. "Oh God."

For a second, I can hear the hum of the Porsche's engine, feel its throb through the steering wheel, Kirby's gun pushed into my side, and smell the rank stench of blood clogging my nose.

A sob catches in my throat.

"Hey," Cade says and moves to sit on the edge of the bed. "It's fine. You're safe now. We're safe now. Everything will be all right."

He gathers me to himself gently, like he's afraid I'll break, until I nestle against him. It hurts to squeeze my eyes shut to quell the tears, but I do it; it's too soon to cry, too soon to fall apart, and it seems unfair to do that to Cade when he must be exhausted and still recovering.

"This isn't your fault," he says. "If anything, it's Kirby's fault or Bridger's, maybe even Stu or Sylvie's. Shit, what a mess that family is."

"You said yourself you wouldn't have pursued this if it wasn't for me," I say.

He combs through my hair with his fingers. "Not exactly a point in my favor."

I listen to the comforting sounds of his heartbeat and soak in his warmth. "What happens now?"

"Tomorrow morning, we'll deal with the cops," he says. "And I'll sit in with Bridger and Stu while they talk to them."

"I didn't think about that," I say. "I suppose there will be questions. And the law firm—"

"I'll handle it," Cade says. "Just let me take care of everything, babe. I've got it."

I manage a smile. "We've bent a lot of rules lately."

Cade brings the back of my hand to his lips and brushes a kiss there. "But broken no laws. Well, none that we'll admit to, although there were some eyebrows raised about your driving."

"I'm not wearing any handcuffs," I say. "That must be a good sign."

"I argued extenuating circumstances," he says. "It was a hostage situation, after all, and once they found the security guard and Bear's bodies and saw the state of the office—I mean, if Rafi hadn't been there to call the cops as you and Kirby left, and come in after me, Bridger, and Stu to break down that door with a chair . . ."

I swallow hard and cling a little more tightly to him, trying not to consider the possibilities. "We should get a sworn statement from the cops who worked the scene. If one of them will say something about Rafi's heroic actions, that will look good to the discharge appeal board."

"Maybe your friend, Detective Miller," Cade says. "He came by earlier, but I asked him to let you rest tonight. Tomorrow, maybe, but no conversations without me present, all right?"

"You're the fixer, not me," I say.

He slips from my grasp long enough to grab something and returns to his seat with a small box that he opens to reveal a diamond and ruby Claddagh ring. "It's not an engagement ring," he says, and I don't point out to him that it could be, that my views on our relationship have changed drastically in the last couple of weeks. "I just saw it and thought of you, and how nice it would look on you."

"And you happened to remember where you stashed it?" I ask.

He ducks his head and grins, watching me from under his eyebrows. "I might have had it hidden in my attaché case the whole time, but I knew you wouldn't go through that."

"It's beautiful," I say, removing it from the box to admire it.

"Now you'll have a heart with your crown," he says.

I throw my arms around him and hug him close. "You know it's not really appropriate or respectable for a woman to accept jewelry from a man she's not married to."

"Well." Cade winks and slides the ring on the fourth finger of my right hand. "Respectability is overrated."

I fall asleep in his arms, content that he is there and that he will manage everything.

*   *   *

Miller's lack of questions and the way his glance flickers to Cade standing on the other side of my bed every couple of minutes makes me wonder what was said when the two men spoke without me, but I'm not brave enough to ask.

Not if it keeps me and Cade from being cleared of any culpability in the deaths of Bear and Kirby, as well as any charges of obstruction into the investigation of Cesar and Heather's murders.

In the end, Miller only eyes the ring on my hand—even if it's not an engagement ring—and probably considers the fact that I wear what is obviously one of Cade's T-shirts and a pair of his pajama pants I've rolled up. "Next time, would you just come to me with all this?"

I frown. "Would you have listened if I had? It didn't seem like your bosses were very interested."

"We could've worked something out before we got here and the lawyers got involved." He taps his pen against his notepad, looks from me to Cade and back to me, and asks, "What are your plans?"

"I don't know," I say.

"McCarrick?" Miller asks. "I imagine there will be questions about the law firm and its future. Certainly the state bar might have some interest."

Cade folds his arms across his chest. "What's your point?"

"Just wondering if you two are sticking around town for a while," Miller says.

"I'll let you know before we buy any plane tickets," Cade says.

"And you'll give me a heads up if you decide to hold one of your three-ring press conferences?" Miller asks.

Cade nods. "I can do that."

*   *   *

Rafi and Evangeline meet us with my car after the doctor signs my discharge papers, and Evangeline hugs me. "I was so worried," she says.

"You sure this is a good idea?" Rafi asks Cade.

Cade shrugs, my backpack that he rescued from his Porsche slung over his shoulder and his attaché case in hand. "I think it's best we lie low for a week. At least until we work out all the details on how everything proceeds from here."

"You're the lawyer." Rafi hands Cade the car keys. "Gas tank is full, and bags are in the trunk."

"What bags?" I ask.

"The bags I packed this morning when I ran home to shower and change," Cade says. "Let's go."

I'm not surprised when he drives us east out of Dallas, across the Ray Hubbard Bridge and through the eastern suburbs of the Metroplex, but I ask, "What about the firm?"

"It'll be there," he says.

"And Miller? The cops?" I ask.

Cade grins. "I told him I'd tell him if I bought plane tickets."

It's midafternoon when we arrive at the cabin in the woods to drop our bags and go grocery shopping. But we reach for each other almost as soon as we step inside, kissing frantically like we've been separated for years, shedding clothes all the way up the staircase as if at some level we both feel compelled to prove nothing is broken, nothing is permanently damaged, that we're alive and together.

The realization crashes over me, but in its undertow are the relief and exhaustion and fear and grief, the remembrance that we watched Bear die, that Kirby took me and left Cade behind, that Kirby died in a car wreck I engineered.

And maybe Cade knows that, because he doesn't ask why I sob into his shoulder at the end. We only cling to each other, exhausted, and sleep.

We sleep and we eat and we make love. We swim in the lake, lounge in the hammock, and roast marshmallows in the fire pit.

Eventually we talk.

But for the first three days, Cade only talks about the Holcombes or the law firm or Dallas in the past tense, as if our lives there are a book that he has closed and filed away on a shelf. I let this be, because I know at some level Cade won't allow himself the luxury of crying on my shoulder after we make love or—and perhaps what he'd prefer—putting a fist through a wall.

On the fourth day, he mentions the idea of moving away, maybe to the Piney Woods, maybe somewhere else, somewhere quieter, where no one knows who we are or what happened at the firm. I don't say anything, even though I know the city calls to him, that he needs to be in the center of things, solving puzzles and charming juries, that if we move away and he settles into life as a rural prosecutor or even as a general practice attorney, he'll stagnate and lose himself.

But on the fifth day, we swing in the hammock together and he sighs. "We're going back, aren't we?"

"I'm not twisting your arm," I say. "But if we go back, we go back on our terms. We just need to decide what those are."

He nods and we don't talk about it anymore.

We return to Dallas in time to tour a two-bedroom, two-bath apartment in his building with a balcony that overlooks downtown and two walk-in closets in the master suite.

On Monday, we sign the lease and begin packing our apartments.

It's Wednesday, though, before Cade goes to the law firm. He returns with all our personal belongings that could be salvaged from his office.

"So what happens now?" I ask.

"Bridger is retiring." Cade pulls his SMU diploma from a box and wipes a smudge off the glass. He leans it against the wall and withdraws his law license certificate next, the gold Texas star gleaming. "The firm is dissolving, so Armando and I are cashing out our shares. We're keeping our client lists."

I fold my arms across my chest and cock my head to one side, trying to read what's behind his grin and those green eyes. "And?"

"And you'll see," he says, drawing me close for a kiss. "But I think you'll be pleased. And proud."

"I'm always proud of you," I say.

He dimples and grins. "I know."

32

W E HOLD THE ribbon cutting for McCarrick & Tamez the first Friday in September at the new offices in a high-rise within walking distance of our apartment. Evangeline and I have our own office, where we can supervise the team of paralegals and legal secretaries and even a receptionist who will keep the firm running smoothly.

She smiles up at Rafi. "I'm saving you a desk."

"Gotta get through school first," he says and straightens his new suit coat. "Now that my discharge is upgraded, I can work on getting my degree."

"You working or eating?" Lupita chides, patting his arm. "I can't tell lately."

"Ay, Lita!" Rafi chuckles. "Can I help it your tamales are my favorite?"

I lean down for the older woman to embrace me and I brush a kiss on her cheek. It took me a week after Cade and I returned to Dallas to work up the nerve to appear at her doorstep. She didn't scold me, but listened, and when I asked if I could help her file the paperwork to receive the benefits for her husband's death in combat she should have had decades ago, she only nodded.

Now, despite the cruel twists of fate that brought us together, I can't imagine my life without her. Given how often Rafi eats with her, fusses over her car, and spends time mowing her yard, I don't think he can, either.

"I don't mind helping you study," Evangeline says. "I may still have my notes."

Cade slips an arm around me. "I'm not sure about these workplace romances. Is there a clause about that in the employee handbook?"

I laugh, but Armando shrugs and glances at his phone. "I'm not an HR attorney. I'll be right back."

"He's nervous about something," I say to Cade. "What's going on?"

But Cade doesn't answer because Stu limps through the glass double doors, still on a cane. I half listen as they chat about Stu's plans for his last year of law school, about the sale of his family's home in Highland Park so Colleen and Bridger can quietly retire in Florida, about the Porsche Cade bought to replace the last one, and Stu finally says, "This place looks nice."

"I'd love to take all the credit for it," Cade says, grinning. "But Evangeline and Reagan worked very hard."

Armando enters, a tall red-haired man close behind him, and I watch our friend point out things around the office. "Is that—" I begin to ask.

"I'm not the only one who likes Texas redheads," Cade whispers in my ear. "His name is Connor."

I stand on my tiptoes to kiss Cade. "It's nice for everything to be out in the open. No more secrets, no more lies."

"Well." Cade shrugs and steals a second kiss. "There never were between us anyways."

I nod, because we've seen where lies and secrets will take us, the dizzying heights we can climb to and fall from, and so we know we'll never be more than what we are to each other.

"There's a private balcony," he says. "And I brought the flask."

Our gazes meet, and as much as I know I should be the voice of duty, propriety, and respectability, I feel myself leaning in, wanting him.

"We shouldn't," I say. "It's your party."

He grins. "That only means we can."

We look around to make sure no one will notice, and then slip away out the side door into the evening.

ACKNOWLEDGMENTS

I REMAIN INCREDIBLY GRATEFUL to Toni Kirkpatrick, who saw the potential in Reagan and Cade and appreciated how it blended genres. A huge thanks, too, to Yezanira Venecia, who helped stretch the text even more. And thank you so much to Rebecca Nelson for so tirelessly answering my billion emails and keeping me on track, and Meghan Deist, who designed the cover that brought Reagan and Cade to life so well and blows my mind each time I look at it. Special thanks to Dulce Botello and Madeline Rathle for all the marketing support.

Thanks to my agent, Jessica Faust, who loved Rafi the most and whose expertise was invaluable in finding a home for this book.

Thank you to my beloved critique partners, Maggie North, Ingrid Pierce, Sam Odierno, Amanda Wilson, and Aurora Graves, who do their best to keep me from Faulknerian sentences and bouncing off the walls in between writing projects by letting me read drafts of their works. Finding my writing community was probably one of the few bright spots to come out of 2020.

Special shout-out to Tobie Carter, Kelly Malacko, Eliane Boey, Rae Knowles, Monique Asher, and the rest of our "loamy" #ThrillsAndChills chat family.

I would be especially remiss in not acknowledging this book's godmother, Olivia Blacke, and the rest of our hockey/book group chat, Ellen Devlin and Danica Flynn (all great writers!) who are always down for game discussions or just some Tomspiration. If you think Cade resembles our favorite hockey player, who am I to argue with you?

At the time of revising the first draft, I was a member of a WFWA Critique Group that consisted of Angelica Lebensfeld, Loretta Capeheart, and Mallory Arnold, whose inputs I found invaluable.

Like many writers, I maintain a full-time day job. Unlike many of my writing colleagues, though, my boss and work team love that I have an alter ego who writes and have been amazingly supportive. To Michael, Joe, Chris, David, Cara, Jenn, Allen, and Ray, thanks for always asking how the book is coming along and coordinating your own pre-order campaign.

Thank you to my Bush Institute VLP cohort, who encouraged me to pursue fiction and pointed out how I could still make a difference for veterans even if it wasn't white papers going to Congress—especially Duane, Boerstler, Thompson, Hutch, Richard, Jen, Tiffany, Cicely, Amy, Blaire, Meghan, and Mary Beth. I won't say I wasn't doing field research when we were karaokeing our way through Uptown, Deep Ellum, and the Park Cities, but . . . I wasn't NOT doing field research, either.

Last but not least, and probably most importantly, thank you to my husband, without whom this book wouldn't be possible. For the last fifteen-plus years together, you have pushed me to go after my dreams, encouraged me to invest in my writing, and even cheerfully stepped in with the kids when I needed time/space to write. For their patience and understanding, I'd also like to thank our two children, who have not and will not read this book until they're in high school (no, for real, PUT THIS DOWN AND PUT IT BACK ON MY SHELF), my sister who was my first reader waaaaaay back in our high school days, and our parents who ignored the notebooks with drafts of my teenage scribblings multiplying in my bedroom.